MW01515240

PHALANX ALPHA

by

Alistair McIntyre

Best wishes,

PUBLISHED BY:

www.the4threalm.com

Phalanx Alpha

Copyright © 2013 by Alistair McIntyre

All rights reserved

ISBN 9781482746778

This book is a work of fiction and any resemblance to persons, living or dead, or places, events or locales is purely coincidental. The characters are productions of the author's imagination and used fictitiously.

Cover artwork by Ryan Vogler

voglerart@gmail.com

http://voglerart.daportfolio.com

The4threalm.com

Alistair McIntyre, the author of this work, is part of the4threalm.com, a group of writers who work, edit, critique and publish collaboratively. He would like to invite you to see more of his work, along with that of several other talented people, at the site below. And be sure to participate in the discussion. We're nothing without our readers, and we want to know what you think!

http://www.the4threalm.com

.

Chapter 1

A long journey through southern Kenya's bleak brightness culminated in the pitch-black interior of a small hut. Doctor William Baird, Billy to his few friends, blinked as the room slowly evolved from darkness. An elderly Maasai woman lay on a simple cot, bundled in blankets despite the abusive heat. The doctor wiped his brow with a handkerchief, composing himself before kneeling beside the ailing lady.

Her face wore a constant frown, the only outward sign of the pain throbbing through her body. Leathery eyelids fluttered halfway open for just a moment, her body not able to provide the strength to fully observe the world. Or not wanting to.

The doctor reached out and touched her forehead. He joined her in a frown and then said in English, "Hello, I am Dr. Baird."

The slim translator standing in the tent's doorway spoke slowly to the woman. Her face twitched and she whispered something back to the translator before addressing Baird in heavily accented English.

"I am dying."

Baird regarded her with compassion, having knelt many times in the presence of those ready to die. Prior military experience had introduced a variety of deaths to the doctor almost daily. After his tour in Iraq as a field medic with the British Paratroopers, 1PARA to be exact, Baird had moved to Nairobi to do aid work. Death knew no borders.

"It would appear that way, but there's always hope for a miracle," he replied evenly, believing that God had raised the dead and could effortlessly heal the cancer raging in this old woman's body, if that was His plan. The translator started talking to the woman in Swahili, but she slowly opened her eyes and spoke.

"I speak English."

The doctor smiled, and then he turned to the doorway as the translator stepped outside and rattled off some harsh words in the local language. Intrigued, Baird followed and stepped into the light, instantly regretting not donning his sunglasses first. After recovering from the shocking brightness, he shaded his eyes with a hand and looked upon a strange sight.

His translator was speaking animatedly with a middle-aged woman standing next to what could only be described as a giant pink man. The doctor observed that the shade of pink didn't come from overexposure to ultraviolet rays. In fact, he'd never seen such a color before. Not many people dwarfed the doctor, who stood at almost six and a half feet tall, but he estimated this giant to be at least eight feet tall. And hairless. Deep black eyes ignored the commotion going on, staring at nothing in particular.

Strange, the doctor thought. *Only in Africa.*

He pulled his phone out to take a picture. While lining up the shot, he asked the translator what was going on.

"This woman says that this oaf is a healer, and she demands to see the woman in the tent. I told her that this was unacceptable, and the poor lady needs to die in peace!"

Baird snapped the picture, and then leaned in close to the much slimmer man.

"Well you should pipe down, mate. No need to start yelling about death in front of a patient."

The translator apologized and reiterated that the crazy woman should leave.

"How does she know the giant is a healer?" Baird asked.

After a blast of language, the translator explained, "Her son went missing by Lake Magadi recently, so she went to find him. With help from the locals, she found the boy. The pink man was with him. The boy's leg was very obviously broken. He had fallen from a rock." The man paused.

Baird looked at him with a raised eyebrow.

"So what?"

The translator swallowed and said, "She claims that before they even got the child to a doctor, his bone had set, and he could stand on it."

Baird frowned.

"Is she sure it was broken in the first place?"

The translator ripped off another verbal barrage at the woman, who returned in kind, annoyance painted all over her face. She made an L-shaped signal with her index finger.

The translator continued in English, "She says his shinbone was completely broken, that the parts of the bones were bent at right-angles."

Baird looked at the ridiculous pink giant, standing perfectly still with a simple white towel wrapped around his waist.

He asked, "I'm guessing this lady wrapped the towel around him?"

The translator confirmed the detail.

Baird mulled the situation over and then said, "Seems to me that I wouldn't hang around with a giant naked bloke I'd found with my son in the middle of nowhere. Unless said giant naked bloke had really healed him."

The translator stared at the doctor, mouth hanging open in shock.

"Just a joke, mate," he reassured the man, then added more quietly, "Look, this woman's probably going to die soon. I don't see anything wrong with letting this guy pretend to do some magic before we take her to the hospital."

The slimmer man just shook his head and moved out of the giant's way. Without a word, the pink man bent at the waist and entered the tent. Baird followed him in and saw the pink man touch the old woman's face with amazing gentleness for such a large creature.

The moment passed quickly. The large man glided gracefully from the tent. Baird watched the giant disappear from view, overheard a brief exchange between the woman and the translator, and then sat in the relative silence, sweating a gallon a minute. He wiped his brow again.

The uneven ground felt less than comfy when he lowered himself down and pulled a notepad out of his backpack. After scribbling a few notes about his initial encounter with the sick woman, he jotted down a couple of words about the other lady and the "healer."

The old woman startled him with a loud cough. Baird looked up and saw her slowly roll over onto her side. After the initial surprise, Baird leapt up and put a hand on the blanket covering the woman, wondering what on earth she was doing.

She shrugged off his touch and said remarkably forcefully, "I feel better; you do not need to worry."

Glancing around in disbelief, the young doctor stepped outside, this time preemptively shielding his sight. The giant pink man and his guardian had disappeared. The doctor stared back into the dark hut.

He smiled ruefully.

"Hope's a wonderful thing, but it doesn't always last."

The translator stood awkwardly, not quite sure what to do. Baird clapped him on the shoulder.

"Come on, mate. Let's get this young lady to the hospital."

***

"Mark, you seen this crap in the tabloids? 'Local Man Saved in Desert By Pink Giant.' Great stuff!" declared Matt Smith, accompanied by a deep guffaw from his expansive belly.

"I'm sure it's right next to 'Pregnant Man Gives Birth to Three-Headed Twin Cats!'" replied Mark Jackson dryly, staring out of his office into the streets of Phoenix.

Smith continued on, undeterred. "The guy apparently drove out into the desert and his truck broke down. That sucks."

"Ironic that your truck would break down when you drive into the desert to dump a body," Jackson added, causing more booming laughter from his friend.

"Either way, the guy broke down, then started marching back to the highway without any water. He says he eventually fell down and started crawling, but then he couldn't even crawl anymore. As the light at the end of the tunnel started getting brighter, here comes a giant pink guy," Smith explained.

Jackson looked at the large Texas-bred man and quipped, "I always figured Jesus was short and Middle Eastern."

Smith slapped his thigh and roared out another laugh before composing himself.

"Guy swears he wasn't hallucinating, but either way, Big Friendly Giant picks him up and holds him for a moment, then miraculously the guy has all the energy in the world to start trekking home."

"I don't know if I would admit that a giant pink guy gave me the kiss of life," Jackson added.

Smith's face turned red as he silently laughed. Jackson thought he might finally have given his oversized colleague a stroke, but Smith recovered almost instantly as the pair's boss burst out of his office and stormed towards their adjoined desks.

"What the hell are you two still doing here? Don't you read the news?"

Smith pointed at the tabloid on his desk and said with a smile, "You mean this crap, sir?"

The smile was wiped off of his wide face when his boss almost screamed at him, "Yes, that is the crap I mean! Get your asses out there and start being reporters for once! We miss the scoop on almost every damn story because you two sit in here and jerk off all damn day!"

Jackson said in as soothing a tone as he could muster, "But this is a tabloid story…"

The boss composed himself for a moment and said in a slightly less life-threatening tone, "Yes, but it's being picked up by all the major papers. They've found Joshua Greaves' truck twenty miles in the middle of God-knows-where. I don't know about magic pink men, but this guy looks like he really did just walk through the freaking desert. Now get going!"

***

"What do you mean, 'She has never had cancer'? That's ridiculous. I saw it myself on the last CAT scan!" Doctor Billy

Baird announced defiantly. The diminutive doctor before him just shrugged her shoulders.

"Dr. Baird, that CAT scan was not done in this hospital, and you do not have a copy of it. All I can tell you now is that this woman has no signs of cancer in her blood or in the scan."

Baird turned away and stormed out of the door. He should be happy for the woman. She had survived cancer! But as much as he believed in God and miracles, he'd never actually seen a miraculous recovery in person. All of the people he'd seen on the verge of death had promptly fallen over the precipice. Of course, most of the people he'd witnessed in their final moments had suffered from multiple bullet or shrapnel wounds to critical organs before passing on.

In a small room in Nairobi's largest hospital, the old woman sat in a chair, something she could never have done two days ago. She looked so alive and vibrant. Baird couldn't believe the state she'd once been in. And now he had a CAT scan saying she'd never even been in that horrible state. The whole thing was surreal, and a bit scary.

"The giant was an angel, Dr. Baird," she said pleasantly, eyeing the skepticism on his face.

As Baird absently replaced his latex gloves with a fresh pair, he wanted desperately to believe that to be true. Logic provided a stumbling block.

Chapter 2

"What's so important that we need to do this in person, Winston?"

In the heat of the Austin sun, hoards of college kids milled around Zilker Park, partaking in whatever the latest outdoorsy craze happened to be. For Andrew Knight, an afternoon of disc golf or soccer typically would hold no appeal, but on this day he would've gladly taken such inane activities over his meeting with Winston Klotzer.

"Look, Mr. Knight, I'm not trying to piss you off," Klotzer replied in the charmingly sleazy manner of private investigators. Knight wondered if anything could stick to this slippery character. "The truth is, I got some photos."

Despite his promise to himself not to jump to early conclusions, Knight's stomach dropped at that last word. He'd hired the greasy New York P.I. to find out information, but now in the moment of potential truth, Knight wasn't so sure he wanted to hear the news.

"I gave you a mailing address for this stuff," Knight pointed out.

Klotzer just shrugged.

"I like to do things in person, Mr. Knight."

"Okay, fine. Sit down and show me what you've got."

The unlikely pair sat down on a bench, just far enough away from the buzz of chattering young adults to avoid eavesdropping, but not so far away as to provoke unwarranted attention. Knight's large stature caused him to loom over the short, round investigator. This guy had come highly recommended for work he'd done previously for Knight's employer, yet Knight's mind automatically went into overdrive to discredit the man and his methods as Klotzer pulled a photo from a manila envelope.

"So, you can see that the subject is in a coffee shop with a tall, dark stranger. I looked through her Facebook friends and didn't see this guy pop out anywhere," Klotzer explained. He caught Knight's eye. "You seen him before?"

"No."

"Okay, next we got a more intimate moment," stated Klotzer as he produced another eight-and-a-half by eleven color printout. The man's insensitive words stabbed at Knight, but he kept his poker face solid despite the pressure brought on by the high definition picture in front of him.

"So what we got here is the same coffee shop, and the subject crying and holding the stranger's hands. Or more accurately, he seems to be holding her hands," Klotzer narrated.

"Yeah, yeah. I got it. I can see it," Knight interrupted. The picture didn't look good. Feelings of frustration and hurt swelled inside the normally stoic Knight. Who would've guessed that a simple picture could stir up such emotions in a soldier who considered himself vastly desensitized?

"So what you want me to do next, Mr. Knight?"

A moment passed as Knight contemplated. Across the way he watched a twenty-something year old girl blaze a trail right through the heart of a hapless soccer team's pitiful defense. She buried the ball into the bottom corner of the goal, leaving the goalkeeper helplessly reaching. The few fans watching exploded into cheers and applause. That was the kind of normal life that a guy like Knight would never enjoy.

"This is suspicious, Winston, but it's not exactly damning evidence."

Klotzer held up a hand.

"I'm not here to speculate, Mr. Knight. It is what it is."

Knight let out a sigh.

"Right, I get it."

"Mr. Knight, I can probe deeper here, but I'll need some walking-around money to cover further expenses."

Knight just nodded. The more he dwelt on his predicament, the emptier he felt inside. He handed the P.I. the envelope he'd brought in anticipation of the man's financial request.

"Yeah, do whatever you need to do," Knight said.

The two parted ways without another word. Knight headed straight back to his truck and sat for a few moments, staring at the clock. He needed to meet Brian at the gym later, but that was hours away. His eyes rested on the soccer game in front of him, but his mind drifted all over. Not so much as a flinch registered on Knight's face when the same girl scored another spectacular goal.

A flask materialized in Knight's hand. He didn't remember pulling the stainless steel vessel out of the glove box, but since it was already out, he unscrewed the top and took a few pulls. The alcohol's burn helped reset his frantic mind to the one question that haunted him the most.

Karen, why?

Chapter 3

"Look, Andy, I'm not going to fight you if you keep dropping your guard like that."

Brian Lehoski ducked the looping haymaker from Knight, slid sideways, and caught his friend just under the ribs with a sharp body shot. Normally the grunt elicited by his trademark strike would bring a smile to Lehoski's face, but this fight gave him no pleasure. He would've cherished the opportunity to finally beat Knight in a boxing match, but he could tell this wasn't the real Andrew Knight sparring with him.

First of all, the two men bounced around the ring with only the empty gym's emergency lighting keeping them from striding right into the ropes. The place had been abandoned for hours, but this was the time that Andy had set for this bout. Lehoski had been up for it, figuring he could blow off some steam after his girlfriend had bitched him out over leaving wet clothes in the washer overnight.

Whatever.

So other than the weird time for the sparring, Lehoski's next clue that something wasn't right was the drunk man sloshing around the ring in front of him. Of course, even a drunk Knight was a force to be reckoned with. They'd got themselves into plenty of bar brawls over the years, and Knight had never let Lehoski down. The guy was an animal. The husk of a man throwing lazy punches and failing to defend himself was definitely not the same creature, not even the same species.

Knight darted forward and threw a blistering cross that stung Lehoski even through his guard. Lehoski dropped his gloves a touch and started to counter, but saw that Knight's hands hung loosely at his sides, and he wasn't even looking at Lehoski anymore. The eyes revealed a depth of sorrow that made an argument over a washing machine seem like nonsense. Staring into the dark space around the ring, Knight spoke in dejected monotone.

"Karen asked for a divorce, Brian."

Stunned, Lehoski gasped a little. He couldn't believe it. Andy and Karen had been together forever, and for as long as Lehoski had known them, there had been no hints at any serious marital strife. Like a lot of men forced into such an awkward situation, Lehoski couldn't come up with any words to say.

"She won't tell me why, either," Knight added sullenly.

The defeat in Knight's voice was totally out of character. Lehoski had ridden through the depths of hell and back with the guy, taking no prisoners along the way. The two of them had survived the kind of shit storms that only the few, the proud, the lucky get to live long enough to reminisce about. And Knight had led every step of the way.

At least Lehoski finally had an answer to a few of the problems bugging him. The drinking was understandable, pretty much required for the situation. Not paying attention to blocking Lehoski's fists made sense now that Knight had revealed the huge distraction plaguing his mind. Knight was a strong guy. He had mental toughness. He'd get through this okay. It was a crap deal, though.

As if a switch had flipped in his head just from the cathartic expression, Knight turned to Lehoski with a smile. Knowing Knight as well as he did, Lehoski could guarantee that he was the first and probably only person that Knight had shared his burden with. The trust made him feel good, despite the circumstances. The strained smile on his friend's face only spelled trouble.

"I'm going to head downtown for a drink," Knight said. "You coming?"

Definitely trouble.

"You sure that's a good idea, man?" Lehoski asked.

Already undoing his gloves, Knight glared back at Lehoski.

"Don't be a pussy, Brian."

"Yeah, that's not helpful, Andy."

"Sandy was cheating on you, right?" Knight said, taking Lehoski by surprise.

That was a memory he didn't feel like dredging out of the bilge of his soul.

"Yeah, she was."

"How did you know?"

That question always had a way of getting to Lehoski. The truth was, he hadn't had a single shred of evidence. Lehoski had merely called his now ex-wife's bluff during an argument, and she'd broken down and confessed. Like everything else with her, the sadness of her revelation had passed quickly. She'd raged out of the house, trashing everything in sight. Lehoski really hated that the kids had had to watch their mother go bat-shit crazy like that. And to think, *she* was the one with full custody, taking care of his kids in damn Vancouver with some yuppie douchebag of a boyfriend. Where was the justice in that?

"I just had a hunch, man," Lehoski replied.

"Yeah, well you should know what I'm going through then."

Actually, this was news to Lehoski. He'd never heard so much as a vague suspicion from Andy that Karen might be cheating. At least Andy was right on one part. Lehoski *did* know exactly what he was going through. The second-guessing and the blame-game didn't stop with the finalizing of the divorce either, unfortunately.

"That doesn't mean you need to go off the deep end, Andy."

With one last angry stare, Knight clambered out of the ring, grabbed his bag, and headed to the showers in the dark. Somewhere in the dim gym, a weight bench was flipped over with a muffled curse. Watching the storm of Knight's fury unfold, Lehoski waited a few beats, then climbed out of the ring and recovered his own gear before walking out into the cool air of an Austin evening. Knight just needed to get all the junk out of his system. Then he'd be back to normal. Lehoski started the stroll home, wondering how long it would be until he got the call to bail Knight out.

He was halfway up the street before he realized his mistake. How could he let his brother in arms down like this? Lehoski jogged back to the darkened gym and clambered over shadowy equipment to reach the locker rooms.

Knight was nowhere to be seen.

Chapter 4

In any other brawl, the drunk guy would've stood a fighting chance, but against an All Big 12 linebacker?

"I don't think so, pal," Officer Landon Bing said to himself as he sat behind his desk.

The guy was in sad shape. On each pass of the cells, Landon observed that the large man just sat in the corner of the drunk tank, staring at the floor intensely. The stare sort of frightened the police officer, who was no small fry himself. He was over six feet tall and worked out plenty in the station's gym. Definitely not the biggest guy, but strong enough to handle the usual rabble of unruly alcoholics.

The guy hadn't said a single word. Driver's license revealed his name to be one Andrew Knight, of Austin, Texas.

"Not much of a Knight," Landon remarked. According to the record on file, Knight had been in a couple of times recently for bar fights. Landon wished that a few of the bars on Sixth would implement a black list to keep this crap to a minimum, but it did provide some entertainment for the large police presence downtown.

Also, it kept some of the hotheads in line when they saw that the police really did respond in force to any violence in one of Austin's largest gatherings of people. If the police didn't provide protection, Landon was damn sure that the tourism board would.

The officer checked his watch and pushed his chair back, ready to do the rounds again. The night was still a bit young to have too many in the tank. At that moment, Knight was accompanied by two kids who'd been picked up trying to start their car while trashed. Two officers had subtly tailed the youths from the bar they'd illegally snuck into. The bar's manager would be getting a phone call early in the morning to let him know about a heavy fine coming down the pipes.

Sucks for him, but them's the rules, Landon thought as he paused at the large jail cell to look in at Knight.

The guy remained in the exact same position, boring a hole into the floor with his eyes. The officer started to get uneasy and shuffled on, ensuring that his other guests were behaving before returning to his desk.

He'd just sat down when his phone rang.

"Two suits are on the way back to you," the receptionist said as the jail area door flew open and two gentlemen in tailored suits stepped through. Both looked to be the same size as Knight, Landon noticed, but only because not too many guys made him feel small. And weak.

He stood and started to introduce himself when the blonde crew-cut demanded, "You're to turn over Andrew Knight to us immediately."

Officer Landon Bing straightened up, not taking kindly to this young buck strutting into his territory and telling him what to do. He knew fine well that he would be handing over Knight to these men, but not without following some semblance of procedure. That way he could feel like he'd handed Knight over, instead of having these two jerk-offs take a prisoner from him.

"I will obviously need to see your paperwork for that, sir," Landon replied firmly.

The brown crew-cut removed an envelope from his fitted jacket and handed it to the smaller man. Landon opened the envelope, saw the correct seal, date, and signature, and sat down.

As he fished for the transfer document he needed to fill out, he said, "This all looks in order. I'll have the transfer made official in a couple of minutes if you two don't mind waiting." He looked up and raised an eyebrow in as pompous a manner as he could muster. Who did these rookies think he was?

"That'll be fine," growled the blonde. Neither felt a need to sit in the provided chairs, both instead glaring fiercely at the local police officer.

Typical Feds. All bluster. He didn't care that either one of them could easily kick his ass down the street and then back up it again. They couldn't touch him inside his own domain.

Landon finished up the data entry and passed the paper and a pen across his desk. The blonde stepped forward and signed it so hard that Landon thought the man's name would be forever engraved in the desk. He started to think that maybe he should ease off on the irritating behavior just a little.

After grabbing the keys, he had the two federal agents follow him back to the cells. Just before the door of Knight's cell, Officer Landon Bing had a revelation about a potentially severe breach of security.

"Could I see your credentials please, sirs?" he said evenly, not wanting to spark a debate.

Both men tried to strangle him with their eyes, but instead produced almost identical sets of identification. The seal of the Federal Bureau of Investigation was prominently displayed and everything looked in order.

Landon had seen more than one FBI badge, but he admitted to himself that a good forgery would easily slip past him, despite his training on such things. He'd need to see one every fifteen minutes to remember exactly what it should look like.

"Thank you, Agent Scott and Agent Farmery," Officer Bing said nicely as he unlocked the door to the tank.

Announcing his intentions clearly before stepping inside, he sternly warned, "Don't get any ideas, ladies. Knight, two gentlemen would like to have a word with you. None of my business, but the law says you go with them."

Knight slowly stood up and allowed the Feds to cuff him. The three left the cell promptly, ignoring the passed out teens lying on the dirty cell floor. Landon couldn't believe that anyone, no matter how wasted, would want to put their face on that floor. God only knew how many times he'd hosed puke and shit out of there. It looked like one of the teens had added a contribution of a similar sort. Landon grunted and relocked the cell door.

***

The two men loaded Knight into the back of a black Suburban. The truck quickly pulled away from the curb once all three were inside.

The blonde man nodded to the brown haired agent, who unceremoniously removed Knight's cuffs. Knight looked up with drunken defiance written all over his face.

"Not so tight next time, Brian."

A frustrated Brian Lehoski looked his friend in the eye and said, "I'm getting tired of this shit, man. You've got to stop this."

Knight shrugged and leaned back in his chair. Lehoski noticed that the snoring started almost immediately.

"Sleep it off, big guy. You've got a hell of a debriefing at the Fort tomorrow morning."

Chapter 5

The newspaper soared across the kitchen, gracefully while folded, chaotically when air resistance flipped the pages apart. A collage of black and white exploded against the wall and slid to the floor.

"Was that really necessary, Mitch?" Cheryl asked her furious husband without even looking up from her grossly overly-romantic novel. The young woman knew it was sappy, even silly, and definitely unrealistic, but the stories beat watching her equally young husband throw newspapers across the kitchen table. At least she was never the target.

"Have you read that crap?" he exclaimed. Obviously she had not because he'd grabbed the paper first, read a few headlines, and then tossed it.

"What is *that crap*, Mitch?" she asked, still not looking up. Despite the short duration of their marriage so far, Cheryl had perfected multitasking during breakfast.

"That *crap* is all this angel nonsense floating around in the papers. Those reporters should all be shot for it," he said, getting far too worked up for eight in the morning as far as Cheryl was concerned.

In any case, she'd read all about it already. The article described the recent appearance of a pink man in the outskirts of Brisbane. The man had apparently healed a lot of sick people simply by touching them. The local authorities had taken this healer to a nearby hospital, and now sick people from all over Australia were heading to Brisbane. Some people were even gathering there just to witness the healing, despite the hospital asking for only terminally ill patients to show up. Cheryl wondered if her Alzheimer's-stricken Granny would qualify.

"You know how I feel about religion," Mitch urged. Cheryl inwardly rolled her eyes, not wanting to lose her spot in her book. The muscle-bound hunk had just gently laid the heroine down on a lush pile of rose petals. She loved these things.

Mitch continued emphatically, "There is no god. There are definitely no *gods*. And since there is no god, there can be no damn angels. This tripe makes me so mad. Weak people out there are probably eating this up.

"And you know what else? 'Angel Heals People!' Really? People get better from all kinds of serious sickness all the time, and you don't see the papers bragging about angels doing it then. This is just religious nonsense."

Cheryl couldn't have cared less about religion either, but she didn't have anything against those who did. The heroine of her story used to be a nun, and she seemed okay. Although at the moment, the heroine, one Ms. Evangeline Clandestine, wasn't being too holy. In fact, God himself would look away. Cheryl smiled to herself.

"This isn't funny, Sharon," Mitch burst out. As the last word left his lips, he finally shut up.

Cheryl slowly looked up and placed her book down on the table. Mitch's widened eyes said it all.

"Who is *Sharon*, Mitch?"

Now her facial expression matched the sudden rage boiling in her chest. Had Mitch's brain contained more than two brain cells, he wouldn't have adopted the look of a teenager caught defiling himself in the bathroom. What could otherwise have been played off as an innocent mistake now proved to be damning evidence of infidelity. Mount St. Cheryl erupted in impressive form.

Words flew violently across the table, mostly in one direction. A chair flew accurately across the table. A man flew desperately out the front door, yelling apology after apology. The door slammed shut, and a deadbolt ensured the lying bastard could never get back in.

The murderous anger receded, replaced with a sadness that only the ultimate betrayal could muster. Cheryl wandered aimlessly back into the kitchen, now a scene of a natural disaster.

He'll be lucky if I let him live, the young woman thought as stubborn resolve replaced her utter sadness. She couldn't let that vile man get her down. And whoever Sharon was had better look out, too. Those thoughts retired to a darker recess of Cheryl's brain as she stared at the phone on the counter.

Tears streamed freely as she reached to call her mum.

***

The sanctuary vibrated with an intense anticipation as Pastor Martin Daniels entered stage right. A vacuum of sound formed in the air, people unconsciously holding their collective breath.

Mark Jackson hoped the obese guy sitting next to him didn't collapse from all the excitement in a writhing mess of flab and pulmonary blockage. That would be the icing on the cake on this Sunday morning.

As the immaculately attired Pastor Daniels opened his notes behind the enormous church's epic pulpit, Mark reminded himself again of all the reasons that he hated church. Alas, all his excuses had meant nothing the night before when his boss had ordered him to attend this service of the Phoenix area elite. Apparently a good reporter would've already jumped at the Christian angle of the Angel story. Mark would've rather jumped off the top of this outrageously tall church building.

Despite knowing his partner in crime, Matt Smith, for some time now, Jackson hadn't realized the guy's devotion to his faith. Of course Jackson had picked up on the Christian undertones, but he hadn't realized Smith was into activities like teaching Sunday School for the kids in his own church. Jackson had been a little surprised when his boss revealed that was Smith's reason for leaving Jackson to fly solo at the charismatic loony bin that morning. He couldn't agree with Smith's religious ideals, but there had never been a question in Jackson's mind that Smith was a stand-up guy, so he shouldn't have been that shocked.

Having said all that, it didn't stop Jackson ribbing the big Texan mercilessly about his heritage and possible relations with livestock.

The atheist newsman turned his head and rolled his eyes openly as the pastor opened in prayer, asking for guidance from God, for God to speak through him, to use him as a vessel. Mark's overly dramatic facial gesture drew negative attention from a nearby elderly lady. Daggers laced the air between their eyes.

If looks could kill, she'd be up for a grisly murder right now. Anyway, she should have her eyes closed while her infallible leader prays.

The decadent building alone screamed hypocrisy to Mark. Why could these people not see the futility of their efforts? All of this money spent on worthless infrastructure could provide amazing help for all the starving homeless men living under the overpass just two blocks away.

Even if the money was set aside, it would be wasted pointlessly. Everything is wasted, Mark thought hopelessly. Why couldn't intelligent people like himself run the country? Setting aside his personal beliefs, Mark focused on the pulpit and realized that he had already missed the start of the sermon.

"God has sent these angels to heal the sick," Pastor Daniels' voice boomed through well-placed, yet well-hidden speakers. The effect created a bone-rattling, ubiquitous noise. "Praise God! Praise God!"

Producing a small device from his pocket, Mark hit the record button and then closed his eyes. Almost immediately a stern finger probed his shoulder, letting him know that he had transgressed in the House of the Lord.

What the hell is wrong with these people?

Agitated, he turned and nodded almost imperceptibly to a three-thousand-year-old mummy in the seat behind him. The man looked freshly dug up after spending a few years at a depth of six feet.

The good pastor droned on in his two thousand dollar shoes, a pair probably similar to those worn at his internationally renowned speaking engagements.

"Based on this passage in the Book of Revelation, it is easy to see that these angels herald the End Times," he exclaimed. The congregation collectively gasped. Mark raised an eyebrow attentively.

"Do not fear! We have been talking for years that we are living in the End Times. Now here is just more proof," the pastor declared.

Mark could physically feel the gullible relief flood the room as heart rates dropped to merely slightly above normal levels. He had to get out of there.

"Having said that, saints, I must reiterate that we are in for dark times ahead," the holy man explained slowly. Mark felt the blood pressure in the cavernous space hit the high, intricately molded ceiling.

These people actually buy into this crap, he thought with surprise. Then he felt more surprised that he'd not realized this truth sooner. Surely he'd known ahead of time that people came to these churches because they believed in something, right? It wasn't just to hear the ramblings of a best-selling preacher. Mark looked around in wonder.

"There is hope, faithful children," the pastor was saying as the offering trays spirited into existence from the ethers on either side of each aisle.

"All I see is fear," Mark observed, a little bit too loudly for the elderly woman on his left. The daggers from her eyes were much less stern this time, tempered by dread of the unknown.

Amazed, the reporter made a mental note that only a crook could wield such powerful influence to turn the good news of miraculous healings into a sham of fear. He shook his head as he passed the offering basket onto the next victim.

Chapter 6

"Why does Connor always insist on making me wait?" Andrew Knight grunted to himself as he sat in the waiting room outside of his boss's office.

Michael Connor had apparently forgotten about the urgency with which he had forced the meeting on this bright Sunday morning.

Knight put his head back against the cool, neutrally painted wall and closed his eyes. An abnormal amount of pressure caused his eyeballs to ache under the strain of his eyelids. Abnormal for someone who hadn't tried to consume their weight in alcohol the night before perhaps. For the past month, these meetings had happened under similar circumstances on a weekly basis.

As the hangover hinted at beginning a drum line on the inside of his skull, Knight opened his eyes and grabbed the bottle of water he'd retrieved from Connor's secretary. Apparently even the senior officers of paramilitary groups needed assistants. A furtive glance her way revealed her pitying stare. Knight didn't need her damn pity. He resumed his involuntary meditation against the wall and hoped for a miraculous recovery before Connor's door opened.

As luck would have it, the door swung open smoothly, silently, the doorframe outlining the dark room within. Either Connor took pity on Knight's current light-sensitive state, or merely wanted a dark room in which to kick Knight's head around in. It didn't seem to matter much either way to Knight. He promptly stood at attention, waiting for an acknowledgement.

"I think we're past that, Andy," Connor stated. "Come on in."

As Knight marched past his boss into the office, Connor poked his head around the corner and added, "Sheila, I'm unavailable for a short time. Except if Albatross calls, of course."

The door closed quietly behind Knight. Inside the dimly lit office, he stood by the two chairs on the inferior side of Connor's great oak desk.

Definitely not standard issue, Knight remarked to himself for the umpteenth time. The boss's taste never ceased to amaze.

"Take a seat, Andy." Connor plopped himself down in his sturdy leather chair and sighed deeply, as if not wanting to go where he now needed to go. Knight had a pretty good bead on why he had been called in. The stink of alcohol that hadn't quite washed out and the black eye gave subtle clues.

Connor pushed his chair back a few inches and leaned back with his hands clasped on his surprisingly still flat stomach. The years had been good to Connor. He hadn't grown the senior officer's pooch that so many cultivated proportionately to the level of their self-importance.

The Army major didn't fall into that category at all. He was a soldier's soldier. Knight had risen all the way up behind his boss, the two serving in various conflicts, both public and private, classified and incredibly classified. Based on their long history, Knight felt that Connor had to have some idea about what was going on. It wasn't that difficult to work out.

After another sigh, a moment of contemplation, Connor started the awkward conversation gracefully.

"Andy, we've known each other for a long time," he began. Knight nodded, emotionless. He'd prepped himself, knowing that his boss would most likely open with a heart-felt lecture. He wasn't wrong.

Connor continued, "We killed side by side, completed impossible missions together, and I think that we even saved each other's lives a few times in between."

Knight could see the slight smile spread on Connor's face as some happy memories resurfaced. The thoughts in Knight's head at that moment remained a bit fuzzy, but he acknowledged that they'd seen some good times together. And bad.

"When your dad died, it almost killed you, too," Connor stated. "I remember it well. You were the best soldier I had, and you witnessed unspeakable atrocities, but the death of your own father tore you up. I know the feeling, Andy. It happened to me, too. It happened to a lot of us in this line of work.

"When you fell into that pit, that pit of sadness, of despair, I couldn't let you go. You became a son to me, despite our relatively close ages," he went on.

Knight started to wonder if his boss had lived a previous life as a preacher. The man had obviously put a lot of thought into what he would say to Knight that morning, but that didn't mean Knight had the patience to listen to it through the driving beat of the hangover assaulting his cranium.

"It wasn't a lot of fun, but we got through that. Together."

Knight's face remained rigid, but under the surface, his resolve cracked a little bit around the edges. Those days had been hell, but not as bad as now.

Connor's tone changed along with his facial expression, anger seeping in.

"Then my own son was killed in combat, out in the boonies in South America on a mission no one would tell me about, on a mission that no one could give a good justification for."

Even though he'd heard the story a thousand times, Knight let Connor go on. A man deserved at least that much when his son was killed. To this day, Connor's face still painted a picture of pain and fury. Only that royal cock-up could bring out such aggression in the man, but he recovered gracefully. A burden lifted from his shoulders. Knight just let the man talk. The guy had some stuff to get off his chest.

"You helped get me through that, Andy. You were like a brother to me."

Knight reminisced about those days. Staff Sergeant Cliff Connor's death hadn't immediately been disclosed to the major. Even when they finally did tell him, they lied about the circumstances, assuming the major would never check. But check he did. And he was pissed with what he found.

The short story was that the boy had been sent in with his squad to kidnap a cartel leader's daughter, who would then be exchanged for an important American oil executive who had gotten caught up in the drug trade and kidnapped. Michael Connor felt, reasonably so, that busting the American out of his isolated prison cell in the mountains would have been far easier than penetrating the compound of one of the biggest drug cartels in Colombia.

Connor's son had led the squad taking point. None of them returned. The mission was a total loss and swept under the carpet until the major beat an American intelligence officer to the verge of a coma to get the desired information. Knight didn't blame him, but helped Connor get grounded again and somehow maintain his position in the military long enough for the pair to move into their current line of work: the private sector.

"Well, now it seems like I need to be a father to you again, Andy," Connor stated bluntly. "You've had your ass kicked three times in bar brawls recently. Frankly, I don't believe that is humanly possible considering the asses I've seen you kick in the past."

Connor paused. Knight didn't give him the privilege of a response when no verbal question was asked. His boss just shrugged.

"I'm thinking that you're getting smashed every weekend, then getting it into your mind that you'll go pick a fight with someone who can beat you down as long as you don't fight back." He paused again, but still received nothing in return.

"Now why would you do that?" he asked. "Well, because of Karen, I suspect."

Knight partially succumbed to the emotions welling up inside. He closed his eyes for a full second, no longer caring that his boss would know he'd scored a hit close to the mark.

"Look, Andy, I know about the divorce."

Connor leaned forward onto his desk now. Knight looked away for a moment, an uncharacteristic sign of vulnerability, of humanity. Many, many people had died in front of Knight, typically due to his handiwork. Unfortunately, his marriage was his most recent victim.

"So I need to kick Lehoski's ass for sharing that little tidbit with you."

Connor sighed and shook his head.

"How many times do we need to go through this, Andy? We keep pretty good tabs on all of you guys. We've got to keep you honest, and the best way to do that is to watch your personal lives. To a certain extent, anyway."

"Is Winston Klotzer one of those watchers?" Knight asked.

"Nice try, Andy," Connor replied. "No, we keep Winston around for external use only. I wouldn't have recommended him to you for a personal service if he'd been one of the guys keeping an eye on you. Those guys stay in the shadows, mostly in the electronic shadows, of your life."

Knight shrugged.

"Andy, my guess would be that you hired Winston to check up on Karen."

"That's none of your damn business."

Connor put his hands out in defense.

"In any case, there're things in life that happen in just such a way to perfectly screw us over," explained Connor steadily. "You're in a bad place right now. I get it. But I won't give up on you. You're a damn fine soldier, a great leader, and most importantly, a good man."

Knight looked up and saw the father in Connor taking over the conversation. The elder man pushed back from his desk and stood board-straight as he delivered his verdict.

"You will report to Dr. Malcolm every day for an hour session, for the next two weeks."

The company's psychologist was the last person he wanted to spend any time with, especially because the man had seemed incapable of keeping his eyes off of Karen on the few occasions she'd visited Knight at work.

Of course, everything had been set up to support Knight's cover story as a military consultant, whatever *that* was. As far as Karen knew, Knight's involvement in military action had ended with his honorable discharge. Technically what he did now wasn't exactly "military" action, but close enough to upset his wife who'd spent more than her fair share of nights staying up alone wondering if her husband had been shot, or worse. The work Knight and his crew did was worth her pain, though. None of that changed the fact that Dr. Brandon Malcolm was a creepy bastard. Knight groaned at the thought of the torture to come.

"Don't give me that crap, son. For the sake of my own job, I need you to stay on base until the doc clears you. In a case like this, you would normally be kicked out of our little organization and possibly worse, but for now this is your only punishment."

When greeted only with a scowl, Connor continued.

"I suggest you take this deal, Knight. I suggest you take it, finish your time with the doc, and get yourself straightened out. I'm not taking your men away from you, but you'll need to reaffirm their trust in you. They know you were shaken up by something personal. They're not stupid, but now you need to show that you're still a team player.

"Things are finally starting to fall into place for us here, Andy. Some good assignments are in the works, and I need you on top of your game."

Knight stood stiffly. He knew that Connor was taking a big leap of faith for him. There was no point in losing both his job *and* his wife. Of course, Connor was missing a few pieces of the story, but the basic premise was correct. Knight's inner turmoil still played games with his emotions. Regret over his wife, anger at seeing a shrink, appreciation of someone still having faith in his worthless self.

"Sir, yes, sir. Thank you, sir," Knight said with a crisp salute. As he thought about his new mental health appointments, he added through gritted teeth, "I won't let you down, sir."

"You'll survive," Connor observed, ignoring the exaggerated salute and deliberate overuse of the word "sir." "You're dismissed."

Knight turned promptly and strode to the exit, resisting the urge to rip the door off its hinges. Why hadn't he just been there for Karen when she needed him? The same question constantly rocketed around in his head. In response, the same emotions of failure and anger always boiled up. There was no escape from himself.

***

Connor watched his friend storm out of his office. Knight had done enough to express his gratitude by not breaking anything. Not like last week.

Connor had tried to do the right thing by Andy. The guy was going through a seriously rough patch, so Connor had given him a bye on his poor behavior over the last few weeks. Unfortunately, enough word had gotten around the base that Rook, Knight's codename, had lost the plot. Albatross, Connor's boss, had come down hard, telling him to take care of it, or he would. Brigadier General Thomas McGarvey was not a man to be trifled with.

Connor sifted through some papers on his desk, an activity that increased dramatically in the private side of his industry. The bosses felt that Connor's great mind should be attached to a desk, instead of out in the combat spaces, where he could easily have that brain taken from him. From them.

The mundane supply analysis report fell to the desk as Connor put his elbows on his desk and rubbed his aching temples. He vividly remembered the talks years ago with the young man who'd just left. Telling a betrothed man to leave his wife-to-be for his job. That his country needed him more than one woman did. That she could find a new man.

That had gone down like a lead balloon.

At the time, Connor really had believed that it would end up being Karen Knight dealing with the sudden loss of her spouse, not Andrew Knight struggling with losing his. The irony stung. Now Connor deeply regretted not forcing his protégé to leave his fiancée years ago. It would've saved them all a lot of trouble, in more ways than one. The office door opened unannounced and more trouble entered.

"Condor, I hope you took care of it," McGarvey declared, implying the worst. The stately general closed the door behind him and turned on the lights, not needing to ask permission. For whatever reason, the good general insisted on referring to all of the men in this organization by their codenames, Condor in Connor's case. It was a bit ridiculous to Connor, but McGarvey made the rules.

Connor stood quickly.

"Yes, sir. Rook will report for psych evaluation immediately with Dove and attend an hour session daily, sir."

"Level with me, Condor. Is that going to be enough?" McGarvey asked in his most practiced CEO voice. "This is our first big shit contract with the government, and we don't want your main man going pear-shaped on us."

Connor knew what the answer needed to be.

"Yes, sir. Rook's the best soldier I've ever had. He'll recover quickly," Connor responded. He felt his illustrious career slipping away into obscurity as he uttered the sentences that would seal his fate, one way or the other.

"Good, good. As a heads up, they're being shipped out soon for a rescue mission in Antarctica. Seems like we have a little lost Angel down there."

Chapter 7

Each tick from the grandfather clock in the hall emphasized one less second until her arrival. The mechanical sound echoed off the hardwood floors of the motionless house, continually breaking the looming silence with its consistency. Knight didn't even notice the external noise. Deep inside his discombobulated head, difficult thoughts swirled viciously, heedless of the damage they caused.

His wife had dropped the divorce bomb on him and had immediately moved out to stay with her sister, Katie. Having never seen eye to eye with Knight, Katie probably reveled in his discomfort and probably orchestrated the entire affair. The word *affair* set off another cluster-bomb in his skull. He really didn't need that right now.

Sadness was an unusual experience for Knight. He supposed most men didn't feel truly sad that often. Sure, watching his favorite team blow it in the Super Bowl had left him feeling moderately depressed for a moment, but that moment passed swiftly, all remnants of the day forgotten until the next time a colleague maliciously ribbed him about the wasteful loss. By that time, the whole situation was more comical than serious.

This was different. These emotions felt as alien as they had when he'd first heard that his dad had died. The sensation of powerlessness haunted the career soldier. In his job, an assortment of weapons and a solid support system empowered him to survive even the most hazardous and life-threatening scenarios. Having common sense and a cool head helped, too. With both his father's death and his current family crisis, none of these attributes seemed to count for much. Too many questions led to far too few answers, none of which added up to anything concrete.

Why did Karen want a divorce? The drinking? No, that hadn't started until *after* her little announcement. At least he was sober now. Moments like this convinced Knight that he wasn't a true alcoholic, at least not yet. With Karen coming over, resisting the urge to get hammered had proved an easy victory. She'd be far less inclined to deal with him as a drunk, slurring mess. He felt like he had an opportunity to flesh things out with her this morning.

Okay, so it wasn't the drinking. Was it the travel? It was true that his new job kept him away a lot. Of course, she thought he was just a military consultant, trekking around the world to inspect training grounds and monitor teaching procedures. He was certainly teaching lessons, but not in the way she thought.

Perhaps that was it. Had Karen found out about his true occupation? She had gotten tired of worrying the nights away while he was in the Army. When Connor had presented a business proposition to Knight, he'd jumped at the chance to serve his country, make a ton of money, and also smooth things out with Karen. The smoothing process had involved a creative spin on the truth, but that was okay if it rid her of the paranoia that he'd be dead at any minute. Right?

Or perhaps the divorce was brought on by the circumstances surrounding their marriage in the first place. This made little sense to Knight considering it was all her idea, but maybe he could've stuck around more to help her out and support her in such a heavy time of need.

Before he could delve deeper into that scenario, a key turned in the lock to the front door. Knight had always intentionally left the deadbolt disengaged to allow her free entry whenever she so desired, but this was the first time she'd come back. His whole being smiled when he saw her silhouette backlit in the doorway, both because he was relieved that she'd actually shown up, and because she apparently left Katie at home. When Karen stepped into the entryway, Knight's smile dropped.

"Hi, Andy," she said, fatigue encumbering her few words.

"Karen, what's wrong?" Knight blurted out. "What happened?"

His wife's beautiful face looked gaunt and grey. Despite asking the questions, he felt like he already knew the answers. He recognized the signs from years before, from their wedding day.

Karen sighed weakly with some effort.

"I really don't want to talk about it," she answered, not meeting his concerned gaze. "Did you pack the stuff I asked for?"

Knight pointed to the stack of boxes lying at the foot of the stairs. Clothes, mementos, even vitamins. Packing all of the evidence of her life ripping away from his own had occurred with a surgical detachment that Knight had developed and honed in combat. Putting thought into the process would've led to emotions that he had no intention of dredging up at that point. Of course, they'd thrust themselves out of the dark depths of his heart anyway.

"Thanks," she said, moving towards the boxes.

Struggling to lift a box that Knight knew to be fairly light, she turned and asked for his help.

"Not until you tell me what's going on, Karen. Is this a relapse?"

Karen paused, closed her eyes tightly, and then started crying quietly.

Disregarding any thoughts of maintaining the barriers built up between himself and his soon-to-be ex-wife, Knight followed his husbandly instincts and knelt on the floor next to Karen, hugging her close. With her head tilted down, long brown hair stuck to the tears streaking down her face. She resisted his embrace for only a moment before melting into the familiar comfort of his body.

"I didn't want you to find out about it," she sniffed. "It's been so hard, but I just didn't want you to worry."

"Of course I would worry, but that's because I love you."

Knight could feel his wife shiver slightly against him, fighting back a full-on bawl. He held her closer. She sniffed hard and composed herself for a moment.

"I've been seeing a therapist. We meet over at the coffee shop on Congress," she explained. Looking up into his eyes she added, "I just didn't want you to suffer with me on this. Not again."

So that explains the stranger in the coffee shop, Knight thought. He'd have to let Winston know about that.

"So you wanted a divorce to hide the cancer? So that I wouldn't worry?" Knight inquired, confused beyond all measure.

Karen nodded, her brow bunched up with the strain of the tears.

"It's bad, Andy. Really bad," she said.

"But you beat it before," Knight pointed out.

She shook her head.

"The doctor says it's worse. A lot worse."

"What's the prognosis?"

"Not long. Probably not even long enough to make it through a divorce," she sobbed.

Knight grimaced, but held her tight.

"I'm a bit lost here, Karen," he said softly, holding her head close to his. "You wanted to divorce me because you thought the cancer would kill you, and you didn't want me to be around to suffer with you? To worry about you?"

She nodded again. Telling her that her reasoning was critically flawed wouldn't help anything. Knight bit his tongue.

"Please, Karen. Let me be there for you."

Karen hardened physically, tensing up incredibly. Was there more that she wasn't sharing?

"Please, Karen. I'll do a better job than last time," he assured her. *That shouldn't be too hard*, he thought.

A weighty silence descended on the pair, the husband and wife huddled on the floor together. Knight gazed at the boxes lying on the floor, hoping against hope that Karen would tell him to unpack them again. He felt her body decompress, as if the stress had located a relief valve and exited her soul peacefully.

"Okay," she said.

Knight gripped his wife as she continued to vent out the pent-up emotions that haunted her. True relief washed over him, despite a shameful lurking suspicion. The situation still didn't make sense to him, but he would be there for her this time. She wouldn't endure this assault alone.

Chapter 8

"Cancer, huh?"

"Yes, sir. This is the second time she's had it, but the prognosis is much worse."

"So exactly what are you asking for here, Condor?"

"Do you have any connections that can get Karen Knight in to see an Angel?"

The phone hung in an electronic silence.

"I can make that happen, Condor," replied Albatross. "Bear in mind what this will mean."

"And what is that, sir?"

"It means that you'll owe me one."

"One, sir?"

"Yes, one. If I need a mission done even farther off the books than your typical assignments, you'll do it," explained Albatross. "And if you or your men fail, it's on your head, not mine."

Connor stared at the picture on his desk of his dead son, contemplating how far he'd go to help out Knight, the closest thing to a son that he had left. Hearing Andy's voice on the end of the phone moments earlier had affected Connor deeply. The young man had held it together, trying to hide his emotions, but Connor knew him too well. This was worse than divorce. Karen was going to die, and Andy felt stranded, impotent, hopeless.

The father figure strode out confidently off the ship and onto the plank for his son.

"Understood, sir."

"Excellent, then I'll make the appropriate arrangements. It shouldn't take long."

That business concluded, Connor felt the relief of ending what he'd thought would be a far tougher conversation. The major was used to sticking his neck out for his men, but this was a bit different. His relief was tempered by a dread of what could go wrong with any deep black operations that Albatross may demand in the future. Brigadier General McGarvey wasted no time diving into the next topic on the agenda.

"So this assistance should improve Rook's chances of success on this upcoming assignment to Antarctica then?" Albatross asked.

"Yes, sir."

"Level with me, Condor. Is Rook going to get his shit together quickly? Can he run this mission? It should be a simple way to get an easy win for the good guys and regain some trust," Albatross suggested with a skeptical eyebrow traversing the wires between the two phones.

Connor knew that his boss was throwing Knight a softball with this one. It really was an easy way to build up respect with the men who'd witnessed some of his more adventurous alcoholic endeavors recently. Flying down to the South Pole to retrieve an Angel should be a relatively simple task. No kind of danger had been encountered with them so far. He did wonder how the creature could survive down there with no clothes, assuming it was naked like all the rest.

Also, why on Earth would an Angel be walking around in such an unpopulated area? Visiting the penguins?

Connor realized that allowing his mind to drift in the middle of a discussion with his boss wasn't the wisest course of action. The only important matter was the topic of a potentially unbalanced Knight leading a group of men into an abusively cold and remote climate.

"Rook can handle this assignment competently, sir," he stated to his boss, who had obviously waited more than long enough for a reply.

"I admire your commitment to your men, Condor," the general stated. "It's your ass if you're wrong, Condor."

"Yes, sir."

After the *click* signaled McGarvey had ended the conversation, Connor slumped into his chair and stared at the ceiling for a moment. The military man didn't feel hopeless, just unsure. Unpredictability wasn't a welcome commodity in his business. Sending an unstable leader into the field left him uneasy, even if the assignment should be perfectly straightforward. Of course, in their line of work, jobs rarely finished perfectly according to plan.

Not to mention that McGarvey obviously had powerful friends. Even the way that the general operated with impunity around the Pentagon hinted that he had some very, very high level support. Private groups like Connor's got hired on to do work that the military wouldn't touch with a ten-foot pole, but McGarvey suffered no backlash from the ops. Connor found it hard not to worry about what failure would mean. The general could easily ruin him. Or worse. Why would a man with as much classified information as Connor be allowed to walk away?

"Don't screw me over, Andy," Connor said to himself as he picked up an inventory transfer request form.

Chapter 9

Chaos ruled the exterior grounds of the largest medical facility in Phoenix, and inside the Angel's current abode, order hung on by a thin thread. The demonstrations and protests outside over fair access to the healing abilities of the Angel remained relatively peaceful compared to those seen in other countries, with only minor scrapes and bruises from the more fervent protestors clashing with police. For Knight, the whole ordeal remained bittersweet.

As he and Karen had circled the hospital in a private helicopter that resembled all of the others orbiting in the queue, he had looked down on all of the unfortunate leagues of humanity. Thousands of the ill and sick from around the country had congregated around the large medical complex, and loved ones desperately sought to have their cases heard. Both the police and the hospital staff had to turn a deaf ear and a blind eye to the suffering citizens pleading for mercy, begging for healing.

He didn't like to admit it, but the scene definitely disturbed Knight at a core level. These were, mostly, United States citizens, all trying to receive the same benefit that he had inexplicably received. Some of the privileged occupants of the other private helicopters coasting in the impromptu choreography over Phoenix surely felt entitled to this treatment. In fact, most of them probably felt it was far below their station to wait in line with the masses for a beer, never mind a full recovery from terminal cancer or full blown AIDS.

But Knight didn't feel special. He never had. All he'd done was call his boss to share the bad news with a good man that he trusted. Less than an hour later, Knight and Karen had been picked up and whisked away to the awaiting air transportation.

Gratitude did not begin to describe Knight's feelings. Even the sad view of a hopeless crowd couldn't fully mitigate the happiness he felt, the joy he experienced over his wife's impending recovery from the disease that ravaged her insides. Looking at Karen now next to him, her hearing protection poofing up her otherwise straight hair in strange places, Knight couldn't imagine loving someone more. She smiled at him, and he reached out to hold her hand. This was her first time up in a helicopter, and Knight just wished she'd had something prettier to look at outside the window.

At least the accommodations were top-notch. Knight hadn't recognized the luxury aircraft, but the helicopter was well appointed, with leather seats and a mini-bar. Slightly different from the military helos he'd spent years cruising around in. The smooth ride felt a bit alien after shuddering around in Blackhawk jump-seats. Incoming bullets typically caused a rough ride in his line of work. Despite the relative niceties surrounding him, Knight felt no connection to the wealth. He leaned his face to the window again.

The newspapers said that some families had pulled relatives off of life support systems around the country and dragged their devastatingly sick family members into this writhing mob. Apparently they felt that they could force the issue with the authorities. Maybe they could get the medical staff and the police to see that their loved one would die at any moment if not immediately admitted to the hospital for the Angel's touch.

Of course, such ill-conceived schemes wouldn't work. Even if they could somehow ford the sea of humanity and get up to the front, the police barricade had strict instructions to ignore all cries for help and to repel all aggressive advances. Knight didn't want to think about how many of these terminally ill patients would fall victim to the desperation of their own loving families.

The pilot signaled back that their time had come. Karen's grip on Knight's hand tightened in anticipation. With a smooth swoop, they were on the ground and following orderlies under the spinning rotors. Inside the hospital, echoes of a distant rabble filled the hallways as Knight and his wife strode hand-in-hand down clinically clean corridor after corridor until they reached the designated waiting area.

The sight perturbed Knight. He'd expected a lot more jostling and jockeying. In fact, he'd just assumed there would be far more people. The waiting room could've easily held twice the number currently occupying the space. Dotted around the large room were small groups of family and friends. In some cases, the patients were obvious, strapped to gurneys and hooked up to medical equipment. In others, nobody looked visibly sick, but even as ill as Karen was, she didn't look like death quite yet.

Knight silently thanked both his lucky stars and Michael Connor one more time. One day he'd ask Connor how he'd pulled this off.

But still, where was everyone? Karen apparently had the same thought.

"Andy, I think these are only the people from the helicopters."

As they were ushered to their specific seating area, a more detailed scan of the room revealed quite a wealthy demographic. Nobody looked haggard or even just middle-class. A collective sigh of relief enveloped the space, all the families thankful that their dying loved one would soon be cured. Knight wondered at what cost.

"I think you're right," he whispered back.

Karen turned to the orderly who had led them from the helicopter.

"What happens to all the people who don't have helicopters?" she asked quietly.

The orderly looked like he'd really have preferred for Karen to have not asked that particular question, but a few heads nearby had turned to hear his response. He composed himself and whispered back.

"There is another group being admitted based on certain requirements."

"And what are those requirements?" Karen asked.

Now the guy looked really uncomfortable, which piqued Knight's curiosity. Ever the advocate of the masses, Karen insisted a little bit louder.

"Okay, okay," the orderly responded, hushing Karen. "Terminally ill and wounded patients can get on a list. We already took care of all the ones residing in the hospital, but we still have only so many beds and so many staff to assist with the huge numbers involved here."

"A list? You mean first come, first served? Or more like a lottery?" Karen pressed.

"I don't know that, ma'am," he replied quickly. "I've already told you more than anyone needs to know."

With that, the man walked off, anxious to avoid correction from his superiors, Knight was sure. So somewhere else in the hospital was another queue of sorts, but who got precedence, the rich or the rest? Knight looked around and wondered if some of these wealthy bastards weren't even that sick to start with. How far would the bureaucracy at the hospital go to make a buck?

With that thought, the double doors at the other end of the room opened and a pair of orderlies and a uniformed cop strolled in and collected the next group of lucky winners. Knight wasn't about to make a stink prior to his wife seeing the Angel, and he was glad that he could be here to share the healing moment with her. It would probably be difficult to get too indignant about the unfairness of the situation without coming across as incredibly ungrateful for the amazing gift that he and his wife were set to receive.

The doors swung open again and another group of escorts grabbed the next contestants. On the other side of the room, two more small groups rolled into the waiting room and sat down in the appointed places. Knight wondered if the two queues of people, the rich and the not rich, alternated back and forth between who got to see the Angel first. Also, how long was the other queue?

Before he could ponder that unanswerable conundrum, his phone burst into song, murdering the happy silence that had previously inhabited the room. He smiled sheepishly and cursed the idiot calling him, despite never giving advanced warning to anyone who might call around this time of day. It wasn't like he'd received that much warning that his wife had been fast-tracked to the top of the most important list in the country.

The caller ID revealed the code for one of the numbers at the Fort. Was Connor calling to check up on them?

"I need to take this, sweetheart," he whispered.

She nodded and gave a weak smile as he squeezed her shoulder one last time before walking into the deserted hallway. Past the waiting room's double doors, the noise of the crowd outside rattled the windows with a dull drone. No security guards stood or sat on this particular hallway, which suggested to Knight that they had secured a perimeter on the next hallway over. Surely someone was keeping the commoners away from the wealthy folk residing with Karen in the waiting room.

"This is Rook," he said into the phone after finally answering it. He had his phone set up to ring for a long, long time before hitting voicemail. Certain calls couldn't be missed.

"Rook, report back to the Fort immediately."

The clipped tone, the general sense of frustration, and the obvious disregard for Knight's predicament all pointed to Vulture. Even in a private paramilitary organization, someone had to handle mission planning and logistics. For a guy with little field experience, Vulture managed to perform the critical job half-decently, rarely putting Knight and his men in insanely and pointlessly dangerous situations.

Of course, some missions would prove impossible, no matter what strategic planning took place beforehand. That small fact wouldn't stop Knight from hating Vulture for every injury and death sustained by the group. The arrogant prick didn't respond well to Knight's attitude.

"You know where I am, Vulture."

"Of course I do. That doesn't mean anything because you got more important places to be. Get on the next helicopter after it's dropped off its passengers. Copy?"

Fists balled in rage, Knight refused to acknowledge the order.

"Copy that, Rook?"

Could he leave Karen here? In her hour of victory? Their moment of redemption, a chance to start fresh?

Connor would shoot him if he didn't follow Vulture's insensitive orders. Knight just hoped that this was damn important and not just some inane training exercise that Vulture set up specifically to ruin Knight's day. He'd lay the guy out *again* for that.

"Roger."

He pulled the phone away from his ear and could hear Vulture prattling on about something, but Knight couldn't have cared less. He hung up and wandered back into the waiting room, pausing just inside the double doors. Watching the back of his wife's head, he considered her possible reactions. She would be pissed, and rightly so. Once again her husband was ditching her because of work, and that had to hurt.

Knight just shook his head and approached his wife. He sat down next to her and just sat in silence for a moment, choosing his words carefully. Karen removed the need.

"You have to leave, don't you?" she said, looking at her hands clasped together in her lap.

"Yeah, I'm so sorry."

A tear rolled down her pale cheek, but she wiped it away with a smile and a sniff. Her reaction was a bit surprising.

"Your job is the only reason I'm here, Andy," she said, still smiling. "I wish to hell that you didn't have to go, but we owe them my life."

Hand on hers, Knight reached forward and kissed her forehead. He truly prayed that she really felt this way, and he loved his wife all the more for hearing her forgive him for his absence. And all the more Knight wanted to punch Vulture's lights out for ruining this life-altering event for Karen. What a bastard he was.

"Just come back as soon as you can, Andy. Okay?"

Chapter 10

"And after the break, we'll be back with world-renowned Angel expert, Dr. William Baird."

Rapturous applause broke out in waves. The walls and floor of the green room trembled with the excitement from the television studio just down the hall. Billy Baird continued to watch the huge flat-screen monitor on the wall as a nice Vietnamese lady adjusted his hair one final time. The water bottle in his hand did little to salve the dryness in his mouth that always accompanied these last moments before a television spot with whatever talk show host had booked him.

How did I get myself into this?

The simple truth was that he hadn't done anything out of the ordinary. Unless calling the British embassy in Kenya and reporting the miraculous healing of a cancer-stricken woman by a giant pink bloke counted as "out of the ordinary." How that single act qualified Baird as the preeminent expert on all things related to these Angels was beyond him. He was just a doctor who used to be a paratrooper. He'd always thought that that was impressive enough.

Now he awaited his summons to the floor. A ludicrously wealthy talk show host was about to interview him on crap that he had no real clue about. Sure, he had canned answers to all of her prearranged questions, but in reality, he didn't know anything about these Angels that any Joe Blow couldn't learn from picking up a newspaper.

The lady attending to his grooming, Sue, removed the protective paper from inside his collar. Apparently she was satisfied that everything was in place, and that he wasn't going to screw it all up now. Even the minute amounts of makeup that they applied made the former paratrooper incredibly uncomfortable. If only his mates knew about this. He'd never hear the end of it.

When he'd asked his mum for advice, all she'd said was, "Take advantage of it while you can, because those numpties will forget you the minute there's some juicier news."

He suspected that there was a great deal of truth to that. A few of the major chat shows still wanted him to make an appearance, but the spots were getting shorter and shorter already. This one would only last about five minutes. A few quick questions and then he'd be done. No problemo.

The attention was nice. He'd never been pampered in his life, growing up in Govan, the Protestant part of Glasgow. Not the kind of place that made life as a Catholic very easy. In fact, it was borderline suicidal at times. Catholicism wasn't just a belief system for Baird; it was a cultural identity. None of his fellow Catholics had attended church regularly, in the same way that none of the Proddies had bothered going to services. It was all about the bloody football.

A bonnie intern popped her head through the door of the green room and motioned for Baird to follow her. Quickly. With a brief wave and smile to Sue, he strode after the power-walking intern.

She had a permanent smile plastered on her face, but she was obviously harassed beyond belief.

Not his problem.

As he walked, Baird noticed two men talking to each other in the hallway. One wore a royal blue shirt and the other an emerald green jacket.

You'd never see such a sight in Glasgow.

Then again, neither one would have any clue about the intense footy rivalry between Rangers and Celtic in Scotland. The blue and the green. The Protestants and the Catholics. Didn't they have enough bloody problems without bothering about ancient disputes that didn't mean a flippin' thing in the real world anymore?

Who cares that some people love the Pope and some don't? Just leave well enough alone.

At the end of the day, didn't they all believe in the same Angels now?

His stressed-out companion flashed him one more strained smile before forcibly ushering him onto the stage. As taught by his coach, he ignored the intensely bright lights as much as he could and strode towards his host with a huge grin on his face, extending a hand for the afore-practiced handshake.

Before sinking into the rehearsed repertoire, Baird wondered what would be in the gift basket at the end of the interview. He could use a stiff drink.

Chapter 11

The members of Phalanx filed into the briefing room and sat down at individual desks not unlike those found in the average grade school. Unlike high school, no paper or pens adorned the plastic surfaces. Times had changed and each person carried a small tablet computer.

Phalanx didn't appear on any public record. Technically they were part of the Rapid Interdiction Force set up by the Pentagon, but a vast majority of the Pentagon had no idea about the group's identity or activities. The RIF made *classified information* look like the front page of the New York Times. The people present all reported to Condor alone, who then reported to a guy codenamed Albatross, whose true identity was always up for debate.

No one in the team had any idea who Albatross answered to, but no one cared too much. The group assembled in the room had been promised the kind of action that elite special forces units would normally handle, except Phalanx got paid a lot more. Most of them were still waiting for the excitement they'd expected, but at least the money was rolling in from the simple escort or courier missions they'd already completed.

In traditional special operations outfits, any action took months of planning due to obscene levels of mostly pointless red tape and bureaucracy, in addition to mandatory recon and intel gathering. After a few close calls and more than one failure to act in time, the upper echelons at the Pentagon decided that a special group was necessary to execute assignments on an accelerated time table. The higher-ups finally realized that certain unfortunate situations demanded a prompt, and typically forceful, response. From this train of thought, the Rapid Interdiction Force was born.

Within the RIF, at least one independently operated private group existed. Phalanx stood at the ready to move on a moment's notice, to save, defend, capture, or kill their objectives. As a designated leader in RIF team Phalanx, Knight held the highest clout out in the field.

The briefing room door opened, and the man with the mission strode in, followed by his administrative assistant, Vulture, whose real name was actually Joe Berkman. Knight shared Berkman's rank within the organization, but not much else. The two came into conflict frequently about mission strategy and execution, especially on days like today.

Knight felt that they had a necessarily abrasive dynamic that resulted in optimum tactics and results. Berkman just thought that Knight was a jackass.

Connor scanned the rows of school-style desks briefly, taking a quick attendance check, before launching into the briefing.

"Phalanx, your next mission may seem beneath you, but I want to begin this session by reinforcing the severity of the issue and the absolute necessity for success," he began.

Some of the soldiers looked at each other amid a sea of eyes rolling internally. Such overt disrespect would never be tolerated by the major had anyone actually expressed any impatience with him or the mission.

Knight remembered the last rookie who had spoken out of turn during a briefing. He had been summarily discharged back into the military and assigned to the kitchen of a base in the desert of New Mexico. Questions were encouraged. Disrespect led to punishment. Such was the life of the Phalanx, America's defenders. At least, that's how Knight thought of the group. Anything less would've made it a lot harder to lie to his wife every day about what he did for a living.

These men and women formed the solid barrier across which no evil could penetrate. Like the Greek battle formation of old, the Phalanx proved impregnable. The team chose their battles based on their strengths, just as the ancient phalanx worked perfectly for specific situations. Or at least, that was the intent. Since the group's recent inception, they hadn't done anything too fun. Most of the men were antsy for that to change.

"This is a relatively simple rescue mission. We have an incredibly high priority target that needs immediate retrieval," Connor continued. "Before anyone gets too excited, let me add that the target is an Angel," he stated with a smirk. Every eye locked onto Connor, suddenly enthralled.

"And the location is Antarctica."

Had the group been allowed to murmur amongst themselves during meetings, the room would have erupted at this point. Knight saw that not one person broke eye contact with Connor. These professionals instantly knew the stakes here.

"Our government has chosen us because almost nobody even knows that we exist. As such, you can operate in places that the average Army soldier cannot.

"The government would like to keep this under wraps for a few reasons, but I suspect an important one is not letting the world know that we acquired an Angel from another continent. As you know, the Angels that have been found so far, or at least the ones we know about, have been very spread out. No continent has received more than one."

Connor paused for a moment to nod to Berkman, who dimmed the lights and fired up a slideshow presentation on the screen behind Connor. Knight saw an interesting list of locations.

"As you are probably already aware, Angels have shown up in Phoenix, Glasgow, Brisbane, Nairobi, Shanghai, and Rio Di Janeiro. They've all been moved into major hospitals in the local areas, in order to give the public access to their healing powers.

"Any of you who doubt the supernatural healing abilities can pick up a newspaper and read all about it," he added, assuming at least some in the room didn't believe in the religious aspect of the Angels.

Knight had yet to make up his mind on the religion side, but he was seriously grateful that Karen had seen an Angel. She'd texted him earlier to let him know she was on her way home.

The Angels had appeared out of nowhere. They had started healing sick people left and right, and they expressed no desire to do anything but. Not a religious man by upbringing, Knight still had a hard time dismissing the Christian angelic notion.

Plus, what did it all mean? Was the world ending as many major pastors preached constantly?

At the end of the day, Knight did not care about heaven and hell. If he hadn't done enough good deeds in the world to secure a place in whatever afterlife awaited him, then he wanted no part of that place.

***

Unbeknownst to Knight, a major event that Connor did *not* share with the group involved the recovery of an Angel by a U.S. Navy ship in the Mediterranean.

Local fishermen had investigated a flash of light in the sea, and the Navy had responded, intercepting the communications in a possibly illegal manner. That Angel was now en route to a secure facility in the continental U.S. After ensuring that the Italian fishermen had no idea about the nature of the flash of light, the Navy let them go on their way. The need for secrecy had been severely impressed upon the ship's commanding officer, for whatever good that would do.

In the event that the sailors reneged on their agreement, their limited information would be of no consequence. They had not actually *seen* the Angel itself or the U.S. Navy ship recovering said Angel.

Connor had received a direct order not to inform any of his own men and women after he inadvertently discovered the news about this Mediterranean Angel. Secrets could never remain secret when more than one person knew about them, but Connor wouldn't be the one to spread the highly classified information, even with a close ally like Knight.

"Another string of stories that you will probably notice in the news in the next couple of days concerns the crowds of civilians desperately trying to see these Angels," Connor remarked. "Some of these hospitals will wish they'd never even heard of an Angel by the time this all plays out."

The image of Shanghai's streets packed with protestors made Connor smile inwardly. Not that he had anything against the Chinese people, but that government didn't have a particularly good track record in dealing with mass protest. It could get interesting.

"Condor, sir?" Knight asked politely, using Connor's codename by necessity, not choice, most likely. Connor gave him a nod.

"When will the government reveal the second Angel to the world? Seems like they'll be pissed no matter where we found it," Knight said.

"That's not our problem, Rook," Connor responded evenly. "The government has other groups to handle things like that, I'm sure. We just need to make our part happen."

Everyone in the room could be counted on to be the ultimate patriot, if for no other reason than to continue getting paid. Connor highly doubted that any one of them would begrudge the U.S. for obtaining another Angel for its citizens. Even if they knew that the U.S. actually already had two in its possession, they wouldn't care. Their country had to come first.

"As a small side note, the Antarctic Treaty of 1959 greatly restricts the use of military forces in the deep south end of the world," Connor announced. After letting the group mull that over for a moment, he added, "Obviously this isn't the first time that we've sent you out with instructions to not get caught, but I want to reiterate it anyway. *Don't get caught.*

"You will be discretely armed, but you must maintain your cover. It's necessary to interact with civilians down there, mostly scientists, but you can't let on to the true purpose of the mission.

"Before I turn you over to Vulture for the more intricate details of this mission, I should point out that the Chinese and the Russians probably have the same intelligence that we do. Time is of the essence."

***

The group rose as the major nodded to Berkman and left the room swiftly. Certain military protocols and etiquettes remained in Phalanx despite the privatization of the destruction the group delivered.

Before Berkman started speaking, Knight turned to his trusty second-in-command, Brian Lehoski, and said, "Karen's not going to leave."

Lehoski stared at his friend and replied, "Oh yeah? What happened?"

"I'll fill you in later, but it's damn near miraculous," Knight whispered.

"Whatever works."

Berkman interrupted the hushed conversation in the arrogant way that only he could.

"If you ladies are just about finished making out in the back, I'd like to explain to you how you're going to sneak an eight-foot tall, pink Angel out of Antarctica."

Chapter 12

Helicopters circled overhead in the blue sky, their rotors pumping loudly as they descended in a well-orchestrated dance to a single landing pad. Unseen to the gathered crowds of increasingly panicky onlookers, hospital attendants rushed to each helicopter to help retrieve the precious cargo. Sterile gurneys transported the amazingly wealthy, yet unfortunately terminally ill members of Chinese society into Shanghai's Renji Hospital.

Despite the view-obscuring makeshift fences and police barricades, Li Ping knew exactly the type of people seeking treatment in this world-renowned medical facility. She had no doubt that this blessed hospital catered now only to the elite, while hoards of terribly sick Chinese citizens, both middle- and lower-class, slowly rotted in the streets outside.

Disgust inflamed Ping. Disgust at her oppressive and hypocritical government, disgust at the hospital's governing body, and a more immediate disgust for the increasingly large contingent of police officers keeping Ping and her comrades away from the Sanctuary of the Healer. China had not adopted the same nomenclature as the Western states. No heavenly angels alighted in this land.

The crowd bustled organically as the numbers continued to grow. Ping felt like she was floating in the gentle waves of a sea of humanity. Those gentle waves gave subtle hints of an unpredictable, growing intensity. A crowd could turn into a mob in an instant with the right catalyst.

As a medical student from the university that owned Renji Hospital, Ping had thought she could gain access to have the Healer touch her cancer-stricken mother, who stood resolutely beside her, flowing gracefully in the currents of the people. They had made it no further than the concrete barricades erected preemptively to ensure the sixteen-hundred bed hospital remained open only to those who could afford the prohibitively steep price of admission. Anger stirred in Ping's gut.

Standing at five feet and three inches, Ping could see over the few rows of people in front of her if she stood on her tiptoes. Balancing in the undulations of the crowd became a little more challenging when fully extended vertically, but Ping had practiced *t'ai chi ch'uan* for years, building strong balance in the process. As she looked over the head of a small woman in front of her, Ping could make out a policeman on a horse, slowly cantering down the line of police decked out in riot gear.

The horseman yelled orders to the helmet-clad and shield-toting men, orders that couldn't be heard above the dull roar of the people around Ping. Her heart almost stopped when she recognized the man.

Officer Zhang, the man who'd killed her brother.

As if feeling the sharp point of her hatred-fueled stare, Zhang cautiously turned his head towards her. Ping didn't cower, confident that the man would never pick her out of the masses, or even recall her face. She assumed that the dog couldn't even remember her brother, beaten to death in the street for associating with antigovernment students at the university. She knew in her heart that her brother had done nothing to undermine the government. He had told her just that very morning that he recently met these new people who seemed so cool and fun.

"He probably didn't even know about their subversion," Ping had insisted when questioned later, earning her a slap across the face. Tears of hot rage then accompanied the streaks of dark sadness on her cheeks. Prompted by such vile memories, those same tears threatened to force their way out once more.

"No!" she suddenly yelled. The people in her immediate vicinity instantly stopped grinding against each other. That section of the human machine started a chain reaction, a ripple of attention across a large portion of the crowd.

Ping's mother looked up at her daughter's defiant face and asked, "No what, Ping?"

The younger woman stared ferociously at the police captain on his horse, strutting behind a wall of concrete. The rage summoned dark ideas about what she would do to that man. All she wanted in that moment was a second alone to drive a knife through his throat.

The urgency of her cry still captivated the immediate crowd, but the outer layers of people started to mull around and bustle once more. Ping blinked hard and snapped back into reality, shaking her head for a moment, her long, dark hair swinging sadly. She turned back to her mother.

"Mother, this isn't right. We must do something," she urged. Her mother returned her intense stare.

"Then do it."

Ping looked around. Even those closest to her had turned their backs once more, more intent on watching the police

Could she do this?

Would the people follow her?

She swallowed hard.

Would the police *kill* her?

The image of her mutilated brother flashed so vividly that she could swear he was lying right in front of her. The sight made her dizzy. The pain welled up. Her mother grabbed her as she staggered, awakening a determined and resolute Ping.

"Everyone, listen to me," she yelled, louder than she imagined she ever could.

Faces turned to her, mostly in annoyance at the interruption. Seeing Zhang cock his head in her direction only strengthened Ping's resolve to do what was necessary.

"It is our right to see this Healer, too. Not just for the rich!" she screamed. The crowd murmured anxiously, disbelief turning into faith.

"Who are they to say we cannot be healed?" she demanded. "Will I watch my own mother die while I stand only one hundred meters from her salvation?"

The people started to respond to her questions, quietly at first, with one eye on the police guard. Ping grew more and more animated, and those around her spread the word throughout the gathering. The mob started to form.

"We must fight!" she yelled, terrified, but beyond angry. As the chant radiated across the mob, they transformed into protestors, standing up for their rights against an oppressive regime. The police held their ground, waiting to see how far these simple citizens would take their cause.

Ping continued to yell encouragement to her comrades, urging them onwards as she started to push her way through the masses. She looked up and saw no media helicopters. Ping would have bet anything that all media were being kept at long range under strict orders.

Fear started to grip her. The police could do anything. Ping knew that she had to act quickly, before the panic paralyzed her. The surging anger in her bones had to last long enough to reach the concrete barrier holding her people back.

A clear path formed ahead of her, people acknowledging her leadership by allowing her the first opportunity to breach the first line of defense. She recalled the first time that she had jumped off of a diving board as a child. Looking up at it, she had known that she must climb the ladder and immediately run off the end, for fear of stalling.

Regarding the concrete barrier in front of her, the same feeling gripped her. With clenched fists, she ran at the barrier, easily leapt over it, and never looked back.

***

The woman stared police Captain Zhang Hao down as he raised his rifle. She hesitated for a moment before he shot her three times in the chest, dropping her dead before she touched the asphalt. His men flinched next to him, yet knew better than to look at him. Many had often considered how such a sociopath could rise so quickly through the police ranks. They looked on in shock, their faces hidden beneath their protective masks.

Zhang's plan to kill the uprising's leader in order to quell the riot failed.

As the echoes of the shots faded, the dam burst. Citizens rushed the suddenly heavily outnumbered police force. Brandishing riot shields and clubs, the Chinese police thoughtlessly beat their brothers and sisters into the ground, mindlessly performing their duties.

From high-rise buildings all around the violence, teenagers collected video evidence with their cell phones and a few deftly slid the information under the door of the country's strict internet barricades. Instantly, the world knew.

***

"Mr. Prime Minister, I urge you to reconsider your position."

"I'm sorry, Jacques, but you have to understand that my hands are tied on this."

"The French people—"

"Are of secondary concern to me at this time. I have to hold my own citizens' welfare as my highest priority."

French President Jacques Guillaume could not believe his ears as he listened to his opposite number across the Channel. How could the British Prime Minister not grasp the severity of the issue? He tried to maintain a composed voice across the telephone lines and felt grateful that George Strachan couldn't see his tired face.

"George, you have surely seen the riots outside my office?" Guillaume asked evenly.

"Yes, Jacques, but there's simply not enough room in Glasgow for all the sick people who want to see the Angel," Strachan replied adamantly. "We have to worry about housing and food for enough people as it is. We're strapped."

"I cannot even go home at night. I have to stay holed up in my office. These people want to kill me, and why?" he demanded, suddenly losing his cool. "Because they think that I have forsaken them."

The French President could hear the Prime Minister clear his throat.

"Jacques, if I let the French into Scotland, I will have to let everybody from the European Union into Scotland. I believe you have visited the city before. It's a small place."

"Then move the Angel to another location that is better suited to accommodate larger numbers of people," Guillaume insisted.

"Where would you have me move the Angel? There's just nowhere that can handle the vast number of sick people in Europe."

The President relented and eased his tone.

"George, just let the terminally ill in then."

"We have run the numbers, Jacques. Even with just the terminally ill from Europe, we cannot support the influx of people."

The conversation entered a brief lull while both sides considered the magnitude of their problem. The French President tried to think of any way to appeal to his counterpart's sense of decency. He could not believe the selfishness of the man, keeping such a powerful tool all to himself, at the expense of others. The French people deserved access to the Angel's miraculous healing ability, too. Since when did the British truly believe in God or Angels anyway?

"So you plan to keep the borders closed to non-British citizens until all Brits are taken care of?" Guillaume inquired.

"We have not decided upon our next course of action, Jacques. Even if we had, I do not think that the information could be shared," responded Strachan flatly.

Jacques Guillaume plotted his next move. The information he had received from Russia that very afternoon could prove useful, but of course only if it produced the desired effect. He paced across the lavish Persian rug adorning the beautifully crafted hardwood floor in his office.

A look through a bulletproof glass window revealed a scene out of an apocalyptic Hollywood movie. Under the dark sky of a late Parisian evening, an incredible pulsing mass of protestors buffeted against rows of dedicated police officers. The Gendarmes had complained about many defections that afternoon as more and more people discovered Britain's power-play. Part of the President didn't blame them, and he was certainly not surprised. His citizens had definitely rioted for less in the past. At least they had stopped setting cars on fire.

Despite the desperate appearance of the volatile situation outside, the President understood that it was mostly for show. His people were expressing their discontent, but they would not openly attack the police over such an issue. Many had just experienced the high of thinking their loved ones could be healed, only to discover a terrible low when the United Kingdom closed its borders.

They felt cheated.

The President felt cheated.

He only had a couple of cards left up his sleeve. As was his way, he went for broke.

"George, do you realize that if you keep your borders closed, there could be serious repercussions?"

"And what would those be? And from whom?" Strachan demanded, his polished accent giving way to his Scottish roots as his anger instantly flared up.

Jacques Guillaume smiled. Oh, how easily his adversary flustered.

"We have been contacted in regards to joining a new alliance. An alliance that would seek to obtain the Angel."

Silence.

"Did you hear me, Mr. Prime Minster?" Guillaume asked, now enjoying his advantage.

"Yes."

"And what do you think, George?"

"Jacques, I think you should explain why you would disclose that information to me," replied Strachan.

Now the President had a decision to make. Whose side would win? Always the betting man, Guillaume went with his gut on a whim.

"Because the French would of course never join such a traitorous alliance. We consider the British to be great friends and would not jeopardize that over such an issue."

Silence.

Jacques Guillaume started to wonder if his gamble had failed. He had hoped to isolate the French from the rest of Europe, in hopes of receiving special treatment. His people needed this Angel.

"I think this conversation is over, Jacques."

Guillaume started to respond, but heard the click of his opponent hanging up on him. The nerve of the man!

After slamming down the phone receiver, Guillaume paced furiously in his office, wearing a groove in the plush rug, staring at the floor.

Why was the prime minister so stubborn? Why was he so stupid? Could he not see the problem?

He stopped his internal rant and went back to his desk. As he sat behind the mahogany behemoth, he weighed his next move. Really he only had one valid option.

The French President grabbed his phone and dialed the number he had for the office of the Russian Premier in Moscow. Guillaume preferred to be on the winning side of a fight.

***

In a sterile doctor's office, a woman sat expectantly, in more ways than one. Dr. Young had scheduled the ultrasound appointment to check on her baby mainly because of a serious bout of flu the woman had suffered from the previous week.

Cathy had experienced horrible diarrhea, vomiting, chills, and fever for two days before finally relenting to her husband's requests to see the doctor. Upon her arrival at his office, Dr. Grant Young had immediately called for an ambulance, trying not to chastise the expecting mother for putting her child at risk.

Fortunately for Cathy, the hospital in Phoenix had received a special guest. As lines of people waited to see the Angel, orderlies rushed an incredibly ill pregnant woman to the front of the queue. One gentle touch from the giant pink man eased Cathy's suffering instantly. After twenty-four hours of observation, the hospital released the overjoyed woman.

Two days afterwards, Cathy had called Dr. Young, complaining about sudden weight loss. She had explained that as crazy as it sounded, she didn't even feel pregnant anymore. For instance, her morning sickness had suddenly ended.

The good doctor had assured her that everything was probably fine. The flu strain had been particularly strong and even after recovery she should have expected to lose some weight as her body recuperated. Also, many women at her stage of pregnancy experienced a change of symptoms. She should feel blessed that the sickness went away instead of intensifying, as some unlucky women discovered.

They'd then scheduled the ultrasound, just to reassure everyone that the baby was fine. Also, the doctor wanted to check up on Cathy to make sure everything was operating correctly upstairs. She'd sounded very distraught on the phone.

A nurse poked her head into Young's office to let him know Cathy was ready to see him.

Dr. Young entered the room and greeted Cathy with a big smile, "Hello, Cathy. How are you feeling this morning?"

Cathy looked at him sheepishly and said, "I feel great, which is why I feel bad. I don't understand what is going on, doctor."

Her eyes pleaded with him for revelation, for security. Young suddenly hoped the ultrasound would only show good news, which was ludicrous, because he had no reason to think that it wouldn't.

He took a seat next to Cathy and immediately noticed a significant reduction in the size of her belly.

You must be imagining things, Grant, he told himself uneasily. *She has lost a little weight, but it's nothing.*

He rolled the scanner across her exposed and lubricated abdomen. His heart stopped as he glanced at the screen.

The baby had disappeared.

"So, Cathy, nothing strange has happened, other than weight loss? And you stopped having morning sickness?" he inquired, trying his best to make the questions sound innocent.

"No, doctor. There hasn't been anything weird other than that."

Dr. Young avoided her inquisitive gaze. What the hell was going on?

Cathy looked up at the screen.

"I should be able to see my baby, right?" Anxiety and fear crawled all over the question. Young removed the scanner quickly and tried to think up a viable explanation on the spot.

"The machine has been acting up for the past few days, Cathy. I'm sorry. I'll call out the technician to fix it today, and we can reschedule for tomorrow," he explained, deliberately forcing out the words slowly. When Cathy gave him a skeptical look, he added, "And maybe your husband could join us tomorrow?"

Cathy brightened at the thought slightly.

"Well, okay, doctor."

The nurse cleaned Cathy up and escorted her to the front desk before returning in a hurry.

"Doc, there is nothing wrong with that machine. We just used it thirty minutes ago on Mrs. Johnson," the nurse insisted.

Dr. Young stared at the floor.

"I could see her womb on the screen, but that baby's gone," the nurse added, verbally prodding her boss.

"Don't you think I could see that, Patty?" the doctor exclaimed, suddenly snapping out of his daze. "And what am I supposed to tell her?"

"I think she has to be lying," the nurse said.

The doctor stood and said, "I don't think so. She would've been in serious danger if anything had happened at this stage in the game."

"You need to tell her, Dr. Young."

The old man wandered towards the door, lost in his thoughts once more. The future looked bleak. How on Earth could he explain this to Cathy? He had no idea what was going on.

He paused at the door, a hand outstretched towards the handle, frozen in mid-step. A crazy idea occurred to him.

Without moving, he asked the nurse, "What did she do last week that was unusual?"

The nurse looked puzzled for a moment, trying to follow where the doctor was headed.

"Cathy went to the hospital, Patty. She saw the Angel."

Puzzlement morphed into serious concern on Patty's face.

"Doc, the Angel helps people. Surely people would have noticed if it stole her baby?"

Imagination steamrolling through his mind, Dr. Young continued to stare at the door handle, just beyond his fingers' grasp. What exactly had the Angel done? How did it heal people?

"Are you okay, doc?" Patty asked nervously, slowly edging towards the door.

Young snapped out of it once more. He grabbed the door handle and opened it slowly, checking to make sure Cathy had left the receptionist's desk already.

"You're right, Patty," he said. "The Angel helps people. In any case, let's keep this little problem between the two of us for the time being."

Patty nodded her assent, understanding the gravity of the situation.

As Patty walked past him and towards her next duty, Dr. Young called after her, "We should call that technician just in case."

Chapter 13

Located over one thousand miles south of Argentina's Tierra del Fuego, the Fossil Bluff outpost offered little in the way of amenities and plenty in the way of brutal weather. The Antarctic research center at Rothera Point operated the small forward outpost at Fossil Bluff mainly as a refueling station for scientists heading to the more useful Sky Blu research station. Of course, most people only traveled that way during the Antarctic summer months, October through March.

September would need to be close enough for Knight's team of five, designated Talos. Connor loved his Greek mythology, typically choosing team names from an exhaustive list of epic heroes and monsters. As always, Knight hadn't recognized the team's given name and had researched Talos briefly on the Internet.

Apparently Talos was a giant metal man who could only be defeated by removing a nail from his back. Knight would've preferred the name of someone who did *not* die a horrible death. Greek tragedy always added an extra element of fun to missions, especially for the overly superstitious.

Knight didn't suffer from belief in anything, never mind old wives' tales, but he knew that Falcon always put her socks on right before left and would never place new shoes on a table. How Knight had come to have such knowledge didn't bear thinking about.

In addition to Knight's executive officer, Brian "Diver" Lehoski, Falcon rounded out a team consisting of Seagull and Kestrel, who had revealed one drunken night that his real name was Dick Treasure. Knight had a hard time believing that Dick received such a name at birth, unless Dick's parents envisioned a career in pornography for their son. What a disappointment he must've been.

Names aside, in Phalanx, the leadership chose only the best candidates for the interview process. These men and woman hailed from all military services and typically ran the fastest, shot the straightest, and thought the quickest. As such, many teams mixed those who used to be Lieutenants or Sergeants in the same duties, to the point that the titles meant very little anymore. Salutes to the squad leader only occurred in drinking games.

Dressed as casually as anyone could during harsh Antarctic weather, Talos team had landed on the short crushed-rock runway at Rothera station, after a hellish flight originating in the British-owned Falkland Islands. If relations with Argentina or Chile had been better, they could've possibly had a shorter flight, but nobody felt like it would have mattered. The treacherous waters at the bottom of the world circumnavigated the globe unhindered by land mass, reaching violent speeds and creating merciless waves and winds. Despite the pilot's warning, the crew of landlubbers hadn't believed the turbulence would be an issue.

They later jettisoned many bags of vomit. A very amused co-pilot had been nice enough to take a few snapshots of Knight hugging the plane's tiny toilet while praying feverishly for deliverance. Kestrel had nicely suggested that the airman return to his seat, lest he lose part of his anatomy that he should hold very dear. The co-pilot had returned to the front with a laugh as Kestrel then buckled and made a ghastly deposit into a brown paper bag.

After a relatively smooth landing at Rothera, Talos had received some flak from the few Brits keeping the station running during the dregs of the dreadful winter season.

"Why the hell did they send you Yanks down here?" the leader of the scientists had demanded. The man's dreary appearance matched his tone. Apparently he'd spent quite some time in the southern reaches of the world.

Another added, "We could've handled this situation very well, thank you very much."

Knight regarded the two men with what he hoped looked like typical American overconfidence. Nobody had informed him of any "situation." As far as Talos were concerned, they were just supposed to be a group of visiting scientists, intent on doing semi-routine work.

Knowing that Lehoski had a much better rapport with people in general, Knight nodded to his XO and stood back

Lehoski looked at the small group of Brits and asked, "Well, what equipment do you have to deal with this situation of yours?" Knight smiled as his friend embarked on a verbal fishing expedition.

The head scientist looked perplexed at the question.

"This was just a simple seismic event. You blokes are borrowing a lot of *our* equipment just to get out there."

Lehoski maintained a friendly smile and said, "Yes, we appreciate your assistance." He concluded that conversation abruptly and asked, "So is our next pilot almost ready to go?"

The scientist stared as hard as a highly educated intellectual could, overtly displaying his disapproval of this team of American field scientists. Knight figured that Talos didn't look or act like any scientists the Brit had ever met, but with the international reputation that Americans enjoyed, that wasn't a problem.

"Yes, McDougal's just pulling the plane around now. We'd been told you'd want to move on to Fossil Bluff immediately, though God only knows why."

The team trudged back out into the snow and pushed against a rigid wind that penetrated to the depths of their very souls. Their high-tech cold weather jackets did their best, but still couldn't fully resist the abusive climate. After five minutes had passed without any sign of a plane, Knight started to think someone had pulled a fast one on them.

Over the whipping wind, Knight said to Lehoski, "Those Brits trying to get smart with the new guys?"

Lehoski pulled down the insulating bandana from around his mouth and laughed.

"I do believe so. It's freezing balls out here. Definitely a good trick," Lehoski replied.

Knight edged closer to his XO. The strong wind gave Knight his first isolated contact with Lehoski since the briefing at the Fort. Knight didn't really entrust much in the way of personal information with the others, but Lehoski had always been a good friend.

"Hey, Brian," he said.

Lehoski turned to Knight, who leaned in close and pulled Lehoski's hood away from his left ear. A jagged scar poked out from under his thick-knit sweater, a souvenir from a cracked-out Columbian drug dealer who Knight had put down with a lucky diving shot from a .45 pistol. The mere flesh wound for Lehoski could've been fatal had the psycho been given just a fraction of a second more to enjoy his heinous existence. That moment had cemented the bond between the two men, but Knight hoped he didn't need to make such a low percentage shot to strengthen that bond ever again.

"Karen got cancer again, and that's why she wanted the divorce."

A confused look filled Lehoski's wind-reddened face.

"That makes no sense, bro."

"Yeah, tell me about it," Knight responded with a smile.

"So by your smile, I'm guessing there's more news?"

"Yeah, Connor got her in to see the Angel in Phoenix. That's where I was when dipshit called me back to the Fort."

It was Lehoski's turn to smile.

"I was wondering. Not like you to be the last one to show up for a briefing."

Knight laughed with his friend.

"Andy, that's seriously great news."

With a nod, Knight concluded the conversation for the time being. The rest of the crew had spotted Knight and Lehoski talking and had slowly edged closer to find out why. They were just work associates and nothing else. They had no reason to learn the intricacies of Knight's private life, so he moved away from Lehoski, figuring that they'd get the hint.

All heads turned to a small hangar not far from the main station building. Above the sounds of rushing air, a small plane appeared. The team collectively stamped their feet, not in irritation, but in an effort to keep warm. Even the short cold exposure could lead to interesting medical conditions, like Trench Foot from World War One.

The plane pulled to a stop close by and they hustled over, not caring if they suddenly looked a lot more athletic than the average American scientist.

Inside the small plane, Talos was introduced to Barbara McDougal, pilot for Rothera station. The team fed her their aliases and chatted with her for most of the boisterous hop across George VI Sound. Apparently Barb was the only Brit on the continent with a decent personality. She chalked that up to her Scottish roots.

Knight also couldn't help noticing that she was the only Brit around with a pretty face. Not that she had much competition from the unkempt scientists they had just left behind. Knight was fairly certain one of them had been female, but he couldn't be sure.

Barbara explained that she was the only non-scientific staff member at Rothera, for the time being at least.

"I'm just the pilot for all of those stuffy know-it-alls," she said with a grin. "I can't understand any of what they do here, and they treat me like crap, but the wages are worth the aggravation."

Knight was just glad they didn't have to pretend to be real scientists, because his eleventh grade physics education definitely didn't cover the required material. Especially since most of his time there had been spent passing notes with his future wife, not learning about acceleration equations. One of his major goals in life was to minimize his time spent as a falling object.

The thought of Karen in that dusty old science room brought back a flood of nostalgia that brought a smile to his face. He'd not really known what was going on back then. He definitely hadn't had a clue that she *liked* him.

Ah, the ignorance of youth.

The exterior world faded a few shades into obscurity as he pictured her long brown hair flowing to her shoulders, framing a picture-perfect face. The small things touched him the most. That scar behind her ear from a childhood dog attack. Knight had been one of the select few who even knew about that permanent mark, that reminder of a horrible day in the life of a young girl. Had the dog still been alive, Knight would've gladly strangled it. Twice. Then brought it back to life, only to tear it to pieces.

Someone punched him on the shoulder, popping him back into the land of the living.

"You must be jiggered after that flight in," Barbara said, her permanent grin only briefly belying an underlying sense of mild concern for her spaced-out passenger. Knight rotated in the front seat to look at this crew in the back. They all returned his brief stare, an acknowledgement from him to them that everything was fine.

"I don't know what *jiggered* is, but I am tired," he responded, sinking his head back into the uncomfortable headrest. The neck support jolted with each jerk of the plane.

Barbara laughed quietly.

"Not going to get much rest on this flight. Sorry," she said gleefully. Knight guessed that the pleasant company of normal-seeming individuals was quite a boon to the pilot's mood after ferrying unappreciative geologists and cranky physicists around. It was so strange. Knight would've thought that the many men on the base would've fallen head over heels for this woman, considering how out of whack the gender ratio seemed to be on the world's most southern continent.

The plane started to descend, and the pilot fixated on the controls, no longer up for a good banter with the passengers. Knight appreciated her professionalism as his seat threatened to eject him through the window with each bump.

After a few moments of intense concentration, Barbara smoothly touched the plane down and brought it to a jarring halt.

"Crap," she exclaimed with an exaggerated groan. "That was almost a perfect landing. Oh well, at least you didn't die."

Knight raised an eyebrow.

"We've had worse," he said, grinning.

The pilot glanced away, smile gone. Was she blushing? She quickly unbuckled and announced it was time to hit the runway. Lehoski winked at Knight , who just rolled his eyes. Another member of the Andrew Knight fan club. Or in this case, the "Bill Moody" fan club. Whoever came up with the aliases needed to take a refresher course. The team left the plane and gathered their bags from the small hold. This time Barbara raised an eyebrow.

"You didn't bring very much for a trip out here."

Lehoski replied, "Well we don't plan on being here very long."

Barbara sighed.

"Those bloody scientists never tell me anything."

Talos looked at the pilot inquisitively.

"They never told me how long you were here for. Usually teams spend a week out here," she said before adding, "Well, typically they stay at Sky Blu, not here in this crap-hole."

The small accommodations on Fossil Bluff did leave much to be desired. Knight guessed out loud that maybe five people could sleep inside comfortably.

Barbara laughed.

"Aye, on your bike. The five of you are going to be really cozy if you want to all stay in there," she explained.

Lehoski looked at Kestrel.

"Looks like you're sleeping outside, man," Lehoski said, punching his squad mate in the arm.

"You know you can't spend one night away from my sexy body, big boy," Kestrel responded, flaunting the goods beneath multiple layers of subzero clothing. Lehoski grimaced, earning a laugh from the audience.

As the team moved their black duffel bags to the snow-capped, yet unimpressive building, Knight tapped Barbara on the shoulder. She turned to him expectantly.

"So what did they tell you about what we're doing out here?" he asked, in a slightly more serious tone than he had intended.

Barbara looked mildly flustered. She probably preferred wrestling with a tailspin to engaging in a serious conversation.

"Well, just that you were coming to investigate this big event that they keep talking about. And if you don't mind my saying so, they were quite put out when they were told an American team would come and handle it."

"Oh, so they didn't expect that, I take it?" Knight asked.

"Oh, no. And they don't appreciate the implications. They're quite an arrogant bunch of arses over there, Bill," Barbara responded, using what she thought was Knight's first name. As far as she knew, Bill Moody was a professor of seismology from Berkeley.

Knight nodded knowingly, having experienced their level of arse-ness firsthand.

Around the pair on the runway, snow drifted along the ground in the respectable breeze, often whipping up sparse clouds as tall as Knight. In every direction he could see nothing but snow covering the barren landscape, except for the slope that the small station sat on. The red building looked very conspicuous on the side of the small hill.

In the opposite direction, a white fog bloomed on the horizon. The sight didn't make Knight any happier.

"So, that's a storm?" he asked Barbara, who also stared to the horizon.

"Probably, but it'll be nothing you guys have to fret about here. That dilapidated shack doesn't look like much, but she's a tough lassie," she replied with a smile. Knight wondered if she really had taken a strange liking to the mysterious American professor. Despite being pretty and pleasant, he'd been married long enough to know better.

"Alright, well, you would know."

"Just don't stay out too long. It would be unpleasant to be caught out in the open by a storm. Even a small one," she warned gravely.

"Sounds like a plan to me," Knight said as they turned and started towards the building. The rest of the team had just reached the bottom of the stilts supporting part of the station.

Through the whistle of the wind, Knight could swear he heard a single popping noise. The direction was unclear, and he swiveled his head quickly, looking for a source.

He started to ask what that sound was when the red building disintegrated. Flaming pieces of wood and insulation flared out of the station. Knight instinctively threw the petite pilot to the ground and covered her with his body. Small pieces of charred debris landed around them. The snow instantly turned to water and extinguished any flames.

Knight dragged the limp body of Barbara behind a mound of dirty snow created by whoever had cleared the runway. Barbara lay unconscious beside Knight as he pulled an M4 carbine from his duffel bag.

"At least I don't have to explain to Barb why an American professor has an assault rifle in Antarctica," Knight said to no one as he unfolded the stock and checked the action.

He whipped around when sounds of gunfire erupted from behind the engulfed wreckage of the small station. Lying prone against the pile of snow, Knight scanned the top of the small hill behind the building. Plumes of smoke obscured his view of the peak, but he could see his team had gained as much cover as could be found at the bottom of a snow-covered hill. Having a better viewing angle than their leader, they returned fire towards a point directly behind the column of smoke.

Trusting their instincts and following their aim, Knight fired a volley into the space behind the black swirling cloud. The distance and wind factors stole any accuracy he might've had, but Knight knew he could at least provide some suppressing fire for his men. He could see one of his team slowly progressing up the slope from the right side of the inflamed building, trying to flank whoever held the top of the ridge.

The gunfire stopped suddenly, but Knight could hear and see his squad yelling and retreating. Not wasting a moment, he jumped over his cover and sprinted towards them. His shots from range were ineffective, and he felt that he could be more useful up front.

An explosion rocked the middle of the slope, setting off a small avalanche that chased his team. The rumbling wave absorbed one of the fleeing Talos members and settled before it could wipe out the rest. Knight sprinted through the cloud of displaced snow, using it for cover as he searched earnestly for his lost man. Urgency pumped adrenaline through his veins as he scrambled across the freshly packed snow.

The cloud around him started to fade, and Knight looked up to see one of his squad at the top of the slope, looking over the other side. Obviously that was whoever had tried to out-flank the enemy. Knight couldn't identify the person since they all wore the same bright orange jackets.

Knowing that his team had his back, Knight focused all of his faculties into his search of the snow. Under the white blanket, one of his men was dying, slowly suffocating under what could be just a few inches of snow. The thought pressed him on as he saw two other orange-clad figures tramping around the snow beside him. He recognized Falcon and Lehoski at the short distance.

"He was over here in this area," Knight yelled to them, the cold air shredding his throat and making his voice hoarse. They assembled on him and searched vehemently.

Falcon yelled, "Over here! Over here!"

Knight turned and saw part of an orange glove protruding from the snow. The three flocked to the site and threw down their weapons. Each of them had a small collapsible shovel on a hip holster. They made short work of the snow and started dragging the gloved hand from the icy depths.

The normally suntanned face of Kestrel emerged from the hole, his skin already a ghastly pale shade. Wasting no time, the team dragged him from his icy prison and laid him on the snow. His breaths came deep and ragged as he tried to replace the lost oxygen in his lungs. Falcon put a hand on his shoulder as he balanced himself on hands and knees. He brushed her away smartly and slowly got onto one knee. His breathing quickly became more regular.

He coughed a few times quite violently before looking up and saying, "What the hell took you guys so long?" The unconquerable smile grew on his face.

"Well, we thought it would help a California guy like you to get accustomed to the climate," quipped Lehoski as he grabbed Kestrel's arm and yanked him to his feet.

"That sounds like a great idea. Why don't we bury you next?" Kestrel replied, patting some of the snow off of his face and jacket.

"Come on, you were only under there for a minute."

"Yeah, but I inhaled half the snow on the slope on my way down."

Falcon punched him playfully in the arm. "You know, it's your own fault. If you hadn't hit that guy in the shoulder, the other one wouldn't have thrown a freakin' grenade down at us."

Kestrel laughed. The guy was pretty new to Phalanx, but Knight could tell he'd fit in easily enough. A good sense of humor was a boon in a job that encountered and skirted with death frequently.

"Well, we should probably see where our new friends are."

Knight watched the fifth member of their team casually jog down the slope towards them. He was glad that everyone was okay and in good spirits, but the ambush more than perplexed him.

"Seagull, what was all this shit about?" Knight said as Seagull jogged closer.

"Two guys on snowmobiles. They booked it after one got hit. Left a nice grenade as a present for us," Seagull explained. "They must've used a mortar to blow up the station. Must've taken it with them, because I don't see anything up there."

Knight thought about this for a moment.

"So we have a couple of guys perched up behind our temporary residence, waiting for us to arrive? How would they know we're coming? Or when?" he asked the group.

"They were probably patrolling the area and saw the plane coming in. Figured they'd blow up the station and maybe take out the plane," Lehoski suggested.

"What did they do after the first explosion? I didn't have a good vantage point because of all the smoke," said Knight.

"Yeah, our fearless leader stayed behind to chat up the cute pilot," laughed Kestrel.

The quip elicited a "Who? Me?" expression from the team leader as the group enjoyed some stress-relieving mirth after a potentially scary situation. Just then, Knight remembered Barbara's unconscious body lying out behind the snow mound.

"Ah, shit. Falcon, go see to our pilot and make sure she's okay. I may have knocked her out when I jumped on her," Knight said, getting a good laugh out of Kestrel.

Knight turned back to the remaining team members and asked, "So what happened after the building blew up?"

"We were getting our bearings, then two guys came running over the slope, rifles out. They didn't fire at first, I guess thinking that we were just civilians," Lehoski explained.

"So I guess our disguises worked," Kestrel chimed in.

"Yeah, it bought time for us to get to small cover and pull our carbines. Soon as we opened fire, they booked it back over the hill," Lehoski went on.

Knowing his men would only fire upon a threat, Knight felt no need to question their actions. He was sure that his boss would be a little upset that they initiated the firefight, but in fairness, those two assholes had blown up their bunk beds. No pre-game nap for the team equaled death for the enemy.

"Kestrel winged one of them when Seagull started pushing up from the flank. That's when the grenade appeared, and we hauled ass out," explained Lehoski. "You know the rest from my end."

Seagull finished the story.

"I went over the hill. Got there in time to see two snowmobiles scooting into an ice valley of some sort. They must've had an escape route planned. It provided them some good cover, because I couldn't tell what direction they were headed."

The two ladies rejoined the group, Barbara looking particularly groggy after having a brick wall lunge into her.

"Sorry about the tackle," Knight said, feeling the need to apologize to the small woman.

She glared at him for a moment and touched a spot on her cheek. Her Scottish red-headed temper flared.

"You could've at least not left me on my face, you git. My cheek has freezer burn now."

The disbelief on Knight's face instantly calmed her, and she stared at her boots.

"Sorry. Thanks for trying to keep me safe."

With the heat of battle escaping from the confines of their insulating clothing, the group became visibly colder with each light gust of ice-filled wind. They followed Knight to a mound of snow similar to the one he had originally left Barbara behind. A decent amount of the chilly air diverted over their heads as they crouched behind the natural barrier.

"Okay, guys. Listen up. We could have more of those assholes inbound at any moment. We don't have a huge amount of information other than there are at least two hostiles with snowmobiles, rifles, and bad aim out there," Knight explained calmly, his warm breath misting in front of his face.

Kestrel smiled.

"You don't need good aim with a grenade at the top of a glacier," he remarked.

"Don't interrupt the CO," Lehoski snapped, glaring at the relatively new guy on the team. Kestrel nodded grimly. There were times for screwing around and there were times for listening. When Knight was laying out a plan, his group had better pay damned good attention. Listening deficiencies got people killed, and not always just the person with the attention problem.

Knight continued.

"Alright, I'm going to report in to HQ. The explosions don't look like they knocked out the shed containing the snowmobiles, so we should be okay on that front, but we want HQ to get the satellites over us to see if they can give us more info," he said.

With a long look around the group, meeting everyone's eyes, he added, "The mission's still a go. We have our coordinates and that's where we're headed. Just now we have to keep our eyes open."

His team nodded their assent. Each one of them looked determined to pay back their hosts for such welcoming hospitality. Only one person in the small huddle looked confused.

"And what am I supposed to do, exactly, Bill?"

Chapter 14

"Gran, did you read about China in the paper today?" Cheryl asked her grandmother.

"Oh, I don't read much, Margie," the elderly woman replied.

Margie was Cheryl's mum, who was stuck in traffic trying to meet them at Brisbane's Princess Alexandra hospital. Cheryl had called her old school pal Tom, who just happened to be a policeman, and who just happened to still have a thing for her. He'd jumped at a chance to escort her grandmother through the zoo outside the hospital, where a massive crowd jockeyed constantly for attention from anyone who would listen.

When Tom had dropped them off at the front door, he'd said something about calling her sometime to go out. Cheryl had smiled politely and nodded, but she was in no mood for that. Not yet.

"So you didn't read about the bombings in Jerusalem either?"

Her grandmother looked at her with that puzzled expression that Cheryl recognized all too well, like she'd just said something highly inappropriate. Cheryl just sighed and looked down the hallway to the doors where the Angel supposedly resided.

She wondered what Israelis thought of the Angels. Terrorists from Afghanistan, or Jordan, or some place like that had blown up three temples in Jerusalem, all because the bastards thought the Angels were messengers of Allah, sent to herald in some kind of new Islamic conquest. Where these nutters got ideas like that,

Cheryl had no clue, but what a horrible loss for all the Jewish families affected by such insanity.

The queue shuffled forward as an armed policeman admitted another patient into the Angel's lair. Cheryl's grandmother inched forward, and then turned to her granddaughter with sudden dread.

"Where am I? How did I get here?"

At Cheryl's gentle embrace, the woman visibly calmed.

"It's okay, Gran," she said quietly. "We're just at the hospital for a visit."

Her grandmother's smile put Cheryl at ease, and she carefully released the woman. With nerves still shot from dealing with Mitch earlier, Cheryl didn't know if she could handle a wild outburst from a confused old lady.

The ceiling above them exploded violently. Burning white light filled the corridor. Pieces of drywall and rebar ricocheted amongst the helpless crowd. The mayhem tilted wildly to the left for just a moment before Cheryl crashed headfirst onto the floor.

A mind-crushing headache and a deafening ringing sensation greeted Cheryl as she slowly regained her vision. With her sight swirling, she struggled to make out her bloody surroundings. Her eyesight returned in time to look through the broken doors leading into the Angel's room, where a giant of a man stabbed the large pink Angel in the chest with a spear.

A scream unlike any she'd ever heard in her life rocketed down the hallway. Lifeless bodies regained consciousness as the painful sound wave careened off the walls. Cheryl writhed in agony, but still kept her eyes on the horrible scene unfolding nearby.

The assassin, covered in some kind of shiny metallic armor, towered over the Angel, who already dwarfed most of humanity. The ceiling lights cut out, finally giving up after the trauma of the explosion. Another scream resonated through the darkness, forcing Cheryl to grasp her ears. She knew that she was screaming in pain, but she couldn't even hear herself over the intense shrieking all around.

The emergency lighting in the hallway kicked on, drenching the scene in dull red. Cheryl could see the Angel struggling against the large spear poking through its chest, but the attacker easily held the weapon steady, just watching its prey writhe. With a flick of the attacker's wrist, everything changed. In a brilliant blue flash of light, the Angel disappeared.

There was no time to scream.

In a deft movement for someone so large, the assailant bounded back into the corridor and leapt up into a large dark, ragged hole in the ceiling.

Bolts of yellow and white light pierced the ambient red glow from the opposite end of the hallway. The voices of orderlies followed the flashlight beams. Pain seared through Cheryl's back and legs as she attempted to move. Next to her, her grandmother lay motionless.

With the appearance of a flashlight beam on them, Cheryl reached out and grasped her grandmother's outstretched hand. In the white light, blood glistened in a deep gash across the back of the old woman's neck.

Strong hands suddenly dragged Cheryl away from the carnage. Stern voices commanded her to let go. She refused.

"Gran!"

Chapter 15

"You're sending me back?"

Knight nodded.

"What if the eejits shoot me down?" Barbara demanded frantically, breaking from cover and standing up into the icy air.

"Seagull saw them driving off in the completely opposite direction, back towards where we're about to go. They won't be on the Sound between here and the base."

"And you want me to come back and get you? How does that work?" she asked, more calmly this time.

Lehoski handed the pilot a small plastic box.

"It's a satellite phone. I'll call you on it when we're ready for extraction," Knight said.

With a nod, Barbara opened the hard plastic case and discovered a small phone inside. She looked around the group with a raised eyebrow.

"So you lot know what you're doing then?" she asked, sounding very motherly.

With a nod from each of them, Barbara seemed as content as she could be. She wished them the best of luck, and then jogged out to her waiting plane. Her departure did nag at Knight a little. Now the pilot had information that would be best kept quiet. Would she be able to keep her mouth shut?

Knight watched her go, knowing he was right about her being safer in the plane than with them. Losing her in part of a firefight would be unforgivable, and terrible for public relations. Despite being as battle-hardened as anyone present, he didn't want to lose a civilian on this mission.

Especially not the pilot.

***

"So what's the plan, Rook?" asked Kestrel as Knight joined the rest of Talos in the supply shed after his call to base. Each soldier had reversed their brightly colored jacket, pants, and hat; a chilly exercise to say the least. They now sported a pure white uniform. The British scientists may have become suspicious of a civilian group wearing all white for a dangerous Antarctic expedition. Only idiots would want to blend in with the snowy landscape. Or a group of elite soldiers who had just been shot at. Reversible clothing may have been a fashion faux-pas in the rest of the civilized world, but Knight found it very useful in his line of work.

"They're putting birds in the air as we speak. We'll have as much satellite coverage as they can inconspicuously spare, and we'll have air support taking off from the Falklands," said Knight.

Lehoski jumped on a snowmobile and pulled down his ski goggles. He started up the powerful motor and yelled, "So we're still on, I hope. I got a present for those dick-holes out there." His M4 hung ominously across his back.

"Yeah, Diver. We're a go. Saddle up."

While waiting for the others to pull out of the shed, Knight felt someone jump onto his snowmobile from behind. A look over his shoulder revealed Falcon settling into the seat. She leaned forward and wrapped her arms around his waist.

"The fifth snowmobile doesn't start, so I need a ride out there, cap'n," she yelled over the cacophony of the other motors leaving the shed.

Knight nodded and prepared to move. Falcon's hand slid down to his thigh. He looked back at his passenger.

"What the hell are you doing, Falcon?"

"Just call me Ariela," she whispered, putting her lips inside his hood.

"Just keep your hands to yourself."

"Come on, Rook. What's the big deal?" Falcon insisted after Knight slapped her hand away from his crotch. "It's not like you're married or anything, right?"

Knight kept his personal life separate from his work life. As such, only Connor and Lehoski knew about Karen, and there was no need to indulge Falcon now.

His passenger finally acquiesced to his silence.

"Fine. Whatever, Rook."

Falcon wrapped her arms around him at a more appropriate level and tapped him to indicate she was ready. The old snowmobile didn't look like much, but the oversized motor shot the vehicle out into the snow with a surprising surge.

After wrestling the controls for a moment to keep the rickety snowmobile going in a straight line, Knight reached up with one hand and clicked on the small headset protruding from under his cap.

"Diver, do you read me?" he asked.

"Yeah, Rook. I got you."

"Lead on," Knight said.

"Roger."

A Global Positioning Satellite monitor had been hastily attached to Lehoski's ride, and he insisted on being the navigator for the mission. The guy was perfectly capable of handling the responsibility. As such, Knight pulled into formation behind Lehoski, not wanting to be accused of bringing up the rear again. Soldiers didn't earn respect by showing reluctance to ride headlong into danger ahead of their men.

After an hour of bumpy riding across open snowy flats and through narrow icy fissures, Lehoski pulled to a complete stop. The hand signal to hold formation appeared, which Knight promptly relayed to the two men behind him. The glassy frozen walls of this particular crevasse wouldn't even allow Knight to pass Lehoski if he'd wanted to.

"Okay, this is the spot according to the GPS," Lehoski reported.

Knight stood up on his snowmobile and peered ahead. The slightly dimming light indicated that they needed to find their target and get out of dodge pronto. Unfortunately, nothing lay in their path ahead.

"I don't see anything, Diver," Knight said.

"Yeah, me neither."

"Maybe it's up top," suggested Kestrel. These were his first words to anyone since being chastised for interrupting Knight earlier. It was good to see Kestrel wasn't dwelling on it, which was a good sign for his chances of assimilating into the team.

The walls on either side of them stood about eight feet high, which was nothing the group couldn't conquer.

"Alright. Kestrel and Seagull, you guys are going to boost me and Diver up over these walls to take a look above," said Knight. He had no idea what he was looking for, but he hoped it would be obvious.

Moments later, Knight had his feet on the shoulders of his two men. He scanned the windswept horizon before him and saw nothing of interest.

Damn.

"Just a whole lot of snow up here," he yelled down. The biting wind assaulted the exposed parts of his face, stealing his breath when he tried to talk. Still on the men's shoulders, he peered in the opposite direction and froze.

"What is it, Rook?" yelled up Lehoski.

After a few tense seconds, Knight let the men lower him down to the ground.

"I don't know what it is, but it's definitely an object of interest," Knight explained as he strode to the other wall of the ice corridor.

Falcon piped up, "I've got to piss. I'll be right back." She disappeared around the corner as Seagull and Kestrel hefted Knight up once more. Knight watched her go for a moment, annoyance at her earlier flirting resurfacing. Was there any benefit to telling her he was married? He wasn't too sure that it would have any effect on her anyway. She seemed like the type.

Knight peeked over the lip of the ice wall and observed the frozen environment, looking for anything out of the ordinary, other than the ominous dark mound rising about fifty yards from his location. Nothing stirred other than the wind that edged around his clothing and managed to find hidden locations to penetrate, creating uncomfortably cool draughts down his spine.

With the coast looking clear, he braced himself and then dragged his weight over the edge. Immediately he spun around and reached his hand down to help Lehoski follow him up. The two men checked their M4s promptly, wary that the Chinese or Russians or whoever could be hiding nearby.

"Stay put. We'll be right back," Knight said to the two lifters. They nodded and sat down on the snowmobiles, hugging their limbs to their chests for warmth. Knight and Lehoski saw Falcon reappear as they left the edge and stepped towards the large dark shape on the snow, rifles at the ready.

"What is that?" Lehoski asked, probably hoping that Knight had been given a special briefing with extra information. Unfortunately, Connor and Vulture had failed to mention this.

"I have no idea," Knight responded absently, his brain focusing more on searching for hostiles than for deciphering the meaning of a strange black formation in the snow.

The irregularity was shaped like a black pyramid with the top half chopped off. As the men got closer, they could also see that one side was longer than the other, giving the appearance of having a rectangular base. Neither soldier appreciated the absolute lack of cover on their short journey.

Knight tapped Lehoski on the shoulder and gave a hand signal for them to split up and circle around the structure and meet on the other side. Lehoski nodded and broke off in a crouch towards the dark shape. After reaching the target, Knight saw that it was much taller than he had guessed. The uniformity of the snow around it made judging size from a distance quite challenging. Instead of being ten feet tall, it was more like twenty feet. Also, the long side of the base had to be at least forty feet, while the short side was only around half of that.

A shiny, incredibly smooth-looking surface coated the exterior of the black half-pyramid. Knight noted that no snow rested on it. Surely anything exposed to the elements for as long as this structure had would be hidden in snow by now? Was the surface incredibly hot and melting the snow away? Knight felt it prudent not to touch the surface, just in case.

The two men met on the other side of the unidentifiable object without complication.

Lehoski immediately asked, "Why isn't this thing buried in snow, Andy?"

Knight stared at the deepest black he had ever witnessed and shrugged.

"I don't know, but I don't see what Connor wants us to do with it," he replied as he bent down and densely packed a snowball. Years of childhood vacations in Colorado winters had trained him well in the art of perfect snowball creation.

After stepping back to what he considered an arbitrarily safe distance, Knight threw the frozen projectile in a lazy arc, striking the black surface about halfway up the face.

Or at least, it should have struck the surface.

"Did the snowball just disappear?" Lehoski asked, wonder mixing with genuine concern.

"I think so," Knight replied, intrigue greatly outweighing concern. "I'll try again."

After multiple attempts yielding the same results, the two men gradually moved closer and closer, until they could've reached out and touched the blackness if they had been brave enough.

Or stupid enough.

In every trial, the snowballs simply disappeared into the shiny face. As close as they stood to the object now, the men could see no obvious reaction taking place. It wasn't like the snowball was melting on impact. It just simply disappeared.

"We should get the rest of the guys up here," Knight announced, realizing that the rest of the squad would start to worry eventually. Had he not specifically said to stay put, he was sure they would have already come searching. The two men headed back to their team.

***

"I knew it," Seagull exclaimed upon walking up to the mysterious object.

Knight and Lehoski exchanged a confused glance.

"Knew what, Seagull?" Knight asked carefully.

The man turned quickly and spoke even more quickly, his words pouring out in an excited flurry.

"The Angels are aliens, Rook. Man, I can't believe this. I actually get to see the first spaceship. This's so awesome."

Seagull paced feverishly around the object as Knight observed him incredulously.

Aliens? Really?

"I don't know about all that, Seagull," Knight said.

The last thing he needed was for one of his men to go home and start yammering on about extraterrestrials. He personally didn't believe in aliens or any supernatural crap, but the Angels certainly made a good case for the existence of *something*.

But maybe Seagull was right about them being aliens. Or something else. Damn, he was confused now.

"There's no sign of any Angel here. That's for sure," declared Lehoski. He looked at Knight for further instructions while the other three wandered around the black structure and threw snowballs at it. It was funny that their first response was also to throw something at the mysterious stunted pyramid.

Seagull came running over to Lehoski and Knight.

"Maybe the Angel's inside?" he asked, bursting at the seams like an adolescent who'd just discovered what his dick was really for.

The look in his eyes pleaded with Knight to make it true. Knight started to think that someone was losing the plot. Concern turned to worry when Falcon appeared in the group and started in on Seagull.

"There aren't any aliens, dumbass," she said in a particularly nasty tone.

"Shut up, Falcon. Shouldn't you be praying to this thing, or something?" Seagull responded bitterly.

As the two squared off with torrents of irrational, yet hate-filled words, Knight stepped between them and had to physically push them apart. This was an easy task, as Knight was significantly bigger than both. Lehoski assisted in crowd control, pulling Seagull back and motioning for an antsy Kestrel to stay out of the fray.

As Lehoski quieted Seagull down behind him, Knight looked Falcon in the eyes and said, "You've got to calm down, Falc. We don't need this shit right now."

His words had little effect on the fiery young woman, so he continued, only having to shake her back to attention a few times.

"Seagull made a stupid comment, but this isn't the place to deal with it."

"You really think this is about a stupid comment about God, Rook?" she spat out. The response surprised Knight, but he didn't flinch.

"We don't have time—"

Before she could open her mouth in retort, Seagull yelled from behind.

"I'll tell you about it, Rook. She's been bangin' Condor for months. That's why she's mad, because I found out and wanted her ass kicked out."

Knight turned and marched over to his subordinate.

Seagull continued his tirade.

"That's the only reason that she's even in this squad, just because she'll screw her way in anywhere. How else would a chick get into Phalanx?" he demanded of no one in particular.

"This isn't the place," Knight roared. "None of that shit matters here. You want to lose your job over some stupid bullshit like this, Seagull?"

That had the desired effect. A lot of the soldiers in Phalanx made good money, but also racked up massive debts to counteract their hefty incomes. Knight had long suspected Seagull for a gambling man. The guy's anxious face looked comical inside the giant white hood of his jacket.

"No, sir."

"We'll deal with this shit later," Knight announced with all the finality of a father telling a son, *Just wait 'til we get home.*

As Knight strode off towards the mysterious object once more, he became suddenly aware of the night approaching and the wind picking up. Both interesting factors for their mission. He wondered how Seagull had found out about Connor's affair with Falcon, though, if it was even true. That situation was very concerning. To his knowledge, Connor was a happily married man. That could change quickly based on this new information.

And what was Seagull's motive here? Honor? Jealousy?

Shit, they did *not* have time for this.

Falcon whipped back her hood and started yelling at Seagull again, this time out of abject humiliation. Knight twisted around to rejoin the fight, but saw a flash in the distance. He felt the whirring of a large caliber bullet whizzing by his head and then watched Falcon's elegant neck disappear in a cloud of blood. The report of the gunshot followed behind the bullet, jolting everyone to action.

Falcon's shocked face rolled off of her shoulders in a ghastly way. Her decapitated body took one more step towards Seagull, who had already started to scramble away. The body flopped forward and a jet of blood shot from her neck, spraying the back of Seagull's white pants. He didn't care to notice.

The four surviving men charged to the black object, the only cover within reasonable range. They dived in beside Knight. He sat in a crouch behind the object, but not so close that he would inadvertently lean against it.

"The shot came from that small rise directly on the other side of this cover. Maybe four hundred yards," he announced.

The men nodded. Despite the circumstances of the heated argument, they had all just lost a squad mate and someone needed to pay. Murderous looks adorned their faces, etched by instant hatred for the enemy.

"Diver, pull the sat-phone and call this in. I want that hill destroyed," Knight ordered. "Seagull, run to the corner down there and take a peek for any incoming hostiles. Just don't get sniped."

Seagull nodded and took off running to the other corner of their protective barrier while Lehoski yelled into the sat phone, not interested in receiving any dilly-dallying from the operator on the other end. Knight listened to the conversation subconsciously as he popped around the corner of the half-pyramid and fired a few shots towards the enemy's last known location. He knew that the bullets were wasted at this range and with the wind, but he let them know their prey was armed. The bark of the M4 always reassured Knight, and he felt the initial edginess of combat ebbing away.

The frigid temperature finally started to soak in. Despite their high-tech clothing, Knight started to feel the chill in a bad way. He knew that they couldn't afford to be stuck out in this environment for much longer.

Where was their support?

"We got two hostiles incoming from the right side of that rise," yelled Seagull from the other corner of their cover.

"ETA on our air support, Diver?" Knight barked.

Lehoski packed the phone away and replied curtly.

"Less than two minutes."

Short bursts of rifle fire echoed down the length of the still unidentified black structure. Seagull and Kestrel alternated popping up to take a few shots at the intruders, who had taken cover on the side of the rise where the sniper had been located. The enemy soldiers also wore white outerwear, and their weapons blended in with the white landscape, a benefit that the Talos team didn't have. Their black M4s reported loudly and flashed brightly as the sun quickly disappeared into the horizon.

Within the myriad of interesting thoughts screaming for attention in his cramped brain, one thought spoke out louder than the rest. At first he didn't see the relevance. The mystery of the black pyramid pricked the inside of his skull.

The snowballs had disappeared into the blackness. What if they simply traveled straight through it, as opposed to actually disappearing? This question begged a much more important one: What if bullets would pass straight through the structure?

A quick look over his corner of the pyramid showed no signs of life. A muffled expletive coursed through his headset. Seagull's voice was instantly recognizable. Just the sound of it reminded Knight for a moment that he and the young man would be having a little heart-to-heart after all was said and done.

"Diver, cover this corner. I'm going to check on Seagull," Knight said to his XO before running to the other end of the pyramid. The freezing air burned his throat even with such minor exertion.

At his destination, the small amount of blood on the snow made the whiteness look like a slaughterhouse floor. Seagull sat on the snow behind Kestrel, who continued to trade bursts with the enemy. The sun finally took its resting place below the horizon, plunging the group into darkness.

Or at least, it should have.

Never had the stars looked so brilliant and spectacular to Knight. Due to totally unacceptable levels of pollution, city life didn't lend itself to epic vistas of the universe. The night sky captivated Knight wholly until he realized that the ominous black pyramid now displayed wondrous stars of its own. The shooting stopped.

Not even the quickly intensifying cold could pull Knight's attention away from the awe-inspiring celestial scene.

A kick at his feet snapped Knight from his stupor. He looked down and saw Seagull in the dim white light of the pyramid's stars. The soldier was clutching his own right arm. Through his earpiece, Knight heard Seagull's strained whisper.

"The bullets shatter when they hit this damn pyramid. I got a couple pieces in my shooting arm, Rook."

Why had the bullets broken apart, but the snowballs hadn't? Did the pyramid know the difference between the two? How could it?

Knight crouched down beside him, his own face probably glowing with an eerie light from the pyramid.

"It's not bad enough to keep you from fighting, right?" Knight said, much more of a statement that a question. The resolve in the injured soldier's face appeared instantly.

"No, sir. Just a scratch."

"Good. Now what the hell is going on with this pyramid?" Knight asked.

And where the hell is my air support?

In response, the area on the other side of the pyramid erupted in flames. The fierce heat filled the air and the booming explosions masked the engine sounds of the jet fighters screaming away into the distance. Death left as swiftly as it arrived.

The four men watched in awe as the half-pyramid lay etched in a burning sky. The flames lapped around the starry prism, which blocked much of the heat from assaulting the soldiers. In fact, compared to the suddenly dire cold that had just descended on them, the heated air felt quite temperate.

"Rook, we got an incoming call," said Lehoski, still crouched at the other end of the half-pyramid. Knight hustled over to his position as Seagull got back on his feet.

Knight grabbed the phone.

"This is Rook, over," he barked.

"Rook, this is Zeus Control. You have an identified civilian helicopter inbound from the northeast. Our planes made audio contact. It checks out, but we wanted you to be aware, over," said the generic voice of a dispatch operator.

"Roger, Zeus Control. Who is piloting this helo, over?" Knight asked, a little confused by the conversation.

"Someone you know, Rook," came the vague response.

A change in the ambient noise of the area interrupted Knight from verbally tearing the operator a new one for dangerous ambiguity. The unmistakable whooping sound of helicopter rotors filled the air. In the light of the dying fire, a large helicopter emerged from the dark night. Lights on the side of the aircraft illuminated the wording on the side.

ROTHERA.

"Holy shit," Knight muttered.

"What's that, boss?" Lehoski asked.

"It's Barbara," he replied as he lifted the phone again.

"Zeus Control, we're taking this chopper out of here. Relay new coordinates of the target to my PDA, over," he ordered.

"Confirmed, Rook. You'll have those coordinates momentarily. Zeus Control out."

The conversation ended. Knight would be having a word with Mr. Connor about the professionalism of the communications staff. Or maybe he'd just punch the dispatcher in the face. The fire burning in his gut from the recent adrenaline surge waned, but he still felt like punching someone, *anyone*, in the face in that moment.

With no more fuel to be found in such a frozen wasteland, the bombs' fires died quickly, leaving a large pool of water where the enemy had once been. Barbara lowered the helicopter slowly, its large searchlight scanning the wet area. Talos could see no sign of any opposition.

"Bodies are probably charred and under the water," Lehoski said.

Knight agreed and then ordered Kestrel to help Seagull get Falcon's body into the helicopter.

"I'll grab the head," he said flatly. As leader, he took the most difficult jobs, be it the most physically, mentally, or emotionally challenging. Retrieving the mutilated head of a fallen comrade ranked high up on the list of horrible jobs.

Now Knight felt blessed by the utter darkness. Falcon's features and injuries were not immediately distinguishable in the starry light. The quickness with which night had come on surprised Knight. It seemed like only minutes ago the sun was still poking its head over the horizon. Time always flew by on missions.

Looking down at Falcon's twisted features, Knight once again understood why codenames were used in his line of work. Having a manufactured identification for someone kept them at arm's length emotionally. That certainly helped when staring into a pair of lifeless eyes bulging out of a separated head.

Ariela.

Damn, he wished she'd never shared her name with him. Now she was someone he really knew.

Crap.

He picked up his subordinate's head with two hands and held it at his side. The sub-freezing temperatures had already taken care of solidifying anything that would have leaked out onto his white uniform, but he still held the head to his side. Knight could think of plenty of other things he would rather be doing at that exact moment.

Barbara's face turned a ghostly pale shade of white when Knight climbed onboard and placed the head on a small plastic tarpaulin that Lehoski had produced. They wrapped the tarp around the head and anchored it to the floor while Kestrel and Seagull attempted a similar feat with the headless body in the back of the helicopter. The pilot stared straight ahead, closing her teary eyes for long periods of time, trying not to vomit.

With the helicopter doors closed, even the small amount of heat flowing from the vents provided the men with extraordinary relief. As the blades spun up faster and faster, the noise in the cabin increased exponentially and more heat filled the cabin. It wasn't shorts and T-shirt weather, but it was a vast improvement.

Knight's hands and fingers trembled with the bitter cold as he removed his gloves and pulled his PDA from a heavily insulated pocket in his jacket. He yelled out new coordinates to Barbara. She looked at him as if he was crazy, but he explained they still had a mission to do, and she had just joined the team by virtue of necessity.

"I just came out to make sure you guys were out of the storm," she yelled adamantly. "I saw that black shape and guessed you'd be heading to it."

"I could kiss you, babe. It's freezing balls out there," replied Kestrel, rubbing his arms, trying to force out the chill.

Barbara rolled her eyes, but Knight noticed the small amount of levity had sufficiently distracted her from the decapitated cargo onboard. When he thought about it, if the body thawed out, things would get sufficiently grosser for everyone on the chopper.

"Diver, when we bail out to collect the target, grab some ice so that we can pack it in the tarps with Falcon. We don't need her warming up in the helo," Knight said.

The XO nodded solemnly.

Winds buffeted the helicopter every step of the way as Barbara cut across the frozen Antarctic plains. The coordinates were actually closer to home than where she had picked the men up, so the situation didn't seem all that bad, under the circumstances. She explained to Knight that she couldn't care less about what his orders were. If the storm approaching from the northeast moved in quickly, they were heading home.

"Barbara. That's not how this works. I have two guys on board who know how to pilot this chopper," Knight explained calmly, but loudly to be heard over the roar of the rotors. "If we need to, we're commandeering this helicopter."

"Don't threaten me, arse-wipe," Barbara snapped.

The anger was very apparent on her face. The green glow of the instrument cluster gave her a ghoulish hue that emphasized her scowl. A gloomy silence engulfed everyone. Lehoski stared at his own PDA, monitoring the group's progress via the GPS link. Kestrel sat back in his chair, eyes closed. Barbara sailed through darkness. Seagull stared at the tarp-covered head of his apparent nemesis.

The two had never been best of friends, but Knight had expected both of them to maintain a certain level of professionalism in the field. They'd got in each other's face just once during a training exercise, and Knight had summarily reprimanded both equally, not caring who did what to whom. Despite the unique circumstances of her acceptance into Phalanx, Falcon had received zero special treatment from Knight. Soldiers were bred from hardship, not coddling. Knight wondered if Seagull had acted out based on an attraction to a woman he couldn't have.

"Here we are, sir," Barbara announced overly politely, pulling the helicopter's nose up into a hover. Snow swirled by in great gusts as the pilot arced the helicopter gracefully in a full circle.

Her interruption rescued Knight from thinking about Falcon, but that meant it was time for him to be a douche bag. Knight didn't like it, but it was necessary.

"Barbara, I need you to give us control of the helicopter."

Her glare could've bored a hole through his skull easier than a nine-millimeter round. The reaction really didn't matter. They had the guns, and she would be a liability if she identified the cargo. Knight decided to attempt a compromise.

"Okay, you're the pilot. Kill the searchlight and put us down. We'll blindfold you while we do what we need to do."

The angry stare reduced in intensity by a few factors of ten, but she was still pissed.

"It's for your own good, Barbara. You do *not* want to know what's going on here," Knight reiterated.

She nodded and gracefully plopped her noisy baby down with a solid thump. The look on her face threatened to turn Knight to stone, or to at least boil his blood inside his body, while he wrapped a makeshift blindfold around her head. Satisfied, he left Seagull in front with her to keep her honest. A quick look at the instrument panel revealed the searchlight controls. He flipped the lights back on and scanned around in front of the stationary vehicle. Good thing he'd had Barbara shut the powerful light off. A solemn figure stood in the bright white beam of the searchlight, directly in front of the helicopter.

"That what we're looking for?" Seagull asked in the relative silence as the rotors spun down.

Knight just nodded.

Knight, Lehoski, and Kestrel dismounted and carefully approached the tall pink figure. The Angel seemed completely unaffected by the billowing snow or the lack of sunlight. It cast a wicked silhouette in the illumination of the searchlight as the remnant of Talos squad closed in.

Chapter 16

Two men sat in a lavishly appointed office, one behind a great mahogany desk, one very consciously in front of the deeply polished behemoth. The power in the room definitively flowed in only one direction.

The phone on the desk displayed an alert from the secretary outside. No beep could be heard. The only indication to visitors that a message had been received would come from observing the eyes of the man behind the desk. All he needed was a quick glance to see that his three o'clock appointment had arrived and was waiting outside.

His titanium, diamond-appointed watch showed five minutes until three o'clock. With a perfectly neutral expression firm on his face, the man smiled on the inside. The three o'clock visitor would bring him a lot more pleasure than the current loser slouching in a chair that was worth more than the man's generic Mercedes.

At the thought of his upcoming appointment, he considered that keeping the special consultant waiting for a few extra minutes would not make any difference. He paid for the time regardless. A few minutes of self-denial might just do him some good in a world where he could have anything he wanted, at any time he wanted.

Now the smile transferred to his exterior as he leaned forward and waved a hand at the pictures on the desk that captivated his current guest. The gloomy look on the other man's face told the whole story. The game was over before it even started.

This would be quick.

"Bryan, now that we know where we stand, I don't think you'll have a problem acquiescing to my request," he said smugly.

As much as he loved the chase, what was the point if you never caught the prey? This lion held the gazelle's throat securely in his ravenous jaws, begging the victim to give him a reason to bite down.

His guest didn't immediately respond. The stare intensified, the man wishing to will the pictures out of existence. No such luck for him there.

"These pictures of you and the twelve-year-old boys in Thailand do not need to leave this office," said the lion behind the desk. "In fact, they will stay quite safe in my vault."

The guest's defeated eyes followed the man's outstretched arm, which just happened to be covered in a suit of such quality that poor Bryan could never comprehend. The extravagantly coated arm led to a perfectly manicured hand that pointed to a gigantic safe built into one of the office's walls. The large grey door loomed ominously.

A man of such stature required a lockbox large enough to hold a lot of leverage. One did not receive such prominence cheaply. As such, many other people served his will due to compromising evidence that he alone held. Or at least, that is what they thought.

Now the small, sweaty man spoke.

"Mr. Murphy, I'm not sure I can agree to your terms," Bryan Fortuna said, stuttering ever so slightly with nerves.

A little backbone from the diminutive man only increased the size of the evil smirk on Murphy's face. As Chief Executive Officer of Celestius, the largest cancer-treating pharmaceutical company in the world, David Murphy had negotiated with many individuals far more skilled that his current quarry. The truth was that in this case, there was not much to negotiate.

"You realize of course that your life would be over, Mr. Fortuna?" Murphy asked politely. Before the question could warrant a response, Murphy added, "Not to mention your boss's career."

Ah, yes. There was the breakthrough.

This peon had a hard-on for his boss and could not bear the thought of ruining her. In Fortuna's industry, information ruled, but pictures of prominent figures with little boys trumped all else.

Murphy felt the thrill of victory as Fortuna's form slumped even more than before. This was a wholly defeated man. Murphy just hoped the worthless child molester did not off himself before carrying out Murphy's orders.

Considering that Murphy was Fortuna's boss's greatest contributor, it stood to reason in Murphy's mind that he would have her ear. Unfortunately, power had gone to someone's head, and Murphy had been denied the access he had expected. Hence, one of his non-payroll employees had followed Mr. Bryan Fortuna on a vacation to Thailand. Now Murphy owned him. He always got his way, one way or the other.

The shattered man simply nodded in disgrace.

"Fantastic," declared Murphy, punctuating the conclusion of the meeting. "Please see yourself out, Mr. Fortuna. Keep me abreast of any developments," he ordered with a smile.

Fortuna had entered the room just thirty minutes ago with all of the confidence that an overly inflated ego could supply. After just half an hour, Murphy had crushed the arrogant deviant's false sense of security, exposing it for what it truly was. This man had never accomplished anything worthwhile in life, never known the meaning of hard work.

Now Fortuna had finally met someone who had achieved everything through tireless fighting. Murphy hoped Fortuna learned something from the encounter to better himself in the future. Education unlocked potential.

The broken man shuffled towards the door. Murphy thought he heard a muffled expletive cursing his name as Fortuna reached for the handle on the immense, dark door. The sound brought another small amount of satisfaction. Obviously Fortuna had worked out that Murphy would own him forever. What a marvelous day.

Perhaps Fortuna was just weighing the heavy potential consequences of his decision. People could die.

He should have thought about that before his little excursion to Thailand.

People most likely would die, but Murphy had a far grander plan in mind. The initial investment would reap unimaginable rewards.

The door swung open smoothly in Fortuna's grasp. Despite his best intentions, Fortuna could not throw the door open, or slam it shut for that matter. A deliberately installed mechanism slowed the door's speed as excessive force was applied. Murphy entertained many guests who would love to rip the door off its hinges as they left, so he frustrated them just one more time. He had control.

With the door fully opened, Murphy grinned again. Fortuna stood before the most beautiful woman he would ever see in person. This was just another perk of Murphy's illustrious job. Candy was a special consultant of a special breed. She floated across the floor past Fortuna's wide-open jaw, his gaze transfixed on her perfect form.

Blue eyes as chilling as ice, long naturally blonde hair falling straight as arrows, and hips to kill for, Murphy's new guest attracted a crowd in any situation. For the next hour or so, she would have to deal with just one man's undivided attention.

The secretary outside announced that Fortuna's time had expired, and he needed to move on. With a subtle push on the man's back, she cleared the doorway. The secretary closed the door with a wink to Murphy.

A wry smile plastered across his face, Murphy stood to meet his most desirable guest.

Chapter 17

Andrew Knight stood rigidly before the desk of his boss. The situation was all too familiar. Low light gave the entire debriefing the hush-hush feeling that it deserved. Connor's intense glare hinted that despite the initial innocent questions, something more serious was in the works.

Knight had a decent enough idea of what that might entail, but focused on the present part of the debriefing. The story so far was nothing to write home about. Connor was reading his notes to recount Knight's tale.

In the monotone that he adopted whenever reading aloud, Connor stated, "So after the death of Falcon and the elimination of the enemy threat, which we discovered to be Chinese in nature, between you and me, Talos boarded a civilian helicopter piloted by civilian Barbara McDougal. With updated coordinates, Talos located the target and secured it onboard."

Despite the lack of an explicit question, Knight knew that Connor expected a verbal confirmation. The man never even lifted his head to give an inquisitive facial expression. Another hint that Knight was in the doghouse for something, and he didn't think it was for the death of his squad member.

"Yes, sir. That's correct, sir."

Some old military habits were hard to break, the drastic overuse of the title *sir* for one.

"There's no mention of what you did with Ms. McDougal after the extraction."

If Connor had asked a question, Knight had missed it.

"Did you ensure that she wouldn't be a problem in the future, Knight?"

Do you mean, did I kill her afterwards? That wasn't how Knight worked. Civilians weren't fodder.

"She was blindfolded before we discovered the Angel. We took the Angel onboard and removed it without her ever seeing it," Knight explained. "She's good."

Connor just gave a gruff *humph* in response. Was that disappointment that Knight detected? He damn well hoped not.

"According to your statement, the Angel accompanied Talos squad without incident, unless the miraculous healing of Seagull counts as an incident."

"That's right, sir."

Now Connor looked up with the weary eyes of a parent listening to a child retelling the moments before a grievous infraction. He massaged his forehead, just above his eyebrows, pushing hard enough that his knuckles turned white.

"Can you explain that to me again?"

Visibly sighing seemed a bit inappropriate, even to Knight, but running through the events of Seagull's healing *again* didn't strike him as fun. In his mind he pictured a greatly exaggerated sigh, with an accompanying theatrical shoulder motion. That would have to hold him over. In fairness, despite the ubiquitous stories of Angels miraculously curing diseases and ailments, seeing one in person or hearing about one firsthand still led to severe skepticism. Knight didn't blame his boss, but he was still irritated about having to repeat himself.

"As previously stated," Knight began, while putting a leash on the desire to tilt his head in a teenage condescending way, "Seagull's arm had been injured by multiple bullet fragments. We believe that the bullets shattered upon contact with the pyramid. That aspect of it is unexplainable with our information, because our own scientific testing had shown snowballs would disappear into the pyramid."

The look on Connor's face said to get on with it, but Knight decided to irritate his boss just a little more. Knight preferred winding roads in conversations. They were easier to hide undesirable information in.

Also, at some point Knight wanted to broach the subject of Connor's indiscretions with Falcon. *That* little tidbit required some buildup.

The thought of Falcon's death prompted a flush of regret. This always happened when one of his own died, whether it was back in the Rangers, or now in Phalanx. She was the first to die under him on a mission for Phalanx. He'd known someone would get killed eventually, but losing someone he was responsible for never felt good.

"Seagull expressed that his injury wouldn't keep him from his duties and he performed them well. So well in fact, I forgot he was hurt at all."

Knight couldn't help falling back into a formal tone for briefing his boss, just another old habit that would die hard.

"On the chopper, the Angel turned to Seagull and put its hand out. Seagull seemed to know what to do. He undid his gloves and removed his outer jacket. Then he rolled up his sleeves, exposing some obviously uncomfortable injuries. At this point, we experienced some turbulence and...."

"Get on with it, Knight," Connor burst out. He jumped to his feet to look into Knight's unwavering eyes. "I don't give a shit about any turbulence. It has no relevance to this part of the debriefing. Just finish it."

As the major took his seat once more, Knight smiled to himself internally. That was a new record time for pissing off his boss with a roundabout explanation. The guy was definitely like a father to Knight, but if memory served, Knight had possessed a penchant for pissing off his own dad frequently, too.

"Yes, sir. The Angel touched Seagull for only a second with its hand, then pulled away and stared at the wall for the rest of the trip. It was weird to see something alive stay so motionless. Eerie."

The air in the office grew thin for a moment as Connor took an enormously deep breath and held it. After an arbitrary count, Connor allowed his lungs to relax and breathed out. Knight assumed the man had taken up stress-relieving exercises specifically to handle him. Even a son could get under a father's skin. In fact, a son could usually do a better job of that than anyone else. With exception of the father's wife, of course.

Now rubbing his temples and clenching his jaw shut tightly, Connor furrowed his brow impressively. The man was under pressure. Knight used this time to stare at the wall and think about the beer he would have later. An ice cold Shiner Bock would hit the spot. Shiner was one of the blessings of living in Texas.

Now his boss looked up and dropped his hands to the desk with a quiet slap.

"Then what, Andy? Was he fixed?"

Knight thought about mentioning his own desire to neuter Seagull after the outburst over Falcon, but then thought the better of it. He actually started to feel slightly bad for Connor and the bureaucratic crap that would probably follow this supposedly top secret mission.

"Visibly, we didn't notice anything, due to his clothing. Seagull claims that he experienced a vague sensation, like having surgery under a strong local anesthetic. Apparently he could feel something going on, but it didn't hurt. After the sensation ended, about an hour later, he didn't have any pain at all."

"Alright. So did you recover the bullet fragments?"

"No, sir. Seagull claims there were no fragments. They disintegrated in some way. I wasn't about to touch him and find out. The Angel still freaks me out," explained Knight.

Connor tapped a finger on his desk lightly and stared at Knight. The arrhythmic strikes on the wood annoyed Knight to no end, but of course he wouldn't let his boss see that. Such weakness could lead to Connor having a new Knight-interrogation trick.

Finally Connor spoke. The words weren't exactly laced with venom, but their quiet volume and mild tone hinted at sarcasm.

"I believe that Seagull made enough of a recovery during the flight to engage in some extracurricular activities at your destination," Connor asked Knight, without actually asking a question.

"Sir?" Knight responded innocently. Perhaps too innocently for a major trained in the ways of soldiers.

"Yes, Andy. I received an unofficial complaint from one irate Major Kennedy today."

And an official complaint would never be issued, Knight knew. Not when someone was on the receiving end of a Grade A beatdown.

Good times.

On the last leg of the journey with the Angel, Kestrel had proven very useful in volunteering to pilot the last plane. To be honest, Knight hadn't even known Kestrel *could* fly a plane. For whatever reason, Lehoski had vouched for the new guy, so that was a good enough credential for Knight. The small prop plane had contained Knight, Lehoski, Seagull, Kestrel, and the subdued Angel. The corpse of Falcon had been off-loaded at a previous stop for a special, secure transport home. Such unique arrangements often drew too much attention, so the Angel rode along in the small plane with the remaining members of Talos.

As a crude disguise, the Angel wore a large set of fatigues and a crude black balaclava. Its hands were secured in front of it with handcuffs. Apparently the Angel didn't particularly care. It certainly hadn't caused a fuss. The plan called for treating the Angel like a special inmate being transferred back to the United States after extradition from a foreign country. So far no one had questioned the eight-foot tall prisoner. As a result of the Angel's great height, the small prop plane seemed even more crowded than normal.

While making an unusually fast landing on United States soil, Kestrel had barely avoided ricocheting the plane between lines of waiting Army jeeps cruising the runway. One of the jeeps had flipped over as a result. Needless to say, some of the Army soldiers on hand expressed deeply negative regard for their mercenary brethren who'd just swooped in and caused all kinds of ruckus.

Knight had ignored the childish harassment, but Seagull had informed the soldiers that they shouldn't have driven their jeeps so close to the plane. After being compared to a cowboy who regularly entered into unnatural relations with his own mother, Seagull had offered the soldier a free colon-cleanse.

The exact words had been, "I will kick the shit out of you."

After the ensuing rumble on the runway, five of the Army soldiers lay in a bruised heap and Knight peeled a sixth off of Kestrel, who had been taken by surprise from behind. At least, that was his side of the story. Knight let the soldier go without further injury. The guy had obviously held his own against Kestrel, who was no small man, so Knight saw no need to reward the soldier with a fist to the face. The man's uniform said Sergeant Hasselbeck. Knight would put the name forward to Connor later.

"We would've offered the medical assistance of the Angel sir, but it was undercover as a drug-dealing basketball center," Knight said innocently.

"I don't need to hear you talk about any of that, Andy. The complaint was unofficial. So unofficially I will request that you and your men grow up and stop acting like idiots. Officially, you lost a soldier out there. Obviously your team needs help learning professionalism."

The words stung Knight deeply, but part of the job was bearing the brunt of the boss's frustration over a serious hiccup in the organization's first important mission. Knight had already ripped into Seagull for his Antarctic outburst, but without Falcon in the picture, Knight didn't think Seagull needed to leave the group. They were a family, and families had issues from time to time.

"Yes, sir," Knight finally replied.

This acknowledgment appeased Connor, and he dismissed Knight with the flick of his hand, an order that Knight was only too happy to follow. He'd bring up the affair with Falcon when Connor was in a better mood. That way he could ruin yet another day for the boss.

***

As soon as the door closed behind Knight, Michael Connor slouched back in his chair and stared at the ceiling, hands locked over his chest. Moments passed by.

Wide rays of light penetrated the drawn blinds, growing in intensity as clouds gave way to unveil the bright Texas sun. Connor stood and strode to the window, never having been one to saunter. The man only walked as if he had a purpose, which he typically did.

Using two fingers of his right hand, Connor peeked through two of the slats in the blinds. Knight marched leisurely away from the building containing Connor's office. From Knight's gait, Connor could tell that getting Karen to the Angel and then going on a mission had done wonders for Knight's wellbeing. Despite the tone of their most recent meeting, Connor looked out the window and felt proud of the young man.

Connor wondered if Falcon's death had jolted Knight back into his old self. That woman had proven to be nothing but a problem since her arrival in Connor's life. Nobody in the group who knew the full situation would grieve her too heavily, assuming anyone did know. There certainly hadn't been any hints at Connor's level that Falcon had blabbed.

The altercation with the Army boys cemented the return of the old Captain Knight. Of course, Connor had expressed disapproval and verbalized some veiled threats, but the father figure in Connor just laughed. Those pricks needed a good whooping every now and then to keep them humble. Nothing more would probably be heard about the scuffle, considering the result. Connor knew for a fact that if his boys had lost that fight, the Army would have widely publicized it amongst their own ranks.

Hell, they might have even claimed victory regardless. Connor didn't believe his counterparts still in the Army to be that petty, but he could never be sure. Assumptions usually led to problems.

So now Knight was back, kicking ass and taking names. This mission was exactly what the doctor ordered. Well, not exactly. The Phalanx doctor had insisted that Knight wasn't fit for a leadership role, but Connor had overruled that sentiment. Apparently he understood the man better than a shrink could.

Another positive result of Ariela's, rather *Falcon's*, death was the opening of a spot in Phalanx. Connor always scouted out new talent, and he had a few more names that he needed to run down. Finally he could hire someone with the proper qualifications, not just a home-wrecking nuisance.

Connor returned to his desk to dive into the eternal stream of necessarily useless paperwork that flowed across his path daily. A brief moment of introspection surprised him.

Such a cynical view of a soldier's death would never have crossed his mind a decade ago. A lot had happened. Results justified his apathy. The Angel was in a secure location, and a personal ticking time-bomb in his organization had been eliminated. Even so, as Falcon's ex-employer, Connor still had duties to perform. The most annoying of these would be the mountain of paperwork to fill out to cover the woman's death. Thankfully Phalanx had some creative writers to invent the cover stories on Connor's behalf. Ariela Rodriguez would of course be made out to be a hero in some glory-filled mission. Connor didn't care, as long as the truth hadn't gotten out, and wasn't just lurking, like a big, angry dog in a dark alley, waiting to strike.

The phone rang three times before Connor reached to answer it. A stickler for details, he hated to leave a line half-finished on a document and insisted on completing the line before answering.

A familiar voice on the other end of the phone said, "There's been an incident."

Chapter 18

Mark Jackson and Matt Smith, the greatest reporters that a failing newspaper could ever ask for.

The thought rolled around erratically in Mark's head as he pretended to pay attention to the tantrum unfolding in his boss's office. Editor-in-chief Charlie Olsen of the Phoenix Press had finally taken a running leap off the deep end. He was in spectacular form, really.

"You two idiots managed to lose the main character in this story? How in the deepest, darkest pit of hell did you manage that feat?" Olsen screamed, pounding on his desk to accent each adjective of hell.

Olsen expected no answer to these questions. Interrogations at the Press often went this way. Jackson and Smith just stared curiously at the man, trying to keep a straight face. Smith had once smirked ever so slightly when Olsen had stomped down angrily and accidentally destroyed his precious wicker wastepaper basket. That facial faux pas had earned another series in the long line of lectures on appropriate behavior in the office workplace.

That this man could possibly represent any level of office standards just made Jackson sick. Rampant and obvious hypocrisy had infiltrated every aspect of his life. Instantly the image of Pastor Martin Daniels appeared in his mind, prompting thoughts of utter dissatisfaction with mankind.

A stern prod to the chest opened Jackson's eyes. He'd dozed off while his short, bespectacled, balding, plump boss continued his irrational rant.

Such a dire interruption could *not* be tolerated, Jackson was told sharply. Once again, Olsen poked him in the chest. Sternly.

"Don't touch me, Charlie," Jackson said patiently.

Olsen glared at him, but did not touch him again. The boss returned to his own side of the cheap and cluttered desk. Jackson was not a very tall man, and he didn't have an impressive physique. The reporter got his way with just his words. Except for one time in Tempe when his Texan partner in crime had needed to step in and subdue a pair of gangbangers who thought that Jackson was a vice cop. Matt had acted swiftly and instinctively, belying his oversized girth. Plus, the guy's fists looked like sides of ham.

Perhaps Jackson's ability to talk his way out of situations benefitted more from standing next to an incredibly big guy than just from his own wit and intellect. The slight, but sinewy, reporter could never go so far as to admit that out loud, so he just accepted that his mouth was his best defense, unless someone was punching it.

The boss resumed the session at a slightly more relaxed tone.

"So where is he?" he asked.

Jackson looked at Smith, who just shrugged. Sometimes Smith was not in a particularly helpful mood. The longer that the rant went on, the closer the day would be to being over. That was how Smith's mind worked. He just had to make it until five o'clock.

The ball was in Jackson's court and Olsen was staring impatiently, as if restraining himself from beating the reporter with a desk chair.

"The subject's gone, and we don't know where, boss," Jackson said.

"Did you check his place of residence?" asked Olsen through clenched teeth.

"Yes, but the landlady hasn't seen him since he paid his rent. Other than that, she really doesn't seem to care. Maybe we should ask her again in a month, when the next round of rent is up," explained Jackson.

Smith stifled a laugh and casually converted the outburst into a bout of coughing. Olsen's head snapped to the big man and his expression showed that he didn't buy the charade.

"The guy was supposed to be here first thing this morning for an exclusive interview, but he never showed," explained Jackson, regaining his boss's attention.

"Doesn't he have a cell phone?" Olsen asked.

After taking a moment to gather his appropriate thoughts and fend off the less helpful responses floating through his head, Jackson replied, "Yes, but he's not answering it."

"What about the police?" snapped Olsen.

"What about them?" replied Jackson.

"Did you file a missing person report with them?"

"Uh, no," said Jackson, not doing a good job of hiding his opinion of that matter.

"Oh, so you don't think it is that important to find our newspaper's savior, Jackson?" asked the boss in a poisonously sweet voice. "We could really use the boost right now."

"The police don't accept missing person reports this early, boss," replied Jackson with exaggerated patience. "They wait twenty-four hours if there's no suspected immediate danger to the subject."

"The only subject in immediate danger here is your job if you can't find this guy," snapped Olsen.

Jackson thought he could see the venom dripping from the words in midair. When Jackson didn't rise to the bait, Olsen continued.

"Okay, well get out there and find Joshua Greaves."

Both reporters stood and turned for the door, rolling their eyes at each other for good measure. Jackson would rather have undergone various Southeast Asian tortures involving bamboo and loose fingernails than listen to anymore crap from his ineffective leader. The meeting had accomplished absolutely nothing. They still had no story, and they still knew that they were supposed to find the subject.

"Don't roll your eyes at me, gentlemen!" roared Olsen.

Everyone in the open area of desks outside Olsen's office perked up at the explosion. The secretary glanced up at Jackson with wide open eyes and a small grin. Apparently the show was good today. Jackson stood in the office doorway and turned back to his boss.

"We're getting killed by online news sites and a shitty economy, guys. We need this story," yelled the chief.

The two men nodded and left the office, carefully closing the door behind them. Olsen hated when anyone rattled the glass in the door while closing it, and neither reporter wanted another speech on effective and appropriate door closure.

As they sat down at their desks, Jackson looked at Smith and said, "Well, at least he's not just blaming us for the collapse of his paper. My back was hurting from the heavy burden."

"To be honest, even if we find this guy, nobody's going to care. This is old news."

"Yeah, everyone wants to hear about the crazy shit going on in the Middle East right now," said Jackson. "That place needed another suicide bombing like I needed another nonsense lecture from Olsen."

Smith was silent for a while, and then asked, "So what happened to this guy, Mark?"

Jackson leaned back in his chair and put his hands behind his head before answering.

"I have no idea, man. No idea at all."

***

"Have you seen my grandmother?"

The older woman looked down at the cute little girl and replied, "No, I have not."

The girl scrunched her face into a wrinkle of terrible concern. In such a small village, everybody knew who she was. News traveled fast in this dusty village on the outskirts of Magadi. Being such a closely knit community, someone should also know the location of her missing grandmother.

"I can't find her," the little girl said emphatically.

The woman looked down at her again. She couldn't be more than six years old, but her harsh life in Africa had already aged her considerably. Worrying about her grandmother probably didn't help.

"Why don't you go back to your grandmother's house and check there? Maybe she's already returned," the woman offered kindly.

"But I've already looked there," the child insisted. Her distress grew with each passing moment.

Tired of the discussion and not worried about the child's suddenly gregarious grandmother, the woman hushed the child and gently turned her towards the grandmother's house. The elderly lady had been known to disappear for long walks recently, so the woman wasn't particularly concerned.

"Go on home," she urged.

Begrudgingly, the six year old bounded off towards the small house. She could run very quickly for her age and reached the doorway in a short amount of time. Life in her part of the world encouraged good running skills.

"Mother, where is Grandmother?" she yelled into the dark house.

Her mother emerged from the kitchen area, exasperated with her child's incessant questions. The child's grandmother had become more and more active every day since the Angel had healed her cancer. She now appeared to be indestructible.

"Child, you need to ask questions in a respectful manner," she instructed her child crossly.

The young child huffed and puffed for a moment.

"Sorry, Mother. I cannot find Grandmother."

The mother crouched down and lightly put her hands on her daughter's small shoulders. She smiled widely for her child's benefit.

"Your grandmother has just gone for a long walk. I'm sure she's fine and will return shortly. It's cute that you miss her, but she'll be back soon," the mother promised.

The child wore a restrained scowl on her face, but nodded obediently and ran outside once more.

"Your old mother probably just shacked up with some man. Probably hasn't been with a man in a decade," called the mother's husband from the corner of the room. He laughed at his own humor.

His wife just rolled her eyes. Unfortunately, he was probably right. Her mother had developed a new love for life and who knew what she was capable of.

She would start to worry if the old woman hadn't returned in another day.

***

From the sky above, the crowd surrounding Renji hospital more resembled a writhing mass than a group of people. The protestors had filled the streets constantly since the death of the young woman who'd led the initial charge. As the older and more tired members of the mob worked their way out, new protestors cycled in to take their spots.

The situation had resulted in only the single death, but more injuries than the hospital could handle. In reality, the Healer could repair all of these injuries, but the hospital's governor had decided that the people could do with an acceptable level of suffering. If they had not fought the police, they would not now need to take up a bed in the crowded medical facility.

Helicopters from all over the city hovered around in the sky above Renji, waiting for their turn to land. The flock of choppers roughly resembled the shape of a tornado, with increasing numbers of them at elevated altitudes. Some waited so long in the mechanical cyclone that the pilots had to surrender their spot in the queue to go refuel, much to their patrons' dismay.

At least three helicopters transporting incredibly ill individuals had arrived on the ground outside the hospital with deceased cargo. The orderlies performed their duties without any outward show of emotion, but certain aspects of the situation were quite ridiculous. Many of the incoming visitors had no chance of survival on the long flight to the hospital. Poor judgment, fueled by a desire to live, led to their untimely demise, but who could blame them?

In an attempt to appease the locals outside, the governing body had recently created a queue for the less wealthy people in the street to gain access to the Healer. Reports had quickly spread throughout the crowd that ten of the rich patrons received the healing touch for every one or two of the less fortunate individuals. The intensity of the crowd electrified.

When word spread that an elderly woman had died while waiting for the Healer's touch, the pent-up fury exploded.

At first there was one glass bottle spinning elegantly through the air. The potentially deadly projectile transformed into an infinite number of pieces upon contact with the concrete, harmlessly peppering the ground in front of some policemen. As they looked up, the space above the crowd gradually filled with anything that the protestors could get their hands on.

Bottles, bricks, and stones ricocheted off of helmets and riot shields. The police geared up for a battle. Officers yelled formation orders above the roar of the crowd, directing the fight in safety behind their men. In well-scripted unison, the lines of armor-clad police advanced their positions, one steady step after another. It would only be a matter of time before the dissidents traded simple glass bottles for improvised firebombs.

The large water guns mounted on top of gigantic black trucks fired a few warning shots before opening up completely on the rebellious crowd. The powerful jet of water knocked down the front lines of the protestors, tossing flailing individuals around effortlessly. The mob backed up as the wall of black approached.

With only a few strides separating the rioters and the police forces, all eyes jerked upwards as the top floors of the hospital detonated. A pulse rippled from the building, knocking down hundreds of stunned onlookers. Bodies lay strewn around on the cold concrete as jets of flame spewed from gaping holes in the upper-stories of the hospital. Pitiful shrieks emanated from amongst the fallen.

The fighting ended instantly, both sides eyeing each other in fear of the other, wondering who had caused this calamity. After just a few seconds, flaming bricks and timber descended into the crowd. Thoughts of protest fled as quickly as those able-bodied enough to pick themselves up. In the exodus, the discombobulated and incapacitated lay trampled beneath those who had fought on their side only moments before. Screams of agony drowned beneath screams of fear.

Few citizens cared to look up and watch a flash of blue light shoot from the hospitals roof. The short blast penetrated the billowing smoke and disappeared into the overcast clouds.

Next to Renji hospital, nearby police regained their composure until the cries from inside reached their ears.

Their Healer was dead.

Chapter 19

Three of the world's most powerful political leaders prepared for a showdown. Though physically separated by continents and oceans, technology brought them far too close for comfort. High definition images of the other two participants' faces appeared in perfect clarity on large LCD monitors. Each stone-faced leader stared stolidly into their respective camera, waiting for the potentially world-changing meeting to commence.

The view on each screen showed a leader from the waist up, just enough visual range to observe their hands resting on expensive desks. Unseen, but presumed present, sat hosts of advisors, observing in silence while their lieges readied for verbal sparring. In more remote locations, secret locations, sat men and women who had much less interest in the content of the discussion as they did in the content of the signals crossing such vast distances. Teams actively monitored the secure lines to ensure no unauthorized parties attempted to be a fly on a wall for the proceedings.

Israeli Prime Minister Amzi Shalev started the video conference.

"Thank you for assembling at such short notice, Prime Minister Strachan and President Davenport," he began in flawless Cambridge English.

The leaders of the United Kingdom and the United States nodded in acknowledgement. They both had a good general idea of why Shalev had called the meeting and would not have missed it for the world.

"I understand that recent events in my country leave you unwilling to travel here in person. As much as I can always promise world-class protection during any diplomatic visit, I hold no ill feelings about your insistence to meet via the Internet."

A wry smile creased Shalev's face only briefly before he resumed.

"Due to the increasingly large hostile element in the European Union, I have not included other nations in our discussion. I do not have to tell you that certain countries are plotting against the United Kingdom as we speak. They wish to gain access to your Angel, and Prime Minister, I understand your dilemma."

Strachan took advantage of Shalev's pause to clarify his position for the record.

"Thank you, Prime Minister," the Scotsman said in his practiced British accent. "I appreciate your understanding that my country cannot possibly support the numbers that would flow in if I reopened the borders. It is a logistical impossibility."

The British leader added nothing about the suspected plans of the EU to forcefully obtain access to the Angel. Strachan knew that Shalev probably had a very good idea about the situation, he may have even been approached to join the alliance, but Strachan had no intention of offering any new information that he had. Relations with shrewd politicians proved difficult enough without giving away information for free. Information equaled power.

Reading between the lines, Strachan saw that Prime Minister Shalev most likely hadn't sided with the disgruntled European nations. Otherwise, this meeting would be relatively pointless. But with Shalev, all was never as it seemed.

The Israeli leader nodded and continued.

"As you know, Jerusalem suffered terribly in the last few days. The string of bombings has left over one thousand of my people dead and many thousands injured. Many have been bussed out to the hospitals of other cities because Jerusalem's facilities cannot meet the needs of this many victims."

Shalev leaned forward on his desk, his completely bald head tilting to a well practiced angle, revealing his infamous scar. As a child, a bullet from a Palestinian's gun had etched a jagged trench diagonally across the top of his head. That bullet had been meant for his mother. The three following rounds had all found their target, killing her in dreadful, drawn out pain.

The assailant had laughed at the misery, goaded the small boy who had dived in front of his mother, trying in vain to protect her. The Islamic warrior had then smashed in the bridge of Shalev's nose with the butt of his rifle, earning the young boy another permanent reminder of the hatred thrust upon him.

The violence had been mindless. They had done nothing wrong. Yet, his mother died in his arms. The pain and anguish honed a skilled, yet ruthless leader. After years of escalating violence in Israel, the population had been all too happy to have a strong man of valor in office, a man who shared their feelings and knew their pain. He owned their hearts, but they had been given freely.

The other two leaders recognized the man's gesture and knew the words that would come next. The display of his past experience always preempted military action.

"The Israeli armed forces will march into the Kingdom of Jordan with a vengeance in precisely one hour," Shalev declared, spitting the words out.

Just mentioning the Jordanians got Shalev's blood going. They had recently provided such useful assistance to the United States and Israel in the form of intelligence and staging areas for CIA operations, but now to stab them in the back. Just like the old days.

"But Prime Minister, I thought the instigators were Egyptian, Afghani, and Iranian? Jordan has done nothing but help us recently," said Strachan.

"They entered our land through Jordan, and that is where we will begin!" yelled Shalev.

Passion accelerated each word across cyberspace, burning a path of hatred. Neither Strachan nor Davenport flinched. They had seen this before and every time had successfully talked Shalev down from the brink of epic conflict with the Muslim world.

"Do not insult my people by calling these animals 'instigators', George," spat Shalev, losing his formality in his anger. "I have over one thousand dead citizens to account for. They will not die in vain the way so many have in the past."

The British leader continued to lead the charge for mediation.

"Amzi, think this through. If you attack Jordan, every Muslim country will immediately attack your people. Are you prepared for that?"

"George, do not patronize me. You know the history of my country enough to know that we have fought them all before. And we will do so again."

Before Strachan could get a word in edgewise, the Israeli Prime Minister continued.

"I would feel better about the situation if I had not heard that British troops are being pulled out of Israel and out of the eastern Mediterranean. I thought we were allies, George," said Shalev.

His disgust coated the words that sought to penetrate Strachan's cool demeanor. The British leader had seen worse and didn't bite.

"As you said yourself, Amzi, I have to worry about my other supposed *allies* attacking my country. I am only consolidating forces to protect the interests of British citizens."

Knowing that her turn would come soon enough, President Meghan Davenport jumped into the fray.

"The limited U.S. military forces stationed in Iraq at this time are fulfilling policing duties only. They cannot be spared to help Israel, and they certainly cannot be expected to suppress any anti-Israeli violence that breaks out in the region due to your actions, Prime Minister Shalev," Davenport stated.

As the United States' first female leader, Meghan Davenport had led a successful first year. Unlike George Strachan, Davenport hadn't encountered Amzi Shalev enough to warrant calling him by first name. Shalev did not feel the same way about her.

He laughed in her face.

"Meghan," he started, as if talking to a child who had just parroted some new information that they had recently heard but hardly comprehended. "You should know by now that all of the serious terrorist threats left Iraq years ago."

Davenport interjected, "That's not true—"

"All that remains in that backward nation," he continued undeterred, "are ignorant suicide bombers who take care of themselves. After all, they can only explode once. The United States has all of the resources necessary to destroy that threat and stamp out this terrorism, yet their leader appears as impotent as the previous few who refused to take off the 'little kid gloves', to use an Americanism," stated Shalev smugly. "At one point I heard one of your predecessors preaching that all American troops would leave that cesspool, but look where we are now. You are still too weak to do what is needed."

Through gritted teeth, Davenport responded, "The United States, and any other civilized country, does not act that way, Amzi."

Now that Shalev had established the first name basis in such a derogatory manner, Davenport said his name in such a way that Shalev reacted as if she had slapped him. He recovered his composure quickly. Strachan sat quietly, observing Davenport trying to establish herself with the Israeli leader.

In a dismissive tone, Shalev said, "The world would be a better place if the U.S. could fight wars with the intention of winning."

When Davenport ignored him, he added more forcefully, "You would still be a British colony if not for the backbone of your forefathers."

The dust settled for a moment while Davenport wondered why she had to suffer this intolerable man. What did she really need him for at the end of the day?

"Amzi, the people of my country are already upset that we have so many troops in Afghanistan, still fighting a war on terror. You propose to expand that war. Do you really think my people will support that?" Davenport asked, now calm and diplomatic.

The Israeli just shook his head in disbelief.

"Afghanistan is a total waste of time and resources. You should dedicate those forces to the defense of your greatest ally," Shalev said reproachfully.

Davenport stared intensely at him when she asked, "And exactly what have you done lately for *your* greatest ally?"

When the response didn't come immediately, she stated flatly, "We'll get back to you, Prime Minister."

A nod to the IT guru in the room killed the Israeli's feed. Davenport clicked a button on a remote lying on the desk and muted incoming and outgoing sound. After a few moments of exchange between the world leaders and their respective advisors, she turned off the mute for her British counterpart.

"Talk to me, George," Davenport said, not caring that Strachan was still in a discussion with his team.

The British Prime Minister turned to the camera, doing his best not to appear too irritated at the interruption. He had worked with countless heads of state in his long tenure as the British leader, but sometimes Davenport proved more trying than certain Third World dictators. As the first female American President, Davenport had proved herself more than capable of the required tasks, but her attitude conspicuously highlighted the large chip on her shoulder. Strachan could handle her misgivings in exchange for what he needed.

"I think we need to protect our best interests first, Meghan," Strachan said carefully. He didn't mind stating the obvious, so long as he could avoid associating himself with a specific idea too early in the discussion.

"Well said, George, but what exactly are our best interests?" she snipped.

Strachan noted the tone in Davenport's voice. He'd never been one for mixing childish emotional inflections with diplomacy. Suddenly tired of games, Strachan laid everything out.

"For Britain, my people are the most important factor in this issue. I need to provide for their defense, first and foremost, especially in the present European political climate."

"So that means using U.S. military forces as a deterrent to your neighbors?" Davenport asked, this time in a more neutral tone.

"That is certainly an idea, yes."

An uncharacteristic silence fell between the two leaders. Time slowed to a fraction of its normal pace as Strachan and Davenport stared at each other from across the Atlantic. As he started to break the silence, Strachan noticed Davenport's eyes twitch to the right of the camera, just for an instant.

She had muted him. The display and network instrumentation showed no sign of the typical mute in use. Apparently his American counterpart had a custom setup that included a few extra bells and whistles. Her quick glance to the side told Strachan that she was probably listening to her advisors and didn't want him to hear their counsel. He wondered if she could still hear him if he chose to talk to his own team.

In the communications room of the White House, President Davenport tried to focus intently on the camera, but she knew that she had glanced at Bryan Fortuna when he'd started talking. It was a rookie mistake that she shouldn't be making at this stage of the game. There would be plenty of time for mulling over her shortcomings later, so she pushed the thought out of her mind.

Fortuna, one of her closest and reliable advisors since her time as a state senator, was explaining the need to bolster Israel's defense in the name of America's own safety. Davenport didn't know if she agreed. She turned off the mute on her outgoing sound.

"George, we need to reinforce our ally. Israel cannot fall."

"Even when they start the conflict, Meghan?" asked a slightly shocked Prime Minister.

Davenport didn't hesitate.

"They were attacked quite violently this week."

"They were attacked by a terrorist organization based in many countries, including one that we have significant military presence in. They cannot just declare war on their closest rival," said Strachan.

"Actually, they can. And they will."

Strachan's brain kicked up a gear, deftly considering the Americans' angle in the dispute. What did the United States stand to gain from helping Israel dismantle the fragile peace that loosely controlled the Middle East? Oil could always be a factor, but they could have caused as much disruption as they had wanted when they went after Iraq the last time.

The Middle East did not possess the most important currency of the current political world: Angels. Or at least they had none that British intelligence had caught wind of. Perhaps the Americans had information indicating that an Angel did exist in that region. Another Angel could prove useful, especially if the rest of the world didn't know where it had originated from. After performing the split-second calculations required of a premier world leader, Strachan made his decision.

"Of course, the United Kingdom will support Israel," he stated regally.

The smile growing on the President's face stopped halfway when Strachan leaned forward conspiratorially and added, "As long as our great American ally will shore up our defenses."

No immediate response came from Davenport, so Strachan explained.

"The troops are going to be in much more danger in the Middle East. We can split that risk if you back up my position locally. Your troops stationed around the U.K. will just be a deterrent."

Davenport politely stated, "The U.S. will be there for its British brother, as usual."

The Prime Minister's jaw-line tensed at her words.

"We're allies, George. Let's keep it that way," Davenport responded before saying, "We need to tell Shalev about our decision."

She turned to someone out of Strachan's view and said, "Bring the Prime Minister Shalev back in."

After a few awkward moments of waiting, Strachan's second LCD flared to life with the face of the potentially belligerent Israeli leader. The man's face held a perfectly neutral expression, not revealing any hopeful expectations of a positive decision.

Davenport laid out the decision of the Western leaders. Shalev nodded with an expansive smile before closing the connection, obviously happy to have Western support. With such strong military help on the way, grander plans could roll into motion. The Islamic world would burn. Neither Strachan nor Davenport knew any of Shalev's ultimate goals when they exchanged formally pleasant goodbyes and signed off.

Once safely separated from cyberspace, Davenport dismissed all of the technicians responsible for the networking system. Every one of them had passed the most invasive of background checks with flying colors, but she still didn't like them to be around anymore than absolutely necessary. Only her closest advisors remained in the room with her.

"So are we sure about this European situation?" she asked to no one in particular.

Confident affirmations came from all around the table, but Davenport only needed to hear one voice in order to put her mind at ease. Fortuna had served as her closest ally for years and had never steered her wrong before. Now that the pair had entered the big leagues of international politics, he had already stepped up to the plate and delivered a few crucial homeruns.

"Europe won't engage the U.K. with our military nearby. The losses would be far too great for the gain," explained Fortuna.

"Some of the Eastern Europeans countries have leaders who've proven irrational and very easily manipulated in the past, Bryan," pointed out Davenport.

"Yes, but they're not stupid. In the past they've acted irrationally when the profits could be huge, but even if they got access to an Angel, so what? They'd have to share it with the rest of Europe and that's a total waste of time. No one will attack Great Britain. I doubt anyone would attack even with just the British military around," said Fortuna.

With a curt nod, Davenport stood up, a common indication for the rest of the room's occupants to vacate the space. They filed out promptly, leaving the President to her thoughts. Two Secret Service agents remained inside as the door closed. Within moments of being as alone as she could usually be, the phone on the conference table sprang into life, ringing emphatically. She answered on the third ring.

Strachan spoke quickly.

"Meghan, another one was just killed. We need to take steps to protect ourselves."

Davenport stared at the wall. Without severe training in maintaining a rock-like poker face, her mouth would have dropped to the floor.

"How do they keep getting to them?" she asked aloud.

"We don't even know who *they* are yet. Initial reports range from incomplete to totally unbelievable."

After a few seconds of pacing around the room with the cordless phone stuck to her ear, Davenport came to her decision. In this matter she knew that Strachan would abdicate responsibility to her. Fortuna had warned her about this situation arising, and she knew the correct response.

"We need to move to Plan C, George."

"So soon?"

"Yes."

"I'll alert the Ministry of Defense."

Chapter 20

"I told you before, I do not know where he is," exclaimed the stout Pakistani woman who Jackson and Smith had come to know only as Mrs. Gadhi.

"So you're positive that you haven't seen him?" Smith asked nicely. Jackson couldn't fathom how the guy kept his composure in situations like this. Jackson just wanted to strangle the information out of the stubborn bitch.

The woman put both hands on her hips and adopted the all too well-known stance that preempted a negative response from any woman, American, Pakistani, or otherwise.

"We went over this yesterday," she started, exasperated. "He is not here and has not been here for the last couple of days."

"This's bullshit," Jackson muttered. Smith gave him an elbow to the ribs. The old woman's angry glare penetrated deep into Jackson's soul. There wasn't anything in there worth keeping, so he figured she could do her worst.

"If you don't believe me, Mr. Jackson, then go ask his pretty little girlfriend," Mrs. Gadhi spat.

"Girlfriend?" both reporters blurted in unison.

"Yes, girlfriend."

"Do you care to elaborate?" asked Jackson, trying his best to grit his teeth and resist the pressure welling up inside. Joshua Greaves' landlady had been less than helpful during their investigation into the man's disappearance. For a guy who'd been found by a random Angel in the middle of the freaking desert, Mr. Greaves was proving to be a total pain in the ass to locate for a pair of regular old newspaper reporters in the city.

"Oh, yes, Mr. Jackson. Mr. Greaves spends at least three nights a week staying with his pretty girlfriend," Mrs. Gadhi confided without hesitation.

"And what's her name?" Smith asked.

The gossipy Pakistani woman jumped at the opportunity to spread some juicy information.

"Emily Nihipali. She lives two blocks away in the big new, fancy apartments on the corner."

Following the woman's outstretched arm, the two reporters saw the giant apartment complex in question. Jackson wondered if the aggravation in Mrs. Gadhi's voice came in part from her clientele jumping ship to the new place on the block.

"Alright, well you've been very helpful, Mrs. Gadhi," Smith said warmly. The guy was smooth.

Mrs. Gadhi even blushed a little.

"Please tell your friends that I have rooms available," she yelled after the two men as they wandered towards their new target. Jackson tried to think of anyone he could refer to Mrs. Gadhi, if for no other reason than to irritate the fire out of them.

It wasn't all bad, though. As difficult as she'd proven to be at times, Mrs. Gadhi was definitely observant, and probably close to being illegally intrusive. Jackson sure wasn't going to move in any time soon.

The two men inquired into the number of Emily Nihipali's apartment at the front office. For whatever reason, the flamboyant gentleman manning the desk took a particular liking to Jackson and promptly provided the unit number and location. On the way to the apartment, Jackson wondered about the legality of the disclosure while Smith ribbed him extensively for attracting members of the same sex.

Once at their destination, Smith took a break from haranguing Jackson and rapped smartly on Emily Nihipali's door. The two men waiting in silence, but Smith's smile showed he wasn't done with Jackson yet. Jackson broke the stalemate as the lock turned inside the door.

"Don't be such a damn red neck," he said.

"Who's a red neck?" inquired a hidden face on the other side of an engaged chain lock.

Smith laughed in response.

"Apparently *I* am, but that's not why we're here," he said cheerily.

Jackson chimed in, "Do you know Joshua Greaves?"

There was a pause.

"Why?"

"Because he promised us an interview about the Angel and then dropped off the planet."

"Oh."

"Is he staying with you?" asked Smith.

"Uh, no. I haven't seen him," the woman announced rapidly, lacking confidence.

Jackson caught a glimpse of a beautiful tanned face in the gap left by the partially opened door. This chick was smokin' hot, probably of Islander descent. Of course, that meant jack shit if they couldn't get her to talk. She obviously knew a lot more than she was letting on.

"We work for the Phoenix Press," Jackson said, trying a new angle. "We're just trying to find Joshua so that we can get his story out there. Share his encounter with the Angel with the world."

Or at least a small circulation in Arizona.

The young woman hesitated.

"We're only trying to print positive things here, Ms. Nihipali."

Her face turned to stone. Resolute, she spoke.

"I've been instructed not to talk to the press."

As the door closed and the lock turned, Jackson didn't even have time to blurt out any kind of persuasive argument. All he could do was sum up the day's events in a couple of words.

"Damn it."

Chapter 21

Seated in the all-too familiar briefing room, the soldiers of Phalanx prepped mentally for the unknown task ahead. Knight sat quietly with Lehoski, Kestrel, and Seagull, who'd recovered fully from his bullet wounds. They all knew that even just the deep bruises left after taking a shot through a bulletproof vest took at least a week of recovery. A penetrating wound healed much slower than that, but Seagull had experienced what very few other people had. An Angel had touched him, closing his wounds and seemingly evaporating the shrapnel. Knight still couldn't get his head around the disappearance of the lead.

The members of Talos dwelt in that quiet place that came after a mission that suffered a loss of life. Eyes were on them, probing for how they would handle it. Even in the briefing room, Knight could feel his colleagues searching his face, watching his interactions with his team. The four men displayed nothing, not giving an inch to any rumors that they were emotionally affected by the loss of Falcon.

She hadn't made many friends amongst the Phalanx soldiers, mostly due to her poor performance scores, as opposed to any of the men discovering any secret knowledge of Falcon's origins in the group. Most of the soldiers had lost much closer brothers and sisters in the line of duty, so no one felt sorry for the lack of grieving taking place. Despite this, at a base level, none of them wanted to lose even their least favorite sister to the enemy. Revenge would be meted out to the next encountered hostile, by the ton.

Heads remained focused ahead, but eyes snapped to attention as Condor and Vulture entered the room unannounced. A small tangible weight left Knight's shoulders as he became a secondary target for his compatriots' focus. Connor wasted no time as he stood before the twenty of his troops that he had handpicked for the next assignment.

"The reports that you have undoubtedly seen on the news are true. Alpha Three and Alpha Six are both dead," Connor announced.

Due to protocol, the Angels had been codenamed Alpha by Connor. A world map materialized on the wall behind the boss, confirming that the Alphas in Australia and China had received the codenames Three and Six. Phalanx had received the list of designators that morning, but the map provided a good visual aid, especially for the mercs that hadn't bothered memorizing the required reading material.

Nobody reacted. The details had been fuzzy, but enough credible news outlets had picked up the stories that Knight knew they would be true.

"Well, more accurately, the Alphas were destroyed," Connor continued. "Both were essentially vaporized, according to the few surviving witnesses and the minimal recoverable evidence.

"In tomorrow's news, the hospital housing Alpha Five has just been obliterated. All we have is that the local bomb experts are completely dumfounded by the source of the explosion. A team from the FBI is being hotshot over there as we speak, in order to aid the limited local resources. Initial reports reveal that there will be no survivors from that building."

Knight recalled that Alpha Five was the African Angel in Nairobi.

"Let me spell it out for you, gents. There is a threat moving undetected that can break into hospitals at will, or simply blow them up. That does not make me feel secure, and it sure as hell does not make our Commander-in-Chief feel secure. As such, measures are being taken to protect our own Alpha assets."

Connor paused to stare down his troops, emphasizing the seriousness of the situation. This was unnecessary. They got it. Well, most did. It would only be a matter of time before this unknown threat reached the United States. Their blood started to simmer at the thought. Mercenaries or not, they were patriots first.

"Alphas One and Four are in transit to a secure facility inside our borders."

So they were moving the Angels from Antarctica and Scotland to somewhere in the United States. This move surprised Knight, but obviously the Brits had been promised a speedy resolution to this threat, otherwise they would never turn over their Angel. The damn thing had brought them enough trouble with their European neighbors that just giving it away would be ludicrous. He hoped that his government wasn't stupid enough to think it could pull a fast one on the Brits and keep the Angel for itself. It was nice to have at least one solid ally in the world.

Knight had another thought.

"Condor, what about Alpha Two, sir?" asked Lehoski, reading Knight's mind, also concerned with the Angel in Phoenix.

"Good question, Diver," replied Connor.

Connor's openness to questions from his employees had always impressed Knight. Connor knew that he stood before a group of highly intelligent alpha males and respected their abilities to think. He had hired them for a reason, after all. It usually made his job easier.

Usually.

"And the answer to your question is: That's where you boys come in.

"An incredibly effective killer, codenamed Tango Delta, be it a group or an individual, is decimating the world's supply of Alphas. As I stand before you, another Alpha is assuredly very close to death. Eyewitness accounts so far are few and far between. We really do not know what we are dealing with at this point.

"Our government, in agreement with the Brits, wishes to protect its assets, but at the same time, the President does not want a monster out there, hiding under the bed, waiting to take out our Alphas while we sleep.

"Alpha Two and Alpha Four are well publicized. We would like to presume that Tango Delta locates targets simply by watching the news, but we cannot assume this. Assume nothing. Alpha One and Alpha Four will be moved, but Alpha Two will be left in place, but with a catch."

Connor paused for dramatic effect, giving Knight a chance to consider the situation.

So the Scottish and Antarctic Angels are being secured, but not the Phoenix Angel. Let me guess where I'm headed.

"Phalanx will be waiting for any bastards who show up looking for a fight. Welcome to Operation Halo Guard."

The next pause deliberately invited questions. Knight took the opportunity.

"That sounds a bit reckless, sir. Why do we need to put Alpha Two at risk at all? This is a very precious commodity we've got here."

"I get my orders and you get your orders, Rook."

The ambiguous answer left a sour taste in Knight's mouth. While his colleagues asked the more generic questions about the logistics of the operation, Knight dwelt on the cop-out his boss had just fed him. All of his life, Knight had honed the ability to listen to other conversations while computing a different subject intensely inside his own head. No detail of the briefing escaped Knight, but the other active part of his brain flew around with afterburners roaring, considering the potentially huge obstacles involved with the mission. No fear coursed through his veins, but concern for his men and for the Angel floated around in the depth of his conscious.

Knight drifted back into full attention of Connor's words.

"We have no pictures or video to share, but the few eyewitness testimonies agree that we are dealing with a giant who utilizes a weapon that generates an intense bright light while it disintegrates an Alpha. Then Tango Delta escapes undetected.

"I cannot tell you why we don't have surveillance of Delta, because it makes no sense. The people in Australia claim that Delta blew a hole in the ceiling and then dropped down into their hallway prior to killing Alpha Three. We can't explain how Delta bypassed all the security so invisibly."

Knight thought of a pertinent question.

"Condor, do we know if this is an individual that hit all three Alphas, or multiple persons working in unison?"

"We have no idea, Rook. It is logistically possible that a single Delta could hit all three targets. The timing would work. We would have seen something though, somewhere. Even if we are dealing with a single, well-trained, giant killing machine, he has a lot of help from the outside. The resources required to cover up this kind of operation are almost unimaginable.

"I personally do not like that one bit.

"The press is going to reveal a new name for this killer. The Demon. Fitting, right?"

A few soldiers snickered at the moniker.

Seagull piped up from beside Knight.

"Condor, sir. I don't know about Angels and Demons, but I swear we saw a spaceship down in Antarctica."

What the *hell* possessed Seagull to bring this up now, Knight didn't know. Talos had internally agreed to *not* talk about it with the rest of Phalanx. This decision had been passed down to Knight from Connor, and Knight had persuaded each soldier to keep their traps shut about the damn pyramid. Knight was at once annoyed with Seagull, but also curious to see how Connor would handle the situation.

Without skipping a beat, the major used an ancient military mind trick.

"No you did not, Seagull."

Taken aback, the man persisted.

"Yes, we did, sir."

Connor glared at Knight.

Oh boy, it looks like Seagull took a large dose of stupid pills this morning.

"Rook, did you see a spaceship?"

"No, sir. Seagull also didn't see any spaceships," Knight answered crisply, not bothering to throw a withering stare in Seagull's general direction. The man had just done something moronic, but he wasn't in fact a moron. He would get the hint that the rest of the group didn't need to know about what Talos saw, or didn't see, in Antarctica.

When Connor turned his eyes back to Seagull, the man concurred, "That's right. My mistake, sir."

"We all make mistakes, son. The best we can do is to learn from them, and not repeat them. You would be wise to remember that."

"Yes, sir," replied Seagull, before folding his arms so tightly that it looked to all of the world like he was trying to hide inside himself.

Connor observed his troops once more and then decided to let them take a break. Knight thanked his lucky stars that Vulture hadn't even said one word. This was the best kind of briefing.

Knight knew well enough that Vulture would try to throw Seagull's little outburst back into Knight's face as a sign of poor leadership.

Whatever.

Connor dismissed the soldiers and watched them all leave, bar one. When the door closed behind the last of the soldiers, the remaining one spoke up.

"Where are the two Angels heading? Do we know that it's really secure from a threat that we have such limited intel on?" asked Knight, still sitting in his chair.

"Rook, you know the place," replied Connor.

"I'm not so sure that I do."

"You had a training op there two years ago. You were part of a team assembled to attempt to defeat the facility's security," explained Connor.

"And if I recall correctly, you failed, Rook," pointed out Vulture with all the smugness the pompous officer could muster. Knight ignored him.

The infiltration team had indeed failed several objectives on that training exercise. After defeating various aspects of the external security, the team had found no realistic way of breaching the facility, mostly because they couldn't locate the entrance. They had followed the attack plan to the letter, yet the entrance didn't show up where the surveillance had indicated. After searching for twenty minutes, one of the men had stepped into a motion or heat sensor array of some kind, bringing the authorities right on top of the assault team.

Not a good day.

The commanding officers organizing the exercise had kept the facility's identity and location as secret as possible, even from Knight's team. Being bright and well-traveled boys, they had worked out the general location easily enough. Most of them had visited the Rockies more than once and could pick out a few landmarks during various stages of the operation, despite being blindfolded for much of the travel.

It was a logical place for such a subterranean base. The Rockies provided excellent natural defenses for any installation, especially one with such a well-camouflaged entrance. Knight still didn't know how they had hidden the entryway.

"Rook, do you have any further questions?"

Knight stood up and strode towards Connor.

"Yes, sir. What if the Demon, if it's even a single guy, straight-up blows the Phoenix hospital to bits? Like the African situation?"

"Rook, we'll have it all planned out."

"How can you account for random explosions like that? We don't know what lengths this Demon, or his backers, will go to in order to kill these Angels."

Vulture announced in his best kiss-ass voice, "Rook, you should watch your tone towards your boss."

"Shut up, Berkman," snapped Knight. Vulture's face lit up in shock.

"Rook, behave yourself," said Connor forcefully. "Everything will be accounted for. You have not even been to the operational briefing yet. You're not walking your men into a death trap."

"How do we know he'll come after us?" Knight asked. In his head, the question was really: *How do we know that the United States hasn't organized the hits on all of the foreign Angels?*

"Rook, so far the world has lost three very important beings in a matter of days. Phalanx is the contingency plan. If the killer never shows, then that is great. If he does show, then I want to be ready to smash him."

"So do we warn the South American authorities?" asked Knight.

"They're already up to speed. We will alter our plans accordingly if they're hit before us. That doesn't mean that we shouldn't plan based on current intel," replied Vulture.

Knight nodded to Connor, and despite the validity of Vulture's comments, walked away saying, "I wasn't talking to you, smart ass. Don't get my men killed."

Chapter 22

After moments of anxious murmuring, the congregation stilled instantly. Mark Jackson knew that the ominous signal could mean only one thing: The good Pastor Martin Daniels had materialized on stage. And sure enough, wearing a rich black suit with a flashy power tie, the man of the hour strode to the pulpit, brandishing his sword of holy literature.

"You're in for a real treat, my friend," Jackson whispered to his Texan partner-in-reporting.

Matt Smith had only agreed to come along to the service on that Sunday morning because his own Sunday school hadn't required his presence. The poor guy had apparently already been awake for hours when Jackson had called. Despite the public levity of his general demeanor, Jackson knew that Smith couldn't sleep through the night anymore. Try as he might, the woes of the world impressed a great weight on his broad shoulders. Even just the disappearance of Joshua Greaves overly stressed him out.

And with all the pressure, some of Smith's former bad habits had made a sudden reappearance in his life. Alcohol helped with getting to sleep, but Jackson of all people knew that even such a minor chemical dependency could lead down a scary, dark road. Perhaps the pastor would bring *something* in his message that would relieve some of Smith's stress.

Doubtful.

"Brothers and sisters," Pastor Daniels declared. "Let me start by thanking all of you for coming this morning. These are uneasy times, and I know that many of you suffer from dark anxiety in these days. Well, my friends, I do believe that God has got some answers for you."

Ah, crap. Here we go, Jackson thought as the pastor started to get the crowd warmed up. The place was instantly abuzz at the prospect of hearing some revelation.

"The incredibly increasing reports of missing people are no coincidence, brothers and sisters," he declared, his voice ramping up in volume and intensity. Jackson estimated the man at around forty-five years old, but the way the guy's face glowed red when he really started preaching should've worried his impassioned followers.

From behind his lectern, Daniels produced a newspaper. Thrusting it into the air was a purely theatrical device, for a vast majority of the congregation sat way too far away to even read the title of the paper. Mercifully, the gigantic digital displays around the sanctuary offered a screenshot of the front page of the Times.

"Demon Hunts Angels!" Daniels announced for anyone who had not watched the morning news before church. "I have preached for years that these days of ours are in fact the End Times. How much more evidence do we need? This is the Rapture, people. The saints are being called home!"

The church's roof strained to contain the spiritual excitement erupting throughout the enormous sanctuary. Voices and hands were lifted to the heavens in exultation. Feet stomped on the ground and for more than one geriatric, the stimulation proved too much as they fainted in their pews.

Jackson's eyes were wide open as he slowly turned to Smith, whose facial expression mirrored his own.

"I said you were in for a treat, Matt, but I didn't think it would get this nuts already."

Smith just stared at him in response. The pastor continued at breakneck pace.

"This front page article of a secular newspaper explains it all without even realizing it. They're spreading the good news without any conscious effort. God is moving!"

This statement elicited another round of raucous applause and jubilee.

"According to this report, most of these disappearances are of people who came into direct contact with an Angel. Do you think that's a coincidence?"

"No!" came the united response.

"Their earthly bodies have been healed by an Angel in anticipation of the Father calling them back home. They were being prepared for His glory!"

Jackson and Smith had to stand at this point to see over the uproarious crowd in front of them.

Are these people freaking crazy? There are a huge number of people going missing every day, and we're supposed to just believe this is all just part of some grand scheme of an invisible deity?

The thought perplexed Jackson, but at least he and Smith would have a story for Monday's morning paper. Despite the demographics of his current neighbors within the four walls of the church, the rest of Phoenix wasn't quite so religiously zealous. It would be interesting to see how the rest of the city would react to knowing they lived among total nut-jobs.

"It's not all good news, however," continued the pastor once the riot had subdued itself to a dull roar. "Satan has summoned forth a Demon to fight our Angels."

A round of boos echoed.

"I know, I know. Trust me, I know. Do not be disheartened, for the Bible foretold this. This is part of the plan. *His* plan.

"But let me share with you some sobering news. These Demons have killed many people in their quest to murder the Angels. Yes, that's right, brothers and sisters, I said *these Demons*. Revelation chapter nine tells of four such creatures 'who had been prepared for the hour and day and month and year, [who] were released to kill a third of mankind.'"

A third of mankind? Is this guy totally insane? He can't say that kind of shit in here with these whackos. They might just believe him.

"The news reports speculate that just one Demon committed all of these atrocities against humanity, but the Bible plainly shows us that four such Demons are at work today, acting as a scourge against us.

"But do not fret over those who die in the Lord's name during this time. Revelation chapter six tells us that 'it was said to them that they should rest a little while longer, until both *the number of* their fellow servants and their brethren, who would be killed as they were, was completed.'

"For their work, we are told they will receive the white robe from God. He will welcome them in. If anything, they are the lucky ones. Their suffering is over."

Jackson felt Smith leaning close to his ear.

"I wish we could leave so that my suffering would be over, but this is going to be one hell of a story," Smith said quietly, probably trying not to draw any unwanted attention from the quieting crowd. Jackson held up his recorder, its red LED indicating that he was capturing every moment. Hopefully the roars of the crowd wouldn't drown out too much of the pastor's message.

"We are in for trials and tribulations. The walk of a Christian is a difficult one. We may be called to give our lives for the Lord in the near future. Christians in the Western world are no longer accustomed to such acts, but our brothers and sisters in China and North Korea have gladly laid down their lives for the Lord in recent years. We will also be taken care of by Him."

The congregation grew still again as the pastor paused, now gripping the lectern with two meaty hands, his arms fully outstretched. His head tilted down towards his notes and open Bible, but Jackson doubted greatly that the man needed either of these resources for this message.

"We will be taken care of by the Father, so long as we meet Him with the correct heart. I hope that all of you are right with God, but if not, then now is the time. It's never too late to sort out your life.

"Even if it's something so simple as respecting your husband or loving your wife more. Or perhaps you lied to a friend yesterday. Maybe you frequently take the Lord's name in vain or look at smut. It could be that you have not been tithing like you used to.

"These are harsh times financially, don't I know it, but believe me when I say God takes care of those who follow His rules."

Jackson rolled his eyes. He knew where this was going.

"Ten percent seems like a lot, but God takes care of the difference."

Daniels rambled on about the economics of heaven, but Jackson had checked out. He couldn't stand this stuff. Huge amounts of money poured into this place, yet he would bet his paycheck that less than one percent of that income actually went outside the walls of the church to help others. That was the point right? For the church to help others in need?

Offering baskets appeared and disappeared in short order, probably taking in a record tithe even for this particular wealthy mega-church. Jackson knew that not every Christian was blind and not every church was selfish, but it was hard to see past the hypocrisy before him to see the general good of the overall group.

He himself gave at least ten percent to local charities, but he didn't need a holy man to tell him to do it. It was common decency, which is something that many people who encountered Mark Jackson would never have guessed that he possessed. The truth was that his friend Matt Smith had got him into it. The big Texan gave big to those who had little. Jackson had to admit that it did feel pretty good to help other people out. His personal self-satisfaction may have seemed to some like a selfish reason to help others.

But so what?

As the music that accompanied the offering faded out, Pastor Daniels feverishly launched headfirst into his next topic. The lack of segue caught Jackson and the rest of the congregation by surprise.

"As all of you know, our brothers and sisters in Israel have endured heavy losses recently," he declared, waving the next page of the Times around erratically.

"The people of God are now moving against the enemy. Muslim terrorists initiated unprovoked and utterly cowardly bombing attacks against Israel, and now they will reap the reward of their actions. The Israeli army is now moving into Jordan in retaliation, seeking to root out these terrorists once and for all."

Interesting platform. What's the connection here?

The crowd collectively leapt to its feet once more, forcing Jackson and Smith to get up again.

"There are no Angels in the Middle East for a reason, people. God's Angels are for God's people!"

That didn't make any sense, if anyone was God's people, it was Israel. The damn guy just said as much a minute ago.

"The Islamic belief system is polluted and corrupted. The Demon has come from their faith in evil. We must fight the good fight! Pray for victory!"

The pastor's face beamed with a color close to that of pickled beets as his congregation roared their support. His diatribe continued for a few minutes, fueled by the fire of his parishioners.

Daniels stopped screaming for a moment. The church still rocked with the momentum of his sermon. He slowly raised a hand to his chest as his torso convulsed slightly. Those paying enough attention to their pastor probably assumed that the Spirit of the Lord was moving upon him physically.

These thoughts ended when the pastor collapsed. Stewards shot out from either side of the stage and rushed him off, out of view. An associate pastor grabbed a microphone and announced that Pastor Daniels had fainted and was okay. He dismissed the service and the rabble poured into the street, much more focused on the subject of the sermon rather than the man who gave it.

Jackson and Smith exited amid the throng. They slowly navigated the human currents until breaking through one edge of the mass. Once free, they both noticed an Indian family walking on the other side of the street, just quietly observing the exodus taking place. Jackson guessed from the man's turban that he was a Sikh. At a previous newspaper gig, he'd worked with a guy who wore similar attire. He couldn't have given less of a crap about what gods the guy did or didn't worship; he'd been a stand-up guy.

Heads in the swarm snapped towards the foreigners across the busy road. Jackson and Smith both sensed the body language of the crowd.

"Oh shit," they said together as they scrambled to evade the rush of people seeking out the target on the other side of the road.

"They're not Muslims, you idiots!" Jackson yelled at the top of his lungs as the rioting Christians easily tossed his small frame to the ground. Covering his head with his hands, Jackson rolled frantically as impassioned legs and feet pounded against him. Smaller patrons of the mass crashed to the asphalt, having failed to scale the human obstacle. Too fearful to open his eyes, Jackson just hoped to make it out alive.

Chapter 23

The level of paperwork involved in private contracting still shocked Knight. He sat at his simple desk in his small office and typed furiously on the keyboard of his laptop. The death of a subordinate definitely warranted some attention, but Falcon's demise was threatening to bring on an early bout of carpal tunnel syndrome. Why Connor needed all of these forms filled out by Knight was anyone's guess. The old man probably just didn't want to do them himself.

When Talos first returned from Antarctica, Connor restricted all of them to the base. Nobody left until the debriefing process finished. With that done now, the rest of Knight's team was free to go, but he couldn't bail until the documentation was complete. Apparently writing a pre-debriefing report hadn't been good enough. Now he was completing the post-debriefing version of his story.

Funny how the truth could change after a quick meeting with the boss. *That* part of the job certainly hadn't changed when Knight moved into private industry.

With the final keystroke struck, Knight leaned back in his supposedly ergonomic chair. The damn thing felt uncomfortable as hell no matter which of the thousands of settings he messed with. Earlier that morning he'd found his feet totally asleep.

Standing, Knight stretched his shoulders and wondered if proof-reading his report was worth the effort. His typing was pretty clean to start with, and Connor probably wouldn't spend a huge amount of time reading it anyway. What was the point in documenting this crap? Was Connor covering his own ass, or Knight's?

Thoughts of Karen entered his fatigued mind when his cell phone vibrated on the table. He hadn't seen her since he'd gotten back, as per Connor's orders. Skipping town probably wouldn't have gotten Knight killed, but he'd been on relatively thin ice prior to the Antarctic mission, so he was trying to behave. Mostly.

Picking up the phone, Knight swore. It wasn't Karen.

"Katie," Knight said neutrally as he answered the phone. His sister-in-law was far from his greatest fan, and he thought she was a total bitch on a good day. How the two sisters had come from the same parents defied rational thought.

"Andrew," Katie responded, taking advantage of his preference to go by either Andy or Knight.

"What can I do for you?" he asked.

"Where's Karen?"

"I haven't seen her for a few days. Been gone on business."

Feeling suddenly drained, Knight wandered to his filing cabinet and produced an energy bar. Any conversation with Katie could really take it out of him. At least she wasn't in the room glaring at him with her probing, judgmental eyes. Knight had no patience for that crap right now.

"She's always alone, isn't she?"

The energy snack stopped halfway to Knight's mouth.

"What are you talking about?"

"You haven't changed one bit, Andrew."

Damn, she was good at laying on the judgment, even across the vast distances that Knight hoped separated them right now. Having said that, she'd probably need to be on the Moon, or maybe Mars, to be satisfactorily far enough away from him.

"Not following you, sis."

As much as Knight disliked her use of *Andrew*, she absolutely couldn't handle *sis* coming from him, and he knew it.

"You left her when she was sick, and you've left her again."

"She insisted that I follow my dream—," he started.

"What about *her* dreams, Andrew?" she screamed. "Do you think her dream was to die of cancer right out of high school? Do you think she wanted to suffer through that alone?"

She was getting an early start on him today.

"This again, Katie? Karen's already been through all of this with you multiple times. Give it up."

"Give it up? Give. It. Up? How about you act like a fucking man and not just marry someone for their fucking insurance money?"

"That's not what happened, and you know it, Katie."

"Then why the hell would you marry a dying woman, Andrew? Answer me that."

He didn't owe her an explanation, but he answered against his better judgment.

"Because she loved me."

"*Because she loved me.* Do you even listen to yourself? How about you loving her? Did that fit in your contrived little equation?"

Knight resisted the urge to launch his laptop at the wall.

"No, of course it didn't. You just wanted the money."

"Not true—," he tried to fit in, but she cut him off again.

"I was with her every step of the damn way when she was sick, Andrew," she said, crying a little bit now. "*I* was the one who went through that with her. Not you."

"I was defending the country. That's not exactly a worthless job."

"Yeah, right. Call it whatever you want. Following the corrupt orders of evil men who had no interest in anything other than oil."

"You know that's not—."

"*That* doesn't matter right now," she said, her voice rising again.

Knight sat down on the edge of his desk. Katie was like a drunken driver in the way she steered a conversation when she got worked up. She was all over the damn road today.

"So what does matter?"

"Do you know where Karen is, or don't you?" she demanded.

"No, I don't know where she is," he said through gritted teeth. "Would you mind filling me in on why this is important?"

Now she sounded almost gleeful as she said, "I'm supposed to be taking her out for a fun time since her terrible husband is never home."

"And she's not there?"

"Where?"

"At the damn house. She's not at the house?" he asked a little less patiently.

"No, that's why I'm calling you, dumbass. You think I would call you for the hell of it? To shoot the shit with my studly brother-in-law?"

"Whatever, Katie."

"Her car's here, but she's not answering her phone."

"Are you sure?"

"Am I sure her car's in the driveway that I'm standing on right now? Are you retarded?"

The plastic body of Knight's cell phone threatened to give in to the crushing weight of his grip as his knuckles attempted to strangle his sister-in-law through the phone lines. Damn, she knew how to push his buttons.

"She probably left you for real this time," Katie remarked snidely.

"Come on, don't be a bitch, Katie. You know that's not true."

She just laughed.

"I spoke with her this morning, Katie, and she sounded fine."

"Yeah, well I'd fake niceness on the phone too if I was about to take my husband's baby away from him."

Now the phone almost fell out of his hand.

"She's pregnant?"

"You are such a dumbass, Andrew."

"Wait, you telling me she's pregnant and never told me?"

"I'm not saying another word—."

"Tell me!"

"Don't worry about it. I'm sure your kid will enjoy growing up with a father who is actually around."

"Don't mess with me here, Katie. I hate you as much as you hate me, but don't do this."

She laughed again.

"She told me she was done with you after you bailed on her at the hospital. You left without making sure she got in to see the Angel."

"But she *did* see the Angel. She told me that it all went fine," he said, getting frustrated to the point of explosion.

"I'm sure she did," Katie said, her voice the embodiment of calm now that she was in full control.

"You're such a cu—"

"Don't bother finishing that sentence," Katie said, interrupting his insult. "Just tell her to call me when she calls you."

Click.

When she calls? Knight's blood pressure dropped by about sixty thousand PSI. She wouldn't call if she'd left him. So Katie was lying. Again. Man, he *always* fell for her tricks. That irritating woman had an uncanny ability to blurt out crazy shit that would immediately launch him into the stratosphere, and then later he'd find out it was a complete fabrication. Even so, he fell for it every time.

So Karen *wasn't* pregnant. What a relief that was. They had enough going on right now without that kind of complication. Although, they'd always said they wanted kids sometime. Maybe it was time to reopen the subject now that Karen's cancer had been cured.

In any case, his wife must've put her phone on silent and forgotten about her date with her sister. Karen had mentioned on the phone earlier that she'd been sleeping like a log ever since seeing the Angel.

He tried her cell phone unsuccessfully. The house phone also went unanswered. Now that was strange. Knight's paranoia started to kick into overdrive. His house was built to a higher specification than Fort Knox, so there was no way she'd been kidnapped. The place would've been ablaze with lights, sirens, and heat-seeking missiles if anyone had breached the perimeter.

But what if it was all true? What if she was pregnant and had left him? There was still the guy in the coffee shop. Was he just a therapist, or was he something else?

Shit.

Had Karen known that he could get her in to see an Angel? Is that why she'd come back to him in the first place? Was it just like Katie had said? His wife had never forgiven him for not being around when she had cancer all those years ago?

All the pain of her leaving him a month ago came welling back up from the deep pits where he'd deposited those dark emotions. Had she used him? It was impossible that she'd known about his job, impossible that she'd known that Connor would get her healed.

Right?

Damn, he'd failed her. She'd needed him around, and he'd been gone. Again. Now she could be off with another man. Of course, *nothing* justified cheating, but he was an absentee husband a lot of the time. Guilt clambered over the feelings of anger and regret and plopped itself on top of the pile of shit churning in his gut.

As cliché as it was, Knight wished Connor hadn't made him dump out the flask he'd kept in his desk drawer until recently.

He needed a plan. Or a drink. Maybe both.

The door to his office swung open, revealing a familiar face looking more intense than usual.

"Bro, what the hell are you doing?" Lehoski demanded. "We gotta catch a flight to Phoenix."

Shit.

He'd have to get Connor to send a car round to the house to check on Karen. Once again, he was walking out on her.

Chapter 24

Sitting alone in the White House's Presidential bedroom could make a person feel small, even insignificant in the grand scheme of things. President Meghan Davenport sat up on the Amish-made king-sized four poster bed that she had selected for her place of rest, surrounded by the ghosts of those leaders who had preceded her. Some great presidents had sat in this room, deciding the fate of the world. Some other presidents had also occupied this room, seemingly hell-bent on ruining the great country that they led. For better or worse, they had all been male.

Davenport felt the pressure, the expectations, the criticism, but reminded herself that everything that she had achieved in the last year could be for naught soon enough. The first female President of the United States of America had a difficult enough time competing with the memories of her predecessors without Israel stirring the already simmering pot in the Middle East. Handling this situation would easily make or break her Presidency.

Not particularly reassuring.

Meghan Davenport, age forty-seven, married for the last ten years in her only marriage. She was a mother of zero, unless she counted the string of incredibly successful businesses that she birthed and raised prior to her term as a state senator in Texas. Shortly after her surprising victory over the incumbent Texas senator on the national scale, Davenport had shockingly claimed her party's presidential nomination after the resignation of a complete failure of a national leader. Over a year in office later and she still wrestled with her inexplicable rise to power.

Roger, her husband, often reassured her that her series of victories just followed the typical trend of her entire life. She didn't need some awkward alignment of the stars to win in every competition she entered. He was right about the trend. Even from an early age, Meghan Davenport dominated everything that she attempted, often sacrificing friendships in the process. Both of her parents had assured her that none of those children deserved to be in her league, so the friendships would only drag her down to their level. The jury was still out on that advice, but Davenport couldn't ignore the end result.

She was the first female President of the United States of America after all. Who else could have pulled it off? She had been groomed and molded for this position her entire life. The businesswoman-turned-senator had materialized into the national spotlight just months before her presidential predecessor held a sudden press conference to announce his withdrawal from the Oval Office. Many candidates pulled out of the race early after discovering just how far into the abyss President Mort Harrison had driven the U.S. economy. Davenport purely saw the dire situation as the greatest way in which she could serve her country.

And she had done just that. President Davenport, the Girl President, had brought the terminally ill economy back from the brink of utter collapse. The national unemployment level had dipped back below eight percent for the first time in ten years, but she clearly stated in each public appearance, "This is not over. Not by a long shot."

The American public was on her side. They now believed in what she believed. They bought what she was selling. In her mind, it was really very simple.

"Don't spend what you don't have."

This mantra had served her well in all of her previous business ventures. The keys to repairing a broken economic system included intelligent leadership, fiscal conservatism, and a few strokes of luck along the way. That was her recipe for success. So far her luck in the financial realm was holding up just fine.

Unfortunately, Prime Minister Shalev's troops had just brutally annihilated the Jordanian army and hostilely occupied several Islamic territories. As a result, Iran's war machine had awoken, with their leader promising to wipe Israel from the face of the map.

Boys will be boys.

Now the United States had to maintain an untenable position. How could they provide support to Israel without taking part in the dismantling of the center of the Muslim world? Shalev's warmongering antics left little choice. The man knew that he could force her hand, knew that she would have to play along as the novice world leader, just following his lead.

Now Davenport wasn't so sure. Jordan itself had not perpetrated any crime. In fact, as Strachan and Davenport had tried to tell Shalev, Jordan had embraced the West and cooperated immensely with their intelligence communities. Of course, Israel had finally found its militaristic messiah in Shalev, one who relished this moment to destroy Islam.

Just great.

The plain clock on the wall clicked its way to nine o'clock in the evening. Ornate didn't suit Davenport. A ten-dollar wall clock from a generic department store reminded her every day that function came before form. Although having said that, she was rather partial to the look of her Amish furniture.

In any case, her husband would soon return from the gym. It was time to call Bryan Fortuna. Why was he so insistent about sending the U.S. military into this conflict between Israel and its many enemies? She had a few ideas, but needed to hear it directly from her closest advisor's mouth.

Davenport slid from the bed, padded straight past her full-length mirror without even a glance, and opened her underwear drawer. Not even Roger rummaged in there. The Secret Service swept the room for listening devices and explosives and poison and radiation and everything else every morning, but so far they hadn't located the phone that Fortuna had provided to her. He had instructed her to keep the battery out of it when it was not in use and to keep it someplace that no one would look for it. The President didn't really care for the clandestine nature of the phone, but in a meeting last month, Fortuna had revealed a disturbing secret. In that moment, a phone that the Secret Service couldn't easily trace or record had become a necessity.

Now back in the bed with the assembled phone, Davenport remarked to herself once more how much the device exactly resembled her Presidential Blackberry, the one that her bodyguards did monitor. Her more discreet phone only contained one number.

She dialed.

The lack of dial tone or ring always perturbed the President, but before she could ponder the meaning any further, Fortuna's quiet voice flowed from the Blackberry's small speaker.

"Good evening, Madam President," came the low and slightly digital-sounding voice.

Fortuna had explained that the unique encryption involved in their private communication lowered the volume of his voice and caused the vague distortion. He claimed that this had the side effect of protecting his identity from any Secret Service listening bugs in the room. The thought of the White House security officers avidly monitoring her love life didn't put Davenport at ease. She could only hope that they had *some* decency.

"Hello," she responded, carefully not speaking his name aloud.

This part seemed rather inane to her. If anyone could listen to their conversations, they would easily work out that Bryan Fortuna was on the other end of the phone line. The content alone would convict him.

"Satellite images show Iran massing ground troops near the Iraq border," Fortuna said.

"I'm aware of that."

"They'll wait until other Muslim nations are onboard and mobilized before they move. Even if we don't bolster our presence in the area, the military assets that we have in place in the Gulf can hold Iran at bay."

"So I'm told, but the problem is what we do if the other countries get involved. Even with air superiority, we would need soldiers on the ground in significant numbers," explained Davenport.

An exhaustive meeting with the top military minds had covered all of this information earlier.

Fortuna responded, "But our intelligence from the Middle East says that Israel already has plans for its neighbors if any of them seek retribution on behalf of Jordan. As far as I can see, we just send our soldiers as defense for Israel while they handle a majority of the heavy lifting on offense."

Davenport had signed off on a plan to do exactly that earlier. Despite not wanting to be the President who let Israel fall at the hands of Muslim oppressors, Davenport had no intention of pointlessly endangering the lives of the U.S. servicemen and women under her command and care. She hadn't shared this plan with Fortuna yet, but she assumed that he would've already found out about it through his backchannel contacts. The President wanted to fish for some more information from her increasingly paranoid and evasive advisor.

"So tell me why we're doing this?" asked President Davenport.

"Because we have to support our main ally in the Middle East. It's a volatile region that just happens to contain a vast amount of a resource that we consider precious. If we lose access to all of those oil reserves, we'll be forced to deal more with the Russians, and you know what that's like."

The Russian Premier hadn't seen eye to eye with Davenport in their first and only meeting. The man just didn't care about his people, or the people of ex-Soviet states. For whatever reason, the bullish man considered Georgia his own personal war zone. About once a year, Russian tanks found an excuse to invade South Ossetia. Yet another international problem that the U.S. President would need to intervene in. It didn't bear thinking about.

"Spare me. We have greater reserves than we've ever let on publicly, plus access to oil off the coasts of Florida and California. And don't even get me started on the plays in Alaska," retorted the President.

"You can't do that without guaranteeing your own impeachment."

"If the Middle East disowns us, the public relations will take care of everything. Americans already feel a sense of heightened patriotism any time the Arab states feel the need to flex their weak muscles. Considering our past, do you think it would be that difficult to turn public opinion against Russia? We've done it plenty of times in the past."

She waited a beat before continuing.

"I think the majority of American people would accept the de-beautification of the California coastline if it meant not dealing with our Russian friends. Plus, the Russians and Saudis have to play ball with us. Who else is going to consume like we do? They still need to sell their oil to reap any benefit. We wouldn't need to use our own supply for long before they begged us to come back."

"Madam President, the Chinese would love to pick up that tab. They would gladly soak up all of the oil that Russia and/or Saudi would sell them."

"But the Chinese will never pay the same price that we do."

"But technically we're using money that we borrowed from China to pay that price. Also, times are changing. China's ambitious plans for further economic growth require a drastic increase in their oil and natural gas consumption in the next decade. Some predictions forecast that China will out-consume us on oil very soon. With that in mind, I believe China will offer much more lucrative deals to their Siberian neighbors than we currently do."

"Touché. Well played. I knew there was a reason that I kept you around," said the President.

"You might not like me so much after what I have to tell you."

After a delicate pause, Davenport asked the question regarding the giant elephant hanging out on the encrypted phone line.

"This is about the contributions, isn't it?" she asked carefully, without using either the word "illegal" or "campaign" anywhere near the word "contributions."

A garbled sound that could only be a laugh zipped down the line.

"Madam President, this goes far beyond campaign contributions of ill repute, I'm afraid."

Davenport didn't like the sound of that. She only knew what Fortuna had previously told her, and that was regarding some potentially illegal campaign contributions that had come to his attention through a hostile contact.

"And what, exactly, does that mean?"

"I only told you about the whistleblower on the campaign contributions so as not to worry you about the rest of it. Unfortunately, things are coming to a head now."

Her head spinning, Davenport pushed on, trying to hide the extreme tension in her voice.

"You need to be specific here."

"Okay, okay. We're secure on this line after all. Definitely more secure than we would ever be having this conversation in public, with all those goons watching your every step."

"They're there for my protection. I'd rather put up with them observing my every step than end up with a bullet in the back of my head," Davenport said.

"True, you have to worry about more than I do."

"Not if you don't start telling me what's going on."

The veiled threat loosened Fortuna's tongue. Now Davenport started to wonder if he was being fully truthful even now. What else was her most trusted confidante hiding from her?

"A man approached me. This man has evidence of not only illegal campaign funds, but also sure evidence of voter fraud."

This wasn't the first time that someone had claimed that the first female President had been elected due to negative votes disappearing, or due to miscounted ballots, or even due to the votes of dead people. Davenport just thought that the American public watched too many movies, an activity that she'd never seen the benefit in. This President would rather curl up with a good autobiography than watch trash on the television.

"Okay, so what does this one want?" she asked.

"This isn't like the previous accusations. He showed me some of his proof and it's astounding. It's hard to see how he pulled it off, to be honest, but my sources confirm that 'hypothetically' this kind of fraud could go unnoticed for a long period of time," Fortuna explained anxiously.

Now a veil of confusion settled over Davenport's bedroom.

"What do you mean, 'It's hard to see how he pulled it off?' What did he pull off?" she demanded.

"He's claiming responsibility for it all," Fortuna said, now sounding frantic as the words rolled off of his tongue. "This guy says that he organized all of it."

Fortuna's words turned Davenport to stone. If her heart had stopped beating in that moment, she would never have sensed it. Everything fell away from her, spiraling out of control. The room disappeared before her unseeing eyes as she withdrew into herself.

What did this mean?

Was her election really just a power play by some random man?

Oh, no. He was not random. This man knew exactly what he was doing. Davenport could already see the writing on the wall. Someone had amazingly planted her in office, into the Presidency.

And the President was sure that her conniving benefactor would call in his favors. Perhaps he had already, without Davenport even knowing it. Why had Fortuna not told her this before? Why hadn't he said the man's name? Would he tell her? If he refused to divulge that information, would that mean that Fortuna was also in this guy's pocket somehow? Did this man have leverage on Fortuna?

Did that man control the advice that Fortuna had been passing on to Davenport for the last few years?

Oh no.

Fortuna broke the short silence, apparently uncomfortable even leaving that much empty air between them.

"Please understand my situation. I only had a few friends to turn to in order to sniff this guy out, to see if he was being truthful."

Davenport knew perfectly well that the "friends" Fortuna alluded to were just cronies that he had dirt on. Now it seemed like his actions had come full circle. Her stomach started to clench in fury, despite the calm, indifferent appearance of her exterior. After this conversation, perhaps she should go to the gym to relieve some of the pent up stress that had just been dumped on her.

As if she didn't have enough on her plate already.

Despite the negative thoughts seeping past her mental defenses, Davenport felt secure that she could get through this problem. Nothing in life was impossible. Starting out with a pessimistic outlook would only lead to failure.

Fortuna continued.

"So my associates uncovered more evidence of tampering, but they couldn't bring it back around to the source. It does look like this guy has kept his hands clean while he orchestrated your ascension."

"My ascension? Please, Bryan," Davenport spat, exasperated with the ordeal, not caring that Fortuna would be fuming about her breach of protocol by saying his name. "This is ridiculous. What's his name? We can trace this back. We have a lot of resources."

Now a void of sound filled the space between them. Now Fortuna didn't want to talk.

"Tell me who it is, Bryan. Who do I have to thank for my good fortune?" she growled.

All the work she had done, all of her toils and tribulations, for nothing! The first female President of the United States was a sham. Meghan Davenport was a phony. The embarrassment pressed in around her, but she suppressed it. She would let those feelings wait for another time.

"I can't do that," whispered the small voice that had shrunk even more in the past ten seconds.

"Yes, you can. I'm your boss, damn it!"

"You don't understand the situation. I can't tell you," he insisted, now more urgently.

"Don't tell me what I do or do not understand."

Somehow her voice had maintained its volume despite the intensity increasing by a magnitude of one thousand. The explosion must've felt like a punch in the face to Fortuna. Davenport didn't care, not in the slightest. This man was on the take, this man that she had trusted with her most intimate secrets. They had shared her defeats and successes. Fortuna had listened to all of her fears and hopes and dreams. Now the disappointment threatened to undo her resolve.

"What did you do, Bryan? What has he got on you? We can fix it. I'm the damn President," she said, now trying to control her tone. She needed to bring Fortuna back into the fold. He needed to be back on her side again.

"Look, I can't tell you anymore than I already have. He'll ruin both of us if we don't play ball. If you don't play ball."

Another pause.

"Meghan, I need to go."

Click.

Or at least, there would have been a click if these damn cell phones had any character.

Meghan Davenport lay back in her bed and considered the ramifications of the ominous exchange. The issues that Fortuna had intensely urged her opinion on were many. How many of those thoughts and feelings originated in Fortuna? How much of his insistent advice grew from the fear of the man who owned him now?

Perhaps she could work backwards. Based on Fortuna's pattern of advice, maybe she could establish motive. Maybe she could even work out what lobby this guy worked for, if it was a lobby. Perhaps it was private industry, or maybe the military? Was he even American?

Most recently Fortuna had strongly convinced the President to support Israel. Was her unwanted benefactor a Jew?

President Davenport closed her eyes and leaned her head back against the rustic headboard. Anxious thoughts rattled around in her head at light speed, seeking an exit, seeking an escape route. The only person in the world that she had to talk to had just betrayed her. The burden was now hers alone.

A sweaty, but cheery Roger Davenport entered the room and immediately moved to comfort his distraught wife.

***

While the President suffered from a momentary lapse in composure, another prominent leader basked in the glow of a private victory. David Murphy reclined happily in an Alcantara chair in the office of one of his many homes. A friend had suggested trying out this relatively new material in an office chair and so far Murphy relished the pseudo-suede feel of the polyester and polyurethane mixture. Certainly a nice change from the typical plush leather chairs populating the rest of his offices.

Perhaps he could get a bedspread made from the fabric, yet another new experience to try with one of his special close friends. He suspected that Tia would enjoy the sensation, or maybe Leah. He smiled crookedly as he briefly fantasized about both of his girls enjoying his new toy at the same time.

But there was business to attend to, so that would all have to wait.

The phones provided to Fortuna, and then the President, hadn't just materialized from thin air. Far from it in fact. David Murphy had money. A lot of money. Money granted an individual easy access to resources not available to the common man. As such, he had called on an old associate to acquire a few untraceable, encrypted phones. This man had initially refused, even without knowing the true purpose for the devices, but Murphy would never have approached the drug dealer without the appropriate leverage.

Murphy had no qualms about delving into the scummy underworld in order to get what he wanted. Often times these shady individuals could acquire high technology through uncharted backchannels. After all, a prudent drug dealer would amply cover his own tracks to avoid unwanted attention. Murphy had a unique ability to provide the motivation to do so.

Because the dealer had a soft spot for the lives of his own family, Murphy ended up with the phones that no one could listen in on. Except for him. The simplicity of the system delighted him. The phone on his end indicated when the other two were in use, and all he had to do was anonymously and secretly join the call. This particular call left the titan of industry feeling giddy, a sensation not that familiar to him.

So his pawn had successfully placed the enemy queen in check. Fortuna had done his job well, revealing just enough to scare the President, but not disclosing enough to incriminate Murphy in the matter. The habitually generous CEO would have certainly compensated Fortuna immensely if not for the man's problem with diddling kids. Nothing in this world could convince him otherwise. Fortuna was hardly a man at all, so he would be treated as such: Just another pawn in this ongoing game of chess.

After years of backing his horse, the pieces had finally fallen into place. Financial support alone had not earned Murphy the access to the President that he desired so adamantly, so now the backup plan came into play. A man did not become CEO of Celestius without thinking a few moves ahead of his opposition.

No, money had not been the answer, the key to unlocking and corrupting Meghan Davenport's moral compass. Murphy had quickly identified the woman's greatest anxiety. Her opposing political party had not managed to exploit this obvious fear, but Murphy had bent the rules of the game slightly in order to gain the upper hand. It was not like she could fight back; she had no idea about the identity her true adversary.

Yet.

Now it was time to initiate the next stage of the process. Murphy would gain what he most desired, and it would be the President who unwillingly gave it to him. Her motivations at this point meant little to Murphy, as long as he felt satisfied with the end result.

Murphy picked up his new toy and called one of the numbers saved into it.

"It's done," said the slightly distorted voice of Fortuna. "Just like you said. So we're clear, right? Me and you are settled?"

The CEO smiled, reclining further into the soft depths of his chair. In the midst of all the excitement, Murphy had failed to notify Fortuna that he alone could monitor all calls made with these phones. Not *failed* really. He just did not trust Fortuna, nor anyone else. People who could be bought for one price could always be bought by someone else for a prize of slightly higher value.

"So I take it that your associate now understands the situation?" Murphy asked, ignoring Fortuna's questions. The pawn did not make demands of the king.

"Yes, we're all in for the holy land."

The smile only widened as Fortuna relayed information that Murphy was already privy to. Murphy listened closely, regarded each word for the hint of a lie, judging Fortuna's current trustworthiness. After the accurate recount of the previous conversation, Murphy nodded to an empty office, content with his domination over his chess pieces.

"So are we straight?"

Again with the questions. Who did Fortuna think he was? It was time to remind the man of the order of hierarchy.

"Where are the Angels being moved to?"

A gasp. A raspy, digital gasp, as if the encryption hardware could not even believe its own electronic ears.

"What are you talking about?" Fortuna stuttered, fumbling in the dark.

Murphy was sure the man could not work out how Murphy could possibly know such a highly classified state secret.

I bought you, Bryan , did I not? What makes you think I cannot buy someone else also?

"Where?"

"I can't tell you that." An immediate and confident response now that Fortuna had had a moment to compose an answer.

"I disagree. I believe that you both know the answer and are physically capable of providing it."

"This is going too far."

He is such a weak man, so short-sighted. This has not gone nearly far enough yet.

"I own a facility."

"Out of the question. Not a chance."

Well at least Fortuna has the brains to work out where this is headed. Or at the very least, he thinks he does.

"The NSA has borrowed this facility many times in the past. It is a secure and very remote location. The good Director of the NSA can certainly provide you with a reference for the place on my behalf. Except, it goes without saying, of course, that my name will not show up on any documents linked to the property."

No response. Murphy enjoyed capturing the other man's entire attention. Interruptions irritated him.

In any case, it was time to show his hand.

"So, the Angels will be moved to my private facility instead of that ridiculous military prison listed in the current plans. Why on Earth would the government lock up the world's most precious life-forms in such a useless place?"

The line remained silent for a moment. Fortuna had reached that deep recess within the abyss. Murphy knew that he owned his pawn completely.

"I will inconspicuously provide you with the required information. I trust that you will make the correct and proper decision in this matter. Or we could skip to the part where I release pictures so damning that your only logical response would be prompt and efficient suicide. Assisted or not is fine with me."

"No, no, it's fine. Just send it."

Fortuna's sigh of utmost depression enlivened the CEO. Victory once more. Triumph heaped upon the triumphant. Would he ever tire of winning? He doubted it.

"I'll take care of it."

The line went dead. Murphy placed the phone in the densely lined hidden compartment of his desk. Despite all of his safety precautions, he could never be too careful with precious assets. The Angels would soon find that out, of that Murphy was certain.

He relished in the success of once again crushing the spirit of Fortuna. Surely the man could not avoid his fate without suicide. Surely he knew what was coming. The demands would continue. Orders would be passed down. When his obedience ceased, his career would be promptly ruined. The control felt secure for the time being, but Murphy knew how temperamental a subject could become. Most of these horrible excuses for humanity eventually developed what they believed to be a conscience.

How long would it take for Fortuna? How outrageous would the demands need to become before the switch toggled in his puny brain? At some point the man would defy Murphy, against all logic and rationale. In that moment, he would seal his own destruction, either by his own hand or by Murphy's.

As long as the pawn performed his most recent role as directed, the pharmaceutical king could obtain his prize. Every beneficial action by Fortuna from that point forward would just be a bonus. Murphy's plan had now entered the critical stage.

Of course, he had prepared for that contingency. The consequences would be dire, but sometimes great men stooped to a certain level in order to help the greater good. The current plan just ruined a solitary degenerate. Murphy would not miss the man when all was said and done.

Murphy stroked his chin as well as any mastermind had ever done. Perhaps Fortuna needed to be brought in after the Angels had been successfully transferred into Murphy's care. An accident could be arranged at any moment.

This is such a dangerous world to live in, after all.

His thoughts turned to other activities. Lifting a perfectly normal phone handset from its cradle on his desk, Murphy had just one more decision to make for the evening. Who should he call now? Tia or Leah?

Or both?

Chapter 25

The black HMMWV convoy rocketed down the streets of Phoenix towards the target hospital. Inside the lead Humvee, Knight examined his PDA, continually switching between the pages showing his various teams. This time Phalanx, in a break with the norm, held more traditional names. Apparently Connor wanted the op to look more professional.

At first glance, giving codenamed operatives *another* designation to work under seemed redundant. It was easier to use Alpha, Bravo, Charlie, etc., because when a member of Bravo called in, each man involved in the mission automatically knew the general physical location of the caller. For Knight, the organizational aspects of the naming convention proved useful. On his PDA, tapping a finger on Alpha team brought up the three names of the members, along with a green heartbeat indicator claiming that each individual was alive.

Knight never wanted to see any life indicators turn red, but he suspected that he would see at least a few on this foolhardy mission. If not his own men, then it would be the hospital staff, or worse, the Angel.

The whole operation stank, and Knight had shared that sentiment in a not-so-subtle way during the mission briefing with Vulture. Berkman. Whatever. As usual, the arrogant asshole had acted aloof, a tactician without the combat background required to understand the mind of a boots-on-the-ground, honest-to-God soldier. Of course, Berkman *thought* that he understood Rook and the rest of the deployed Phalanx forces, but to Berkman they were just resources to manipulate.

So not only was an important American Angel at risk, but the lives of nineteen privatized soldiers as well. Not to mention the civilians and local police forces.

The Humvee plowed through a red light, swerving left and then right to dodge cars driven by unaware drivers. Knight jostled back and forth, his hand holding a death grip on the "Oh Shit" handle above his head. As someone who hated backseat drivers, Knight just kept his comments to himself as the driver weaved across the street again.

Knight hoped that the concentrated security presence would convince any would-be assassins that a frontal or aerial assault would be futile. None of the previously attacked hospitals had any serious defense in place, just various forms of civilian police to keep crowds in order. The Brazilians would be wise to not follow America's lead in defending their Angel. Knight didn't have any further intelligence on that situation, but was sure that they would take equivalent steps as the U.S. had done, instead of taking the sane action and hiding their Angel from harm.

It was ludicrous to set this trap. A hospital was no place to stage an ambush, if that's what the higher ups were thinking. Phalanx's presence had better be enough of a deterrent, or some innocent people could easily get hurt.

After the explosion at the hospital in Kenya, Knight had wanted to move the Angel to a location more isolated from civilian populations. Vulture had explained that this proposal was impractical.

Of course it was. It wasn't like Berkman had any dying relatives in the hospital. Maybe if he did, his tune would change. Knight's wife had already been seen by the Angel, so now as far as Knight was concerned, he didn't have any need of the thing. That didn't mean that he shouldn't do all in his power to keep the Angel alive to heal others who did need it.

He shook off the tempting thoughts of putting Berkman's head through a plate glass window and flipped through the pages in his PDA once more, ensuring for the tenth time that his men's heartbeat monitors still worked. Technology was great, but only when it worked. How many American soldiers had died because of equipment failure? It sucked to think about.

Knight's radio came to life, grabbing his attention while the Humvee skidded around a corner.

"Rook, this is Halo Overlord, over."

Command was calling in. It was Connor's radio operator.

"Roger Halo Overlord, this is Rook, go ahead."

"Be advised, Alpha Seven is down, copy?"

Shit.

The Brazilian Angel had been taken out.

"Roger. What intel do we have, over?"

In the short transmission delay that followed, Knight started issuing new orders to his teams via his PDA. Obviously Tango

Delta wouldn't already be at the Phoenix hospital, assuming one team perpetrated each attack, but instinct had gotten Knight's blood flowing and a change in plans was necessary. He was getting antsy now that he knew that Phoenix would almost certainly be the next target.

Michael Connor's voice filled the silence, needing no introduction.

"Rook, witnesses confirm previous reports. Flashbang upon entry, followed by swift execution of Alpha Seven. Tango Delta exited before anyone had recovered. Most eyewitnesses have permanent hearing and sight impairment from the flash."

More good news.

Connor continued.

"As a result, change to contingency plan Zulu Zulu Bravo."

That was the relief that Knight was looking for. Now Phalanx needed to extract Alpha Two immediately. An armored transport would meet them at the hospital to take custody of the Angel. Knight could've jumped for joy, but instead just allowed a slight grin. Obviously Connor had convinced the Rapid Interdiction Force leadership to not sacrifice his men and the Angel on a ridiculous plan.

"Roger that Halo Overlord."

As soon as the last word left his lips, Connor was talking again, obviously not waiting for a response as he sat in the Fort in Texas.

"In addition, all intel suggests that Tango Delta is inbound to your position. ETA unknown. We still don't know if a single hostile, a group of hostiles, or multiple groups of hostiles are involved."

Knight had considered this question in depth since the second attack. A series of staggered attacks by multiple groups seemed like the best shot at first, but that would involve that many more people. Secrets were hard enough to keep between just two friends, never mind between multiple teams who presumably worked for the same boss. A single team could've logistically committed each assassination, but it would take an amazingly well-trained group. It would take a team like Phalanx to pull off.

Knight shared that sentiment with Connor.

"Don't get cocky, Rook. Get your asses in, and get them out again safely. This is our moment."

Sensing the end of the exchange drawing near, Knight asked for the status of Kilo Kilo, known only to a select few as Karen Knight.

"Nothing yet, but try not to worry too much about that. Halo Overlord out."

Easy for you to say.

The timing was impeccable. The hospital lay just ahead. Knight appreciated the last minute save by his boss on the mission strategy, but not the lack of info on his wife's whereabouts. Like everything else in his marriage, it would just have to wait.

"Whew, and I was getting worried we'd be doing some real work today," said Lehoski, sitting across from Knight on the other bench in the back of the Humvee. Seated next to him, Kestrel grinned wide and happy.

Since the death of Falcon, and Connor insisting Seagull stay behind on this one, Talos, currently designated Alpha team, consisted of only three men. As soon as Seagull got straightened out again, he'd be allowed back in. Eventually Connor would fill Falcon's empty spot, but until then, Knight had to make do with what he was given.

He quickly tapped in the confirmation code for contingency plan ZZB while the Humvee zigzagged through traffic. They were close to the hospital, but there was still plenty of time for his men to absorb their new orders.

"So what's Kilo Kilo, Rook? Anything we need to know about?" Kestrel asked.

"You heard Condor: Don't worry about it."

The convoy screeched around the last corner and pulled up to the emergency entrance of the hospital. The lead truck deftly dodged an ambulance entering the ramp from the opposite direction, prompting a blast of the horn from the confused ambulance driver.

"That's how we roll," yelled Kestrel as he popped the Humvee's rear door latch.

Phalanx erupted from the Humvees before the drivers had even brought the large vehicles to a complete stop. The group's M4 carbine rifles led the way into the hospital, itching for a chance to discharge metallic death. Knight hoped that the hospital staff had been made aware of the recently fluctuated situation, but soldiers carrying guns typically got their way no matter what.

As per Knight's pre-arrival instructions, Charlie and Delta teams immediately headed for the hospital roof. Knight suspected that the enemy had a habit of breaching the relatively soft hospital perimeters from above. If by some miracle the enemy target made it all the way to Phoenix in the next fifteen minutes, there would be a sweet surprise lying in wait.

Bravo team setup shop at the hospital emergency foyer, ensuring a clear passage for Alpha and Echo teams upon returning with the intended package. Bravo's leader, known as Pelican, explained to a very perplexed head of hospital security that the Angel was leaving. Right now. The poor receptionist fainted as teams Alpha and Echo sprinted past her, following the pre-ordained path to the large emergency operating theater holding the Angel.

Leading the charge past gawking onlookers, both patients and medical staff alike, Knight scanned ahead, checking every face for any signs of deceit. There would be no more surprises on his watch. He rounded the last corner on his mental map of the hospital and stopped short.

He could see straight through the glass window next to the OR door. The theater was empty.

The Angel wasn't there.

A security guard came puffing up the hallway behind the Phalanx soldiers. Before he could open his mouth, the irate Knight was on him.

"Where is the Angel?" he demanded.

The overweight guard paused, bent at the waist, trying to ease the pain in his gut from his uncharacteristic display of athleticism in following the soldiers. Knight grabbed the man's shirt and lifted the sweaty face.

"Where. Is. The. Angel?"

Through a cough and stutter, the terrified man spurted out, "OR Three, sir."

The teams needed no directions. They hadn't just been catching some nap time on the way to the hospital. Each man had studied the hospital's layout until they saw the place as a ghostly aura every time they closed their eyes.

Knight called in to Bravo team.

"Pelican, find out why the hell they moved Alpha Two without telling us. Rook, out."

Lehoski cursed furiously as the men raced back through the hospital, unfortunately retracing some of their previous steps. While Knight made a mental list of the preparation tasks remaining, his radio squawked abruptly. The panicked words flowed quickly, chilling his blood.

"Contact, fifth flo—"

Chapter 26

"Welcome to this special meeting of the Celestius Board of Directors. If you will all please take your seats now, the Chairman will be with you shortly. Thank you."

Along the wet bar lining the lengths of the grand board room, decanters filled whisky glasses with haste. Despite the sudden flurry of movement, all eyes followed Murphy's gorgeous assistant to the immense double mahogany doors guarding their sacred chamber. Her slender figure floated from the room with a sophisticated sensuality that every board member found intoxicatingly enticing. The same thought crossed each mind: Only the best for Murphy.

Within moments of the last director claiming his chair, the Chairman of the Board appeared in the doorway, a trademark presidential smile gracing his face. The guy certainly had charisma in bucket-loads, which the uneducated often mistook as a sign of a lack of ruthlessness. Every director in the room knew that crossing this man was probably the last mistake in life that they would ever have a chance to make. If they didn't find their own way to promptly leave this world, Murphy would assuredly make their fate expedient.

Having said that, as if death wasn't enough, Murphy had been known to posthumously, albeit anonymously, slander the good names of mostly good men who had failed to meet his sometimes exorbitant demands. Only Murphy was capable of digging up some of the secrets that leaked out of this board room. For most of the directors, they found security in not needing to worry if their boss knew their deepest and darkness secrets. It was a reassuring fact that he already knew what ghouls hid in the shadows of their past. There was nothing left to conceal, which brought a certain level of freedom.

In the meantime, they didn't have to wait long for their boss to shatter their every expectation for the unusual board meeting.

***

"Gentlemen, Directors of the Board, thank you for joining me at such short notice. I promise that even Mr. Sanders will not regret leaving his third mistress in as many weeks to be here with us today."

Ten years ago, Greg Sanders's face would've lit up like a crimson Christmas tree at such a public declaration, but now he just laughed it off with the rest of the gang. Murphy always found little ways to reaffirm his grasp on every one of his directors' lives. Announcements of guilt in one crime or another were commonplace and expected at any board meeting. One unspoken rule had risen as a result: These outbursts of secret truth did not leave the mahogany-paneled chamber under any circumstances.

Murphy reached the far end of the room to take his position at the head of the long table. The densely black marble sucked all of the light out of the room, leaving an atmosphere thickly layered in the mysterious.

Without so much as a signal from Murphy, two knock-outs entered the room unannounced. The barely clad beauties efficiently distributed glasses of champagne down each side of the conference table, pausing just long enough at each director to cause a potentially dangerous spike in blood pressure. Once again, lucky eyes remained transfixed on long legs until the large doors drifted securely shut. After a few moments of awkward silence, Greg Sanders decided to challenge his boss's confident smile.

"So what's this all about, Murphy? Are we celebrating anything in particular, or just your latest victories in the bedroom?"

This got a few muted laughs and Murphy's smile transformed into more of a shrewd smirk than a genuine symbol of happiness. He let a pregnant pause build before sating the intrigued minds of his cronies.

"Gentlemen, I am here to share with you the glorious future of our company. Today we will have in our possession the most precious commodities that this planet has ever seen."

"We're getting into the oil business?" asked one director with a chuckle.

"No, Dale. This is far bigger than oil. We already rely on the clowns running that industry far too much in our pharmaceutical endeavors.

"No, sirs. What I bring to you today will forever change this company. We will bring in more revenue in the next year than we have made in the last five combined."

A void of sound followed a few gasps from those seated around the table. After years of following Murphy and enjoying the benefits of his stellar accomplishments, they couldn't bring themselves to discount the outlandish promise. "Five times" would be deemed lunacy in any other boardroom in America, but if anyone could pull it off, David Murphy and his board all knew that *he* could.

"Don't you want to ask me how I intend to do this, gentlemen?" Murphy asked with a boyish grin.

A series of shocked nods responded.

"Alright then. Let's start off with some classified pictures of our new treasures."

The wood panels behind Murphy split apart silently to reveal the gigantic high definition screen hidden in the wall. Upon seeing the subject of the first image, all of the men seated at the table suffered an involuntary intake of breath. The realization of imminent incredible wealth was not lost on a single director. The extraordinary beauty of the women who had recently served them didn't hold a candle to the gorgeous bank statements that the directors had already conjured up in their minds.

"So owning one of these so-called Angels probably gives most of you a raging hard-on, but I am here to tell you today that we are now taking ownership of not one, not two, not even three, but *four* of these magnificent creatures."

The English language failed to describe the monetary lust taking place in the dark boardroom. Communal greed wasn't a sin within the confines of their sanctuary. Betrayal, deceit, disobedience, these were the sins that condemned a man to death here.

A voice cut through the thoughts of dollar signs and celebration clouding the attention of the directors.

"So what do we do with them?"

Murphy took a moment to revel in his own greatness before sharing his vision. The idea had formed effortlessly upon learning of the top secret Plan C, a clandestine agreement between the United States and the United Kingdom. In the event of an imminent European invasion into the UK over access to the Angel in Scotland, the British would airlift the Angel to the U.S. for safekeeping.

So it appeared that the American President had sold the idea that defending the Angel on British soil created an untenable position. An island that small could easily be overrun by the combined combat forces of Europe, and the U.S. couldn't possibly invest a majority of its military prowess to protect even its dearest ally. If push came to shove, the only option to protect the citizens of the United Kingdom would be to remove the object of the Europeans' desire. What was the point in maintaining possession of an amazing, healing creature if most of the British population couldn't leave their bomb shelters for fear of the fiery death brought by European cruise missiles?

As the nuclear bombings of Hiroshima and Nagasaki had proven a century prior, nothing convinces a foreign government to see your point of view faster than a whole bunch of dead folk.

Of course, who truly benefited in an agreement such as Plan C? As of today, the arrangement greatly benefited David Murphy due to carefully crafted influence over a peon who intimately advised a pawn. The thought undeniably rubbed Murphy the right way. The

President of the United States of America, the world's most powerful world leader, answered to David Murphy. Well, at least indirectly.

Convincing that idiot Fortuna to reroute the Angels away from a military prison to Murphy's very own secure facility had proven easy enough. The man's backbone had completely withered under the crushing pressure of Murphy's threats. In the end, the result would be the same. The man would fall, one way or the other. In any case, Murphy took solace in knowing that his own future had once again received reinforcement.

So back to the question at hand. What would they do with all of these amazing creatures?

"Not that long ago, (you may remember this story) a fellow entrepreneur pulled in a total of fifty million dollars from over three hundred suckers for an *almost* space flight. These men and women of significant wealth just wanted a unique thrill that a vast majority of the populace could never afford: A ride through the heavens.

"Now just imagine what these same billionaires would part with in order to avoid a miserable, illness stricken existence prior to painfully passing into a vague afterlife. In fact, don't imagine. Just watch."

Murphy stepped out of the way as all eyes focused on the graph displayed on the giant LCD wall. The shocked expressions etched on his cronies' faces lit up Murphy's insides. This simple bar graph showed absolute success. Nothing in history had ever brought such fantastical reward, monetary or otherwise. The numbers really spoke for themselves. Hundreds of the world's wealthiest citizens wanted to be freed from their mortal chains in their advanced ages. What was recovery from colon cancer worth? Who'd pay one hundred million dollars for an Alzheimer's cure? Did the world's richest consider a billion dollars too steep to survive Parkinson's? The answers respectively were: *everything, anyone with one hundred million dollars*, and *not even close*.

"Gentlemen, what we're offering here so far surpasses that space flight parlor trick that if I need to explain it to you in any clearer terms, you don't deserve any part of this unique opportunity," Murphy said with no pervading tone of jest.

A falsely timid voice of reason spoke out.

"But what about the rumors of all the disappearances? People are saying it could be the start of the Rapture, Murphy."

The whole room laughed along with the speaker. Murphy joined them before responding, "Gents, if there is a true Rapture taking place, I don't think any of the names on this list or any of the men in this room need to worry about getting taken up on high in Zion."

A fresh wave of laughter enveloped the boardroom.

In truth, only Murphy knew the full extent of the sometimes malicious actions he had taken in order to achieve his own wealth. Of course, none in the room with him could be classified as anything other than sinners by any god of any religion. How many had cheated on their wives in the last twenty-four hours? Probably half. How many had stolen from those too naïve to even realize they were being robbed? All of them. Heaven had no place for these men, and Murphy didn't need to waste time worrying about his own soul. He certainly had enough to worry about just wondering where he would spend all of his even more overflowing wealth.

The voice of reason continued with its true confidence.

"Seriously though, Murphy. There could be some substance to these reports that all of these people reported missing had been healed by an Angel in the weeks prior."

The chairman had read the news articles and a few intriguing police reports on the matter, but he still had no real answer to the question. How could anyone explain why a pregnant woman's baby had vanished from her womb after the woman had received an Angel's touch? The doctors and scientists meticulously examining her certainly had no resolution to that question.

And as long as the question remained unanswered and did not affect his latest business enterprise, Murphy couldn't care less about what happened to those people. His paying customers were most likely only going to need to pay him once for his regenerative service. What happened to them beyond that point was none of his business. Still, he had to respond regardless.

"First of all, our latest clientele do not care. I had the foresight to broach the subject to test the waters. These are all successful men and women who have been winners their entire lives. How do you think these titans feel to pay someone to empty their colostomy bags or to feed them through a straw at regular intervals? How would *you* feel in that situation?

"They're tired of the humiliation and restrictions of growing old and frail. Even if they blow their life's work on this one purchase and it brings them a few weeks of boundless youth, they will say it was easily worth double again."

Murphy paused for a moment before moving on.

"As for the disappearances, I think you'll find that any geezer or old hag who has just been given their youth back is not going to stick around with their ungrateful offspring or mooching friends. Most likely you'll find most of those missing people out living their lives to the fullest and embracing all that they had missed for the last few decades," Murphy said, a perfectly "I am the teacher and you are the student" smile giving just the right level of condescension.

The room joined in a brief chuckle, not really fooled by the explanation. Steps would need to be taken in order to cash in on their opportunity. Deals would need to be made on an accelerated schedule to assure payment before this Rapture nonsense gained more steam.

"Alright, gentlemen of the board, before we get into the details of your new assignments, I propose a toast," Murphy announced.

He raised his glass and looked around the room as his associates followed suit. After all that he had done for them, these men would follow him into the depths of hell. If hell actually existed, he'd make sure each of them reached that dire final resting place to spruce it up a bit prior to his own grand arrival. Fortunately, he had nothing to fear. Only he commanded the greatest power on the planet.

With a half-grin he continued, "Here's to playing god, and to never needing an Angel."

A chorus of "Cheers" echoed around the room as the men drank to their own health. With that handled, there was only one business matter left to address.

"Gentlemen, I would like to introduce you to our newest spokesman."

Around the table, Murphy could see a mixture of blank looks, suspicious glances, and conspiratorial nudges. None of them had any idea who was about to enter the boardroom, yet a few were pretending to be a part some fictitious inner circle with the boss. Just another game. Murphy tapped on the intercom button and asked his secretary to show his guest in.

A couple of seconds later, a tall, rugged-looking man cautiously stepped into the inner sanctum of Celestius. Murphy could see the man was uncomfortable, but he would have him trained in public appearances in no time. It wasn't the man's personality that Murphy required.

The first medical doctor to find and report on an Angel. *That* was the man's value. In the real world, it didn't mean shit. Sure, he'd found an Angel, but he didn't know any more than anyone else did. Of course, investors didn't know that. Murphy smiled and pointed to an empty chair at the table.

"Welcome, Dr. Baird."

Chapter 27

Chaos asserted control in the hospital. Doctors and nurses in scrubs of various colors darted around the bustling corridors, trying to follow the security guards' evacuation directions. Patients and medical staff alike gawked at the Phalanx teams mobilizing around them. The poor souls didn't even have half a clue as to how scared they should be in that moment.

Sparrow from Charlie team hadn't responded since calling in the alert. Worse, Knight's handheld display showed no heartbeats for any of Charlie.

This was bad. Very bad. It was time to move.

Knight yelled into his radio.

"Echo, get that fucking Angel and get it out of here. Now!"

"Aye, sir."

"Delta, split and take southeast and southwest stairs to the fifth floor. We have to find Charlie."

"Roger."

Lehoski and Kestrel followed along close behind Knight as he reached a bank of stairs and ascended quickly. Echo split off from Knight's team and headed for the operating room holding the Angel. Bravo team still manned the foyer, but Knight didn't see the point in that anymore.

"Pelican, tell the cops to get all civilians out of here, then secure the area directly over OR Three. Get up and hold that position," he barked. "I'm taking Alpha team up the northeast stairs to help find Charlie team."

Various forms of "copy" and "roger" returned on the comm lines, mixing in with the reports of Alpha team's boots on the concrete stairs. They rounded the corner for the third floor, taking two at a time, not a heavy breath among them.

Knight's mind ran a mile a minute as he considered the mission. He'd lost four men, apparently on the fifth floor. The hospital had four major staircases around the critical zone where the Angel was. He'd sent men up two stairways and he'd taken another. That still left one unaccounted for.

"This has got to be a different assassination team, right Rook?" Kestrel asked, interrupting Knight's thoughts.

Knight reached the top of the stairs and grabbed the door to the fifth floor. He paused, rifle ready.

"Yeah, looks like it."

"We don't even know if it's a single hostile this time," chimed in Lehoski, raising his rifle towards the door. He nodded at Knight.

Knight yanked the door open, allowing Lehoski and Kestrel to burst into the hallway. They immediately covered the left and right corridors. Knight followed them in and swept straight ahead with his M4.

"Clear."

The trio hustled forward.

A pair of soldiers from Bravo cautiously opened the door at the far end of the hall, coming up from the other staircase. All the men pointed guns at each other for just a moment, trained instincts kicking in. Knight gave the signal for Bravo to start sweeping the other side of the fifth floor. Alpha team would head to the unmanned staircase and check to see if Tango Delta had escaped down there.

With a cry of surprise, a police officer flew across the hall in front of them. A scream echoed from a room on the right. Kestrel moved to help the officer while Lehoski and Knight swung right into the doorway that the officer had just vacated. Inside, a doctor stood panting wildly, his face red. He was yelling.

"I can't leave my patients!"

Knight approached the man slowly, gun barrel to the floor.

"You gotta get out of here, it's not safe, doc."

"I don't care, I'm not leaving my patients."

The cop came trundling past Knight.

"You just assaulted a police officer. You're coming with me."

The doctor's face transformed instantly into that of fear.

"No, no, you can't let him take me," he blurted out. "These people could die."

Knight looked at his watch. This was taking too much time.

"Screw it. Just leave him, Officer."

The cop stopped in the middle of cuffing the doctor. The man looked embarrassed that a doctor had just thrown his ass across the hall, but the guy with the biggest gun usually made the rules. And the M4 was a tad bit bigger than the 9mm Glock in the cop's holster.

"Okay, whatever."

The officer left and the doctor regained his composure. He turned back to his patient, who'd been watching all of this wide-eyed from his bed. Alpha left and continued. The team communication channels remained eerily silent.

"Status report."

"Echo is at OR Three with the package now."

Knight rounded a corner with his rifle raised.

Empty.

"Rook, this is Humm." Humm was short for Hummingbird, one of the men in Delta. "We found two of Charlie. Bastard killed Sparrow and Finch."

At the news, Knight paused. He scanned the hallway in both directions. Everything was quiet. Only the random *beeps* and mutterings of medical equipment met his ears. Kestrel and Lehoski spread out, covering other angles.

Tango Delta had been on this floor. The Demon was here. Somewhere.

Knight motioned his team to fall in.

Alpha team's footsteps bounced conspicuously off of the tiled walls. Their boots sounded dangerously loud to Knight as they progressed towards the fourth stairway.

"Where's the rest of Charlie?" whispered Lehoski.

The trio reached the final corner before the stairway. Knight peeked around the edge of the sterile white wall and got an answer to Lehoski's question. He turned to his two men.

"Cover me."

The three popped smoothly into the corridor. Lehoski and Kestrel posted at covering positions, watching both directions.

Knight crouched down next to the missing pair from Charlie team. He updated the whole team through his radio.

"This is Rook. I've found Robin and Kite. Both dead. Throats cut open."

Silence.

Knight looked around uneasily. They were dealing with a team of pros. No way could the whole of Charlie team get taken out like this by scrubs.

"Humm, report."

Silence.

Then a whisper.

"Rook, this is Penguin. We found Hummingbird and Heron. Same shit. Both dead."

Lehoski and Kestrel both looked at Knight. A deep-seated need for violent vengeance filled their eyes. He shook his head and pointed in the directions they were supposed to be watching for incoming.

Damn, this was getting worse. He'd been talking with Humm only a minute ago.

"Orders?" Penguin asked, agitation evident in his voice. With just one word, Penguin made clear to Knight what he wanted to do, and what was going to happen when he found the enemy. Unfortunately, Knight couldn't just send Penguin and his buddy off to die.

"Get into secondary defensive positions."

Knight jumped up with Kestrel and Lehoski in tow. They headed for the stairwell.

Time to head back down.

"We don't have enough men to hold all these positions," Kestrel muttered. Knight silenced him with an angry glance. He didn't need to be told what he already knew.

Knight kicked the panic device on the stairwell door, swinging the large door into the wall hard enough that it locked into the open position. He peeked into the doorway with his rifle and scanned up and down the stairs. Footsteps reverberated from above. He shifted across the doorway and crouched behind the wall, pointing his rifle at the stairs leading down from the floor above. Lehoski lay prone on the floor, his gun trained on the same spot. Kestrel crouched against the wall and covered their asses.

A doctor's bootie stepped into view, followed by the rest of a doctor in green scrubs. Alpha team relaxed and stood. The doctor stepped past them and proceeded down the hall. Lehoski started to go after the man, but Knight grabbed his arm.

"It's his funeral. Not our problem. We've got to get to that Angel."

Knight and his men took the stairs three at a time and burst into the first floor of the hospital. They double-timed it to the operating room where the Angel had been staying. Shouts echoed from inside the large room. Lehoski and Knight exchanged a glance.

Now what?

Echo team members stood just inside the OR doorway, pointing fingers and yelling incoherently over each other. Upon Knight's entrance, they all shut up and stood at some form of attention. A tall pink man stood in the center of the room.

"What the fuck is *that* still doing here?"

No one offered to answer Knight's question. His tone wasn't exactly inviting and he knew it.

"Someone had better answer me here, and fast."

The four members of Echo team glanced furtively at one another, none brave enough to talk to their pissed off boss. One of them finally coughed and said, "It won't leave, Rook."

Damn it, this whole mission was botched. He'd already lost Charlie and now the Angel was screwing around. And where the hell was Penguin? And he still didn't have a visual on the bastard killing his men. This was spinning out of control.

"What do you mean *it won't leave*?"

"We tried asking it to move and that didn't work. Dumb bastard doesn't speak English."

Emboldened, another Echo guy spoke up.

"We tried to push it, but that asshole's a strong mofo."

Great.

"Okay, we're out of time, take up defensive positions along this hallway."

The men scattered, covering both entrances to the OR and posting a small perimeter as best they could. Every man put an eye on the ceiling, knowing that's how the hostiles usually attacked the Angels.

Knight crouched by the door and looked back at the Angel. The pink bastard seemed totally unaware of any danger. It just stood there staring at the wall, totally oblivious. Just perfect. Looking up, Knight started to question his decision. Should his team have stayed up one floor and tried to hold that position? He'd felt too exposed there, but now he could see they weren't in any better shape in the OR.

A deafening explosion ripped apart the ceiling above Knight's head. He rolled away as the flaming debris hit the ground all around him. The OR wall stopped his progress with thump to the head. The room buzzed loudly in his ears and everything seemed dark. The lights must've been knocked out.

In the disorientation of it all, Knight's mind wandered to the same place it always did. He wondered what his wife was up to. He wondered if he'd see her again.

Not a helpful thought.

As his hearing slowly returned, Knight could hear the cacophony of a handful of carbines showering the ceiling with lead. Vision came back a lot slower. Everything remained a blurry mess of fire and tracer rounds. He raised his rifle and held fire, waiting for whatever was going to descend from the gaping hole above the darkened OR. He didn't need to see straight to shoot straight.

His men ceased firing and now crept slowly forward to get better shooting angles. Still the Angel just stood in the middle of the room, ignoring a piece of fiery acoustic tile smoldering on its shoulder. The sight creeped Knight out. These damn Angels couldn't be human.

Then Knight's mind cleared enough to remember the next part of the attack.

"Everyone get back!"

They looked at him with anxious expressions, but didn't immediately retreat. From the opening above, a small metallic sphere fell through to the floor and bounced with a *clank*. Assuming the worst, Knight leapt towards the device, trying to cover it up.

But he was too late.

Chapter 28

With the mission underway, Michael Connor sat at his desk, sipping a single malt from the Isle of Skye in Scotland. No joy passed from the glass tumbler to his taste buds. Men were dying.

As a soldier, he'd always acted instinctively, trusting his gut and his brains to connect the dots. Success after success had proven the concept. When the shit hit the fan, Connor could be relied on as *the* guy who would get his men out of the muck. Surrounded by hostiles, a few well-placed shots and perfectly deployed assets could turn a situation in a heartbeat.

Now the old major sat in a chair while men in a different state were dying at his command. He felt useless.

He told himself that the scotch wasn't a coping mechanism. It's not like he was getting drunk. The bite kept him sharp.

Sure it did.

His computer monitor showed the same display readout that Knight could monitor from his handheld device. Vital signs of soldiers had redlined in various places. Shit, the whole of Charlie was gone. Delta was incapacitated, as good as dead. According to the radio traffic he'd heard, Knight had holed up the survivors around the Angel. Not a good idea, but what the hell could Connor do about it? Knight must've known something he didn't.

A retired quarterback watching his old team blow it in the big game. What were his options? Calling Knight now would do no good. The situation had spiraled far too deep for that. They were in it up to their necks with nowhere to go and no one to drag their asses out.

Another sip of Talisker from the glass. The alcohol burn hardly registered.

The phone on his desk lit up, bells ringing.

"Condor."

"Condor, this is Foxtrot. We've lost comms with Alpha."

A squall started forming in his gut.

"Where are you?"

"In the trucks waiting on delivery of the pack—"

"Get your asses in there *now*," Connor yelled, uncoiling his frustration.

"But, sir—"

"Your team is dying, soldier," he barked. "Get in there and *do* something about it."

Hesitation.

"Roger, Condor."

The line went dead. Condor dropped the phone on the cradle and flopped his face into his hands. Had he just committed more lambs to the slaughter? Did he need to tell the General?

Fucking Thomas McGarvey. Albatross.

What was *his* game? What was his stake in this crapshoot of a mission? Connor had a hard time believing that the local National Guard couldn't have handled it officially and effectively. Instead of a massive level of resources carrying out a simple mission, Phalanx had been sent in undermanned and with too little time to plan. Yes, that was the whole point of the group, but Connor had never wanted to just throw away the lives of his soldiers wastefully.

Did McGarvey feel the same way?

It was time to find out. Connor ripped the phone off his desk and started dialing.

Chapter 29

Mark Jackson looked at the dirty floor and wondered where the line was. Not any specific line in the nasty linoleum, but the line between dedicated investigation and out-and-out harassment. He was standing in the cereal aisle of a grocery store that just happened to be down the street from Emily Nihipali's apartment.

The apartment in which, until recently, Emily had spent a lot of time with her boyfriend, Josh Greaves. Despite Jackson and Smith's most ardent efforts, Mr. Greaves was still missing.

An elderly lady stopped at the end of the aisle and stared down the two men loitering amongst the breakfast foods. To avoid her suspicion, Jackson grabbed a colorful box off the nearest shelf. A stupid mascot adorned the packaging, promising thirteen different essential vitamins and minerals within.

"Can you believe people eat this crap?" he asked Smith, disgusted.

Smith just grunted, continually checking over his shoulder.

"There's no way this is healthy for anyone," Jackson continued. "The food colorings alone probably cause cancer."

"I like them fine," Smith said.

It wasn't too much of a stretch to imagine the oversized man indulging in garbage cereal. Jackson observed his uncomfortable partner in crime. As much as Jackson didn't care for skirting legal boundaries in the process of getting a scoop, Smith *really* abhorred it. Getting caught stalking Emily Nihipali wasn't something either man looked forward to. In fact, just confronting her in about thirty seconds was going to be awkward enough.

And right on cue, here came their mark.

Every day, Ms. Nihipali got home from her job and went straight to the local gym. Not a fancy place, but affordable on what Jackson presumed was her meager salary. And each day after her workout, she stopped off at this grocery store on the way home. They'd only trailed her for a few days, but in each visit, she'd headed down the cereal aisle last of all.

Unless she had a small army of children hiding out in her apartment, Jackson assumed that the woman ate cereal three or four meals a day, based on the rate she consumed her bran cereal of choice. The stuff tasted worse than rabbit food to Jackson. He'd stick with a cup of coffee and a cigarette as his morning ritual.

She wandered down the aisle, scanning the displays for the box she desired. About ten feet from the two reporters, she stopped suddenly and slowly turned her head in their direction. She looked less than pleased to see them.

Understandably so.

"I'm calling the police," she said casually, turning around with her basket swaying under her nicely toned arm.

The reporters had already decided that Smith would handle the talking since he was far more pleasant than his accomplice.

"Please, ma'am. Don't do that," he urged. Smith's thick drawl seemed slightly exaggerated to Jackson, hopefully an attempt at southern charm. "We're really just concerned about Josh."

She whipped around and stormed towards the large man, her finger pointing furiously.

"Stop lying," she growled. "You just want a story."

Smith put both his hands up and took a step back in defense.

"That's how it started, ma'am, but I can assure you that now we're just as worried as you are."

"I doubt that," she snipped.

But she didn't run away. She stood her ground and glared at the pair of them. Did they have her now?

The rage in her eyes subsided. Her shoulders slumped a little as signs of exhaustion set in.

"You been sleeping okay?" Smith asked.

"How I sleep is none of your damned business," she snapped with a lot less ferocity than before.

Jackson watched the tall, beautifully athletic woman debate with herself if the two journalists really did just want to help. It was true that they were crazy with curiosity. She was obviously withholding information, and they had no idea why. At the same time, concern over Josh Greaves' disappearance definitely factored in more and more as each day passed.

"Look, both of you go wait at my car while I pay for this stuff," she said. Then she glared at Jackson and added, "I'm sure you've been following me closely enough to know which one it is."

He nodded sheepishly, embarrassed by the declaration, despite having steeled himself for her response. Was it just because she was so pretty that she got under his skin a little?

The two men strolled casually over to Nihipali's SUV and tried to wait next to it without looking like a pair of rapists on the prowl.

"How come they always single *me* out as the bad guy?" Jackson asked.

"Because you look like an asshole," Smith replied, smiling wide.

At least the day was looking up. They might even get a story. Or a trip to jail.

"You don't think she's calling the cops, do you?"

"No, I think she's ready to spill the beans," Smith answered. "Whatever beans she has to spill, anyway."

Jackson nodded and watched as Emily Nihipali left the grocery store and made a beeline for her vehicle. As she drew closer, Jackson saw tears forming in the corners of her eyes. A pang of guilt hit him, followed by a haze of confusion.

What was wrong with him? He'd never felt bad about causing an interviewee grief. It was his job to find the truth, no matter what. Why else had they ambushed her in a grocery store?

She directed them into the backseat as she climbed into the driver's seat. After a moment of collecting her thoughts, she started the car and then turned up the radio. Loud.

"I think I'm being followed by more than just you two idiots."

That was news to Jackson.

"What do you mean?" Smith asked, his deep voice traveling over the obnoxious pop music blaring from all sides.

"Everywhere I go, I keep noticing these same two guys. They're never together, but I see one or the other just about everywhere," she explained. "It's really creeping me out."

"Do you think it's related to Josh?" Smith asked.

She scrunched up her face a little as sadness welled up. Jackson's usually stone heart cracked at the sight.

"I don't know, but they started showing up after he left."

"After he left?" Jackson echoed.

She nodded.

"Maybe you should tell us what happened," Smith suggested. "Maybe we can help you."

After a final glance between the two, she acquiesced and shared her story.

Last week, Emily had woken frightened in the middle of the night. Sweaty and panicky, she'd assumed it to be the result of a nightmare. To calm her nerves, she'd gone to the kitchen for a glass of water.

When she'd returned to the bed, Josh was gone. After a few minutes of walking around her apartment in the dark looking for him, she'd gotten worried and had turned on every light. There'd been no sign of him anywhere.

"So he just left without saying anything?" Smith asked.

A single tear formed in her left eye, bubbling, but not ready to break free quite yet.

"That's the thing," she started. "I'd set the alarm before bed like I always do."

She left it at that, as if her explanation covered all the bases. Jackson and Smith just looked back at her, expressions saying, "So what?" Realizing their confusion, she elaborated, a little bit frustrated.

"The alarm system beeps any time someone opens a door or a window."

"Are you sure that it works?"

"Yes, I had it checked out the next day, just to be sure."

"So what happened after you couldn't find him?"

"I called the police, and they showed up, but they weren't buying it."

"What did they say?"

She sighed and looked up at the ceiling of the SUV. The loud music had little effect on her.

"They just told me that they'd file the missing person report and get back with me."

Phoenix's finest at their best.

Although, the story did bring up some interesting questions. Jackson's first would've been to ask if Josh had even been in the bed when she'd woken up to get water. Despite her gorgeous looks, the cynic in Jackson always won out. He thought of some gentle phrasing for the question, but before he could pose it, Nihipali made the point moot.

"So the next day, a bunch of guys in weird suits showed up," she said. Jackson tried to keep a straight face, but he had a feeling that either this was a crazy lady, or they'd just struck gold.

"What kind of weird suits?"

"The kind you see on TV. Haz-mat, or whatever they're called. They said they were with the FBI Missing Persons Unit, but that seemed strange after the police had been so skeptical with me the night before."

Jackson couldn't help himself, so he interrupted.

"What'd they do?"

"I had to wait outside in a black sedan while they did whatever it was they did."

Smith jumped in.

"Did you see any equipment that they took into your apartment?"

"Uh, they rolled a giant vacuum cleaner thing out of a van and took it inside."

Jackson was getting optimistic again.

"Did they remove anything from your apartment?" Smith asked.

She looked out the window for a few moments before answering.

"When I first noticed Josh was gone, I could've sworn I saw his boxers in the bed, but I was in such a panic, maybe I just imagined it."

"You think they could've taken your boyfriend's underwear?" Smith asked.

Her face fell slightly.

"I don't know," she said quietly. "Maybe they did, maybe they didn't. At this point, does it really matter?"

The sad tone in her voice created an awkward tension that had Jackson squirming in his seat.

"Did you happen to see any labels on anything? Any ID tags or anything?" he asked, just needing *something* to fill the silence.

Once again she appeared to delve into the recesses of her memory for any shred of evidence. Unfortunately, she just shook her head.

"Well, thank you for your time, Ms. Nihipali," Smith said.

Jackson added, "Yes, you've been very helpful."

She looked at both of them earnestly, as downtrodden as an abandoned kitten.

"Do you think you can find him?"

The answer was negative, but of course, they couldn't share that.

"We're going to do our best to find Josh," Smith said. "If you have any questions, here's my card. Call me at any time of day or night if you think of anything else."

She nodded and took the card out of his beefy hand. The two men started to climb out of the SUV when the woman muted the radio and said, "Wait."

They both poked their heads back in.

"I remember one thing, I think."

Jackson's whole body tensed. What was it with this woman and dragging out explanations?

"When they took me to the car, I got a look into the back of the big van where the vacuum cleaner came from," she continued.

Jackson could've strangled her at this point.

"There was a duffel bag inside with the word *Celest* written on it, or at least, I think that's what it said. It was partly blocked by a box."

Smith got her to spell out the word and thanked her again, reminding her to call if anything else at all came to mind.

The reporters walked back to Smith's truck, the Texan all smiles again. He punched Jackson in the arm.

"Looks like we've finally got a lead."

Chapter 30

Knight wandered through the upper levels of the hospital. A couple of doctors walked by without even a glance, others observed him curiously. That was understandable. His head floated along just beneath the ten-foot tall ceiling.

He slipped into a stairwell and headed down a few floors. He paused just beyond the door to the fifth floor. A few moments passed as he looked around, waiting.

Turning suddenly, Knight found himself staring at Sparrow and Finch. Sparrow asked what he was doing, but Knight didn't respond. The soldier was asking the question, repeatedly. Knight's right hand shot out, driving a smooth blade into Finch's neck. Blood jetted out of his throat as the knife drew back and slashed at Sparrow. The poor guy had barely had enough time to yell a single word into the radio before the knife cut out his throat.

Knight grabbed both men by the fronts of their fatigues and carefully lowered them to the ground, checking over his shoulder to see if anyone had noticed. They hadn't. The doctors and security guards were all preoccupied with the soldiers waving guns around downstairs.

A noise. Something that got Knight's attention. He darted down a hallway faster than Knight thought possible. After a few turns, Knight found himself in the hall leading to another stairway. Robin and Kite came into view and waved to Knight as he slowed to a casual walk. Without any hesitation, Knight lashed out with both hands and drove a knife into each of their necks. The two men didn't know what hit them as they watched the life drain messily from each other's bodies.

With the agility of a jungle cat, Knight leapt over the pair of fallen soldiers and shot into the stairwell. Up one flight of stairs, and then Knight was racing along to another stairwell. Nobody paid him any heed. Then he was down the stairs like a rocket, and then moving more cautiously into the fifth floor from the other side of the building.

With the stairwell door slightly ajar, Knight could see Humm and Heron creeping past. They didn't notice the door. Knight slipped out gingerly, slashed both of their throats, and then ducked back into the stairs. Up one floor, back across the length of it, then down the same stairs he'd gone up only moments before, more slowly this time.

He stepped down the stairs and saw two soldiers pointing guns at him from the open stairwell door. Knight recognized himself, his actual self, in the doorway signaling for Lehoski to lower his weapon. The soldiers made way, and Knight had the bizarre experience of walking past himself onto the fifth floor.

Penguin and his partner, whose name Knight couldn't immediately remember walked across in front of Knight. Penguin's left hand was covered in blood. They must've been heading to the stairs to meet the actual Knight downstairs at the Angel. Instead, Knight's blades shot out and shanked the two men. Penguin, juiced up from the murder of his best friend Hummingbird, drew his pistol as he lay bleeding out. He took aim, but Knight grabbed his wrist. The dying man's mangled vocal chords couldn't even scream as his wrist shattered in the vice-like grip. The pistol fell harmlessly to the floor.

Knight headed down to the second floor. Guarding the intersection directly above the Angel, Pelican and the remainder of Bravo team were vaporized when Knight tossed a grenade at them. The explosion obliterated the area on the floor directly above the Angel's location in the operating theater.

Then Knight was dropping a small metallic sphere through the gaping hole in the floor, ignoring the hail of bullets flying up towards him. After a few seconds, the ground shook with the detonation. Knight dropped through the hole gracefully.

In his peripheral vision, Knight could see some unconscious bodies from Alpha and Echo teams scattered around. Directly in front of him, the Angel stood, mouth agape in a terrible scream. He thrust a giant spear into the Angel and watched as an electrical shockwave jolted through the weapon. The room filled with a brilliant blue flash.

The room quickly normalized. Instead of the Angel, there was only a black, smoking burn mark where it had stood.

Knight swiveled around the motionless room. The medical equipment had tumbled all over the place at one point or another. He stepped towards a bloodied soldier against the wall. Despite the red covering most of his face, Knight again recognized himself, now resting unconsciously. Knight turned to the right, where a cracked mirror revealed his true identity.

Knight then reached out and put a gloved hand on the head of his real body.

***

Flecks of dim light slowly pierced the gaps between Knight's closed eyelids. Groggy from his forced slumber, he slowly realized that he was lying on the floor of the operating room, his back pressed against the wall. He had that feeling of waking from an insane nightmare, but the details flitted away, as they always did.

Clumsily, he pushed himself up into a sitting position. As his head moved even just a fraction of an inch, the world shot around at crazy angles. Ignoring his body's protests, he forced himself up, everything spinning away from him. He collapsed back onto his rear.

Promptly, he vomited all over the floor. Each convulsion ripped pain through his ribs. He couldn't tell if he had a few bruised ones, or if his ribs were actually broken, but his back felt like a hot knife was being inserted with every cough.

His head felt bludgeoned. That was about the only word for it. His view lolled around drunkenly as he sat as still as he could manage. A second round of hurling threatened.

He looked to his left and saw a stainless steel cart lying on the floor. A crimson gash on the corner of the cart looked like blood. Knight touched the side of his head gingerly, and his hand came back with the same red stain. At least he'd found the culprit for his hangover. If he'd had more strength, he'd have punched the cart, but he was sure he'd just throw up again if he tried.

Plus, his wrist already hurt like hell.

After yet another wave of nausea, Knight slid back down onto the floor. Lying on his back with his knees bent offered slight relief from the dizziness. He understood the head injury, but why was he so damn tired? His body felt like he'd just barely survived eight rounds with Mike Tyson and a tiger.

A noise grabbed his attention.

Had the Demon come back to finish the job? Knight could hardly move, and his brain was only half-functioning. He didn't really care about living or dying at this point.

He could vaguely remember the ceiling exploding and the small grenade falling. He'd tried to smother it to protect his men, but he suspected that he'd not made it. For one, he was still alive. With the mess strewn all over, Knight couldn't make out any of his team.

Another noise. The banging of a door.

Knight risked another episode of painful heaving and lifted his head off the cool floor. Paramedics were rushing towards him from the end of the hall. A security officer was wrestling with the door to a stairwell, trying to get it to stay open.

The medical personnel stopped suddenly. The looks of horror on their faces didn't grant Knight much solace. What the hell had happened?

With as much effort as he could muster, Knight propped himself up on his elbows for a better view. The sight before him made him wish that his vision was still blurry. All around him, the bodies of his men lay battered and bloodied. None of them moved. Not even a twitch.

The operating room started spinning wildly as Knight swept his eyes across the whole scene. In the corner where the Angel had once stood, now all that remained was a giant black scar on the floor, wall, and ceiling.

The dim room faded to black as his head thumped back onto the floor.

Chapter 31

Celest.

Why couldn't they find anything about this damn word? Was it a brand? Was it a company? Even Google didn't seem to have much to tell them, unless they were looking for a psychic or a punk rock band with the same name. Jackson did proffer the clairvoyants services to Smith, just for a little extra assistance, but his partner wasn't in the mood.

The usual, carefree Smith was on sabbatical apparently, because the large man sitting at the desk across from Jackson was a man on a mission. He'd never known Smith to get so wrapped up in any of their cases. The guy probably just had the hots for Emily. Jackson couldn't blame him.

Jackson pushed his laptop out of the way and pulled out the one resource that he'd never consider using for anything useful in any investigation: a copy of the Phoenix Press. He started in the sports section, just to get warmed up to the terrible writing. Looked like the Suns were in trade negotiations with a few players after one of theirs went missing a week after seeing the Angel. Apparently professional athletes couldn't handle the sniffles. For the kind of money those bozos were getting, Jackson would've played with amoebic dysentery. *That* would make the other team think twice about guarding him.

The disappearances were getting weird, though. So many people who got healed by the Angel just fell off the face of the planet. Reports were sketchy, but some claimed people just found a pile of empty clothes where their blessed relative should be. Were all the touched folk just hiding out naked in the Arizona desert in one of those jacked up cult compounds, dancing round a camp fire and singing about tall pink men? Jackson wouldn't put it past them. People were stupid and worshiped just about anything these days.

Other than a promo for the Cardinals, nothing else popped out as worthwhile in the local sporting world. None of his colleagues' pieces in the meat of the paper offered any intellectual distraction, so Jackson noisily flipped over to the obituaries. Smith glared at him, probably for the excessive paper crinkling, but it was hard to tell today. The littlest things had set the big man off. Two hours previously he'd berated the boss for the usual early morning barrage of empty threats. That had been entertaining, to say the least.

Maybe Jackson could lure ol' Charlie out for round two, just to spice things up.

Any thoughts of shenanigans flew straight out the window when Jackson read through the fourth entry of the obits. Even after a second and third read, he couldn't believe it.

"Shit, Matt, you gotta see this."

Smith's initial angry reaction faded instantly when he saw the name.

"Emily's dead?" he asked.

"Looks that way."

The pair sat in silence, listening to the dull roar of the office around them. Emily Nihipali's sudden death brought up far more questions than it answered.

"Did we do this?" Smith asked.

"Don't start down that path, man. If someone offed her for talking to us, that's on them, not us."

The look in Smith's eyes told a different story.

"If we hadn't gone after her, made her talk—"

"Stop. We were just doing our job."

"That doesn't mean we have no responsibility here," Smith whispered harshly. The two men had slowly leaned closer and closer together over their shared desk as the exchange progressed. They could be damn sure that *someone* was eavesdropping in a building full of scummy reporters. Their current level of intimacy probably drew more attention than a more casual conversation.

"Let's go for a walk, bud," Smith said.

Jackson nodded and followed his partner out into the Phoenix heat. It wasn't even three o'clock, and it was already abusively hot. Why didn't he move up north again? Oh yeah, because being snowed in for a month every New Year totally sucked.

Traffic zipped by at a relatively fast clip compared to the end of the lunch rush an hour before. The two men tried to stay in the shade of the office buildings as much as possible as they wandered down the sidewalk, destination unknown. The sounds of cars and pedestrians and construction made it hard for the two of them to hear each other. Jackson could only hope that any unwanted listeners faced the same challenge.

"Do we agree that this is fucking suspicious?" Smith blurted out. It wasn't like the mild-mannered reporter to swear.

"Yeah, man. The only other interviewee who died the day after an interview with us was that gangbanger who was going to testify against those mafia assholes."

Smith just nodded and kept staring straight ahead as he walked. It was a lot to process. Emily wasn't some violent thug who didn't deserve the air that he breathed. This was a good person with no criminal record. This was a girlfriend looking for her missing boyfriend.

It was tragic.

"We've got to work out what this Celest stuff is about, Mark."

"Yeah, but we're pissing into the wind on that one."

"We owe it to her. There's a connection somewhere."

The men reached the corner of the block. A small group of late lunch-goers assembled behind them as they waited for the crosswalk to give them the go-ahead. Jackson looked to his left at the sudden roar of a large engine. A black sedan shot around a pickup and bored into the intersection, angled straight for the pedestrians on the corner. Jackson froze.

Two hands grabbed him from behind and launched him into the street. He shut his eyes in a midst of squealing brakes, terrified screams, and the *thump* of metal colliding with flesh.

Jackson lay on the pavement for a few seconds, his body seized up, unresponsive to his desperate will to move. The world just buzzed around him. Everything seemed grey and fuzzy. He just *couldn't* move.

Someone pulled him onto his feet and slapped his face. Sound returned in a blaring instant. Color drained back into his sight.

Jackson and Smith paid no heed to the pickup honking at them for diving into the street. The awful scene on the corner of the sidewalk arrested their attention. Eventually the honking died out as the pickup driver also noticed the trail of destruction left by the errant sedan. Seven bodies lay in twisted heaps, scattered around like fallen pins at the bowling alley.

Except, these pins were covered in blood and bent in unnatural ways.

A few bystanders moved in to assist in whatever futile manner they could. Most people just stood and watched with various degrees of shock and disgust on their faces. A few talked on their cellphones, but Jackson doubted any had thought to call the police. Smith whipped out his phone and dialed emergency services before Jackson could act.

Some punk kid stepped in front of Jackson, taking HD footage of the nearest broken body. The reporter snapped.

Smith hauled Jackson off of the young man, and whispered in his ear that enough was enough. They had to go before the police arrived. Sure enough, sirens approached. The two men headed off, ignoring the pathetic taunts from the kid whose nose now gushed blood all over the sidewalk.

"Did you really need to slam his face into the concrete twice?" Smith asked, his breathing a little heavy from the exertion of escaping a crime scene.

"Little shit deserved worse."

They reached the alley that ran behind the offices buildings. Cutting down the side street granted access to the rear door of the Press. Smith held the door open for Jackson, but blocked the doorway for a second. He turned.

"You okay to go back up to the office?"

Jackson nodded.

"Yeah, man. A little screwed up, though."

"Yeah, we could've been killed."

Jackson knew that Smith had saved his ass, but he couldn't bring himself to thank the man. Later, but not now. He had a lot to digest.

"They tried to kill us, Matt."

"We don't know that."

"You fucking serious, man? Do they need to send you a fucking signed invitation to your own funeral?"

"Calm down. I'm just saying that we don't know for sure."

"A *black* sedan, which I'll remind you is the kind of car that Emily sat in while her apartment was raided, just tried to kill us, then drove the fuck off. That's not clear enough for you?"

"I'm not saying it wasn't, I'm just keeping an open mind."

Jackson forced his way past Smith and started up the stairs.

"Screw that, Matt. They killed her and now they want to kill us. You can keep an open mind, but close the damn door."

Chapter 32

"Julius, take a look at this."

Julius Savage peeked around the computer monitor on his desk.

"What is it?"

The small room was dark, the way his three employees insisted upon, but Julius could easily make out the scowl on Tracy Tam's face in the glow of her screen. Her two partners in crime were crowded around the display.

Must be important.

The giant of a man unfolded himself from the office chair designed for normal people. After a quick stretch and a yawn that gained more displeased looks from Tracy, Julius walked his six-foot-eleven frame past two empty desks to reach Tracy's. Her henchmen made way for their boss.

"Argus, Sarah, shouldn't you two be doing something useful?" he asked.

They both grinned sheepishly and Argus pointed over Tracy's shoulder at the monitor.

"Okay, Tracy. So you wanted me to see some satellite passes. What's up?"

"I wouldn't expect a manager to spot the problem here," she snorted.

She really was a lovely lady. Shame she was so damn good at her job. People management classes were developed specifically to deal with this chick.

"I did your job for ten years, Tracy." She grunted. He resigned himself. "Let me take a look."

At first, nothing really popped out. She had eight different windows open, showing screen captures from various satellite feeds in the last week. Julius tried not to assume what was coming next. Eight was a key number recently.

The shot over Antarctica was particularly exciting.

"So what do you guys think?" he asked, still cycling through all of the windows.

"Anomalies," Tracy announced.

You don't say.

"You're going to have to do better than that if you want my job, Tracy."

"These blips show intense heat activity in very remote areas."

"I can read a satellite display, too," Julius said, loving every minute of driving Tracy crazy.

"I don't think that part of Antarctica has a small, underground industrial complex, so *something* hot obviously crashed there. I mean, these readings are off the graph."

Julius looked to the two spectators, which drove Tracy nuts.

"You guys connect the dots yet?"

Tracy heaved a great sigh and said, "They popped up around the same time that the Angels appeared."

Oh, she was good.

"So?"

"Seriously, Julius?" she blurted, incredulous. He just looked at her innocently, despite wanting to jump out of his skin with excitement. "They're spaceships."

Argus stifled a laugh. Sarah elbowed him in the ribs, and Tracy added a disparaging look for good measure. So apparently Julius's team of analysts hadn't come to a consensus. Maybe it would've been easier if any of them had the same information that Mr. Morris had entrusted to him alone. That would take away from the fun, though.

"I take it that you disagree, Argus?"

"Yeah, I mean, think about it," the young man said. "There are what, six Angels in the world—"

"Two, if you don't count the four dead ones," Sarah interjected with a grin. Julius had picked up that she always had smiles for Argus. As long as he didn't catch them doing the dirty on the copier, he didn't care.

"Right, whatever. Point is: it's not eight."

"So what? There could be two more out there that we don't know about," added Tracy.

If only they knew.

"Good work team. You know the drill. Forward all that crap to me, purge it from your drives, then forget you ever saw it."

With a printout in hand, Julius stepped into the hallway. The bright corridors of the National Security Agency always took him by surprise after hours hidden away in his dark cave. He'd rather keep the lights on, but his team begged him to keep the lights low.

Apparently it helped the youth of the day operate. Julius was only thirty-five, but his direct reports made him feel like fifty. How could things change so quickly in the space of a decade?

The walk to his boss's office didn't take long. The man appreciated efficiency.

Julius knocked on the door.

"Come," came the one word response.

"Mr. Morris, I've got some satellite passes to show you."

Mr. Morris, all five-foot-three of him, stood to take the printout from Julius. The diminutive, balding middle manager didn't look like much, but Julius knew that he was a shrewd operator. Saying the guy had trust issues was a glaring understatement. Julius always watched his back for a potential knifing.

"I am sure I do not have to tell you what this is, Mr. Savage."

Julius didn't hear a question, but replied, "No, sir."

"This information is stolen property."

"Uh, who did we steal it from?"

"Not *we*, Mr. Savage. *Your* team stole it."

Julius kept calm on the outside, but his heart started racing a mile a minute.

"I don't understand, sir."

"Mr. Savage, these satellite shots are stored on a hidden, encrypted sector of the network."

Damn it, Tracy.

"Obviously you did not realize that, or you would not be here in my office," continued Mr. Morris.

Julius stood straight before his boss and tried to avoid looking down on the man. The guy hadn't offered him a seat, so he wasn't taking one.

"So what happens now, sir?" Julius knew the tension had crept into his voice.

After giving Julius a few seconds to contemplate hara-kiri, Mr. Morris smiled for the first time in Julius's experience.

"We are in the intelligence industry, Mr. Savage, and your young apprentice seems even more adept than you at that age. I am quite impressed."

Julius relaxed a touch, but waited for the inevitable hammer to fall. Mr. Morris's smile had no glee behind it.

"We will, of course, be transferring Tracy Tam into a more suitable role for her skill set."

Well, there it was. Could've been worse.

"And you need to forget that you saw these pictures. These are extremely classified and far beyond your pay grade."

"Sir, real Angels don't need spaceships."

"What's your point?"

"People need to know about this."

"Who?"

Julius furrowed his brow.

"Everyone."

"Do I need to remind you about the NDA that you sign on a yearly basis?"

"The public don't need to know about everything we do, but this—"

"There are no 'buts' here, Mr. Savage. Get back to work, and do *not* go rogue over this. It is *not* worth it. I will make sure of that."

Julius didn't move.

"Is there a problem, Mr. Savage?"

"No, sir."

Mr. Morris sat down and picked up a pen, ready to continue whatever task Julius had interrupted with his office visit. Without looking up, his boss barked, "Then why are you still in my office?"

Chapter 33

How did I end up here?

Baird once again looked around the opulent sitting room of Malvin Kent. The unusual name had come from the combination of the names of his two grandfathers, Malcolm Kent and Kelvin Rutherford, giants of industries past. A childhood full of jests towards his uncommon name had given way to startling success in his own right. Of course, a business had a greater chance of success when bankrolled by a billion dollars worth of inheritance.

All of this Kent had revealed in the first thirty minutes of the conversation. At the present moment, the elderly gentleman had excused himself to answer the call of nature. Baird didn't look forward to reaching eighty-five years old. The man he dealt with today had infinite resources available, yet couldn't even go for a piss unattended by his nurse.

This would be an easy sell. These powerful men that Murphy sent Baird to chat up offered very little resistance to the proposition. They need only give one hundred million dollars, and Celestius would make sure that the fogies would be cured of any and all ailments within forty-eight hours of the money clearing. To a guy like Kent, a hundred million wasn't even close to his total net worth, so Baird didn't foresee any problems. Murphy had definitely done diligent research on all these old fogies.

The large oak door opened and Kent reappeared, shuffling his aching feet across the Persian rug covering an antique hardwood floor. Baird quickly adopted the "open" look that his appearance coach insisted upon: sit comfortably, don't fold his arms, and smile. Always smile.

Easier said than done. His out-of-practice cheeks hurt like hell from all the smiling.

Kent sat down in his black leather recliner with a huff. Baird waited patiently while the older gentleman caught his breath. The attendant stared at Baird accusatorily. Was that because Baird's visit had caused physical distress to the patient, or was it because the attendant's services would no longer be needed if and when Kent accepted the proposal? Baird wasn't supposed to discuss these matters in front of *anyone*, but Kent had insisted his nurse stay, as his heart could peg out at any moment. Baird had pointed out that he was a medical doctor, but Kent had only snorted in response. The older men got, the less they gave a crap about social graces.

"Alright, Baird, you've explained the medical research that your company's done on these Angels, and I'm satisfied."

The joke of *that* was that even Baird didn't understand a single bit of the research, so it was highly unlikely that Kent did. That hardly mattered. As long as the codger signed up with the program, Baird would continue to receive an astronomical salary.

"Just one question remains, son," Kent continued. "How long do I have?"

Baird didn't like where this was going, but tried not to let his smile slip.

"How long until you can see the Angel? Well, as shown in the marketing materials, we'd get you out there in—"

Kent interrupted him.

"No, son. You misunderstand. When will I disappear like all those other folks who see the Angels?"

Damn it.

Baird had hoped to avoid this discussion. Every time it was such a chore.

"There's no established link between the healing process of the Angel and the disappearances, Mr. Kent. It's all coincidental, or—"

"Bullshit. Just level with me here, son. I got a lot of things to line up for after my healing, and I want to know how long I should plan ahead for."

"I can assure you—"

Kent held up a hand, hushing Baird.

"This conversation's over if you won't play ball with me."

Baird sat in silence for a moment, his happy demeanor faltering while the cogs turned at a million miles an hour in his head. Celestius had promised Baird that the Angels didn't cause the disappearances. They had stacks of research and data to support the claim. The company's private investigators had uncovered hundreds of viable explanations for why people were vanishing. Everything was aboveboard, otherwise Baird would've walked away from the insane amount of money they'd offered him to sell this product.

He would've walked away. Right?

Now Baird was faced with a choice. Either he could stick to the truth as he knew it, and risk losing this customer, or just agree with the guy and move forward.

What was the worst that could happen?

Kent looked at Baird expectantly, but as the Scotsman started to speak, his common sense caught up with him. If he admitted that Celestius was selling a service that they knew caused harm to people two weeks down the line, all kinds of problems would be slapping *him* in the face. No, he couldn't do that. Better to upset Murphy on this one rather than make a huge blunder. If this business fell apart, it would be Baird left holding the bag. *He* was the spokesman.

Still, it was hard to remember to *not* trust the hand that was feeding him.

Baird nodded to Kent and stood up, ready to head for the door.

"Whoa, whoa, whoa there," exclaimed Kent, each breath more ragged than the last. "Let's not be too hasty there, son. Sit back down so that we can work this out."

Once Baird was seated again, the old man leaned forward and produced a pen from his jacket.

"I'll just assume I have one week to go. Where do I sign?"

Chapter 34

Nobody else in the room knew what'd happened. None of them would ever know. The assassination attempt was their little secret.

Well, at least Jackson considered it to be a botched hit job. It wasn't every day that a car flew into a crowd of people in broad daylight. Jackson continued to work on Smith, trying to convince him, but it wasn't working. Yet. The big man was either in denial or just playing devil's advocate.

"Okay, I might have something here, Mark."

Jackson looked up from his desk.

"You ever hear of a company called *Celestius*?"

"No, but that's damn close to Celest."

Smith nodded.

"I thought so, too, so I looked them up. Pharmaceutical company based in Houston. Did that big cancer drug, Inverestium, a couple of years back. Stock set some kind of a record after that homerun."

"Okay, Matt, but what's that got to do with Emily? Or us?"

"Well, one of the little details that got lost in our notes kinda ties this together."

Jackson stared at his colleague, waiting for the other shoe to drop, but Smith seemed intent on reading something on his desk. What the hell was it with people not completing a whole damn thought?

"Matt."

"What?"

"What detail?"

Smith finally looked up.

"Oh, right, sorry. Was just reading something. Uh, yeah, the detail. She called and left us a message that one time. Didn't think much of it then, but she described the font on the 'c' in Celest."

"Right, I remember. She said that it looked like it had a vine twisted around the first letter."

In response, Smith turned his laptop towards Jackson.

"A fucking snake," Jackson groaned.

"Yup. Looks like we got a match."

"So what else you got?"

Now Smith had a big grin. Obviously this was something good.

"I went to high school with the CEO."

"Bullshit."

"Nope. Swear to God."

"So who is it?" Jackson asked, still not buying it.

"David Murphy. We're both from Houston."

"There's got to be a lot of guys called David Murphy from Houston. How do you know it's him?"

"Not every David Murphy has a dad who paid for the high school's football stadium."

Jackson had to agree that that would be pretty memorable.

"Also, the guy sucked at quarterback, but his dad was the biggest donor, so David was QB."

"Let me guess, you were O-line?"

Smith flexed his giant arms.

"You bet your skinny ass I was."

Jackson just smiled as he shook his head.

"Okay, but do you know anything that might help us here?" he asked.

Smith leaned back in his chair and Jackson heard the lumbar support groaning under the strain. The guy had broken a few office chairs in his time, and each time Jackson had laughed his ass off. Smith was a good sport about it.

After searching the dusty old memory banks, Smith told Jackson about Murphy's brother.

"I can't remember the guy's name. I don't even think it was a real brother. A half-brother, I think. Different last name."

"I can hit up some ancestry websites if I really want to know this stuff, Matt."

"Just let me finish. This guy was full crazy. Totally nuts. Played linebacker. Hospitalized three or four quarterbacks in one season. Guy was a couple years older, if I remember right.

"Anyway, I'm pretty sure he went off and joined the Army. Never heard about him again, but that doesn't mean he's not still around."

Jackson let the information digest. What could he glean from all of it? Surely *something* useful was in there. Just as he thought of a frightening scenario, Smith beat him to the punch.

"Man, you're slipping in your old age, Mark. A few years ago, you'd have knocked this one out of the park already. Think about it. Murphy owns a medical drug company that is investigating a guy who saw an Angel. Lady who goes to the press dies soon after. Murphy has a psychotic brother who has military training."

"That's a lot of speculation for a guy who doesn't even believe the driver of that car was trying to kill us."

With a grim look, Smith said, "Let's say that I'm leaning over on that side of the fence now."

Jackson was troubled. He leaned in over the desk to talk more quietly.

"That's not a pretty picture you've painted for us, Matt. If you're right, we have a nutcase soldier out to get us."

Both men sat for a while, deep in thought. Sometimes life got heavy enough that the next course of action wasn't even an immediate concern. Sometimes a guy just needed to take a step back and think about everything.

Jackson took the lead.

"So you think you have an *in* here? Can you just call this David Murphy guy up and ask him to grab a beer?"

"We got on okay in high school, but that was a long time ago. Seems like I could try."

That was good enough for Jackson. He turned back to his computer and brought up the homepage for Celestius. If nothing else, the website was sharp. These guys had dropped some serious coin on the face that they presented to the world. That made sense. If Jackson was experimenting cancer drugs on cute little bunnies and kitties, he'd try to make sure the public focused on how colorful and user-friendly the website was. Maybe he should've gone into marketing instead of journalism. It definitely couldn't pay any worse.

The thought of another cup-noodle dinner didn't inspire Jackson's appetite, but there wasn't much choice. He didn't have time or money to splurge on sustenance. Smith always said that quitting smoking would help free up some cash. Jackson disagreed, saying that he'd need to take up heroin or cocaine just to get over his potentially homicide-inducing nicotine addiction.

In fact, the last cigarette in his last pack was calling his name. He stood up and was heading to the door when Smith called him back over.

"You think these things are aliens?" Smith whispered.

"What things?" Jackson asked, confused.

"Keep your voice down." Smith looked over both shoulders briefly, scanning the room for any eavesdroppers. "The Angels, Mark."

"What're you talking about?"

"Think about this. What if Josh Greaves was abducted from the apartment when Emily got up to get a drink in the middle of the night?"

"Have you lost your damn mind, Matt?"

"No, it's just... Well, it's just all too crazy."

"No, *you're* just too crazy," Jackson stated flatly, loud enough for everyone to hear. Faces all over the office turned to see what was going on. Smith looked at Jackson very disapprovingly. Jackson shrugged and headed for the door, but turned as he opened it.

"Next time, don't interrupt my smoke break unless there's a black sedan heading my way. Okay?"

Chapter 35

A blank, sterile landscape blurred all around Knight as he fought to keep his eyes open. Even in his deepest alcoholic binge, he'd never felt so fuzzy, so disoriented. So drunk. His head slowly rolled from side to side, straining his physical limitations, yet he felt no frustration at his inability to function. Overall, he felt great. Warm sensations coursed through his neck and face, alleviating all worry.

A sudden movement in his peripheral vision took Knight by surprise, but his eyes wouldn't track the dark blob floating across the room. Very quickly, Knight stopped caring. Heavy eyelids forced themselves shut, ignoring Knight's weak protests.

Behind his closed eyes, Knight witnessed the dream again. There wasn't really another description for it. He was just along for the ride, totally powerless to affect the outcome. Over and over again he watched the deaths of his co-workers, some closer friends than others, some just relative strangers. That didn't matter, though. When a brother died, it didn't matter if Knight hated the guy's guts or not, *someone* would pay.

The closing moments of the dream faded into the indistinct shapes of what Knight established to be a hospital room. This time, his eyes focused long enough to make out the bed that he lay propped up on. An IV protruded from his arm, and somewhere an EKG was beeping away at a slow, steady pace. His sight started to fail as the drugs exerted their power over him again, the wave of calm washing away his anxiety. At the last second of consciousness, that damn dark blob scooted across the room and disappeared.

And then Knight was staring at the stark room in absolute clarity. He could only tell that significant time had passed by the darkened light piercing through the shutters on the window. To Knight it had only felt like a particularly long blink.

The doctor at the foot of the bed looked up from his chart and smiled. He held up a finger and glided from the room.

Must be the dark blob.

Knight sat in solitude for a few minutes before a nurse stopped by to check on his IV and to ask him the usual questions posed to a recently unconscious patient. He remembered his name, he knew where he was, but no, he couldn't tell the nurse about his last memory before passing out. When the nurse gave him the pitying eyes, he pushed his head back into his pillow and responded, "Oh, don't' worry. I remember it just fine. I just can't tell *you* about it."

With an unprofessional *hmph*, the nurse marched out of the room. Knight opened his eyes in time to see the nurse brush past Connor in the doorway. So that was where the doctor kept running off to. He probably had orders to summon Connor as soon as Knight woke up.

How nice of him.

Before Connor could open his mouth, Knight was on him.

"Where is Karen?"

"Wh—"

"Where. Is. Karen?"

Connor smiled and leaned forward onto the rail at the end of Knight's bed.

"I see that the meds are wearing off, Andy."

"Yeah, and someone's going to find out my fist still works if you don't tell me where Karen is."

The smile dropped.

"Look, Andy. We tried to find her—"

"*Tried?* What the hell does that mean?" Now Knight's heart monitor was beeping faster and faster. The irritating noise only drove his fury as it eeked past the wall of calm and tranquility erected by the pain meds.

"You need to calm down, Andy," Connor said, more sternly. "We'll find her."

Knight just stared angrily at his feet, hidden under the sheets. He *really* wanted to kick something. Something fragile. Something expensive.

"Do you know where she could be?"

That was a very good question.

"No," Knight said, a little uneasy now. His anger was quickly making way for anxiety. "I haven't heard from her since the other day."

Connor seemed to sense Knight's tension. He reached out a hand to Knight's foot, which was the weirdest empathetic gesture Knight had ever received from another man. That didn't seem to matter so much. Karen's disappearance took all of Knight's attention as another wave of chemical bliss enveloped him. Slowly his thoughts turned back to the dream, but this time he wasn't asleep.

With a pat on Knight's leg, Connor withdrew his hand and got down to business.

"Andy, we've got to go through a few things from the hospital."

The hospital. Right, the dream.

"I already know what happened, Mike."

Knight was aware that he was drifting around the room. His head felt so heavy, but not in a bad way. Keeping his head upright seemed impossible, like spinning a large plate on top of a thin stick.

Connor interrupted Knight's reverie.

"We don't have time for this, Andy. I need you lucid."

With that, there was a tug on his arm. Knight looked in that direction, the process of which took far too long. He didn't care. He didn't even care when he saw the red trickle leaking across his forearm and running down onto the floor. That sucked for whoever had to clean that mess up.

"This bastard who killed half your guys, we got some video of him from the CCTV in the hospital. Not the best quality, but good enough to scare the shit out of me."

"He slit their throats, Mike."

Connor froze for a moment, his eyes suddenly sad.

"Right. That he did."

Connor's voice came from all around, but from nowhere in particular. Knight's head lolled around, searching for the noise source. A slap on the leg brought him back to focusing on Connor at the end of the bed. How had Connor gotten way over there?

"Pay attention, Andy. Do you know you walked right past this guy?"

The dream played back in his head. Walking down the stairs and seeing himself and Lehoski waiting at a doorway. How was Lehoski doing anyway? Knight's best friend's wellbeing started to form into a question for Connor, but that train was too slow leaving the station. Some of the dots connected, and coincidentally, a raging headache started to set in. The psychotic leprechauns were back to their old tricks and throwing sledgehammers around between his ears.

Oh yeah, Connor had unplugged his IV.

Damn it.

Knight was surprised by how fast the pain came on. The meds had faded far too quickly, or maybe time had just gotten screwed up while Knight was high. Either way, he couldn't even open his eyelids. The bright white lights burned his eyes, like he was staring into the sun.

"Yeah, I know. Guy looked like a doctor," Knight said.

"How the hell did you know that?" asked Connor, shocked.

Knight waved for Connor to continue the story.

"This is important, Andy," Connor snapped. "You just corroborated Kestrel's story, and I know you didn't talk to him since the incident."

Knight lifted his hands to his face. Pain darted through multiple points in his limbs. Had a car run him over? He felt broken.

At least he was alive.

He dropped his hands.

"You're probably going to tell me next that Tango Delta is a nine or ten-foot tall tin man. Right, Mike?"

Now Connor just looked confused.

"Wait, Andy," he stammered. "Are you saying that you saw this thing? In its true form?"

"Not exactly," Knight said.

He quickly ran through what he knew, ignoring Connor's incessant questions. The whole dream sounded much more terrible verbalized. Witnessing the death of friends repeatedly hadn't numbed Knight, which he would've thought it would, hoped it would.

"You realize how crazy this sounds, right, Andy?"

"I'm not making this up."

"Maybe the drugs got to you while you were out."

"Mike, think about it. How would I know all this shit?"

Connor's face paled as he stared at the wall above Knight's head.

"So you think Tango Delta transferred its memories to you?" Connor finally asked, sitting down in the chair next to Knight's bed. The old guy looked about one more outlandish revelation away from fainting.

"It seems that way," Knight said. "I'm guessing that's why my head hurts so damn much."

Connor laughed mirthlessly.

"Or because you got thrown across the room when that grenade went off," he explained. "There's a whole slew of cameras set up in that OR for recording surgeries. They'd been using them to record some of the Angel's healings, so we caught most of the incident."

Knight just sat in silence, resisting the urge to wince at the pain building behind his forehead. Connor leaned forward.

"You did a brave thing there, Andy," he said.

"What're you talking about?"

"Jumping on that grenade. Or trying to, at least."

"Yeah, didn't do much good," Knight said, wincing. "I didn't make it."

Connor stood.

"No one else even tried. Rookies probably shit their pants when that device hit the floor. This is why you're so important, Andy. *Someone's* got to keep their head in those situations."

"Whatever."

A stillness hung in the room, but a hectic rave was taking place within Knight's brain cavity. Talking provided a decent enough distraction.

"So the Angel's gone, right?"

Connor nodded.

"Damn."

More silence passed.

"So you think this thing can disguise itself?" Knight asked, a bit uneasy at the thought.

"Considering the video footage shows something different to eyewitness reports, intel is saying that it can project images into a person's head, disguising it from people nearby. In a weird way, it sort of makes sense when you take into account the information dump into your brain. This thing has some serious mental powers."

"That's pretty handy."

"Agreed. Wish we had that kind of technology."

Knight tried to straighten up a bit in the bed. A train of hurt coasted across his shoulders and neck. Connor jumped forward to assist.

"Right," Knight grunted. "But who does have that kind of tech?"

Connor shrugged and replied, "We have no idea."

Knight looked at his old friend and said, "Well, we also don't have any ten-foot tall terrorists on the watch lists right now, so I'm leaning in a different direction here."

"Which direction's that, Andy?"

"It's an alien."

"Tango Delta? We've considered it. Hard to digest, even with the evidence we're looking at."

"Not just Delta," Knight said, grimacing in pain just with the movement of his jaw. "I'm talking about the Angels, too."

Connor nodded, keeping his thoughts to himself. After a pause, he called for the nurse.

The nurse entered the room, raised an eyebrow at the broken intravenous connection, but kept quiet. After a quick sterilization, Knight's IV was reinserted and the calming tones of morphine quickly took effect. Part of Knight wanted to stay sharp, to be tough, but with the drugs pushing the pain out of his body, the painkillers sounded more and more like a great idea.

"Time for you to relax, Andy. It's a lot to process all at once," Connor said. "In the meantime, we're going to get you home."

Connor paused on his way out the door to add, "And we'll find Karen."

Chapter 36

"Welcome to this special edition of World News Events. I'm Michelle Morioka."

In the electronics department of a giant department store, more and more people started to crowd in around the live feed of the increasingly popular cable news show. Ever since the remarkable appearance of the Angels, international news had exploded, especially as the mysterious creatures started dying.

"On tonight's show, I'll be joined by a panel of experts on the current world situation, but first—"

The pretty, perfectly coifed anchor turned to a new camera, indicating the imminence of important news.

"People the world over are going missing in alarming numbers, and now the civilian populations of many countries are speaking out."

The crowd of shoppers watched as Ms. Morioka provided narration behind shocking video feeds from various locations around the world. Most onlookers got sucked into the footage so deeply that only snippets of the woman's strong voice had any impact. The general explanation sufficed.

In all of the countries that had counted themselves blessed with an Angel, massive riots had now broken out. The violence against the governments was unprecedented, as many of the protestors blamed their governments for allowing people access to the Angels without determining the risks. Statistics darted across the television screen, indicating the popular belief that most of the sudden disappearances of loved ones could be tied directly to contact with the Angel, or to contact with someone who had already received treatment from an Angel.

Another commonly held opinion was that the governments of the world had kidnapped all people who had seen an Angel. Many civilians demanded that the governments release these innocent victims from prison. Others insisted that the governments had already culled anyone who'd seen an Angel.

The shot switched back to the studio, where Michelle introduced her guests to the viewers.

"Tonight I'm joined by economic analyst Craig Erikson, world-renowned pastor Martin Daniels, and our good friend, Dr. Amy Baranowski. Thank you all for joining us this evening."

The crowd watched as the camera provided a quick shot of each participant, who each gave the obligatory nod to their host. Michelle reiterated the disturbingly high rate of disappearances of those who'd come into contact with an Angel, before yielding the floor to Craig Erikson.

"Yes, Michelle, this is incredibly disturbing," he began. This was obviously not his first television appearance, and he maintained eye contact with the host instead of staring directly into one of the cameras. "I will seem cold and heartless here, but all of these people burning down their cities in protest are really missing the big picture. They're upset that their friends and family are going missing, but this is starting to go beyond personal grief.

"What we're seeing now is a situation where *too* many essential members of society are going missing. I'm only able to talk about the U.S. and the UK, since Kenya and China haven't released much information, but I would suspect it's the same. What we see now is that our ability to function as a civilization is starting to feel the strain of so many people dropping off the face of the planet.

"This is simply not sustainable, economically speaking. We need people in their jobs, doing the work that keeps our society running. Most of the people who visited the Angels directly were terminally ill patients seeking healing. They weren't typically highly contributing members of society. They relied on their caregivers. Now we are seeing that those same caregivers aren't showing up for work anymore, and we can't find them."

Michelle interrupted him as soon as he paused for a breath.

"So you're saying that these caregivers are far more important than most people would assume?"

"Absolutely," Erikson answered. "Think about it. Who is going to work harder than someone who *needs* a job to support a dying family member? That kind of motivation isn't natural in our workforce, where, let's face it, most people are just cruising for a paycheck."

"Good point," Michelle said. "Now, what about rumors that so many of high society and the wealthy were given special access to the Angel? Do we know if those people have disappeared also?"

A few more passersby in the department store perked up at the mention of the wealthy. The audience now fully blocked a three-way intersection, obstructing the path for any potential television buyers. Half of the store clerks had joined the group already; not one made a move to disperse their fellow watchers.

"It was just a matter of time before those rumors started," Erikson said. "Their origin is probably with middle-class people who struggled to get a relative or a friend in to see the Angel. The assumption would be that their access was hindered due to a lack of financial resources. If only they could pay to see the Angel, then they'd be allowed right on through.

"But of course, that's ludicrous. Once again, I can't speak for other countries, but this is America. That kind of class warfare would never go unnoticed, or unpunished.

"In any case, our focus right now needs to be on identifying key job functions that are vacant right now, and then fill those jobs with qualified individuals. We can't afford to lose our entire workforce here, and the statistics show the rate of disappearance is *not* getting any better."

Michelle thanked the analyst for his time and brought Pastor Martin Daniels, live from Arizona, into the frame.

"Pastor Daniels, what are your thoughts on this mystery?" Michelle asked.

"First off, I apologize for not making it tonight in person. I'd originally planned on it, but the congregation here is growing by leaps and bounds each day, and I'm getting a bit overwhelmed with the demand for new services," explained Daniels. He laughed easily and added, "In fact, I have *two* late night sermons to give tonight, and another first thing in the morning."

"So you obviously attribute the swell in your numbers to the Angel phenomenon?"

"Oh yes, definitely," the pastor said. "I mean, sometimes God needs to reach down and give His people a firm slap in the face to get their attention. The Angels have had quite an impact on God's green Earth, and I don't think we can discount what's going on here."

"And what is going on here, Pastor Daniels?"

Even the nonbelievers in the department store audience felt gripped by the depth of devotion and focus in the pastor's eyes. His dramatic pause had many in the crowd leaning forward as the anticipation became almost unbearable.

"Simply put, Michelle, this is the Rapture," he announced firmly. *"That's* what's going on here."

"The Rapture, Pastor Daniels?" Michelle asked, with just a hint of skepticism passing through her mental filter.

"Michelle, the Bible is clear on this. We've known that we've been living in the End Times for a while now, and it should come as no surprise that in our age of decadence and debauchery, God would call His people home.

"The Angels are here to heal the sick and to save our souls. People see these miracles, and they finally believe in the truth: the Jesus truth. Just look at my congregation. We've quadrupled in size since the Angels showed up, and we were a pretty big church to begin with," Pastor Daniels said with a smile.

"So you're saying this is just a marketing tactic for God?" asked Dr. Amy Baranowski from off-camera, incredulity dripping from each word. The camera switched to her briefly, to catch her facial expression. No one watching cared to wonder why her microphone was even active while Daniels was talking.

The pastor's smile didn't falter.

"That's one way to look at it," he replied. "He's been in the advertisement business for a long time, but most people haven't been paying any attention."

"Right, the advertising business," Dr. Baranowski said evenly. "So was one of the goals of this ad campaign to end up with all the Angels dying? That doesn't seem like a very prominent show of power by an omnipotent being to me."

Now the pastor lost his smile and adopted a very serious tone.

"As I'm sure even you are aware, Doctor, spiritual warfare is nothing new."

"Spiritual warfare? Ha! So how are these 'spirits' of yours taking physical forms?" she said, not angrily, just in abject disbelief.

"In the same way that these Demons are taking a physical form to kill the Angels," stated Daniels. "I don't pretend to understand the logistics—"

"Right, the *logistics*," Baranowski cut in, talking over Daniels while the satellite feed tried to keep up. "You're going to sit there and talk about the logic behind imaginary friends of yours fighting against imaginary friends of your imaginary enemy?"

Not losing his temper, but also not taking such a berating lying down, Daniels replied, "Feel free to share your best explanation then, *doctor*."

After a slight hesitation on Dr. Baranowski's part, Michelle broke in and ended that segment of the show, thanking her guests one more time for their participation. After the brief dismissal, the camera focused in on Michelle once more.

"Now we turn to the United Kingdom, where organized protests are bursting out of control in every major city. Despite British Prime Minister George Strachan's attempts to appease the populace, his efforts have found little traction amongst the conflicting groups of protestors."

While Michelle continued the narrative, footage from every corner of the British Isles played. The scenes varied from formal marches in the streets, to youths lobbing Molotov cocktails at police officers.

"Many of the violent protestors are reportedly not affiliated with the original protests at all, but are merely taking advantage of an opportunity to commit various crimes, including arson and looting; however, a majority of those involved claim to have strong investment in their cause.

"On one side, protestors are upset that they have no access to the Angel. They demand that their loved ones receive the special treatment that only the Angel can provide. On the other side, people are upset that their loved ones were allowed to see the Angel in the first place, as they have now vanished suddenly. Rumors of clothing being left behind by the disappeared are unconfirmed at this time.

"Those fighting for the right to see the Angel have been totally shut out of the hospital in Glasgow, Scotland where the Angel has resided. This has led to rampant speculation that the Angel is no longer there. No reports of an attack, such as those seen in Kenya, China, Australia, Brazil, and now the U.S., have surfaced."

A shot of European naval vessels coasting through nondescript water appeared next to Michelle on the television.

"The buildup of European military assets around the United Kingdom is now in decline, as European leaders withdraw their aggressive stance. The island nation had been surrounded in recent weeks by an increasingly large number of naval vessels from around the continent. In response, the U.S. Navy was sent to fortify defensive positions around England and Scotland primarily.

"With the European forces now in withdrawal, questions are being raised about the meaning of the action. Do European leaders now consider the Angel not worth fighting over, due to the recent rash of mass disappearances? Or do the European leaders know something that the general public has not been made aware of yet? For example, is the Angel even in Glasgow anymore? Are the rumors true?

"As always, as soon as any news on the subject of the Angels arises, you can tune in here with us at World News Events to find out the very latest information."

The camera panned away slowly in a parting shot as Michelle Morioka gave her signoff and faded to a commercial for the dog food that dogs prefer.

Chapter 37

David Murphy sat at the desk in his study, doing nothing. The sensation was very strange, doing nothing. For the last two decades, he'd always been doing *something*. Or someone. Ha, that brought a smile to his face.

But he wasn't happy. He had a problem, one that he couldn't seem to solve despite his ample resources. Even reminiscing about the last few hours with that new escort he'd called in couldn't force the troubling situation from his focus. Hell, that was the whole point of her coming over. But no, he still wasn't happy. Not at all.

He scratched a fingernail idly at a nick in his desk. How had he never noticed this before? Maybe some of Marissa's gaudy jewelry had marred the finish. Glowering at the imperfection, he picked at it furiously, exacerbating his gloomy mood. Eventually he slammed his clenched fist down on the desk. The piece of shit would be replaced by lunch.

Of course, a slightly damaged desk wasn't the root cause of his anger. No, his rage was fueled by the knowledge that he was about to ask someone for help. That person was closer and dearer to him than any other human being, and Murphy had definitely assisted his brother innumerable times, but seeking the aid of others always tore Murphy up. He was an independent man. He ruled over a great pharmaceutical empire. He bedded every woman that he desired. He did *not* need help.

Except right now.

The phone seemed miles away as his hand reached for the receiver. Slowly he gripped the device and gingerly brought it to his ear. He really didn't want to do this, but it was the simplest way. He punched in the number and waited only two rings for the recipient to answer.

"Hello," the voice said.

"Hello, Shaggy," Murphy said.

"Still with the cartoon references, David?"

"Don't use my name on the phone."

"You done screwing that model yet?"

So his brother was keeping tabs on him now? That was interesting. He looked around the room aimlessly, as if he could spot a surveillance device with just a glance. Tomorrow he'd have the whole place swept for bugs. Again.

"I need a favor."

Silence.

"I need two reporters taken care of. Quietly."

"Don't you have people who do that for you, David?"

"Don't you ever listen? *Stop calling me that.*"

"Fine. I'm just tired of all the codename bullshit already," the voice snapped. "What've these two done?"

"That's irrelevant, but if you must know, they've been snooping around a little too closely for my liking."

"Must be serious if you're willing to employ the big guns."

Truthfully Murphy admitted, "My men failed miserably."

"They're not pros."

"I pay them enough to call them professionals."

"Money doesn't buy success when you hire idiots."

"Look, I helped you out very recently, if you recall," Murphy stated.

A pause.

"That's right. You did."

Murphy let the conversation simmer for a moment.

"So you can handle this, brother?" he asked, knowing the answer, finally glad to use some damn leverage in the exchange.

"Tell me their names, and then consider them gone."

And so Murphy did. Nowhere in his being could a trace of guilt be found, not even hidden in what could be considered a conscience. Two men had taken it upon themselves to investigate Celestius, and Murphy's plan was in too a delicate stage to risk any unneeded press. Like most aspects of Murphy's life, it was just business.

Plus, the tragic deaths of two members of the liberal media wouldn't leave so much as a skid mark on the underpants of society. Murphy was really doing the country yet another favor.

You're welcome, America.

Before his handset had even reached the phone cradle, his thoughts were already drifting to calling Marissa back over for round two. It was time to do *something*.

Chapter 38

She'd left him again. Knight hated to admit it, but it seemed like his sister-in-law had been right. Just thinking about that stupid woman roused the primal urge to put his fist through a wall.

Katie. That bitch.

Desperate to get out of that depressing hospital room, Knight had convinced Connor to let him recuperate from his relatively minor injuries at home. The amount of pain medication they'd pumped into him didn't really line up with the scrapes and burns he'd received from his encounter with the Demon. Could be that they wanted him sedated when they revealed his wife had gone missing.

He rubbed the back of his head gingerly. The knock back there had definitely been a good one. Even the warm sensations of the whisky in front of him didn't quite have enough potency to eradicate the pulsing thud in his skull, but it was a start. Thoughts of Karen running off with another man could've been exacerbating the headache just a tad.

Katie's snide remarks rattled around in his mind as he took another swallow straight from the bottle. Had his commitment to his work really driven his wife away? Had he failed in his duties as a husband? He'd thought Karen respected his occupation, or at least what she thought his occupation was. Perhaps his job had been an easier pill to swallow when she'd known he was a soldier, risking life and limb for her country. Maybe she just didn't have the same patience to wait around for a mere military consultant.

As if she'd know what that really meant anyway.

Another pull on the bottle caused an all too familiar warming down in his chest. As much as he would've loved to dive right back into the booze, he slid the bottle away. His was a dangerous path. What if Karen showed back up again randomly, claiming she'd been wrong, she'd made a mistake, and she was so sorry for it all? That remorseful attitude would change really quickly if she found a stumbling drunk waiting for her.

None of it made any sense, though. Her car was there in the driveway. All of her things were still in the house. Knight had even found her cell phone, *not* set on silent. And to top it all off, when he'd arrived home, the shower had been running for no reason. She'd just up and disappeared, as if into thin air. It just didn't add up. Had she really just ditched her entire life to run off with this so-called *therapist?* Maybe the Angel caused people to go nuts; had the government researched these things before unveiling them to the public?

Anger boiled inside, partially heated by the alcohol roiling around in his empty stomach. Why hadn't his damn private investigator warned him about this? Knight wasn't paying Klotzer to sit on his greasy ass doing nothing. He should've picked up on this long ago. Winston Klotzer's name still showed up in the recent call history of Knight's cell phone, a sad indicator of Knight's lack of social life. He tapped the number and waited for the answer.

"Mr. Knight—"

"Shut up, Winston," Knight barked, leaping well over a line that he could've avoided crossing. "Why didn't you tell me that Karen was leaving?"

"I—"

"Don't lie to me," Knight said. "I'm paying you good money here."

"Look, Mr. Knight," Klotzer said. "I understand you're upset, but I need you to calm down."

"Calm down? *Calm* down?"

"Yes, Mr. Knight. You've been drinking, and you need to cool it."

"You're walking a dangerous line here," Knight growled. "This isn't about me here."

"Yes, it is. It's all about you, Mr. Knight," Klotzer explained. "Well, and this here information I got for you."

Knight stopped jumping down the guy's throat for a moment. What information could Klotzer have? Some rational explanation for his wife's disappearance could've gone a long way, but suddenly a heavy burden fell on Knight like a ton of bricks. The reality of his plight felt like he was on the wrong side of the tree when someone yelled, "Timber."

"Sorry I blew up there, Winston," Knight said, embarrassment looming over his anger. "I'm screwed up right now."

"Don't worry about it," the P.I. said, dismissing any slight. "But you need to see this stuff."

"It doesn't matter anymore, Winston."

"Come on, sure it does. You know my policy of not discussing client information over the phone, so why don't we meet, and we can go through this stuff together?" Klotzer asked, as if the two were best friends.

"No," Knight said sullenly. "She's already gone. What good's it going to do to rehash it all?"

"Okay, okay. I'm just gonna send it to that mailbox address you gave me back at the start. Should have it tomorrow."

Knight leaned back on the sofa and sighed loudly at the ceiling.

"I don't care," he said finally. "Whatever."

After a brief pause, Klotzer said, "Mr. Knight, cheer up. I know you're hurting now, but it's not the end of the world. Relax. Watch some TV or something. Just avoid the news."

The P.I. was obviously referring to all the news reports of people vanishing a week after receiving the Angel's touch. On a good day, Knight could easily discount the information as scare-mongering. On a day like today, he just didn't want to think about it at all. There was no Rapture. His wife was just fucking missing, and there was a plausible reason for it. Plus, it had only been a few days for her, not a week, if Knight could even choke down any of that religious bullshit.

"Bye, Winston."

After ending the call, Knight tossed his phone into the recliner to his right. Five minutes ago he'd have rocketed a fastball straight through the window, but now he just felt defeated. What did any of it matter now? Karen was gone, and he was still there, sitting on the couch she'd picked out. He rubbed a hand across the soft fabric.

Furniture had never been his thing, and the price tag had shocked him, despite his ample earnings, but still, Karen knew what she was doing. This was a fantastic sofa.

But like everything else in his damn house, what did it matter if he was there on his own?

Some air, that's what he needed. A bit of separation from the memories of his wife's eye for interior design would help. With that, he grabbed the whisky off the coffee table and headed for the back deck. That was his realm, untouched by any female influences. A built-in grill, some simple chairs, and a deck were all that he needed back there. Yeah, that sounded good.

Before he'd reached the back door, his work phone rang loudly in the empty house. Knight actually jumped at the sudden sound, so wrapped up in his thoughts that the slightest noise had caught him off guard. He stared at the small device, wondering what Connor wanted. Knight felt like he'd only just gotten home. Was his boss calling to check up on him, or calling because he already had a task for him? Either way, Knight knew he couldn't ignore the call. He put the bottle down and grabbed the phone.

"Rook," Knight said after answering.

"How you holding up?" Connor asked, genuine concern in his voice.

"Fine."

Both men weighed the silence, an unspoken exchange taking place. Knight wasn't *fine*, but they both knew that.

"Rook, we've got a job for you."

"Great."

"You know I want you to rest, to get all your ducks in a row, but this is a matter of national security," Connor said.

Knight had never turned down a mission in his life. That would've been a sign of weakness, of cowardice. But his current emotional state was ragged, even a bit fragile. Phalanx needed Rook, a decisive man of action, a leader who got shit done. Could Knight fulfill that role? And there was still the question of why Connor was specifically asking *him* to run this op.

"Why don't you send someone who wasn't blown up twenty-four hours ago, Condor?"

"Albatross asked for the best," Connor replied. "He asked for you."

"Playing to my ego won't get you very far, boss."

"This is a big deal, Rook. There will be significant bonus on this one."

"I already make enough money to support a single guy."

"Still no sign of her?" Connor's tone had changed slightly with this question. Rook ignored him.

"When do I need to be back at base?" he asked instead. Looked like he'd have to get his shit together, cancel his pity party, and get his ass in gear. At a minimum, the distraction would do him some good, help him forget about Karen.

"You're to go directly to Bergstrom. Cardinal will meet you there with further instructions."

With no witty sign-off, or even a simple goodbye, Rook hung up the phone and went to grab his gear. Flung far from his mind, an open bottle of whisky stood defiantly on the dining room table.

Rook didn't even glance in its general direction as he left the house and headed for Austin-Bergstrom airport.

Chapter 39

In the wee hours of the next day, Rook stood inside another man's house, decked out from head to toe in dark grey. The ultra-flexible suit was specifically designed to contain all traces of the user, allowing them freedom to roam around without leaving DNA all over the place. It reminded him of the Tyvek suits he'd seen forensic investigators wearing at crime scenes in TV shows, only not so baggy. Under the suit, he wore CSPBA, or Concealable Stab-Protective Body Armor, standard issue for defense against small-caliber weapons and knives. Perfect attire for the kind of work Condor had assigned to Rook.

From his perch near the front door, Rook could see Cardinal, a fellow Phalanx operator, hovering across the open downstairs area. The large man, garbed identically to Rook, was covering the backdoor, the only other entrance to the house. In a car outside, Bluejay monitored the street, awaiting their mark.

Whereas most of the soldiers in Phalanx had chosen single-word designators, Bluejay had gone with a complex name that had to be amalgamated in order to meet company standards. He was out of the military, but Rook still couldn't get away from inane bureaucracy.

All three men kept to themselves, which was perfect for Rook. He had nothing to say.

Breaking into the home had been a breeze after remotely deactivating the burglar alarm. One of the techies at the Fort had hacked the code for the alarm and programmed it into a key fob for Rook. To avoid spooking their target, Rook had then rearmed the alarm, but with the interior motion sensors deactivated. Condor had promised that the target didn't have automatic alarm activity notifications being sent straight to his phone.

Rook had had limited exposure to spies over the years, but his current target was by far the least paranoid of the bunch. If anyone played with the alarm at Rook's home, he sure as hell knew about it immediately. Then he'd drive home with a few friends to make sure the intruder suffered some old fashioned hospitality.

Prior to boarding the flight from Austin, Cardinal had passed Rook a note detailing the login credentials to the online workspace for this mission. Using his company phone, Rook had accessed the secure server and read his orders. The specifics may have turned the stomachs of lesser men, or at least gone against the conscience of the layman, but Rook understood the situation. He'd fought for his country before and had seen firsthand the results of traitorous bastards giving the enemy intel on friendly positions and movements. Now he had a chance to root out a mole and mete out some honest justice, which differed from the charades exhibited in court rooms.

"Movement."

Bluejay's voice in his headset quickened Rook's pulse just a touch, just enough to know that he was still human. A healthy amount of tension would help him react quickly, instinctively. Too much excitement would lead to a mistake.

"White sedan approaching from north end of street," Bluejay continued. After a few seconds, Rook heard the telltale sounds of a car pulling into the driveway just on the other side of the front door. Bluejay confirmed. "Looks like our guy."

Cardinal snuck across the small room and took up a post just inside the kitchen. He was hidden from view from the front door, but close enough to help Rook when needed. A car door closed outside, the sound muffled by the structure of the house.

"Target approaching front door," Bluejay said. He counted off, "Three... two... one..."

Bang on time, a key entered the lock. Rook took a deep breath, slowly exhaled as the door swung inward towards him. With no glass in the door, and no glass on the wall next to it, the target didn't even notice Rook's looming presence while stepping into the house and closing the door behind him. Eyes already adjusted to the low light, Rook waited for the smaller man to reach for the alarm panel, which beeped frequently to ward off less motivated intruders. Rook's heart thumped in his skull, despite his breathing exercise, as his eyes bored into the back of his prey. This man had no idea how close to death he stood right now. Was Rook a bad man for secretly getting a buzz from the power he held over another human life in that moment?

Just before the target's fingers touched the buttons on the alarm panel, Rook launched from the shadows and tackled the target to the floor. The smaller man squealed in shock as Rook flipped him onto his stomach and easily manhandled his wrists into padded plastic cuffs. It wouldn't do for the man to have blatant evidence of restraint on his body prior to his demise.

Rook hauled the traumatized man to his feet and nodded to Cardinal, who had already stepped from the kitchen to disable the alarm and lock the front door. No need for any other unwanted visitors at this time of night. The two Phalanx operators whisked their docile captive to the center of the living room. Whether the shock of his assault had worn off or whether the target's eyes had adjusted enough to reveal the noose hanging from the ceiling fan, Rook would never know, but the small man started to struggle like a cornered wolverine. An end table flew across the room, its contents skittering into the dark. Cardinal caught a flailing heel in the shin. And that was enough of that. A meaty fist plowed into the spy's defenseless gut, leaving him wheezing and gasping for air.

Ever the professional, Cardinal stopped at just one punch. Some Phalanx members would've mindlessly beaten the subject to a bloody pulp, but that was why Cardinal and Rook were here, and those guys weren't. Rook hoped the big man had taken enough off the punch not to cause too much internal damage that would show up in autopsy. Of course, with this little bastard's history, it wasn't hard to believe someone had sucker-punched him earlier in the day.

Before they could move the target into position, Rook's cell phone vibrated to denote a received text message. He read intently for a moment as Cardinal kept one eye on him and one eye on the moaning captive. Rook turned to his partner.

"Damn it. Team Two's done already," Rook said, glaring at his objective. "Let's finish this spying piece of shit and get out of here."

Cardinal nodded. Their mark didn't struggle violently, but his head came up and he tried to wiggle backwards, away from his fate.

"Spying? Oh shit, oh shit, oh shit," he exclaimed, squirming in a panic. "You guys killed Smith, didn't you?"

Even in the dim light, Rook could tell the face of the man going by "Mark Jackson" had turned ashen with fright.

Good.

After neither man responded, the target spewed forth all manner of threats, promises, indictments, but like all of his kind, he eventually fell back on begging, pleading, lying.

You'll find no mercy in me, you piece of shit.

"Let's get this done," Rook said. Cardinal nodded.

With very little effort, the two soldiers lifted the criminal onto a chair. The soon-to-be-deceased writhed around and kicked the chair over. Rook and his partner let the idiot fall awkwardly to the ground. While Cardinal retrieved and repositioned the chair under the noose, Rook lifted the small man off the ground by the front of his shirt.

"Oh god, my shoulder," he cried. "I think it's dislocated."

This was unbelievable. Rook grabbed the man's upper arm and forcibly jerked it to the side. A cry left the man's lips, but the shoulder joint was still in one piece. The guy was fine. Well, as fine as a death row inmate could be.

"I'm starting to think this suicide should be slower, and much more painful," Cardinal muttered as he restrained the man's legs.

As much as the man deserved to die, this wasn't fun. Rook wasn't that kind of guy. It was just sad to listen to the guy implore his captors to spare him. That was probably the little sneak's purpose, to make Rook feel sympathy for him. After a few more moments of struggle, Rook wrestled the guy's head into the noose while Cardinal held his legs in place.

"Please don't do this," he whispered. "I haven't done anything wrong. I'm not a spy, just a reporter. I don't know who you think I am, but I'm not." To his credit, the guy wasn't sobbing all over the place like some did.

"Shut up," Rook muttered as he made sure everything was in place. He'd have to do this fast so that the bastard didn't wriggle out of the noose as soon as the two men let go of him.

"Wait, wait. You don't understand," he said, getting louder. "Those Angels aren't what we think they are. They're owned by some company called Celestius. You have to let me tell someone."

Rook had never heard of Celestius, and he didn't care. The guy was stalling.

"The Angels are making people disappear," the man said. "The public needs to know."

With that, Rook nodded to Cardinal. In seamless choreography, Cardinal stepped away and Rook kicked the chair from under the traitor's feet. The rope snapped taught, but due to the short distance the man fell, his neck didn't break. Rook watched as the man's face darkened. After a minute of pointless struggle, the body jerked more feverishly, more urgently. A minute later, the body was still.

That was their cue. Rook removed the padded cuffs from the dead man's wrists. The pair of Phalanx operators exited the house through the backdoor and crept along the back of the house. The fence in the backyard offered no challenge as the men vaulted over it and cut through the neighbor's yard. Intel said no dog lived here, so that was a plus. Rook hated killing innocent animals.

The neighbor's yard backed onto a side street where Bluejay waited with the car to whisk the trio away. In the dim moonlight, no one noticed two large men scaling a fence and casually entering a nondescript sedan. And just like that, the defenders of America sped off into the night.

Once underway, Rook used his cell phone to report in to Condor, who was safely sequestered away at the Fort.

"Team One heading home," he said. "Target neutralized."

"No problems?"

"None."

"Good," Condor said. Rook appreciated his boss's trust in him. No further explanation of the mission's success was required right now, but Condor had other thoughts on his mind apparently. "That information dump we talked about at the hospital, Rook. It's possible that it went both ways."

Condor probably intentionally referred to the previous conversation ambiguously to prevent Bluejay or Cardinal from overhearing anything that might sound too crazy. To Rook's knowledge, only he and Condor knew about the Demon's interaction with his brain.

"So they could know something that I know?" Rook asked.

"You are privy to certain details that would interest a certain third party."

Rook stared out the passenger side window of the car and mulled over the implications of that statement. What information could the Demon glean from his brain that would serve its own purpose? His eyebrow cocked a little at the realization.

"The location of the next one," he stated. Out the corner of his eye, he could see Cardinal trying very hard to appear disinterested in the conversation. Next time, Rook was bringing a Bluetooth headset for some damn privacy.

"Exactly," Condor confirmed. Rook knew the secret location of the surviving Angels. Condor and Vulture had told him during the hospital mission briefing that the Angels had been moved to the secure facility that Rook had once been paid to break into, unsuccessfully. Seemed like the Demon would want to try its hand at the same task. "You interested in some revenge, Rook?"

In the window, Rook's grim reflection stared back at him. "You have no idea."

Chapter 40

The monotonous *whump* of the helicopter rotors enveloped Rook, tempered by his isolating headset. Had the ride across the Rockies not been so rough, the repetitive pulses of the blades could've easily lulled him to sleep. The early discharge from hospital was starting to catch up to him, in addition to not really sleeping the night before. Rook wondered if the hanged man's body had been found yet. Intel said he was a loner, so it could be a while. Either way, neither Rook nor Cardinal had left any evidence behind.

One of his fellow passengers yelling to another brought Rook back into the present.

"Hey, Blackbird, why we gotta follow Rook now?"

Blackbird, Kilo squad's leader, regarded the man as if he'd just farted in front of the President.

"Because Condor said so."

"Didn't Rook just get his last team killed and shit?"

Rook didn't know much about him, but his codename was Buzzard. Judging from his current demeanor, the guy was a prick. First impressions were rarely far off the mark.

Blackbird wasn't taking the bait.

"It all pays the same, Buzzard."

"It doesn't pay shit if Rook gets us all killed."

"Enough," Blackbird snapped. The giant of a man nodded to Rook when he said, "If you had even half a brain cell between those two big-ass ears of yours, you'd know Rook has the biggest score out of any of us to settle with this fuck."

Buzzard leered at Rook, who in turn refused to look away.

"Don't fuck this up, Rook," he sneered, before smugly breaking eye contact and nodding to the guy sitting next to him.

The rest of the squad just sat and watched, listening to the exchange over their oversized headsets. Rook wasn't sure how many agreed with their more vocal counterpart, but he could respect them for at least not openly showing insubordination. Sure, Phalanx wasn't military, with all the decorum that entailed, but even in a civilian company publicly badmouthing the boss wasn't the best strategy for career advancement. And usually it wasn't tolerated.

Rook tilted his head towards Blackbird, all at once thanking him and acknowledging that the squad leader still had more pull over his men than their new CO. Screaming at Buzzard for his stupidity wouldn't get Rook anywhere fast.

Still, how many of these men would blindly follow him into battle with such a proficient enemy? How many had even received a full briefing on Rook's last encounter with the Demon? When the killing started, would he turn around and find all these men awaiting orders? Or would he be left stranded, wishing Lehoski'd been healthy enough to come along?

Brian.

Poor guy was in a bad way apparently. So bad that Rook hadn't even been allowed to talk to him. It was strange. Rook had the images from the Demon's attack playing nonstop through his mind, but nowhere could he pinpoint Lehoski going down. Maybe his friend had taken the Demon on after the memory transfer had taken place. Or maybe the memories weren't one hundred percent accurate.

Lehoski's isolation wasn't the only strange thing going on at the Fort. When Rook had inquired on the status of Kestrel, whom he hadn't seen since the showdown in the operating room, Condor just gave some bullshit answer about Kestrel being sent home for a couple of weeks on leave. Since when did anyone in Phalanx get permission to take a leave of absence at such a crazy time? After a few more prodding questions, the boss had finally revealed Kestrel was suffering from a few mental issues after a near brush with death in the hospital. None of the memories that the Demon had transferred to Rook showed anything in particular about Kestrel's fate, so Rook just had to trust Condor's word again.

Without warning, the boss's voice filled his headset.

"Rook, the Alphas have been relocated."

This was a surprise.

"Where are they?" Rook asked.

"The point is that I'm not going to tell you, Rook," Condor responded, his voice fuzzy in the speakers of the headset. "Tango Delta could be monitoring your brain, we don't know. Just know that the Alphas are gone."

That sounded kind of paranoid to Knight, but who could really know?

"Roger, Condor."

Left to his own thoughts again, Rook started to draw out his plan on his handheld tablet. The Demon had entered via the roof during each attack, so odds were that would be its first maneuver. How did it get onto the roof, though? Aerial transport? Did it somehow scale the outer walls? He looked up at his men, all patiently watching him, waiting for his orders.

Damn it. He just didn't have enough information to prepare for this assault. People were going to get hurt, he could feel it.

Despite the intense concentration involved in considering contingencies and placing assets on the drawing board for this defensive scenario, Knight's attention wandered. What was Karen doing right now? He hadn't thought about her at all since Connor had sent him to Phoenix with orders to execute that spy. The task at hand had commandeered his full attention. Now he paused in his deliberations, her face disrupting his train of thought.

Damn, she was pretty. Even if she'd cheated on him, even if she was cheating on him at that exact moment, Knight realized that he missed her. Why was it so hard to just erase all traces of the woman from his mind? The answer was obvious, even to him. He couldn't just instantly forget years of great memories shared with the woman he loved. A grenade had detonated in his heart when he'd realized she wasn't coming back, that she wasn't even going to call him. Shit, even just a phone call to tell him *why* she left would work. How could he get any damn closure? All he had were suspicions and paranoia.

And then add in all this shit about people just vanishing—

"Rook, you about ready, man?"

Rook looked across to Blackbird and nodded.

"Yeah," he responded, quickly falling back into step. He started tapping away on his tablet, sending visual instructions to his men's handhelds while he spoke. Cardinal's squad in the chopper flying behind them was also listening in. "Tango Delta begins his assaults on the roof, so that's where we're going to set up. We don't have enough men to cover all the buildings, so we'll get some assistance and heavy firepower from the military personnel on base to cover other roofs."

He paused to check his men's faces. In the fading light of the sunset, all were rock solid, attentive, confident, angry.

"Whatever happens, watch each other's backs, and report *anything* unusual," he said, his words falling like hammers. "Tango Delta can change its appearance, but so far it hasn't talked. Get verbal confirmation of identity from anyone nearby. Don't get caught out."

In response, Rook received various iterations of acknowledgement. He looked each man in the eye, searching for any doubt, any hesitation. He found none. Even Buzzard's face mirrored Rook's own resolve.

Content for the time being, Rook peered out at the scene whipping by below. Massive trees blurred as the helicopter sped what seemed like mere feet above their tips. Of course, the darkness and the speed amplified the effects, deceiving Rook's vision. The helicopter slowed and banked over the top of the hill and the shadowy outline of their destination appeared, nestled inconspicuously in a pit cut between two hills.

No wonder we couldn't find this place, Rook thought, remembering the excruciating frustration of the exercise he'd once been assigned to, trying to locate this base. That particular mission wasn't really that long ago, but with all that had happened recently, the memories had dimmed significantly. Even now, he didn't have much intel on the base. Most of it would be underground, cut into the rock itself. Aboveground, one wide building stood surrounded by three smaller buildings.

The pilot interrupted to announce their final descent. The whine of the rotors changed pitch as the bird glided smooth as silk down to the landing pad below. Without a noise, Kilo and Lima squads flowed from the two choppers and assembled in the open. Rook looked his men over and got a warm feeling as his adrenaline started to kick in.

By morning, the world would be short one Demon, Rook could feel it.

Chapter 41

"Bryan, how long have we known each other?"

Bryan Fortuna stared at his boss's back as she stood, examining a portrait of Thomas Jefferson. Had that painting always been there? Fortuna couldn't remember, but it was hard to know for sure with his mind still reeling from the surprise invite to the Oval Office. Usually they kept to a precise schedule for their daily meetings, a result of President Davenport's discipline-oriented ethos.

Another clue that something was amiss was when the President had dismissed the ogre known as Agent Greg Townsend of the Secret Service. The towering man had glared at Fortuna knowingly before exiting the room. But how much did that really matter? All conversations in this famous room were recorded, and who was to stop the Secret Service from installing a few hidden cameras?

But most of all, he worried about what the President had to say to him that she didn't feel required using those encrypted phones he'd gotten for the two of them. Or maybe she had another reason for not utilizing that communication method. Normally a very composed man, a mandatory trait for someone in his position, Fortuna felt beads of sweat forming on his neck, despite the cool temperature of the Oval Office.

"I asked you a question," the President snapped as she suddenly turned to face him.

Fortuna blinked, feeling incredibly exposed in the expanse of the office.

"Uh, right," he stammered. "Sorry, Megh—"

"*Madam President*," she said, in a factual, not necessarily angry tone. Either way, this wasn't a good development.

"Right," he said. "Years."

"Years, indeed," she responded, staring at him, picking him apart with her eyes. Meghan Davenport stood an inch shorter than Fortuna, but in her realm, with home field advantage, she was a giant. After a few uncomfortable moments, she motioned for him to take a seat as she made her way to her own chair behind the great desk.

He acquiesced, barely controlling the nauseating urge to glance over his shoulder. The other shoe was about to drop, he just knew it. The President met his uneven gaze.

"Bryan," she said, voice flat as a windless lake. "How long have you been fucking little kids?"

Oh no.

Fortuna's stomach sank into the subbasement. How the hell had *she* found out?

Murphy.

It had to be. That snake had sold him out.

"You have no proof—"

A sad sigh from his boss revealed Fortuna's latest error.

"An innocent man would've immediately denied such allegations, Bryan," she said somberly as she produced a manila envelope from a drawer in her desk. Slowly, painfully slowly, she removed picture after picture, some in shocking detail. Her eyes focused on Fortuna's face, her gaze growing sterner with each passing second. Fortuna couldn't directly look at her, but he couldn't bear to see the pictures either.

Were these the same photos that David Murphy had acquired? It was impossible not to appear even more of a creep while furtively glancing at the condemning pictures, but he had to establish a common thread. Were they the same? Damn, he just couldn't remember. The fear and anxiety thrust upon him in Murphy's office had blurred his memories.

"Are they even teenagers, Bryan?" she demanded. Before he could respond, she growled, "Don't even answer that."

Crap, what was he going to do? Where was this going? It was impossible to focus with those little faces staring at him.

"You disgust me."

"I—"

"Shut up," she snapped. Now the President rose from behind the desk and leaned forward, looming over Fortuna, who cowered shamefully in response. "Here's how this is going to go. You're going to tell me who my so-called benefactor has been all these years, or I'm going to release these pictures and have you locked away for a long time in a Thai prison."

"But he'll kill me," Fortuna whispered sheepishly.

A bizarre, bemused smirk appeared on Davenport's face.

"You think you'll survive in a prison in Thailand as a white pedophile?" she asked.

"You don't understand—"

"Stop right there," she cut in. "I *do* understand. You're more scared of this man than you are of me."

While the gears whirred furiously in his brain, Davenport lowered herself back into her chair. Everything about the woman oozed *power*. Did he have an out here?

From the moment he'd entered the building today, Fortuna had felt a noose tightening around his neck with every step. Most of the employees pointedly ignored him, while those meeting his gaze responded with nothing short of disdain. Escape by that point was futile, and now the situation had culminated in a total shit-storm. Buying some time presented itself as the only viable option.

"Why didn't you just use the phone I gave you?" he asked.

"I handed it over to the Secret Service," she said, waving away his question. "It didn't take them long to work out that the phone was designed so that a third party could easily eavesdrop on any conversations."

Murphy again. Why hadn't he thought of that? The lying bastard had been spying on him the whole damn time.

"I'm going to need protection."

Davenport laughed.

"I think you should pray your fellow inmates wear some protection."

He shook his head.

"No, I mean, if I come onboard with you, I need protection from this man. You don't know him. He'll stop at nothing to kill me. You already know he has the resources."

The President leaned back in her chair, elbows on the armrests, fingers forming an elegant steeple in front of her tight lips. Was she going to buy it?

"Okay," she said finally. "That can be arranged."

A wave of relief washed over Fortuna, but the President broke into his calm.

"What's to stop you trying to disappear if I let you go?" she asked.

"Where would I go?" Fortuna fired back. "I'm screwed either way. I mean, what's your motivation here for letting me live?"

Davenport's eyes narrowed.

"I hope you're not insinuating that I'd kill a U.S. citizen to cover my own ass, Bryan," she said. "You're a piece of shit that I'd gladly sweep under the rug, but I won't sign off on your death as long as you resign your post and give up your disgusting habit."

As if it's that easy.

"That's enough for you?"

"Your passport has been revoked, so you won't be leaving the country legally any time soon. If you touch a single American child, I can't imagine the devastation that would coincidentally rain down on your life."

"Is that a threat?"

"Are you in a position to ask that question?" Fortuna had never seen his boss exert her influence in such a way. He was a bit taken aback. She *would* kill him.

"Bryan, I'm giving you an opportunity to change your ways two-fold," she explained, leaning forward onto the desk. She counted the points off on her fingers. "One, you can get out from underneath this bastard who has your nuts in a vice, and two, you can break free from molesting children."

"He'll release the pictures if I cross him," Fortuna moaned, finally breaking around the edges. What the hell would his parents say if they saw those pictures?

God, please kill me now.

"Who do you think you're dealing with here, Bryan?" she asked, feigning offense. "We'll change your identity and provide you with ample protection while we take this guy out. You have nothing to worry about here, unless you can't keep your urges in check."

Fortuna stared up at the ceiling, purposely avoiding Davenport's expectant eyes. She was offering him a good deal. A fresh start on this side of the Pacific certainly beat the alternative. Could he really live on the straight and narrow? He liked to think that he wasn't addicted, like he didn't have a real problem. It was his choice after all—

"I need an answer, Bryan."

"Give me until tomorrow to get my stuff in order," Fortuna stammered. "I'll come back, and I'll give you everything I have on this guy."

She pondered that for a moment, then nodded slightly.

"Okay, Bryan. You have until tomorrow morning. First thing."

He stared down at his feet until the pressure from her glare bored through his shame. As soon as their eyes locked, she spoke.

"Don't screw this up."

***

Driving away from the White House, alone in his car, Fortuna weighed his options. In truth, right now he only had one: the one that Davenport had just offered. It was time to get a counter offer. Keeping one eye on the horrendous traffic of Washington, DC, Fortuna dialed in a number from memory. As the phone rang, he made a note to erase the device's memory as soon as he got home.

"Good evening, Mr. Fortuna," David Murphy said in that arrogant, condescending way of his. "So nice to hear from you, albeit slightly unexpected."

Fortuna skipped the formalities and promptly laid out Davenport's plan to Murphy. As soon as he finished, a dump truck swerved across three lanes to make a left turn only three feet in front of Fortuna's black Mercedes. The primal urge to scream out the window and honk maliciously subsided quickly when Murphy started talking.

"So you didn't tell her my name?" he asked.

"No, of course not."

"Alright," Murphy said, apparently appeased by that. "I think you should ignore her advice and join the winning team. You will find the benefits far more appealing, I assure you."

"You want me to come to you?" Fortuna asked as he changed lanes suddenly without using his blinkers. The Chevy truck behind him laid on the horn as his small Mercedes darted around a stalled vehicle and sped through a yellow light.

"That would be best," Murphy said, his tone already hinting at his boredom with this exchange. Fortuna wondered what kind of a woman he was keeping Murphy from at this moment. "It's time that you were brought up to speed on the full extent of my operation. The operation that *you* have helped create."

Could he trust this guy?

Fortuna cruised to a stop at a red light and considered his situation. Basically, he was a degenerate criminal with no moral values, or at least, that's how his President had painted him. Would she really let him escape punishment and live a life of relative luxury after committing such heinous crimes?

The light turned green and he eased through the intersection to join the next congested line of cars.

He knew Meghan Davenport far too well. She wouldn't be able to sleep at night with scum like him loose on the streets. Even if he made it through the first stages of her supposed plan, Fortuna would be in cuffs, or worse, within a month. No, he was probably safer around other criminals.

"Are you still there, Mr. Fortuna?"

It was time to take the plunge.

"Just tell me where to go, Murphy."

Chapter 42

In the small gaps between dark clouds, stars peppered the blank canvas of the night sky. The contrast between the bright points of light and the absolute darkness of the space between took Knight's breath away. Sure, he'd seen a similarly clear celestial portrait on his recent excursion to the Antarctic, but the outlandishly bizarre nature of that trip hadn't afforded him much time to just pause and watch the galaxy revolve.

After a couple of hours of idleness, the frigid mountain air was starting to become uncomfortable. Despite the thermal clothing he and his men had donned for this mission, the chill worked through the layers and effortlessly invaded their bones. Spread out across the wide rooftop, Blackbird and Cardinal tried inconspicuously to generate some heat, rubbing gloved hands against their arms.

Knight and his two squad leaders crouched behind cover in three of the corners of the squat, square building. Kilo and Lima squads waited in the two roof-access stairwells, ready to burst out at the first sign of their enemy. On the roofs of the smaller buildings in the complex, and on the grounds below, military personnel patrolled anxiously. No one was sure quite what to watch for, but each man figured he'd know it if he saw it.

The glowing numbers on Knight's watch told him it was time for another check-in.

"Radar, status," he said into his headset microphone. The narrow arm of the device brushed against his frozen cheek with each word.

"Clear, Rook."

"Roger that," Rook said. "Stinger teams report."

"Stinger One clear."

"Stinger Two clear."

"Stinger Three clear."

"Roger, Stinger teams," he said. "Keep an eye on the sky."

The scary thought that the Demon utilized a flying transport vehicle had driven the decision to activate a few surface-to-air missile teams. As soon as the radar got a hit, those teams would be raining pain on the Demon. In addition, plenty of soldiers patrolled the grounds below, instructed to challenge all individuals encountered, so Rook was confident the Demon couldn't sneak in from ground level. So unless the bastard could make itself invisible, its options were damn limited.

Jet fighter support was en route, but the ETA was still murky. The channels between Phalanx and the Air Force were not as crisp and clean as they needed to be. For a critical situation like this, any bureaucratic delay could needlessly cost friendly lives. Maybe if Condor was allowed to just pay the Air Force for strategic assets, the process would go faster. On the other hand, that was a recipe for corruption if Rook had ever heard one.

Quiet thunder rolled across the heavens above. Knight glanced up somberly, remembering Karen's odd love of violent storms. Now that he thought about it, that characteristic probably explained how she could possibly love her crazy bitch of a sister. The spell cast over Knight by the nostalgic feelings for his ex-wife shattered at the slightest hint of Katie. Unfortunately, that malicious cow could be Knight's only link to Karen if she decided to hide from him forever. Or he could just wait for Connor's crew to find her. It was quite a surprise that they hadn't already, based on Knight's previous experience with that team.

"Rook, you hear that?"

Cardinal sounded uncharacteristically worried.

"Hear what?"

"The thunder," he said. "It's not passing."

Rook hadn't even noticed. He'd been too caught up in his reminiscing.

"Radar, status."

Rook forced himself to take a few deep breaths in the silence that followed. The cold weather already had his muscles taut, but the tension increased with each passing moment.

"Radar clear, Rook."

"Like hell it is." Cardinal again. The man was spooked.

"You got eyes on a target, Card?"

The big man hummed while he searched the night's sky.

"No," he said, disappointed. "It's just not right, though. Thunder doesn't do that."

Rook's skepticism faded fast as the gentle rumbling continued. It didn't make any sense. There was just the moon, stars, and some scattered clouds above them. No shadowy outlines floated anywhere, and in any case, the radar was empty. Still, the sound was definitely creepy. It was like listening to a thunderstorm miles away. But such prolonged thunder would surely result in lightning eventually.

Then in amongst the gentle thunder, a deeper sound emanated. Rook turned his ear to the sky. What was that noise?

The strange sound changed pitch exponentially, all at once becoming too high for Rook to even hear. The noise was more of a feeling now, grating on him worse than nails on a chalkboard. As the sensation intensified, Rook grit his teeth, but kept his eyes open, no matter how much they wanted to clench shut in a futile attempt at blocking the pain.

The irritating tone stopped as suddenly as it had started. Rook looked over and caught Cardinal's eye. Cardinal started edging towards the door to the stairwell that his Lima team was sheltering in. Rook started to tell him to stop, but then he became aware of a dull humming noise filling the air. Cardinal must've heard the same, because the huge soldier broke into a dead sprint across the roof top. The guy was deceptively fast.

When he was just three steps from the door, the dark night bloomed into painfully brilliant light. A focused stream of lightning struck the roof just feet from Cardinal, totally enveloping the man. Rook froze, wide-eyed. The beam quickly darted from where it had caught Cardinal mid-stride. Rook's mouth dropped open.

Cardinal was gone.

The roof beneath Rook's feet trembled, and his ears ached from what could only be described as the dull roar of an avalanche of gravel inside a quarry. Floodlights all over the roof flashed to life, revealing giant, rolling clouds of dust spewing into the air in the wake of the strange beam. Was this some state of the art satellite-based laser technology ripping through the reinforced roof of the building? Through all the chaos, Blackbird's voice filled the open channel with curses as he ran back towards Rook.

"Lima fire, Lima fire," Rook barked, invoking the keyword for a full retreat.

But he knew it was too late. Before any of the men had even had a chance to turn around in the tight stairwell, the streak of fluctuating light zigzagged across the small enclosure for the stairs. Rooted in place, Rook watched in shock as a giant bluish pulse zipped down from the clouds, following the trail of the beam. A deep *whomp* splashed over Rook as the pulse made contact with the stairwell. He closed his eyes as a strong gust buffeted his chest and face, but then almost instantly the flow reversed direction, billowing against his back for a moment. Then the night stood still. When he slowly opened his eyes again, the beam, to his relief, had disappeared. But the scene before Rook didn't look quite right. Something was missing as the dust swirled through the illumination from the floodlights.

The stairway entrance was gone. Completely gone. Now all that remained was a charred crater where good men had once stood in defense of their country's best interests.

Ominous humming resounded across the roof once more.

"Kilo fire, Kilo fire," Rook yelled as he broke for the remaining stairwell.

He ripped the door open and saw Kilo frantically pushing down the stairs. Rook made a note to thank any survivors for not bailing out as soon as the situation had turned to shit. He glanced back and saw Blackbird loping towards him, his dark face grim.

"Stinger One has visual. Requesting permission to fire."

Rook looked up and saw a small blue orb growing in both size and intensity in the middle of the sky above the building.

"Take the shot," he screamed as a bolt of blue light ripped out of the sky and obliterated Blackbird.

Survival instincts flung Rook through the doorway. He rocketed down the stairs four at a time, not caring if he could make it, just knowing that he had to. He hit the first switchback in the stairs and crashed against the wall. Feeling no pain and running on full adrenaline, Rook launched himself bodily down the next flight of stairs as the previous flight exploded in brilliant blue.

The blast shot Rook into the wall hard. The world spun in all directions as he fell headlong down yet another flight of stairs. Something broke his fall with a grunt as curses erupted from all directions. Rook found himself in the midst of a tangle of arms and legs as he broke free of Kilo squad and burst through the closest door, desperate to escape the stairwell.

His head scattered and his heart racing, Rook collapsed in a heap. When he tried to pick himself back up, his left shoulder screamed in agony. Rook followed suit. Through the blinding pain, he let loose a guttural roar and regained his feet.

Kilo squad stood uneasily before him in a dark hallway. Half looked terrified enough to bolt at any second. The other half wore the faces of men who feared nothing. Buzzard of all people locked eyes with Rook.

"Where's Blackbird?" he asked, an accusation heavily present in his tone.

"The lightning got him," Rook replied. The image of the squad leader disappearing in the burning light tore Rook up.

Buzzard took a few aggressive steps towards Rook before two of his fellow squad mates restrained him.

"You did this to us, Rook," he yelled. "You bastard. You've killed us all."

Rook ignored the raging man for a second and listened. The lightning had ceased again. He wondered if the missile teams had scored any direct hits. The threat could be over.

Or it could be just beginning.

Either way, it was time to establish dominance.

He marched straight at Buzzard, whose buddies had released him from restraint. Rook could see the guy's lips moving, but he didn't hear a word of the abuse. All he saw was the insubordinate look of a frightened man with no other recourse but to lash out against authority. As Rook pulled within range, Buzzard cocked back an arm, intent on backing his words up with actions.

Rook stepped inside the punch, taking just a glancing blow to the right shoulder. Buzzard's expression changed from contempt to shock as Rook's left hand drove like a jackhammer into his gut. Ignoring the ensuing coughing fit, littered sparsely with four-letter words, Rook grabbed the man by the collar and slammed him up against the wall.

"We do *not* have time for your shit," he growled.

Buzzard's face twisted in pain as he fought to catch his breath and keep his feet under him. To add to the man's discomfort, Rook relieved Buzzard of his pistol and shoved it up under his chin. Rook's shoulder protested vehemently, but the endorphins blocked it out, leaving the promise of a painful tomorrow, should Rook survive the night.

"I *will* shoot you if you don't get it together," he promised. "We're *all* in a bad spot, and I only need team players here."

None of Kilo squad came to Buzzard's assistance, proving Rook's suspicion that he was a legendary douche, even among his peers. When the emasculated man nodded his acquiescence, Rook released him. Rook turned to the closest man, Cassowary if he recalled correctly, and passed Buzzard's piece to him. The guy took the weapon with a face like stone and turned to Buzzard.

"I'm giving you back your gun," he said. "But if you decide to shoot Rook in the back over this, I'll gut you myself."

For added effect, he whipped out a six-inch-long blade and whirled it deftly through his fingers. Buzzard's eyes widened, but he silently took his weapon back and re-holstered it. Rook inwardly sighed in relief. At least some of his squad was still on his side. He opened his mouth to mention the lack of lightning during the minor altercation, but then a succession of muffled blasts echoed down the hallway. The floor merely vibrated, so Rook's heart sank at the implication as his exterior team reported in.

"Rook, Stinger One is down," said the panicked voice. "I repeat—"

"Stinger Three is also—," another voice chimed in.

Rook looked at what was left of his men. They'd all heard the call. Their anti-air support was wiped out. Even the most stoic among them grimaced.

A frazzling beam of light ripped through the ceiling nearby and cut a smoldering swath in the floor, straight across the width of the hallway. The noise reminded Rook of standing too close to a milling machine, with a series of pops and fizzles thrown in as pieces of the floor and ceiling shot out in all directions. A fire extinguisher mounted to one wall exploded, deafening the soldiers. That was their cue.

Rook gave the signal for his men to get back to the stairway. From his place of honor in the back, closest to the burning arc of lightning, Rook was at least glad to not see any of his men frantically peering back at the carnage. Up ahead, the first man to reach the stairs kicked at the panic device on the door. It didn't budge. Two more joined the first in pummeling the door, but the entryway refused them stoically.

"What the hell?" Buzzard exclaimed. "We *just* used this door."

With no time for listening to any whining, Rook fanned his men out across the small hallway. The men in front lay prone, with crouched soldiers behind them, followed by a row of standing men, all with rifles at the ready. Four abreast in the hallway was all they could manage. Nobody said anything about the door at the opposite end of the long hallway, which came into view each time the deadly beam took a break from ripping the whole building apart. Nobody mentioned the pile of dead soldiers, charred to a crisp on the other side of that door.

With a jammed door behind them, and an erratic death ray before them, Kilo had nowhere to go and nowhere to hide. All watched, powerless, as chunks of the ceiling caved in ahead. The men laying prone in the front got restless, not quite edging away from the growing cloud of dust and debris, but obviously not happy.

The noise of the beam stopped for a few seconds. Kilo collectively looked to Rook, who just continued to stare into the dense brown cloud ahead. The emergency lights flickered.

Not good.

"Rook, we're going to fucking die."

This frantic voice belonged to one of the men whose name escaped Rook. Two of the guys near him shared the terrified look of the first. Cassowary, standing behind the vocal one, gave the man a kick in the ass and hushed at him.

"Can it, Song," Cassowary muttered gravely. The other two stared straight ahead, but how close were they to bolting?

Rook examined his surroundings again. What options did they have?

What were the odds that the beam would immediately kick back on if Rook led Kilo across whatever was left of the hallway ahead to try the door to the other stairwell? He looked at the evenly spaced office doors leading off of each side of the hallway. Would any of those have access to the outside? Probably not. If they had glass, it was certainly strong enough to resist any of the small arms that Kilo had brought along. As Rook thought about calling one of the ground teams outside to ask for advice in escaping this locked-down, secure compound, a dark figure emerged from the dissipating dust cloud ahead.

The ceiling was probably eleven feet high, but this creature's head reached almost the whole way. The low glow of the emergency lights reflected back off of every surface of the creature's attire, which Rook took for armor. Both sides stared at each other as time moved through a stream of molasses. Rook's heart beat all the way up in his throat as he stood transfixed by his nemesis. Why wasn't it moving? Why was it just watching them?

Out of the corner of his eye, Rook noticed Songbird trembling. A thick sheen of sweat washed down the man's pale face.

"Song, don't do anything stu—"

The Demon's foot twitched.

And Songbird was up and running, charging the Demon one on one. The man's barbaric scream filled the small corridor. His rifle came up as Rook and Cassowary both yelled at him to stop. He only made it one more step. A bolt of lightning seared through the ceiling, vaporizing Songbird in a heartbeat.

"Weapons free," Rook yelled, leading by example, filling the small space with a blanket of lead.

In amongst the deep barks of their assault rifles, Rook could make out the distinctive high-pitched zings of metal ricocheting off metal. As he ejected his magazine and reached for a new one, Rook observed the bright sparks appearing all over the Demon's armor. Bullets were useless.

"Buzzard, put a grenade on that bastard," Rook said, keeping his eyes on the enemy.

The Demon lowered its head slightly, ignoring the kinetic lead pummeling its body with such little effect. Rook watched as the Demon's head came back up and the giant rushed towards the firing squad. Rook's target disappeared from view as a shock of lightning ripped through the ceiling right in front of him. The energy repelled Rook back against the wall. Coughing and out of breath, Rook gathered his senses in time to see the beam of light zip back up into the sky right as the Demon materialized in the midst of his charred men. Buzzard stood holding his grenade, staring in wonder and fear at the enormous armored creature before him. The man glanced back at Rook for a second, terror etched in his face. Without anything more than that, Buzzard pulled the pin on the grenade. The small fragmentation device dropped to the floor.

In a blur of motion, the Demon's arm shot out, connecting with Buzzard's midsection. Almost instantly, Buzzard's body vanished from view, crashing straight through the jammed door behind him. Rook looked back at the live grenade lying on the floor and the invincible adversary looming over it. Half of his men were groggy from the lightning tossing them around the small hallway.

"Fall back through the door," Rook heard himself yell.

With only seconds until the grenade detonated, Rook grabbed a couple of the closest guys and dragged them through the open door. Before him lay the mangled remains of Buzzard, who'd been almost cut in half by the Demon's punch, before smashing through a sealed door. A few more men hustled through the doorway behind Rook, who latched onto the last of them and forced them down into cover.

The explosion in such a confined space blew out Rook's hearing so badly that even his vision blurred. Driven by his mounting rage towards this Demon, he staggered to his feet and clumsily peered out through the open door, rifle at the ready. Even his desensitized stomach churned at the grotesque display in the hallway. Charred pieces of his squad lay scattered everywhere, with trails of blood a mix of black and red. The smell was horrendous. Some of the men had been crawling towards the safety of the stairwell when the grenade went off. None moved now.

And still standing next to the epicenter of this disaster, the Demon wobbled on its feet, an arm outstretched to lean on the closest wall. A deep scar was wrenched into its armor along the length of one leg, a result of its arrogant proximity to the blast. The beast made no sound as it limped its way back to a huge gap in the ceiling, where ragged pipes and cabling bent in at all angles.

Piercing through the disgust and defeat controlling Rook, a dark fury grasped onto his trigger finger. Seeing nothing but red, Rook stepped over the mutilated corpses of his men, firing off burst after burst from his rifle. He hardly heard the reports, a mixture of his sustained hearing loss, and his intense concentration on his hatred for this Demon.

His anger only grew as the monster ignored him, slowly making its way down the hallway. It gave no hint of caring as each group of bullets pinged harmlessly off its armor.

Rook's rifle clicked empty and fell to the floor. His pistol materialized in his hand automatically. Stopping his march, he took time to aim and drilled a few shots into the ragged crease in the Demon's leg armor. A grim satisfaction overcame him as the silvery giant silently turned to face him.

That got its attention.

With his foe now staring at him, Rook drove a pair of rounds into its faceplate, but once again to no effect. When his handgun stopped firing, Rook produced what he liked to call his work knife, a seven-inch-long KA-BAR Mark 2. Leading with the carbon steel blade, Rook embraced his anger and rushed his nemesis, screaming with all the brutal urges his body could muster. He'd never felt so alive, and he never even considered the stupidity of his frontal assault.

The knife arced through the air with a hiss, but in a moment of confusion, he tumbled forward into empty space. His rage ebbed as he turned to find the hallway devoid of any trace of the Demon. Breathing hard, he got to his feet as the few remaining live members of his squad ran up to him. While they talked, he stared up into the night's sky through the gaping hole above.

"Man, Rook, you're a crazy son of a bitch," one man was saying.

"I can't believe you charged him with a knife," another added, in awe.

"Are we going to go after the bastard?" the first asked, obviously chomping at the bit for some action.

Rook lowered his gaze to them.

"No."

Their shoulders dropped, and their chests lost a little bit of their pump at the single word they didn't want to hear. Rook didn't need to look around the scene of the massacre again to know that he'd lost enough men on this mission.

"How did it escape?" he asked, feeling eerily calm in the wake of the storm.

"Um, this blue light shot down over its head," one man answered.

"Yeah, then it put up its arm real quick like and zipped up into the sky faster than you can believe," finished another.

Oh, he could believe it. He'd been *so* close to raking his knife across that armor. It'd been right in front of him. But he'd hit nothing but air.

A vice clamped around Rook's head. His hands lifted and dug into his skull, futilely seeking to relieve the pressure as he twisted and thrashed against the nearest wall. The pain enveloped him body and soul as he watched memories being forced to the forefront of his consciousness. He saw the helicopter riding in, his conversation with Condor. The recollection slowed there as Condor said the Angel had been moved away from this facility.

Not here.

The strange voice resounded over and over again in his head as his vision returned to him and the pressure eased all throughout his skull. Rook tumbled to the floor, not even feeling the rough edges of debris pricking at the exposed skin on his hands and face. A step too late, his men grabbed him, hefting him up. They swiftly transported him down the hallway, his feet dragging uselessly behind as his tired eyes started to fade.

In the background, he heard one of the bewildered men ask, "What's not here?"

Chapter 43

"Mr. Murphy, the helicopter will arrive in ten minutes," the Scandinavian voice said through the speakerphone adorning Murphy's desk. When the CEO didn't immediately respond, the voice continued, "You asked to be informed of his arrival."

"I'm aware. Thank you, Dietmar," Murphy responded. The line went dead without further formality.

Dietmar Carlsson, the head of site security for the newest addition to Murphy's empire, was a gargantuan Swede with years of experience in his country's special operations unit. The Särskilda Skyddsgruppen, or SSG for short, dabbled in all the fun parts of military life that elite soldiers crave: infiltration, sabotage, espionage, combat intelligence, and even high stakes rescues. Of course, the SSG, now known as the SOG, concealed the names of its operatives quite well, but no information remained hidden from David Murphy for too long, especially when vetting such an important candidate within his organization.

The stereotypically fair-haired and blue-eyed giant kept to himself mostly and lacked what many would consider traditional people management skills, but Murphy had no complaints. The populace of the facility, both scientists and soldiers alike, all feared Dietmar immensely and followed his orders without retort. It was nothing if not efficient, but what else was to be expected of a man whose cold eyes told subordinates he'd rather kill them than deal with their petty problems?

Murphy cut a trim outline against the window taking up the entire west wall of his office. Was the twenty-foot-tall ceiling absolutely necessary for such a room? Standing before the equally tall window, watching the birth of a glorious sunrise, Murphy considered every penny well spent. Cubes of ice clinked against his lowball glass as he gently swirled the whisky within. Lesser men would berate Murphy for not using a snifter to enjoy such an expensive scotch. And adding ice? Ludicrous insanity. Murphy had no time for such picky frivolities. At six in the morning, he would savor his alcohol in whatever fashion it pleased him.

Now with an empty glass in hand, Murphy started for the door. Work beckoned. There was no rest for the wicked. He smiled at the thought as he placed the glass next to a crystal decanter on a small mahogany table near the door. Before reaching for the ornate door handle, he enjoyed a sizeable sigh. It was good to be David Murphy.

He exited the office, very content with life. With the arrival of his guest, Murphy could dispose of a particularly worthless annoyance. Perhaps the pawn knew that, but that was doubtful, considering he'd actually chosen to seek refuge with Murphy instead of the relative safety of the U.S. government. Had his associate slipped into protective custody, his inevitable demise would've just taken that much longer to find him. At least this way, Bryan Fortuna could vanish at a moment's notice, care of Dietmar Carlsson, more than likely.

And not a soul in the world would care, Murphy thought to himself as he traversed the wide, spotlessly clean corridors of his latest marvel.

Speaking of annoyances, Murphy had ordered Dr. William Baird to report for duty at the facility. Hiring the man had at one time felt like a masterful stroke of genius, but *Billy* Baird had proven himself to be quite a nuisance since his recent arrival. First of all, what person past the age of twelve still went by *Billy?* So childish. Murphy would have none of that. The man was William.

William's initial task had been to talk to clients in order to provide a knowledgeable and affable face for Celestius. Baird had fulfilled that role reasonably well, ensuring the steady stream of income that the company desperately needed to continue in its extravagantly expensive research.

Now Murphy just wanted the Scotsman to hang around in the facility, greet any clients who came to visit, and keep his nose out of everything. The man was ex-military, so Murphy had hoped Baird would spend his time down at the shooting range, or working out, or hell, even running on the beautiful trails surrounding the place. Fences, guard posts, and patrols ensured that no employee left the grounds without Murphy's permission, so escape wasn't a concern.

Instead, Baird had embarked on a personal mission to piss Murphy off. He insisted adamantly that his medical training could be of great use to the science teams working on the Angels. Considering Baird's military background, Murphy just didn't think that was a prudent idea. Some secrets needed to stay under wraps a little bit longer.

He turned a corner and entered one of the many observation decks. The deck was nothing more than a hallway with a bank of one-way mirrors running the length of it, angled down to provide a great view of the lab space below. Murphy could show off his achievements without disturbing the scientists and technicians in the research labs, once the workers got used to living under a magnifying glass, of course. That acclimatization took far shorter than Murphy would've imagined. Working in an environment where someone could be secretly watching from two or three floors up would irk Murphy to no end, but that's why he was on this side of the glass and not the other.

Investors just loved to see the progress being made live and in person. From up on the deck, the money-bags could observe the action without getting in the way, and more importantly, without knowing what was truly going on. From this distance, even the most astute observer couldn't work out exactly what the scientists were studying. That left plenty of creative freedom for Murphy in his narration during tours.

As he continued on down the hallway, Murphy watched his little worker bees buzzing away with their various experiments. They didn't know everything about these Angels yet, but they would. It was only a matter of time. Even in just the short period he'd had the creatures here, his teams had made marvelous strides. Each group was isolated from one another, maintaining some level of division and secrecy between the disciplines. The members of each team worked together, ate together, and probably slept together for all Murphy cared. The scientists had all signed away rights to publishing any of their work, but none so far had voiced concerns that they'd also signed away their lives. At the end of the day, it just wouldn't do for any of the smarty-pants to work out Murphy's ultimate goal. That would not do at all. Precautions and contingencies abounded for such a development.

To minimize the number of people interacting with Fortuna, Murphy had the helicopter landing on the roof pad usually reserved for more prominent guests. The honor would be lost on Fortuna obviously, but at least this way, if he disappeared mysteriously, that many less eyes would've beheld the pedophilic waste of oxygen. Just the thought of the man's despicable appetites awoke an urge in Murphy to just shoot the bastard on sight. He'd always considered himself to be a calm and calculating man, but the more he dwelt on Fortuna's barbaric crimes, the more inclined he was to rid the Earth of such a monster.

Fortuna would be treading on thin ice during his stay with Murphy. That much was certain.

Reaching his destination, Murphy entered into one of his sub-offices, a term given to any of a number of rooms designated as alternate sites for him to work. Not many people had the pleasure of being received in Murphy's holy of holies, which he had just left. No, she'd have to be damn beautiful and grossly charming for that honor. He poured himself a scotch from the ubiquitous decanter and seated himself behind his grand oak desk. For some reason, he'd opted away from mahogany for this particular office. The oak felt more *American*, that was all.

After a minute or so, Dietmar called ahead to announce Fortuna's imminent presence at Murphy's front door. Two minutes later, a bewildered and frightened child rapist sat in a very comfortable chair before Murphy's desk. Dietmar remained, just a few steps behind Fortuna, who furtively turned his head every few moments. The notion was futile. If Dietmar intended to kill Fortuna, there was nothing the ex-political advisor could do about it. After a few awkward moments for the trembling soul, Murphy nodded to Dietmar, who silently exited the office. The Swede had already searched Fortuna for any weapons, and with the simple push of a button under Murphy's desk, Dietmar and a small army would rush into the room.

Once they were alone, Fortuna, who'd watched Dietmar every step of his way out, turned to Murphy and said, "I'm so screwed."

"You'll be fine."

"You don't underst—"

A dark glance from Murphy abruptly halted the man's whining.

"I am well aware of your predicament, Mr. Fortuna," Murphy started. "This president cannot afford *any* signs of weakness in her stay at the White House. As such, I do not see her going to the press to reveal a child molester in her stable of advisors."

Fortuna interrupted. "But they might if they think the information that you hold is more damaging—"

And again, a subtle glare caused Fortuna to simply trail off. It was hard not to smile. Murphy wondered, and not for the first time, that perhaps he should invest in writing a parenting book. His casual dominance over mere mortals would translate well into the realm of the father-son relationship.

"And what good would that do?" Murphy asked. He leaned forward slowly while Fortuna waited anxiously. "What's the upside for Davenport's administration? They out you, then I can still release my information about voter fraud and financial discrepancies in her campaign."

Of course, Murphy had caused those illegal activities on her behalf, but that would take decades to establish. With the sheer wealth he had thrown into that effort, his hands were still immaculate. Plenty of other men and women would see the inside of prison walls for their complicity, but he hovered far above, pulling strings, and then cutting the marionettes loose at the right moment. Many of his puppets still hadn't even realized the ties had been completely severed yet.

"As you can clearly see, Mr. Fortuna, as long as you stick with me, you are more than covered."

Fortuna glumly nodded, and then stared at the floor. Never had Murphy witnessed such a dejected face. Murphy wondered if he put a gun in front of Fortuna right now, who would the pervert decide to kill, Murphy or himself? Perhaps having him killed would actually be a blessing to this pedophile. That was something to think about. There were certainly worse things than death.

Chapter 44

"Holy shit, it's good to see you awake."

For Knight, waking up in the same bland hospital room wasn't quite as thrilling as it was for Connor. His boss was standing by his bedside, a hand on Knight's shoulder.

"When the boys dragged you back unconscious, I wondered if you were ever going to come back to us," Connor continued.

Sluggishly Knight pulled himself up into a sitting position. Connor fiddled with the buttons on the side of the bed to make it more comfortable. Knight had seen the type of controls before, with the instructions depicted by big, colorful drawings that a monkey could follow. The slight change in elevation sent Knight's head swimming.

"The boys said that you grabbed your head and fell down before you passed out," Connor said cautiously. Knight could tell he was fishing. "Did, uh, the Demon talk to you again?"

The Demon. That bastard. He'd ruined Knight's life in an instant.

"Where's Brian?" he asked.

Connor's face recoiled momentarily, before meeting Knight's stare.

"Uh, Brian's still in isolated ICU. He's not doing so well, but the doctors aren't giving up."

Knight lifted a leg and made to exit the bed.

"I want to see him."

Connor stuck a strong hand on Knight's shoulder and guided him back into a more reclined position. Still weak from his ordeal, Knight couldn't resist him.

"You can't," he said sternly. "*Isolated* means you can't go see him."

A sigh heavy with regret welled up in Knight. Releasing it into the world didn't provide any relief.

Karen.

His beautiful wife, gone.

"I can't do this alone," he said quietly.

Connor's voice softened as he said, "As soon as he's better, you'll be the first in there. I promise."

Knight looked up, knowing that his eyes betrayed his sadness, an emotion reserved for the weak. Soldiers didn't get depressed.

"Karen's gone, Mike."

"We'll find her. I have men out looking—"

"You're not listening," Knight exploded. "She's fucking *gone*."

Connor backed up a pace and frowned at the outburst. Not many people would dare raise their voice to him like that. Knight was past the point of caring.

"The Demon opened my eyes," he said, settling back down. "I know what's going on. His English isn't very good, but it's like he dumped a video documentary into my head."

The dull throbbing throughout his cranium was hopefully just a temporary side effect of the Demon forcefully violating his brain. He massaged his temples while he spoke, but it didn't seem to help.

"First, the Demon worked out that I was protecting the Angels without knowing what they really are," he said. "So, he told me the story."

"He?" Connor asked.

"Yeah, it's a guy," Knight said before continuing. "I can still see all of these images running through my head. It's like I was there, like these are *my* memories."

The plastic chair scraped against the floor as Connor pulled it away from the wall and slowly sat down. Eyes cast down, Connor stared under the bed, focusing on nothing. A sad shake of his head ended with his gaze on Knight.

"I don't know—" Connor said. His words faded lazily.

"You don't believe me."

"It's not that, it's just—"

"Just what?"

Connor huffed.

"It's a lot to take in, don't you think?"

"I haven't lied to you so far," Knight pointed out.

"Right, but—"

"I'm not crazy, Mike."

One look into Knight's eyes sealed the deal.

"Okay, okay," Connor conceded. "Tell me more."

"Twenty creatures showed up on his planet. Angels. They went around healing the sick and injured, and asked nothing in return. They were celebrated as gods, sent from above as some kind of blessing. Sound familiar?"

"Unfortunately."

"Yeah, and then people disappeared."

Knight grimaced at the thought. The part he'd left out of his explanation was that he could more than just watch the events taking place. He felt everything that the Demon had felt, including the pain of losing a spouse. Knight recognized that particular emotion perfectly, and the unbridled anger that followed.

Connor had turned into a statue. The man didn't even blink. Knight had never seen his boss so flustered.

"I think he can stop it," Knight said carefully.

"The Demon?" Connor mustered.

"Yeah. I'll try to explain," Knight said. "Eight of the Angels took off, literally. They got back into their spacecrafts and took off. The Demon and a few others pursued in whatever vehicles still worked. Almost everything by this point was falling apart because all their resources were poured into solving the crisis."

"So there are more of these things?" Connor asked. The concern in his voice was evident and well founded.

Knight saw through the Demon's eyes as it pulled into Earth's atmosphere. The Demon had checked instruments, to the best of Knight's knowledge, and determined that he was all alone. Another thing Knight had in common with him.

"Yes, but the Demon doesn't know where they are."

"So we thought the Demon was the enemy, but really he's here to save us from the Angels?"

The images of the Demon searching frantically for his dead wife cycled through Knight's mind in a frenzy of anxiety and fading hope. An ominous silence filled the room until Knight spoke again.

"He's here for one reason, and only one reason: Revenge."

"I don't understand."

Knight shared the Demon's anger when he snapped, "He doesn't give two shits about us, or any other life on this planet. He's here to destroy those Angels and won't stop until he does. This is absolute payback for wrecking his life."

Connor stared at the floor. This had to be quite a bomb to just drop on someone. Knight himself would've had a hard time taking someone else's word for it, but the images and memories were just so vivid and *real*. This was happening, and it wasn't going to get better on its own.

"Look," Knight started more softly. "Before the Demon left, the scientists worked out the Angels were more mechanical than organic." Connor's face came up from staring through the floor. "They're more like factories for these microscopic organisms that spread into living things through touch. These bugs fix up a human body to create a perfect host that produces enough of these little shits to form a swarm."

A disturbing video played through Knight's mind. In it, a montage of death rippled through countless variations of the same scene. One second, there was a perfectly healthy-looking body. The next, it vanished, leaving no visible trace.

"The swarm reaches a certain size and then consumes the whole host, leaving nothing."

"Nothing?" Connor murmured as the revelation steamrolled over him. "So the disappearances—"

"Yeah."

"But how long does that take? I mean, after the Angel touches someone."

"There's no guessing. The swarms took a different amount of time to form in every victim," Knight explained before a thought hit him. "Is Seagull still alive?"

"Yeah, he is."

Knight's eyes dropped to the floor. "Shit, Seagull's still here, but Karen's not."

Poor Karen. At least she died painlessly.

"Damn it, I screwed up," Knight said, fuming. "If I hadn't taken Karen to the hospital—"

"That's *not* your fault," Connor interrupted sharply. "There was no way in hell you could've known this was going to happen." Before Knight could interject, Connor kept going. "What you did was out of love for your wife. Who wouldn't want their wife's cancer to be cured?"

Knight glowered and punched the mattress, but he couldn't refute Connor's logic.

"So these swarms are too tiny to see with a naked eye?" Connor asked.

Knight sullenly nodded.

"What happens then?" Connor prompted.

"It gets worse."

Connor looked ready to burst, so Knight continued.

"On the Demon's planet, the whole environment started to change. People developed breathing and digestive problems. It was a mass extinction. Piles of dead bodies everywhere. No one could escape. And it wasn't just in the air. It was in everything. Even people using artificial air tanks still had to eat and drink. Their food and water were contaminated."

The final memories of the Demon on his home planet were painful to watch. Everywhere his people clutched at their throats, some stumbling around blindly in a halting daze, others struggling just to crawl. One of the fortunate few, the Demon wore some kind of breathing apparatus as he climbed aboard his ship. The Demon's rage burned in Knight's gut as the creature took one last look at his dying kin.

"A fully-developed swarm that's just eaten its host can spread through the air for a short time. Any plants or animals nearby will be infected, and the process starts again. In plants it's the worst. The organisms don't consume the plants, but they do change the plants to produce a chemical other than oxygen."

Connor's shocked face hid nothing.

"What're you saying?"

Knight took a deep breath, savoring it.

"I'm saying that if we don't stop this process, and these bastards get into our trees, they'll spread like wildfire. And we'll have no air left to breath."

***

"Condor, truth be told, we've found some weird shit that supports Rook's claims."

Connor stood behind his desk, staring incredulously at his boss. McGarvey had chosen not to sit, so neither would Connor. He'd left Knight's room about fifteen minutes ago and had managed to catch the general before he bailed out for a round of golf.

"You've got to be kidding me. Why haven't you told me about this?"

"We had no idea what we were seeing until this morning," McGarvey continued, nonplussed. "And now that you know, you need to keep a lid on it."

"A lid on it? Have you lost your mind?"

"You've lost yours if you think you can talk to a superior officer that way," McGarvey snapped.

Connor backed off, choosing not to remind his boss that he left his rank behind when he took on the head job over Phalanx. Someone had to do it, to protect the United States' best interests. And so Connor had, sacrificing all of his hard work in the Army for the greater good. And now his boss was telling him to lie about the most important development in human history. Of course, that wasn't all McGarvey had instructed him to lie about.

"Lehoski's dead," Connor stated.

"What of it? You knew this would happen."

"Knight's asking about him."

"I don't care, Condor," McGarvey said. "That man is the key to all of this. We can't afford him going off the deep end because his best friend just died. He's already lost his wife for God's sake. Can't you gift him some ignorant bliss?"

You sent his wife to the Angel.

"And whatever you do, Condor, do *not* mention that other thing about his wife. The truth could be the end of the guy."

The truth shall set you free.

"Did you know the truth about the disappearances when you sent Karen Knight to see the Angel?" Connor asked, as bluntly as possible.

"What exactly are you accusing me of, Condor?" McGarvey responded angrily.

"Do you need me to write it down in small words for you, Tom?"

McGarvey slammed a meaty fist onto Connor's desk.

"You're dangerously close to the line there, Condor," the general growled.

He's not denying it.

"Condor, you're not seeing the big picture here. Why do you think that we're protecting these Angels, even after we've learned what they can do?"

Something heinous no doubt, you fat bastard.

Despite the desire to reach across the desk and strangle his boss, Connor started to sense that it was time to play ball, or to at least give that impression anyway. Maybe he could still fix all of this.

Now McGarvey was pacing back and forth across the office, lost in his little dream world.

"We're going to weaponize this ability, Condor. And do you know what we're going to do with it?"

Connor hazarded a guess. "Vaporize the Middle East?"

McGarvey stopped walking and turned to Connor with a smug grin on his face.

"Atta boy, Condor. I knew you were the right man for this job."

That's not a very glowing endorsement.

"The sacrilegious sand turds have been bitching up a storm because they didn't get blessed by an Angel, while the rest of the world enjoyed the supernatural health benefits. Well, we plan to give them all the Angel they can handle. But there won't be any curing before the vaporizing starts, though. I can assure you of that."

"So how is all of this research and weaponizing possible?" Connor asked. "I mean, if you're here talking to Phalanx about it, this isn't official U.S. government business, is it?"

"Right again," McGarvey said, his expression growing serious once more. "My brother owns a giant company with all the necessary resources to study the Angels and develop the solution to America's little Arab problem."

Chapter 45

Secret Service Agents Bridenbecker and Sauza let themselves into one of the White House's so-called "war rooms." In reality, it was just a conference room with cozy chairs and a long table, plus all of the modern technical gadgets required for flashy presentations and telepresence. The two men had stood guard over many meetings in this kind of room, but never had they received an invitation to sit at the table.

President Davenport could see the eagerness through their poker faces. She had to give them credit. They were damn convincing, but she'd made a career out of reading people, and she could tell that she'd gained a couple of votes in the next election by bringing these boys into the discussion.

When she'd cut Fortuna loose, she'd not been quite as stupid as Bryan probably expected. At her request, Agent Townsend had sent a surveillance team, consisting of Bridenbecker and Sauza, after Fortuna. According to the live audio feed she'd monitored during the small operation, Fortuna had driven like a bat out of hell, worrying the agents that they'd already been made. Having ridden in a car with the man, Davenport still highly doubted that. He drove like a maniac on a good day.

And this was most certainly a bad day.

With the assistance of a helicopter, the agents had tracked Fortuna to a private airstrip. He'd boarded a private Gulfstream

G550 and promptly fled the area. How convenient. The plane's tail number revealed a series of shell corporations as the owners, but right now in this meeting, Davenport hoped to discover the answer to the true owner's identity.

Also, they'd borrowed a few Air Force and NSA assets to inconspicuously track the aircraft. Davenport had assumed that Fortuna's associate was a person of great wealth and resources, so an impromptu escape via private jet hadn't been out of the question. She'd gotten this far trusting her instincts, and now that the shit had hit the proverbial fan, she wasn't about to stop now.

"Okay everyone, let's start from the beginning," Davenport announced as her latest arrivals took seats around the table. She nodded to Townsend, who in turn motioned for Bridenbecker and Sauza to speak up. The two men tersely described their pursuit of Fortuna and how easy it was to work out which plane the man had departed on.

"It was the only plane that took off within two hours of the subject's arrival," Sauza explained. "And we got eyes on the subject with night vision as he walked up to the aircraft."

Simple enough.

Next, an abnormally tall liaison from the NSA spoke of coordinating their satellite passes with the Air Force. The man, who cordially introduced himself as Julius Savage, displayed some satellite images on the big screen and used a laser pointer on it while he talked excitedly.

"A pair of F-35s trailed the G550 across the country and relayed coordinates to my team," Savage said while the animated map followed his words. "We pinpointed the aircraft's destination as a privately owned airstrip in west Texas. From there, the only traffic observed was a helicopter that landed at a private facility near Big Bend National Park."

The cursor on the satellite display centered on a point just inside the Texas border with Mexico. Davenport's heart sank. In the dark room, with everyone's attention on the presentation, she hoped no one noticed the color draining from her face. Unfortunately, she could see her new most-trusted advisor out the corner of her eye, staring at her, probably realizing the same thing Davenport had. One of Fortuna's last acts in office had somehow gone unnoticed in the whirlwind of the investigation against him.

"So how do we know he's there?" she asked, swallowing hard after her voice caught twice.

Savage replied, "When the G550 landed, it was still the middle of the night. Not much traffic around, so we didn't have much to track. But more importantly, my associate here found something interesting."

He waved a hand that looked like a SCUBA diving flipper to the small Asian woman on his left. Her scowl made Davenport wonder which part of Savage's phrasing could've possibly upset her.

"Fortuna made a phone call to this place right after he left here," the woman said, her innocuous words somehow sounding insubordinate. Rather than reprimand her, Davenport turned to Savage, who seemed to be the one in charge.

"How sure are we, Julius?"

The small woman cut in before Savage could respond.

"I just told you that Fortuna made the call, so he made the call."

Davenport glared at the bespectacled woman, matching the intensity behind those eyes. This young lady thought that she knew it all, but Davenport's main concern at this point wasn't Fortuna anymore.

"What Ms. Tam meant to say was that she triple-checked this information and got confirmation from two other sources in the NSA before coming down here," Savage blurted out, obviously far more concerned for his job than his associate was for her own.

The President just let it go. It was small potatoes compared the eight hundred pound gorilla in the room.

"So who owns the plane?" she asked the group.

Ms. Tam immediately chimed in, "David Murphy."

Davenport waited for further elaboration from the NSA analyst, but none was forthcoming. At what point did a brilliant, yet obnoxious mind outlive its usefulness?

The younger woman rolled her eyes as proficiently as the most indignant teenager ever could.

"He's the CEO of Celestius, which is a large pharmaceutical company based out of Houston."

Interesting. A man like that would have plenty of money to throw around to influence politics. She could already feel the crosshairs being taken off her back on one hand, but then reapplied from a new direction.

"Thank you, Ms. Tam," Davenport said calmly. "Can I assume that Murphy also owns this facility where Fortuna has presumably holed up?"

"Yes," Ms. Tam stated.

How the hell had they missed this? The NSA had vetted this facility when Fortuna suggested it. What was that guy's name, the one who'd signed off on the intel on this place? She'd have to check the reports, but she was sure it was something like *Morris*. Now it appeared that the damn compound was owned by the same man who had facilitated Davenport's highly successful presidential run.

So now what? Did she reveal that she'd stupidly allowed the Angels to be relocated to a place that was owned and operated by her secret benefactor? That was assuming David Murphy was in fact the man pulling her strings for the last few years. All the evidence pointed that way. This was *not* going to look good in the public eye.

Uncomfortable with the silence that followed, Savage started to ramble on about the number of shell corporations and fake names Tracy Tam had sifted through in order to locate the truth. Davenport had no need for such details at this point, so she cut him off. This was going to hurt, but she had to remain accountable.

"There's something that most of you don't know."

Chapter 46

Connor wandered back from his office to the small medical wing of the Fort, intent on seeing Knight again, but also deliberating over what to say to his friend. The process of meandering down a hallway felt comfortable, despite his lack of experience with it. Typically, Connor knew exactly where he was heading and knew exactly what he'd do when he got there. Now, he wasn't so sure. In some unknown amount of time, he distractedly reached Knight's room.

It was empty.

All inner soul-searching and contemplation ceased in a single heartbeat. Connor marched down the hall to the doctor's office. Without a knock, he barged right in. The man on the other side almost flipped backwards out of his chair at the sudden interruption.

"Where is Andrew Knight?" Connor demanded.

The doctor stammered something about the general, but Connor had no time for this. He put both hands on the man's white coat and lifted him not-so-gently up against the wall.

"Where is Andrew Knight?" he repeated through gritted teeth.

"Albatross's men took him."

Connor released his grip, but didn't budge. "Where?"

The doctor cowered as if Connor had hit him. The temptation to bludgeon this peon definitely crossed Connor's mind.

"Where is he?"

Finally the doctor looked Connor in the eyes.

"The brig."

The brig? What the hell was going on here?

Connor stormed across the corridor and bounded down the steps three at a time, something his old, tired knees would be sure to remind him about later. For now, he felt no pain, only anger. While McGarvey had courted Connor in his office, his goons had snatched Knight. But why?

Connor paused as he reached the lower basement landing. This was serious. McGarvey had brought in his own forces to lockdown Knight. They were probably active military. That meant Connor had little pull over them. If he rushed in headlong, guns blazing, McGarvey's men would call their boss and get Connor locked up as well. That wouldn't do anyone any good. He'd have to play it cool if he wanted to save the world. Based on his conversation with the general, Connor was fairly certain McGarvey thought he was on his side, so he had to move fast before that opinion changed.

A small, locked cabinet at the bottom of the stairs contained a toy that could come in useful pretty soon. He used his master key to open the door, grabbed one of the black boxes inside, and deposited it in his pocket. Feeling a little more confident, he headed around the corner. Two guards stood stoically outside one of the cells. These weren't run of the mill prison or county jail cells; they were small suites with a bedroom, living room, and bathroom. But, being deep underground, there were no windows. One door in or out. That was it.

"Stop right there, sir."

Connor paused when one of the two men raised his hand with a small black device pointed at him. His heart raced. What was this? He quickly scanned from side to side, but there was nowhere to hide in the cramped corridor. His hand twitched, trying to will Connor into action.

No, it's not time for that yet.

"Look into the camera please, sir," the man said, moderately exasperated.

It's just a camera.

Palpable relief filled Connor as he smiled for the camera. After a few seconds, the guard motioned him forward. It must've been some form of ID check. Up close, Connor noticed one guard had a fresh black eye forming. Connor advanced and quickly slipped into the room as the guard unlocked the door.

"How's it going, Mike?"

Knight was seated on a bland three-seater sofa wedged up against one wall of the narrow room. The room was about as neutral as possible, but definitely livable. No matter what though, the lock was still on the *outside* of the door. Knight didn't take his eyes off the news report playing on the wall-mounted television. Connor plonked down next to his friend and watched a few minutes of the report. It was more of the same. Riots, disappearances, and general anarchy filled the headlines. Now all the vanished people were finally starting to cause a serious public outcry.

The numbers had grown to the point where the world economy was now being affected, and people everywhere were freaking out. One statistic showed a ballooning suicide rate amongst those left behind with no one but themselves. Even Phalanx had been hit. One guy had shot himself after his sister disappeared, and another had actually disappeared, presumably from interacting with one of the Touched, as the news wanted to refer to them.

If only they knew the truth behind that label. Maybe they should just call them the Condemned. Or are those the lucky ones? The ones who escape the trials and tribulations of a dying planet?

But it wasn't too late. Connor regarded Knight for a moment. The Demon had obviously revealed all this information about the Angels to Andy for a purpose. Somehow the Demon still thought Knight could get it access to the Angels, in order for it to exact its well-deserved vengeance.

"Andy," Connor said quietly, despite knowing the futility of the action if the room was bugged. "Did the Demon tell you where it's hiding out?"

Knight continued to watch the TV as he replied, "He has a freaking spaceship, so I'd imagine he's there." Connor stayed silent for a minute. Knight turned to him, "I always know where the Demon is, Mike."

"You do?" asked Connor, more than a little shocked. Knight's eyes went back to the news.

"And he knows where I am, too."

"How's that possible, Andy?"

"When he dumped all that info into my head, he established some kind of a permanent connection. I didn't really notice it until after those idiots outside dumped me in here."

"From the looks of one of them, you didn't go easily," Connor said with a smile.

"I don't like to be touched."

"So is the Demon talking to you now?"

"No, not really."

Had Knight found out about Lehoski's death? The guy seemed even more depressed than earlier when he'd mentioned his vaporized wife. And Connor had *never* known Knight to sit and watch TV, even the news.

"Does it talk to you often?"

"I honestly have no idea, Mike," Knight said, sounding impatient. "It's really hard to explain."

"Sure, sure," Connor said.

A plan came to mind. It wasn't brilliant, but perhaps it could be enough to stop the madness instigated by McGarvey and his brother. A lot would depend on just how good this Demon really was.

"They're in a compound north of Big Bend," he said. Knight went camping there frequently with his wife, so Connor knew his friend would be able to pass along a good location to the Demon. "It's pretty remote, and fairly expansive, so it shouldn't be too hard to find."

Knight said nothing in return.

"I'm not trying to rush you or anything, Andy, but we're kind of on a time crunch here. Albatross is part of a scheme to use the Angels' powers to eradicate every living thing in the Middle East."

Still nothing from his friend. He shook the man's shoulder a little.

"Andy, don't you get it? If they somehow manufacture and release these nano-whatevers over there, there will be no containing it. North Africa, Eastern Europe, India. Think about it. That's just the start. It's like these dumbasses don't realize vaporizing humans is exactly what the Angels want."

How could his friend be so cold about this? This was a damned nightmare waiting to happen. These idiots wanted to accelerate the destruction of the human race, even if they didn't see it that way. There was no coming back from this once these swarms started proliferating everywhere. Any research involving the Angels needed to be about halting, curing, or even reversing the process, not exacerbating it.

With Andy still ignoring him, Connor eased his hand into his pocket. The suspicious movement got nothing out of his friend. Connor's fingers touched the small device concealed in his pocket. If this didn't drag him out of his funk, nothing would.

"Andy..."

Chapter 47

Karen.

No matter how many times he tried to rationalize or justify his actions, it always came back to his own damn failure. She would still be alive if he hadn't taken her to see the Angel. She wouldn't even have had the opportunity if not for his job, the job that she hated. The job that had forced her away from him, into the arms of another man.

Therapist, my ass.

But that hardly mattered at this point. He would've taken her back with no questions asked. She deserved better.

Her voice filled his ears. Before his imagination could conjure up a spiritual or ethereal origin for her sad words, his eyes spotted the small voice-recorder sitting on the coffee table. Knight had been so distracted that he hadn't even noticed Connor place it there.

His heart crumbled to hear such melancholy pervading his wife's usually upbeat speech.

"Dr. Williams, I wanted to tell Andy about all of this, but I just couldn't."

"Why are you showing me this, Mike?" Knight asked, suddenly perplexed about the content of this recorded discussion, and why his boss had a copy of it.

"Karen, don't you think he deserves to know? He loves you."

"Mike, what the hell are they talking about?" Now he was getting angry. Connor just sat next to him, staring blankly at the small black device on the table.

"I can't do that to him. I know that he wants children, but how can I tell him my chemo is going to kill our baby?"

"Baby?" Knight blurted out.

"It's his child, too, Karen. He needs to know. He won't blame you for this."

"Damn right, I won't."

"I don't know, doctor. He's got a lot going on. I don't want to hurt him anymore than he's already hurting. I love him too much. Isn't it enough that I'm dying? Losing both of us would be too much."

Connor reached over and clicked the playback off. Knight just stared at the recorder. His mind whirled all over the place. It was so much to digest. All of his preconceived notions about his wife had just been shattered by eavesdropping on such a short conversation. She wasn't cheating, and—

"The pregnancy was real, Andy," Connor said quietly. "I had her medical records checked before I showed you this."

Knight was still shocked, still all jumbled up in his head.

"How did you get this?" he asked.

"Your P.I. sent it to a Fort mailbox. I figured you'd given the address to Winston to hide this stuff from Karen. I intercepted it on your behalf."

"Did you only get it now?"

Connor's silence told most of that story. His words finished it.

"Albatross didn't want you going AWOL on us," he explained quickly. "I was instructed not to tell you about this."

Knight jumped to his feet.

"That motherfu—"

Connor grabbed him as he made for the door.

"I can get you out of here," Connor whispered sharply. "But you gotta stay calm."

Knight shrugged away from his friend.

"She didn't leave me for some other guy," he snapped. "She loved me."

"Yeah, I know, Andy."

"And she had a baby. *We* had a baby."

The fury grew and grew with each word. These were supposed to be happy words, words of new birth and fresh beginnings. Instead, Knight was only left with the charred cinders of a hopeful future; a future he hadn't even known about until now.

"He took this from me, didn't he?" he asked.

Connor nodded silently.

"I'll fucking kill him *and* his damn brother."

"I know you don't need this right now, but Brian's dead."

The solemn look on Connor's face did nothing to temper Knight's anger. Instead of wistful thoughts of his best friend and wife, all Knight could see in his mind were the tragic images of the Demon's lost love, of that overwhelming feeling of utter decimation. Now that he'd lost everything, now that he suffered in that void, Knight could feel that kindred bond cementing between them. When everyone was gone, all that remained was burning hate.

"Revenge."

"First, we need to get you out of here," Connor said as he gently lowered Knight back onto the couch.

"Those Angels are going to fucking burn, Mike."

"Yeah, just hold that thought."

Knight watched as Connor straightened his shirt and rapped on the door. The lock noisily unlatched and the door swung inward. Connor stepped between the guards posted on either side of the doorframe. A loud pop sounded and a buzzing noise met Knight's ears. He saw one guard fall away, stiff as a board, but twitching uncontrollably. Fast as lightning, Connor elbowed the second guard in his surprised face. Following the man to the ground, the ex-Army officer delivered vicious blows in quick succession, leaving the target bloodied and motionless. Breathing heavily, he poked his head back through the open door.

"You just going to watch, or you want to help me tie these gentlemen up?" he asked.

Knight stepped to and bound the one on the left with his own plastic cuffs. They removed the radios and guns from the men, and then also removed their boots. Knight was surprised that the stench of their damp socks didn't rouse the men as soon as he and Connor shoved the cotton footwear into their mouths.

Connor ejected the cartridge from his spent Taser.

"Come on, Rook."

Knight followed the older man up the stairs to the main level. A short jog across the courtyard outside had them standing in the entrance to the barracks.

"Gentlemen, we have a mission," Connor announced loud enough to even distract the PlayStation gamers in the back of the long room. He quickly broke down the situation for his troops. The words barely registered with Knight as he fueled the fire blazing in his heart. His parents were dead. He had no brothers or sisters. His wife was dead. His only friend was dead.

The squad huddled around their leader, not quite standing at attention, but at least paying attention. Knight watched confusion turn to acceptance as each man weighed Connor's words and made their own judgment calls.

"The Angels are going to exterminate our species if we don't act now," Connor said. "Anyone you hold dear who has come into contact with an Angel directly, or even with someone down the chain, is going to be dead soon, if they aren't already."

Alarmed expressions filled the room. Not everyone knew someone who'd touched an Angel, but how could any of them know if girlfriends or wives had somehow interacted with a contaminated individual? How could they know if they themselves had become infected? The men subtly edged away from each other. Knight fought back the urge to scream at these morons for thinking it made any damn difference now. His rage was approaching irrationality, but he didn't care. He wanted to dive over that precipice headfirst. He wanted that boiling, raw emotion to pour over and burn everything.

"So where this leaves us, gentlemen, is with a Demon heading towards the lab where these Angels are being held," Connor said, milking the crowd. "I'd say it's in our best interests to make sure he gets his chance to kill them. And to save us."

The men all gave assent, some grunting, some passing comments to each other. Knight wondered if they knew that this went directly against Albatross's plans. Connor had forgotten to mention that part. The boss clapped his hands together.

"It's time to save the world, gentlemen."

Chapter 48

Murphy stormed into his compound's security center, his characteristic calm wavering.

"What the *hell* is going on out there?" he demanded, slamming a fist onto the nearest sleek console for good measure.

Dietmar was hunched over the shoulder of whichever one of his minions was manning the main video monitor. The gruff Swede glared at his boss.

"Unidentified flying objects."

"UFOs? Plural?" Murphy said. Unease was creeping all over his skin.

Dietmar simply nodded, clicked a few buttons on the console, then indicated to the enormous bank of monitors built into the long wall. On the center display, a mess of blurry colors meshed together.

"What is that?" Murphy demanded.

"Aircraft with good radar profiles," Dietmar said in crisp English.

"Shoot them down," Murphy commanded.

"We only have eight SAMs—"

"Fire them all *now*."

His security chief nodded to his subordinate, who in turn started pushing buttons on his keyboard and relayed the information to whomever else needed to know it. Murphy watched the side screens as streaks of flame erupted from automated surface-to-air missile batteries hidden around his facility. At the time of construction, he'd actually doubted himself when adding so many, but observing the series of aerial explosions was worth the significant investment. At least, it was until he saw Dietmar's calculating eyes narrow while watching the feed from an external wall-mounted camera.

"What's wrong?" Murphy asked. Was this trepidation that he was feeling? The unknown factors here were overwhelming.

"I don't know," the taller man replied absently. He called up the feed onto the main display. A small group of figures had materialized in the courtyard outside and were stalking towards the entrance.

The security guards crouched behind concrete barricades nearby totally ignored the newcomers. Surely they could see them? But Murphy watched in horror as the men just stared into space, as if the courtyard was completely empty. The whole room stood in silence as they remotely watched the inevitable unfold. Two of the strangers walked right up to the oblivious guards. Murphy's breath caught as the camera operator zoomed in. The abnormally large men stood twelve feet tall if they were an inch, dwarfing the guards who continued to ignore them.

"Demons," Dietmar growled as he lunged for the nearest phone.

It was too late. Large, shiny protrusions appeared in the Demons' hands and then disappeared into the backs of the unwary guards. Murphy stood in shock, as the two guards crumpled behind the barriers. At Dietmar's sharp instructions, other guards aimed rifles at the general vicinity of the intruders and opened fire, blanketing the area in lead.

Fortuna and Baird entered the security center, finally heeding Murphy's earlier call. Murphy had summoned both for different reasons: Bryan Fortuna to ensure he was close by if Dietmar's services were needed, and William Baird for his British Army experience. Both men froze at the sight of the images displayed on various screens. In each, the guards followed Dietmar's instructions as closely as possible, walking machine gun fire across the yard, hoping to score hits on these seemingly invisible Demons. How the Demons managed this feat was beyond Murphy, but more concerning was the lack of effect the bullets were having. At least the bastards hadn't broken the defenses at the entrances.

In the wall of monitors, one screen caught his eye. A giant fireball roared across the sky, bathing the courtyard in a ghastly glow. What was this madness?

The flying inferno rocketed straight into a wall of the main building. In the security center, the lights dimmed for a moment as the floor shook under Murphy's feet. As the smoke cleared on the screen, Murphy could see the Demons making their way towards a gaping hole in the wall. Dietmar relayed orders for all guns to fire on that spot, but the bullets still just bounced off.

"William, you were a paratrooper, correct?" Murphy asked, still transfixed by the streams of bullets on the monitors.

"Aye," Baird responded. "A medic."

Is he still harping on about his medical experience?

"I need fucking guns, not bandages. Take a team down to the containment area and secure it," Murphy ordered. The Scotsman immediately looked to Dietmar.

Insolent bastard. He should jump at my command.

The Swede's incensed glare held Baird in place for only a moment before he nodded his assent. Baird marched promptly from the room. A few of the security guards responded in kind when Dietmar barked their way.

Throughout the entire ordeal, Bryan Fortuna merely watched. Murphy observed the waste of human life for only a moment before making his decision. There was no way that the President could prove his involvement in any of the political shenanigans he'd instigated to get her into office. Hell, she probably hadn't even worked out who truly owned this facility yet.

With the Demons attacking now, it seemed completely plausible that poor Mr. Fortuna died in the crossfire. Murphy leaned close to Dietmar, whose glower would've frozen a lesser man. Murphy whispered his intent, and the former special operative nodded ever so slightly. So it was done. Bryan Fortuna could now be considered a casualty of an intergalactic war, or just a pedophile who deserved a bullet through the skull many years ago. Murphy's justice system was simplistic, but highly effective, much like Dietmar's management approach. The security chief was still barking orders to his men as the Demons breached the outer walls. Multiple monitors showed security teams retreating from their positions to take up new positions on the building's interior.

Murphy made to leave, but stopped when the man at the console piped up.

"We've got another unidentified contact, sir," the man said, wincing as if he was about to be clipped on the side of the head.

Dietmar looked at the screen.

"That's radar."

"Yes, sir."

"What does that mean, Dietmar?" Murphy asked.

"The others only showed up on thermal," the Swede said.

"Yes, sir."

Murphy was getting a bit antsy.

"Just shoot it down."

The man at the console looked first at Dietmar, and then Murphy.

"Sir, we used all the surface-to-air missiles."

"Fine," Murphy spat. "Take care of this, Dietmar."

Murphy ignored the security chief's hateful stare. There was nothing left to do here. He ordered Fortuna to go wait in his room and made for the door. While one of Dietmar's men took care of Fortuna, it was time for the CEO to execute an exit strategy.

Chapter 49

Knight surveyed the chaotic scene once clear of the helicopter's rotors. An inferno blazed somewhere inside the main building of the complex, evidenced by the billowing tower of smoke pouring into the night sky. Powerful floodlights illuminated sections of the smoky column, creating a ghostly effect. Knight led the charge up behind one of the auxiliary buildings, which wasn't much more than a large concrete block.

Connor appeared at his side as the last of the men disembarked, and the black helo swooped gracefully into the dark.

"Rook, what's the status?"

"I'm just Knight now, Condor," Knight replied. He'd had a lot of quiet time on the ride down to south Texas to harness the berserk fury yearning to break free and destroy everything in sight. Rook was the persona of a company man who followed the head guy's orders without question. When Knight found out that McGarvey was screwing around behind the scenes, Rook died, leaving just Andrew Knight in its wake.

"Fine, whatever, Andy. What's going on over there?"

"There's more than one Demon up there now," Knight said. He didn't need to peek around the corner to know what was going on. Once he'd got into a certain range from the Demon, he'd pretty much had a continuous feed from the suddenly verbose extraterrestrial. It was actually jacking with his senses to have the images streaming so heavily in his mind. He was having a tough time trying to sort it all out *and* interact with his own surroundings.

Connor looked alarmed. "How many?"

"Ten or so."

"Oh my… where did they all come from?" Connor asked.

"Outer space."

Connor glared at Knight. What Knight didn't share was that the ten or so Demons running around in this research facility were likely all that remained of their entire race, the remnants of a world annihilated by the Angels. During the final stages of apocalypse, these lucky few had commandeered the most able bodied spaceships and taken off in pursuit of the Angels. Now they were here, and they wanted revenge. Knight would do everything in his power to make sure they had that opportunity. He had a world to save.

"Don't worry about it, Mike. They're on our team. One remotely piloted his ship into the front of the building to create that huge hole," Knight said, nodding to the pillar of smoke still roiling upwards. "Looks like someone got lucky with a few missiles and knocked the ship out."

"Looks like all they did was give an opportunity to create an easy entrance," Connor pointed out. His brow furrowed suddenly. "Wait, *missiles?*"

The look on Connor's face spoke to the lack of intel on this foolhardy trek into enemy territory.

"Guess we got lucky," Knight said. "Time to go." He started to round the corner, but Connor grabbed his arm.

"You sure they won't kill us, too? The Demons, I mean."

When they were still in the air, Knight had looked at every one of his squad mates, allowing the Demon to register their identities. Knight had taken an extra second when he'd locked eyes with Seagull, who was returning to field work for the first time since the Antarctic expedition. At least externally, the guy appeared to be solid. That could all change when the bullets started flying, but Knight didn't exactly have a choice. Connor had recruited anyone willing to help. Within moments of identifying his team for the Demon, and not without a bizarre nauseating sensation for Knight, the Demon had transmitted the information to the other Demons, separating out these friendly humans from the less friendly ones inside.

"Yeah, I sorted it out," Knight said. Connor didn't look one hundred percent convinced, but Knight didn't give him another chance to argue. He hustled around to the other side of the building and bolted for the gaping hole where the ship had crashed. A small one-foot-tall section of concrete was all that remained of the wall, so Knight cleared it easily. Once over, a giant shape stepped out of the shadows, barring Knight's path. He stopped promptly, having known this encounter was imminent. The less-informed squad behind him yelled, screamed, ducked for cover, and pointed rifles. Knight turned and ordered them to stand down. The chatter quieted slowly and guns were lowered.

Before Knight loomed the giant Demon, encased in its smooth, silvery armor. Knight stepped right up to the creature, proving its harmlessness to his squad. He'd have been lying if he told anyone that his heart hadn't beat just a little harder standing this close to such a powerful creature who'd already massacred so many of his soldiers. Behind Knight, his men gradually left cover and cautiously formed up behind him. Their anxiety was palpable. Knight was acutely aware of a wave of cold sweat running across his whole torso. The cold gusts from outside chilled the sweat to uncomfortable levels. Knight really didn't want to shiver in front of this monster, but that wasn't really up to him.

Not a monster.

I know, sorry.

It was hard conversing with someone who could read his thoughts and sense his feelings. Dealing with his wife's ambiguous social cues was way easier than this.

Had been easier.

She was dead. She was gone. She wasn't coming back.

This fueled the fires once more. Knight's shoulders tensed up as the urge to roar at the top of lungs fought for release, but his hard eyes were the only external sign of the chaos brewing inside. The plumes of acrid smoke contaminating the ruined room definitely didn't help pacify his violent urges. A few of the men in his squad coughed at the intense burnt stench all around them.

Must find Angels.

The Demon's primary point of reference, other than Knight's subconscious, was American television, so he often used terminology from media outlets. Knight was sure that *Angel* wasn't the exact word the Demon would use to describe these heralds of the apocalypse, but he probably also didn't appreciate the nomenclature of *Demon* for himself. The alien hadn't explicitly expressed any—

Do not care. Go.

Knight broke his train of thought and signaled to his men to follow. The first doorway they encountered had no doors, just shattered hinges. In the middle of the doorframe lay a smoldering Demon, much taller than the one standing with Knight, at least when it was living. The crater and general destruction pointed to an RPG. Looked like this science facility was better prepared than the average laboratory, at least when it came to alien invasion.

Come.

The Demon stepped over his smoking comrade. Knight followed suit. A horrid scent wafted into his unwilling nostrils as he crossed over the dead alien. Two steps later and the smell was gone, replaced by the all too familiar stink of battle. Shell casings littered the unnecessarily ostentatious marble floor, which was replete with impressive gouges and small craters. Patches of black, crispy residue graced the light grey walls where explosive ordnances of various types had been used. Parts of the ceiling hung down in tatters, while others were missing entirely. Knight made eye contact with the men behind him and silently pointed up to a few exposed areas they needed to watch.

The hallway zigzagged to the left, then to the right. Sounds of gunfire echoed the length of the sterile passage. As they traversed the corridor, Knight noticed streaks of bullet holes marring the grey walls in ragged arcs. The cacophony gained in volume with every step. Knight glanced behind him. All of his men followed closely, their facial expressions not quite as tense as when they first set eyes on the mammoth Demon leading the way. To accomplish this mission, they needed all the help they could get. In desiring to rid the planet of Angels, who better to employ than a Demon?

The Demon halted for a moment and turned to Knight.

Nualaan.

Nualaan?

Not Demon.

Nualaan's rudimentary English sufficed to get the message across. Knight tried not to think of the metallic ogre as a Demon, but it would be a difficult habit to break. *Nualaan* silently marched on to the next ninety-degree corner in the path. As they reached it, a bullet-ridden Demon crawled around the corner, its jerky movements agonizing just to watch. The creature's armor seemed inferior to that worn by Nualaan. Having said that, it wasn't like Knight was an expert in extraterrestrial accoutrement. Nualaan regarded his compatriot for only a moment before removing the great spear from the sheath on his own back and driving the tip through the armored head of the fallen. The body convulsed for a split second before an arc of electricity shot down the length of the spear. After a bright flash of light that blinded Knight momentarily, nothing remained of the wounded Demon other than a scorched patch in the floor tiles. Knight stared in shock at his associate.

Never retreat.

Knight turned to his men, whose eyes had become like saucers.

"Don't ever run from the fight, or the Demons will put you down," he said. They just stared at him in response. There was no time for further explanation. The Demon charged around the corner.

Knight kept close on Nualaan's heels, despite the creature's far greater stride.

Why was that Demon not in armor like you?

Civilian.

Civilian?

Warriors were already dead.

The sounds of rifle reports and grenade explosions grew rapidly as they approached a T-intersection ahead.

Need Angel location.

After this announcement, the Demon stopped suddenly and grabbed the body of an unmoving guard propped against the wall. The monstrous hand enveloped the guard's cranium. Nualaan effortlessly lifted the man off the ground, prompting no resistance from the guard. After only two or three seconds, Nualaan dumped the body and proceeded to repeat this process on a handful of other bodies strewn across their path. Knight and his men followed wordlessly, waiting for some kind of explanation. After interacting with the last of the recently deceased, Knight sensed a brutal rage erupt in Nualaan. In a blur of motion, the Demon spun and drove the unlucky guard's head straight through the wall. A few men gasped. Nualaan just continued down the hall.

Too dead to know location.

In the middle of the T-intersection of hallways, another of the Demons lay charred, one arm completely severed from its body. Nualaan regarded the corpse without emotion. Experiencing all of another being's feelings so vividly still felt alien to Knight, but the absence of emotion stuck out just as much as the most intense rage.

Nualaan had said the last Demon was a civilian, that not all of them were warriors. Knight knew a thing or two about warriors, and Nualaan definitely fit the bill.

Assassin.

That explained the cold reaction Nualaan had to being around all of this death. It also explained why the Demon could so easily penetrate hospitals to destroy the Angels. What Knight couldn't explain was why the human guards were able to down so many of the Demons. In the hospital, Nualaan had forced images into people's heads to hide his presence until it was too late. Surely these other Demons could do the same?

"Hey Rook. Check this out."

Knight turned and saw Seagull holding one of the dead security guard's rifles.

"Infrared sights on this shit," Seagull said, admiring the weapon.

At least that explained how the Demons were getting shredded. Seagull replaced the gun on the dead guard's lap. Only a desperate soldier would ever trust his own life with an enemy's weapon.

Now the sounds of a firefight were very close, possibly even around the next corner. The demons were still advancing steadily against the waves of security guards blockading each slightly tenable position. So far there had been no sign of the Angels, and apparently Nualaan couldn't glean information from any of the corpses. *Someone* in this building had to know where the damn Angels were.

Knight suddenly had a thought.

Yes.

Nualaan had read his mind even before Knight's own brain had analyzed and comprehended his own thought process. Trying his best to ignore Nualaan's fluid mental intrusion and the urgent brutality welling up inside, Knight turned to Connor.

"Connor, there was a helicopter on the roof when we arrived," he said.

"Right."

"Who do you think would want to escape in a helo when his complex came under heavy assault?" Knight asked, a wicked smile on his face.

"Murphy."

Yes.

"I'd put money on that bastard making a run for it," Knight said.

Dizziness suddenly threatened to overcome him as Nualaan rifled through the present and past perspectives of his fellow Demons. After consulting this dynamic database, Nualaan faced right at the T-junction, away from most of the gunshots. In Knight's mind, he could see through a Demon's eyes as it bounded up a nearby flight of stairs. In the glow of emergency lighting, Knight could see the signage marked "Helipad" with an arrow pointing up the stairs. Needing no further encouragement, he raced down the hall with his squad in tow.

His legs burned with fatigued exertion. He couldn't even remember the last time he'd slept properly. Each mental interaction with Nualaan drained his already low energy reserves, especially when Nualaan decided to exchange vast amounts of information between multiple sources. This strain was transferring from Knight's brain into his body, only he hadn't felt it until he started running on concrete legs. Counteracting this exhaustion, a deep-seated hatred for David Murphy provided all the motivation necessary for Knight to fly down the hallway, aimed directly at the stairwell door ahead.

That bastard knew my wife would die if she touched the Angel.

Yes.

If I'd touched her after, I would be dead, too.

Now he dies.

Damn right.

Right as Knight ripped the door open, the space around him exploded with a familiar sound. A stream of gunfire flowed from the stairway landing above. A few bullets whistled by his ear, but thankfully only the noise of the rounds' rotation hit him. A strong hand on his collar whipped him out of harm's way. After sliding across the polished tile floor on his back for a few yards, a couple of his men popped Knight back onto his feet. Nualaan was already rushing up stairs, heedless of the lead ricocheting off of his body armor. Knight growled and charged the open doorway.

Leave some for me. I have a score to settle, too.

Chapter 50

Even in the confines of his office, the muffled sounds of gunfire unnerved Murphy. He'd used the phrase "life or death situation" many times in regards to business decisions, but only now did he fully grasp the concept. If he didn't get out tout de suite, well, he wouldn't have to worry about high-priced call girls anymore.

For the third time in as many minutes, the phone on his desk rang. Who the hell even had that number? He tried to ignore the incessant ringing and rummaged through his desk, searching for the USB drive that contained certain leverage over certain people that he'd need to deal with in the wake of this fucking debacle.

It wasn't there.

Murphy slammed the drawer shut hard enough that one side slipped off its antique rail. One of his guards had the audacity to look at him with concern.

"Make yourself useful and answer that fucking phone."

The man hustled to the desk and picked up the receiver while Murphy kicked his desk, scuffing his Alden Oxfords in the process. Marring the calfskin of his classic American footwear only further distracted him from the serious problem at hand. In his race to erase an entire culture from the globe, he'd partaken in a few favors from various nefarious sources. The USB drive he'd previously removed from his safe had his fail-safe blackmail material should those individuals ever come calling.

After storming around the room knocking over anything not firmly bolted down, Murphy realized his man was addressing him timidly.

"What is it?" he demanded.

The guard with the phone covered the handset with one hand and looked towards the other guard, who just ignored him, obviously enjoying watching his counterpart squirm under pressure. Even in his current rage, Murphy respected that notion.

"Sir, it's uh, President Davenport," the guard stammered.

Murphy marched over and snatched the receiver out of his hand. A familiar female voice awaited Murphy.

"David, how are things go—"

"I don't know how the *fuck* you got this number, Davenport, but I do not exactly have an overabundance of time to talk. Get to the point."

"I'm the President of—"

"Spare me your indignation, Madam President."

"Fine," the president snapped. "Put Fortuna on."

"No."

"And why not?"

"Add it to the long list of shit that I know, and you do not." Murphy kept looking at the door to his office, half-expecting it to crash open at any second. He was losing his cool in this conversation. A rookie mistake, certainly, but what else could he do at this point? Invisible monsters were threatening to destroy his entire empire for fuck's sake. It wasn't exactly business as usual at Celestius today.

"Why is he there?"

"He's a friend."

"Funny, Bryan never mentioned you," she said, sounding particularly smug. "Or maybe he did." His life's greatest accomplishment was sinking into oblivion, and this woman just wanted to play games? Did she seriously have *no* idea what was going on here? An explosion rocked the floor, just to put an exclamation point on that fact.

"Murphy, what the hell was that?" she demanded. *Now* she wanted to talk about something useful. Murphy jammed his free hand into his pocket and touched something plastic. The damn USB stick. That brightened his mood somewhat. His ex-Soviet investors had an overwhelming desire to see his plan played out in the Middle East, and Murphy had admittedly been slightly worried about ex-KGB contract killers seeking him out as a result of his current setback.

Now let's see those Russian bastards come after me when I hold their financial information hostage. The FBI will be more than happy to sift through it and freeze the more lucrative accounts.

"I don't care about what you think you know about me, Meghan, but I would greatly appreciate you sending the National Guard down here."

The floor shook thrice in quick succession as multiple detonations reverberated around Murphy's crumbling estate. On the phone, Davenport was nattering on about something immaterial.

"Sooner rather than later, Meghan."

At that very moment, the doors to his office swung open. Murphy's heart froze, but then calmed at the sight of Dietmar, stoic as always.

"We're leaving. Now," the Swede commanded.

Murphy nodded, not really listening to Davenport's incessant nagging on the other end of the phone.

"Listen, Meghan," he said, shutting her up for a second. "Good luck running for your second term if you let the Angels die."

With that, Murphy tossed the phone on the floor, not taking the time to hang up. He smiled thinking about the world's most powerful political figure yelling into a phone, demanding an answer of him, yet receiving none. Who was she to presume she could force anything from him? Granted, not everything was going to plan, but with every good plan, there was a solid contingency or three.

David Murphy was down, but he was far from out. His disposable science team had made decent progress in their short time with the Angels. Hopefully the next batch of nerds would be able to expound on the work done by the previous team. Dietmar's men should've already taken care of the scientists down in the labs, just in case any had considered breaching their NDAs. Then it would be time for some good ol' fashioned American mass production. The U.S. auto industry had tanked impressively in the last decade, but visionaries like Murphy still understood how to make *stuff*, especially when that stuff would change the world forever. With briefcase in hand and a smirk on his face, Murphy happily filed out of his office in Dietmar's swift wake.

Chapter 51

When Connor had confronted the remnant of Phalanx with the plan to stop the Angels, he'd immediately known who would come and who would not. Some of his soldiers, like Knight, fought mostly for principle. Yes, the money was good, but ultimately, they answered to some higher calling. They risked life and limb to defend their families and country. The others, for better or worse, were just mercenaries, in it for the cash. These two groups coexisted easily enough, but in moments like this, few amongst them would switch sides, even under threat of apocalypse.

So when Seagull had been the first to step forward, the young man's voluntary action had surprised Connor. That was definitely one man whom Connor would've lumped into the merc category, but there was also an adventurous side to Seagull. When a chance to take part in a controversial mission, especially one that didn't align with Albatross's goals, popped up, Seagull had jumped at the opportunity. Wary at first, based on the man's previous outing in the field, Connor had had no choice but to trust the younger soldier. Redemption was as good a motivation as any. Only six other men had stepped up, making a squad of nine with Connor and Knight included, so beggars couldn't afford to be choosers at that point.

But of the seven volunteers, Seagull had been the first.

And now Seagull, whose true name was Paul Sharpe, lay dying, bleeding out before Connor's downcast eyes. The dark, smoky stairwell had shitty visibility, so Connor couldn't see what was going on above, other than catching the flare of random muzzle flashes. The fighting had advanced up a few flights, leaving Connor with the sole casualty so far. The ex-major removed his USP .45 from its holster, not wanting to become the next victim while tending to his soldier.

When Knight had darted after the Demon, Seagull had wasted no time in rushing headlong up beside them. Unfortunately, a group of four security guards had cut him down, riddling his torso with gaping, bloody holes. The guards then performed a leapfrog style of retreat, two falling back at a time while the other two suppressed the Phalanx men. The Demon had clambered after them, but the big alien was limping something fierce as it tried to mount the stairs, greatly hindering its speed.

Connor had immediately crouched at Seagull's side. Only a few seconds later, the only squad member with any sort of medical experience bent over Seagull and assessed the wounds as fatal. With just a simple, sad look, Peacock had told Connor all he needed to know. In between Seagull's wheezing, gasping breaths, Peacock had plunged a morphine spike into the man's hip. Connor hoped that the powerful sedative would at least ease the young man's passing. Peacock had checked with his boss to make sure he was okay, and then headed up to join the fight.

Now only Connor remained, with Seagull's shivering body in his arms. Ragged holes in Seagull's shirt and ballistic vest attested to the bastards' use of cop killer bullets, essentially hardened, armor-piercing rounds. Thinking of the specialty bullets brought back memories of a heated exchange Connor had once engaged in with a gunnery sergeant about whether or not Teflon-coated rounds had better armor-piercing attributes than uncoated. He'd known for a fact that the Teflon hindered the bullets passing through Kevlar, but the sergeant had chewed his ass out over the disagreement. Alcohol had been involved, and later a fight had ensued.

Seagull coughed up another glob of blood-filled something onto his chest. The man's vacant eyes grew dim as his failing body shook to the point of convulsion. Connor hung on tightly, staring the boy in the face as his eyeballs rolled back into his skull. If there was any chance at all of Seagull being cognizant of his surroundings, he wanted the boy to know he wouldn't die alone. He deserved better.

With one final kick, Seagull lay motionless. Apparently whatever the Angel had done to seal up Seagull's previous gunshot wound didn't possess the strength to heal him a second time. The corpse felt heavier than the body, but Connor knew that to be an illusion brought on by the same raw emotion causing his throat to feel so swollen. Even in middle age, Connor knew what he had to do. He wasn't leaving this poor bastard to rot in this hell hole. With a grunt, he hefted the lifeless, awkward lump onto his shoulder.

Each step sent pain roaring through the insides of his knees, especially the left one, where a piece of shrapnel had shredded his ligaments in his youth. Now the physical strain of his life's occupation was catching up to him, and in a hurry. By the time he reached the first landing, he still had plenty of breath left, but his left knee was on fire, as if lanced by a flaming poker. At the second landing, just another ten steps up from the last, the gunfire above ceased. The grinding of the bones in his knees did not.

By the third landing, his legs were shaking with each timid movement. He felt like such a frail old man, being done in by cartilage decay. Twenty, hell, even ten years ago this would've been a walk in the park. What he felt most of all now was shame.

And that feeling didn't leave when Peacock and Emu appeared on either side of him to relieve him of his burden. At first he struggled against them, refusing to fully acknowledge his weakness, but then for the sake of Seagull's remains, he acquiesced. Between the two younger men, Seagull hung limp, his lifeless feet thumping on each step as the soldiers hustled him up to the top. On the way up, they stepped over the bodies of one, two, then three of the guards, each with an assortment of bullet wounds, but all sharing a hole in the back of the cranium. It was prudent to make sure the enemy never got back up.

Knight stood by a large door, the only exit off the final landing in the stairwell. The corpse of the fourth and final guard lay sprawled at his feet. The grim look on Knight's face twitched at the sight of Seagull's dead body, his blood now slowly forming red puddles on the concrete as Peacock and Emu held him steady.

"Take him down to the next floor," Knight said. "We're about to blow this door."

Everyone assembled on the landing below, except for the Demon, who remained at the sealed door. A small helicopter symbol above the frame hinted at what lay in wait on the other side. Now huddled closely around their fallen brother, each man paid

Seagull the courtesy of a sad look that quickly turned to grit and determination. They'd lost brothers before. They knew how to channel the loss into action.

Above them, the Demon attached a small black box to the door. Backing away from the door a few steps, the creature just stared at the box. Knight turned to the gathered men and told them to brace themselves. The vague warning drew a few concerned looks.

The sudden blast deafened Connor. Instinctively, his eyes slammed shut, and he grabbed the sides of his head with his hands. He opened his eyes quickly, and saw Knight yelling from the top of the stairs, motioning for the team to follow. Connor's hands shook as he pulled them from his ears. Slowly the dull noises formed into coherent sounds as Connor mounted the stairs with his men.

At the top of the stairs, the two heavy doors lay in pieces, the blackened remains scattered across a fifty-foot-wide section of the roof. The small explosive device's power was incredible. Connor regarded the Demon with even more hesitancy than before as he stepped onto the windy rooftop. In front of them, the rotors of a black McDonnell Douglas MD 600N started to warm up. A door on the left side of the roof from the Phalanx team burst open and eight of the facility's security team rumbled out in a textbook protection detail formation. With no cover nearby, Phalanx hit the deck collectively, waiting on Knight's signal.

From the open doorway emerged a giant of a man. He took only a half step before noticing the armed men lying prone to his right. The G36 assault rifle in the man's hands hinted that this was not the CEO of Celestius. A light hanging above the doorway revealed a pair of cold eyes discerning the nature of Phalanx's sudden appearance. Half the guards kept their eyes on Phalanx, the other half looked to the big blond for guidance. Connor just wondered what the big guy planned on doing with the G36's under-barrel grenade launcher attachment.

Knight acted first.

"Put your weapons down," he yelled.

Now all of the guards turned to their leader. Time crawled by as his men started to slowly lower their sights to the rooftop. The helicopter's rotors now whipped around at full speed, thumping loudly against the air. Connor looked to Knight, but the younger man only had eyes for the men across the way. Just when Connor thought the enemy would surrender peacefully, all hell broke loose.

A muffled pop sounded from the G36. The enemy leader started running for the helicopter. Knight screamed for his men to scatter. Connor leapt to his feet, feeling the sharp pangs in both knees. He dived as the grenade exploded in the open doorway behind him, the one the Demon had blown up earlier. There was no time to worry about that. Guns barked everywhere. Bullets whizzed by in all directions. Another grenade exploded, farther away this time. By the time Connor brought his M4 carbine to bear, the fighting was over. He could see the eight security guards lying mostly still. A few moaned, and one crawled for the open door nearby. A single shot from the Phalanx side halted his progress.

Up ahead, Connor could see Knight running forward for the chopper. The big man had already made it inside, but the windows were too tinted to see anything inside. A loud pop reverberated across the rooftop. Moments later, the helicopter door opened and the limp body of a pilot flopped out onto the roof. In the shadow of the door, the big bastard's G36 unleashed a few rounds towards Knight, who hit the deck. Phalanx all honed in on the chopper, firing in short bursts as the door closed and the helicopter started to hover slightly.

As the helicopter smoothly arced into the sky, Connor held his fire and watched as the Demon pulled out its spear. Standing this close, Connor could make out the intricate design of the blade mounted atop the weapon. A meshwork of thorny vines met at the tip. Within that twisted mass, a blue glow quickly grew into a blinding light enveloping the Demon. Connor watched in awe as the creature pointed the spear towards the fleeing helicopter and the blue light zipped off the tip of the spear and curved to match the chopper's trajectory. The flying projectile quickly caught up and impacted the helpless vehicle amidships. Chunks of the helicopter jettisoned out in all directions as a blue fire engulfed the entire cabin section. Casually, the Demon replaced the spear on its back, presumably just watching its handiwork.

Knight's shouts diverted Connor's attention from the floating inferno. He was approaching a man in a suit, who had materialized on the roof, near the doorway the guards had all emerged from. The suit had been as enraptured by the exploding helicopter as Connor had, but now the soldier yelling in front of him changed that. Panicking, the man pulled out a small pistol. Before the man drew a bead on Knight, Knight put a round through the man's elbow.

Connor waved the other Phalanx men back as they all crept forward, weapons raised. He gave the signal for them to establish a perimeter. Happily he noted that none of his men were dead, but a couple limped awkwardly as they sought to establish a perimeter on the roof. The Demon just ignored Connor, standing by his side silently, observing Knight as he loomed over the howling suit on the ground. Connor moved in closer, curious to know what the hell was going on.

"Murphy," Knight growled, his carbine centered on the man's skull. The touch of the warm barrel grabbed the man's attention.

"You don't understand," Murphy yelped. "These Angels are the only way we can win this war."

Knight just bored holes through the man with his stare. Connor had never seen his friend this pissed off before. Murphy grimaced and moaned before continuing rambling on.

"You must've lost friends in this fucking war, too," he said, each word pained. "We all did. But I can end it. We can end it. Kill these monsters, and the Angels can help us."

Still no response from Knight. Connor started to worry about what was going to happen next.

"We've harnessed their power," he said, his voice breaking wildly now. "The Middle-East will be wiped out. No more terrorists. America would be safe."

When Knight continued to ignore him, Murphy's eyes grew wide.

"They killed my parents. On 9/11. Give me this. Give me my revenge," he croaked.

Now Knight spoke, his words full of ground-up hatred.

"Did you give the order for Phalanx to kill two reporters in Phoenix?"

In a bizarre juxtaposition, Murphy laughed while gripping his mangled arm.

"Ha, so that's who you boys are," he said gleefully. "Phalanx."

Knight tapped him on the forehead with the barrel of his rifle.

"Ease up there, cowboy. We're on the same team," Murphy said, not looking any more worried as he laughed again. "How did it feel murdering them? You look pissed, so were you the one who did them?"

As Murphy rattled on and on about Knight killing the two reporters, the soldier swung his rifle behind his back and casually unholstered his pistol. When Murphy saw this gesture, his words slowed down, but didn't stop.

"You're my puppet, you ignorant—"

Before Connor could intervene, Knight's hand rocketed out. Murphy's jaw cracked grotesquely as the pistol made solid contact with the side of his face. His scream pierced the air. Connor took a step forward to break it up, but Knight waved him off with an evil glare.

"Where are the Angels?" he barked at Murphy.

"No—"

That was enough.

"Come on, Andy. We don't have time for this," Connor implored him. "Just let the Demon read his mind."

In response, Knight stood up and shot Murphy in the knee. The man's cry reached a whole new pitch as Connor watched, surprisingly disturbed by the scene. He'd seen some serious shit in his time, but maybe he'd been stuck behind a desk for too long now. He was slipping.

Murphy's shrieks turned into slightly coherent words as Knight pointed the pistol at the other knee.

"No!" he exclaimed. He gestured wildly towards the open door. "Take these stairs to the elevator. Subbasement Two. Follow signs for Containment Area."

Knight pointed the gun at Murphy's head.

"Holy shit, I'm telling the truth," Murphy exclaimed. Connor spoke into the boom microphone attached to his ear, relaying instructions for Phalanx to converge on the door. Unfortunately, that put the scene with Murphy in plain view of everyone. Murphy turned and pointed at Connor, but kept his frantic eyes glued on Knight.

"That guy called you Andy, right? You're Andrew Knight, right?"

The pistol remained trained on Murphy's cranium. Knight's face revealed nothing other than utter disdain.

"I healed your wife!"

As Phalanx rallied up on Connor, Knight spoke quietly, seemingly oblivious to the audience. Connor could tell that each word crawled out from a deep, dark place inside his friend.

"No," he said. "You killed her."

Then the pistol emphatically uttered just one syllable, loudly.

Chapter 52

Five minutes later, Knight trotted down a long, dimly lit corridor in the second subbasement with the remainder of Phalanx in tow. He'd opted to take the stairs all the way down instead of the elevator mentioned by Murphy. The security operation in this damn place exceeded anything Knight could've imagined. No doubt somebody still manned a command and control center somewhere in the immense facility, and they'd be all too happy to trap Phalanx inside a moveable steel coffin.

So the stairs it was. By the time they reached the last flight, Knight's legs had started to get that wobbly, jelly feeling. The adrenaline shooting through his veins after the discourse with Murphy had finally worn off, leaving him feeling clumsy and unsure of himself. The piece of shit had deserved death certainly, but Knight suspected his interrogation tactics perhaps stepped over the line. Never had Connor tried to intercede on a target's behalf.

Up ahead, an illuminated sign hung from the ceiling, with an arrow pointing to the left. *Containment Area.* Instantly, Nualaan transferred this new data onto the few Demons remaining alive. The transaction took less time than before, since more Demons had died while ransacking the place looking for the Angels, but the intensity still jarred Knight something fierce. He paused briefly before the intersection below the sign, shaking the cobwebs loose in his head, trying to focus.

A hand tapped him twice on the shoulder, and Knight looked up to see Peacock pass by and peek his head around the corner. The man's helmet shot right off. His head snapped back at a peculiar angle, and his stiff body gracefully floated to the concrete floor.

"Shooter!"

Knight lunged forward, grabbed the dead man's collar, and yanked him back out of the way. No more shots fired. Nualaan stepped to the corner and pulled out a small device that Knight recognized only too readily. As the Demon hurled the flashbang, Knight noticed pock marks and deep gouges all over the silvery armor across Nualaan's chest. Maybe that explained why he wasn't so eager to jump in front of heavy fire anymore.

Armor cannot last forever.

Nualaan hadn't spoken directly to Knight in a while, and the silent words caught him a bit off-guard. The bang was intense even behind the protection of the wall. Cries of surprised anguish filled the hall. Knight definitely could relate. He waved two of his men to dart across the intersection as he and Emu popped from cover to lay down suppressing fire. To his surprise, three guards stumbled blindly out in the open. A few bursts from Phalanx's rifles dropped the men dead.

An eerie stillness descended upon the scene. Staring down his sights, Knight could see smoke drifting lazily from his barrel. No other movement caught his eye until one of the fresh corpses twitched. Multiple rifles engaged the dead target, causing unnatural convulsions before the body settled for the last time. After the loud outburst, only a dull ringing remained in Knight's ears, despite his hearing protection. He tapped Emu on the shoulder and signaled him to follow as he stood and stepped down the corridor, weapon ready.

"Halt!"

Knight froze. The undeniably Scottish voice had come from up ahead, near a reinforced blast door of some description. Only now that he was in the corridor could Knight see that a cut-out on either side of the walls at the end could provide cover for a couple of enemy combatants.

Shit. We're standing out in the open with nowhere to go.

Knight waved the signal for his backup to cover both of the partially hidden recesses ahead. There was nothing else to do except wait.

"This whole tunnel is wired to blow," the bodiless voice announced. Knight noted the confidence. This wasn't some frightened pissant trying a last-ditch bluff.

Connor spoke into Knight's earpiece.

"Andy, let me talk to him."

Probably not a bad idea with my current track record.

"Sure," Knight whispered.

"Don't do anything hasty here." Connor's bold, senior officer voice was only enhanced by the echoing acoustics of the corridor. "We're on the same team."

"I don't know who you are, but we're not on any team together," the Scot replied.

"It's over, soldier. Murphy's dead."

After a brief silence, the man said, "Prove it."

Connor laughed quietly.

"What do you want me to do? Throw his head down the hallway to you? Come on, soldier. How do you think we found this place when all those Demons upstairs couldn't?"

A pin dropping would've deafened everyone. Connor continued.

"So you agree that he probably told us how to get down there? Good. Now, there's some serious shit you need to know, soldier."

"Like what?"

Connor whispered in Knight's ear to tell him about the Angels' true purpose. After a moment of contemplation in which the desire to lob a frag grenade at the idiot obstructing his mission seemed tempting, Knight pushed aside his more volatile urges. They could only save the world if they got this last defender to let them through. He took a deep breath and hastily ran through the Angels' sordid past and the small point about them trying to terraform Earth into a toxic wasteland for their own purposes.

"People turning into swarms of nano-bugs that will destroy the environment? Sounds a wee bit far-fetched to me," was the Scotsman's only response.

You'll have to go far to fetch your head if you don't let me through this damn door.

Connor interceded, perhaps due to some paternal instinct receiving violent undertones from Knight's stance.

"What's your name, soldier?"

"None of your bloody business, old man."

"Fair enough, soldier," Connor said without skipping a beat. "I don't need to tell you that the touch of these Angels makes humans disappear. Think about it. It's not just some string of coincidences here. These Angels are exterminating us."

"Like I said: sounds far-fetched."

"Okay, then you should know that Murphy and his brother were weaponizing the vaporizing effect of the Angel's touch in order to eradicate our Islamic friends over in the Middle-East."

Now the Scotsman replied with the first hints of uncertainty.

"That's not true," he said quickly. "This is medical research, that's all—"

"Grow up, soldier," Connor snapped. "You think a complete dick-hole like David Murphy is going to sink his fortune into developing an all-powerful cure to all of the ailments that his drugs treat? That's a shitty business model."

Knight. The Angels.

While Connor continued his pointless debate with the Angels' last guard, Knight looked at the tall Demon behind him. In his huge armored hand, Nualaan held yet another odd-looking device. Where did he keep pulling these things from?

A blurry image filled Knight's vision. He shook his head violently as his brain rejected the data being forced upon it. Even behind tightly shut eyelids, the multicolored image morphed and grew in intensity.

What is this? Stop it!

Angels are transforming.

Okay, okay. Just turn it off!

Just like that, the images snapped off, allowing Knight to see properly again. He rocked on his heels as his center of balance fought the cyclone of spatial ambiguity left in the wake of the Demon's breaking and entering. An army of little men ran through his skull, pounding on his brain cavity as impressively as during any hangover he'd ever suffered.

Tell the man now.

Tell him what? I still don't under—

TELL HIM TO LOOK AT THE ANGELS. NOW.

Chapter 53

"So you want me to look at the Angels, do you?"

I want *you to open the damn door.*

The man wasn't cooperating, and Knight didn't have time for this. Despite having very little idea about what was going on, he could sense Nualaan's rapidly expanding unease about the Angels on the other side of the giant doors ahead. What other options did they have if this idiot didn't comply with Knight's request? They couldn't risk the bastard detonating whatever explosives he'd used to rig the corridor.

A dim blue glow appeared on the far wall on the right side of the corridor. Knight signaled to his men: One target, right. They nodded, but no one had a clear shot. The Scotsman's quiet words were barely discernible. It sounded like he was asking someone to link his phone directly into the Angels' Containment Area. After a few tense moments, an audible gasp echoed down the hall.

"Bloody hell," the man exclaimed. "I'm coming out. Don't shoot me."

Knight waved all the Phalanx rifles to the floor and told the man to reveal himself. A tall man with the bearing of a soldier cautiously stepped out of hiding. No weapon was in his hands, just a small black device. Knight raised his rifle and his men copied the gesture.

"Easy, mates," the Scot shouted as he slowly bent to the ground. He dropped the device on the floor with a click. "It's just my phone. The hall isn't wired anyway. Just a wee bluff."

The man's easy smile enraged Knight. He sprinted forward and grabbed the man by his collar.

"What's your name?" he demanded.

"Baird," the man answered, his voice not wavering in the slightest.

Typical British smugness.

"Baird, open this fucking door. Now!"

The man broke free of Knight's grip with a simple twist of the wrist and backed away a few steps, awaiting any retaliation from Knight. When Knight did nothing more than glare, Baird typed a code into the security panel on the wall. While the man's attention was diverted, Knight closed and opened his gloved hand a few times, checking for any sprain from the Scot's defensive maneuver. Everything seemed in order, so he readied up by the door. After a series of hisses and beeps, the giant grey mass slid down into the floor, unveiling a mad scientist's laboratory beyond.

"Welcome to the Containment Area, gents," Baird announced as he crossed the threshold. Knight followed cautiously, panning his rifle around the room, checking for any ambush. There was no reason to fully trust their new amigo just yet. Reading Knight's mind, Baird remarked, "Easy, mate. All we've got to worry about in here are these three pink bastards."

The Containment Area was a wide space, but not very deep. To the right side of the room stood a large closet of sorts. The bright yellow sign above the entryway read, "High Voltage." The interior was mostly dark other than a few red LEDs piercing the gloom. To Knight's left, a short staircase led to a platform containing a workstation of some kind. The blast doors that Baird had just opened lay in the center of the width of the room, so Phalanx stared straight at three enormous transparent cylinders. Each probably stood fifteen feet tall by five feet wide. The shadowy outlines of three tall figures could be seen in the midst of the swirling white gas that filled each tube. An unusually dark blue ambient light covered everything other than a few white spotlights targeting the highlights of the room.

Baird hopped up the stairs on the left to access the workstation. He pushed a few buttons, probably entering a password, then slid a wide lever to its lowest position. The vibrations of a powerful motor could be felt through the floor. Moments later, a humming noise was accompanied by a *whoosh* as the white gas in each containment cylinder evacuated from view.

"We keep the Angels in a form of stasis when not in use," Baird explained as the fog swirled. "I'm just clearing the air out in there to see what's going on. The infrared camera I looked through a minute ago showed some weird—"

Baird seized up midsentence as the clouds dissipated in the tubes. He killed the motors for the pumps that were pulling the gas out. The room grew deathly silent.

"What the hell is that?" Connor blurted out, the only man who could find his tongue.

Standing inside the purged cylinders were not three pink aliens. Instead, black, writhing masses in the shapes of the giant aliens presented themselves to Phalanx. The bodies looked to be made of liquid tar as the surfaces flowed and swirled slowly under intense spotlights.

Too late.

Knight turned to Nualaan.

What do you mean?

Look.

In each cylinder, the oddly precise outlines of the Angels' bodies melted from view. Emu gasped, expressing everyone's concern in one poignant syllable.

"Shit."

What's going on?

It is starting.

What is?

The end of your world. This is the signal. The Angels transform into swarms to lead the integration into your planet's ecosystems.

What swarms?

A second later, it was Knight's turn to curse. Inside each cylinder, a black sphere rose from the ground. In the lights, the surfaces of the spheres resembled nothing Knight could describe. The eddy currents rippling across the exteriors of the spheres twisted and contorted seemingly at random, but it was hard to draw his eyes away from the controlled chaos. The spheres started to expand horizontally, forming short cylinders at first floating in midair, but then making contact with the inner surfaces of the containment tubes.

"Oh, shite," Baird said, fear creeping into his words. "They're trying to break out."

What do we do? Can you kill them with your spear?

Spear is not strong enough. We need more power.

"Where the hell are we going to get more power?" Knight wondered aloud.

"Oi, Demon bloke," Baird yelled. "Can't you just zap them with that spear of yours?"

Knight answered on Nualaan's behalf. "No, it's not powerful enough."

The transparent material of the leftmost containment tube started to crack. At first, just a tiny hairline fracture, but then a vast array of intersecting spider webs. Knight looked wide-eyed up at Baird, who still manned the desk.

"Baird, what can we do?"

After a moment's contemplation, Baird punched a button on the desk.

"Pick up, pick up, pick up," he muttered.

"Yeah, this is Reynolds. I'm still here in the security center," said a voice across some hidden loudspeakers. "What in the shit are you doing down there Baird? And did you just purge the chambers?"

"Aye, but just listen," Baird snapped. "How do I refill the tubes?"

"You can't, bro. That gas is destroyed each time it's evacuated out. The readings from this end show the reserves are too low to fill all three chambers right now. Shit, you don't even have enough sedative for one."

"What other options have we got?" Knight called up.

"Who is that?" Reynolds said anxiously. "Who else have you got down there? I'm showing a whole bunch of people in there with you."

"Doesn't matter, Reynolds," Baird said. "We have to destroy these bastards. They've mutated into something else."

"I can see that. Sort of."

The middle chamber started to splinter under the strain of the expanding blob inside. A few pieces of the container tinkled onto the metal walkway surrounding the Angels.

"So what can we do?" Baird demanded. "Didn't you guys design in a kill-switch?"

"Look, you're not going to like this—"

Now the third chamber formed a giant crack, far more audibly than the others. Knight motioned for his men to fan out.

"JUST TELL ME," Baird yelled.

"It was never finished."

"What was never finished?"

Reynolds sighed loudly, filling the whole room with his disappointment.

"The engineers are still waiting on the final piece of equipment that connects the main power for the facility into some kind of lightning generator. They got the idea from that Demon that kept killing all the Angels." Reynolds paused. "Holy shit, there's a Demon in there with you!"

"Aye, I know. Tell me about this missing equipment."

Longer and deeper fissures formed in all three chambers as Reynolds' disembodied voice explained the situation. The engineers needed a custom power switch that would branch the main power into a giant battery. He didn't know the scientific specifics, but these were the layman's terms that he'd been given. This battery would then discharge into the three chambers, vaporizing the Angels.

Can we short the main power into this battery with a piece of conductive material?

Nualaan's English was getting better by the minute. Knight relayed the question to Baird and Reynolds.

"You'll have to go into the room at the other end of the Containment Area," Reynolds said. "It's going to be one hell of a spark, but I don't even know what you'd shove in there. It needs to be about seven feet long, if I remember correctly."

Nualaan pulled the spear off his back. Knight noted that it was only six feet in length.

That's not long enough.

I will make it work.

A loud crunch grabbed everyone's attention. The chamber on the left wouldn't hold much longer as the black cylinder inside it grew ever shorter, and ever wider. Footsteps echoed down the main corridor behind Knight, the one that Baird had pretended was booby-trapped. Three more Demons stalked their way into the

Containment Area. The huge volumes of communication flowing between the four reunited Demons boggled Knight's inferior brain. Even though it wasn't on the forefront of his mind, he couldn't ignore the bizarre ramblings going on in the background.

After declaring his intent with a surprisingly detailed visual representation, Nualaan made for the "High Voltage" sign. The other three Demons, one of whom was a good twelve feet tall, followed, their anxiety so strong that Knight couldn't help feeling worried also. They'd almost reached the adjoining room when the first chamber shattered completely.

The black mass expanded out into a razor-thin circle, suspended motionless in the ruin of its prison. At first no one moved, but the stalemate didn't last long. First one, and then two of the Phalanx soldiers opened fire on the hovering disc. Knight yelled for a ceasefire, but it was too late. Seemingly immune to the bullets, the disc morphed into something like a fist the size of a footlocker, then zipped lightning-quick towards its two assailants. The fist slowed as it enveloped the first man above the waist. His muffled scream lasted only a second.

Swarm.

Behind Knight, the Demons were clambering around inside the power room, for lack of a better descriptor. In front of him, the swarm was darting from man to man, engulfing their bodies for ten or so seconds each, then moving on, leaving nothing but the ragged stumps of legs behind. As the swarm left each body, the remains of the men's thighs flopped down, the legs bending at the knee before falling over.

The swarm latched onto the man next to Knight, who dived backwards. Connor gave a half-hearted grunt as the back of Knight's helmet smashed into the bridge of his nose. The older man toppled backwards into Emu's arms. Knight tripped over Connor's lifeless legs, sending all three men to the ground. The swarm's newest victim's blood-curdling cry was cut short as the swarm decimated his body. Beyond, the second containment chamber bulged around its midsection, ready to burst. Knight and Emu scrambled to their feet and dragged Connor's unconscious body behind a giant brace running up the wall near the exit.

Help!

Whether the swarm possessed any true intelligence or not, Knight had no idea, but as soon as the four Demons emerged from the small room with their lightning spears in hand, the black mass rocketed towards them. Much faster than their human counterparts, the Demons scattered instantly as the swarm missed and silently impacted the wall, breaking against the obstruction fluidly. In a single pulse, the swarm reformed. Knight and Emu remained crouched in a protective formation beside Connor, rifles raised, for whatever good that might do. A clinking noise drew their attention back to the middle of the room.

The second swarm's about to break free!

One of the Demons gained its feet instantly and ran back into the power room. The swarm thrashed from location to location, trying in vain to catch the other three nimble Demons as they dodged and wove their way to safety. In Knight's mind, he could sense the panic and distress of two of the Demons, but from Nualaan he got nothing. The assassin glided like a ghost, totally untouchable and fearless. The other two moved more erratically, waving their energized spears around in futile hopes of making contact with the swarm. Knight just sat on the floor with Connor and Emu, the only other Phalanx members still in possession of their heads. What in the world were they supposed to do?

Peeling his eyes away from the fight in progress, Knight observed the Demon inside the power room, ripping protective panels and cover-plates off the walls. In his head, Knight suddenly experienced an epiphany, followed by a short-lived jubilance. This glee faded quickly, replaced by the grim realization of imminent death. Spurred on by the shattering of the second chamber, the Demon drove one end of its short spear into an exposed outlet, and then punched an armored hand into another receptacle on the other side of the room.

The powerful spotlights dimmed to almost nothing as a deep *hum* filled the cavernous space. Knight could feel the vibrations in his bones, but the prickly sensation across his skin gave him more pause. In front of him, the second chamber was completely destroyed. An amorphous blob now resided in the empty space. A glow formed around the base of each of the three chambers. In the one chamber still intact, the swarm inside suddenly broke, fragments of it whipping around in a fury. The white glow below continued to grow as the hairs on Knight's neck stood on end.

The power room exploded in fireworks. The charred body of the brave Demon launched from the mouth of the room and slid across the floor. Knight instinctively covered his boss's vulnerable body. A bleep sounded from somewhere on the platform to Knight's left. He looked up. Standing stoically at the workstation, Baird hovered his finger over a button, watching the swarms.

"See you in hell."

He hit the button.

With an ungodly crack, lightning fired in each chamber, blinding Knight. Pain drove his eyes shut, but the ghostly white etching remained, floating around in his darkened vision. The artificial lightning was astonishingly quiet after the brutal initial contact. Knight opened his eyes, hearing only the fizz and pop of three bolts of pure electricity ripping through the chambers. The leftmost had been totally destroyed already by the first swarm. The rightmost remained sealed as the energy burned away the swarm inside.

The center cylinder was broken apart. To Knight's horror, a dark mass swam in the air around the crackling electricity.

"Oh crap, it missed," Baird yelped as the shape flew towards him. He ducked behind the workstation just in time as the mass swooped over his head. Instead of striking again, this new swarm made a beeline across the room, ignoring the remainder of Phalanx, and collided with the first swarm. A flurry of chaotic activity broke out between the two. The stormy coupling hovered around the room, separating and then rejoining over and over, each time more viciously.

Initially, Knight's hopes rose, wondering if this violent interaction would kill off one or both swarms. His heart sank as the turbulent mass quieted down, revealing a terrifying result.

The swarms had combined.

Baird leapt from the workstation platform as the deadly black mass darted in his direction. Knight held his breath, but at the last second Baird dropped to the ground. The super-swarm skimmed across his back, leaving a fleshy gash over one of his shoulders. He cried out incoherently, but fought to get up. Nualaan appeared at his side to propel him back onto his feet. The other two Demons struck out at the immense swarm with their electrified spears, trying to divert its attention. Each crack of the spears drew only a fraction of the hostility this smooth black sphere held for Baird as it stalked after him.

"We've still got enough charge for one more shock," boomed Reynolds' voice over the PA. "Get the swarm into one of those broken chambers, and I'll remotely fire the sequence."

Baird made eye contact with Knight as he hobbled past, making his way towards the chambers.

"I've got a wee plan, mate," the man grunted through clenched teeth.

Knight stood and watched helplessly as the Scotsman disappeared into the shadows of the smoking cylinder. He backed up as the swarm approached, still harassed by the three Demons, but seemingly hell-bent on reaching Baird.

He killed the other one.

This swarm will not stop until he is dead.

Standing defiantly inside the scorched containment chamber, Baird ignored the glow emanating around his feet and hurled abuse at the swarm.

"Get at me, you stupid bastard!"

As if sensing the plan in action, the swarm paused, hovering just a few feet away from Baird's face. Now the shocks and prods from the Demons did nothing to affect this hateful mass. Knight felt the hairs on his neck standing once more as a humming noise grew in intensity. The sequence was starting, but the Angel wasn't in the chamber. Beside Knight, Connor started to rouse.

"What the—?" he muttered, groggy from his incapacitation.

"Shhh," Knight snapped, pointing at the standoff in progress.

The sphere started to shake, at first more like a twitch, but then eventually in raging, spastic convulsions. Sparks flew as the Demons repeatedly thrust rippling spears into the mass, trying to compel it forward.

It hates him too much.

"Up yours, you—"

Baird's final words were lost in the mix as the swarm lunged. The bystanders instinctively shielded their eyes as the lightning smashed through Baird and swarm alike with a resounding *crack*. Knight struggled to open his eyes even slightly as the energy pounded between the electrodes.

As the smoke cleared, the stench of burned flesh spread to Knight's nostrils. He coughed, but forced himself to look on as the wispy mist parted. Both Baird and the swarm were gone.

Chapter 54

Exiting the ruined Celestius facility passed by in a blur for Knight. His well-trained autopilot forced him to continually check his surroundings for hostiles, but he was only going through the motions. If any remaining security guards got the drop on him, it would probably be the end.

All the surviving group encountered on their way out was silence. Silence, and dead bodies. The Demons had done a hell of a job mopping up the defensive forces before heading down into the Angels' lair. Few hallways in the facility were free of human corpses. Fewer still contained dead Demons. Not until he stepped over the first deceased Demon he'd found earlier did Knight snap out of his funk. The charred remains looked exactly the same. Nualaan crossed over the body without a second glance. Apparently Demons had different ideals on respect for fallen brothers.

Just a random person.

Knight stopped, standing next to the smoldering wreckage of the crashed spaceship. The pale sunrise peeked over the top of a building outside, casting its yellow rays through the ragged hole made by the doomed spacecraft. He pointed back to the dead Demon, but Nualaan just kept walking.

What about burial? You're just leaving him?

We don't touch our own dead. That is a bad omen.

You touched dead humans.

I also touched them when I killed them. It is not the same as touching our own dead.

Connor and Emu watched the silent exchange, probably confused. On one side, Knight gesticulated towards some dead alien. On the other side, the three living Demons just climbed out of the broken building, seemingly ignoring the concerned human. When Knight gave up and clambered after Nualaan, the two remaining Phalanx men followed.

"Hey, Andy. I need to tell you something."

Knight stopped and turned to Connor. After a nod, Emu wandered off a few yards ahead, not looking comfortable hanging out alone too close to the aliens ahead of him. Standing in the breaking of a new day, Connor looked guilty as sin. For what, Knight wasn't sure.

"Look, when I told you earlier Brian was dead," Connor said. "I didn't tell you the whole story."

"Okay."

"He died in the hospital, Andy," Connor said, sighing as he unloaded a great weight off his shoulders. "Brian didn't make it out of there alive."

"But, I already know what happened in there," Knight said, suddenly confused. "I saw it through Nualaan's eyes. He didn't kill him."

Connor's face took on a pained expression.

"Nualaan, huh?" he said. "Well, I hate to be the one to say it, but your new friend didn't share everything with you."

The response fostered an anger in Knight, even before he knew any facts.

"What do you mean?"

Connor looked past Knight and started walking slowly after Emu and the Demons.

"Andy, after he dumped his memories to you, he did one more thing before leaving."

"Mike, get to the damn point," Knight snapped. "Just tell me."

Connor stopped and faced his friend.

"Brian was downed, but the video makes it look like he was trying to pull the pin on a grenade. Before he could, the Demon ran him through with that spear of his."

"Holy shit—"

Knight felt Connor's hand on his shoulder, but he avoided the man's searching eyes. In his head, conflicted emotions rattled around endlessly.

"I should've told you earlier, Andy, but we didn't think you'd handle it well enough to finish your mission."

"It can't be true."

"Andy, look at me. Why would I lie about this?" Connor asked. "Kestrel, I mean Dick, watched it happen. That's why he's gone on leave. The guy crashed hard under the guilt he felt for not stopping the Demon from killing Brian."

That was it. Knight charged after Nualaan, yelling at the top of his lungs.

"Hey! Get back here."

His words fell on deaf ears.

The distance between himself and Nualaan closed rapidly. Reaching his target, he shoved the big Demon with all of his frustrated rage. To Knight's great dissatisfaction, the bigger creature hardly budged; however, Nualaan did turn to face him.

He was going to hurt me.

"So what? You didn't have to kill him."

What would you rather I did? Maimed him?

"You could've just disarmed him."

Knight lunged forward, but Nualaan was faster. Knight's arm felt like it was being crushed in a vice when the Demon grabbed him and held him easily at bay. Emu pulled his rifle up towards the Demon, but had no shot with Knight in the way.

"He was my friend, you bastard," Knight growled.

You tried to kill me before you knew who or what I was. How is this any different?

When Knight gave no response other than staring at the ground, Nualaan went on.

Your race shoots first and asks question later all the time. This is no different. I had a mission, just like you did, and one human threatened my success. You would have done the same.

The penetrating wisdom of the Demon's words struck a painful chord in Knight. Nualaan must've sensed the defeat in him, because the Demon released his iron grip and started walking again. Knight just followed, as downcast as he'd ever been. Karen was gone. Brian was gone. What did he have left? Connor was staring at him, but the soldier couldn't meet his boss's eyes, couldn't explain why he was trailing helplessly behind his best friend's killer.

None of this matters.

"How do you figure?" Knight mumbled.

This planet's ecology is already changing too much, even without the Angel swarms.

Knight abruptly stopped, all other thoughts thrust from his mind.

"What do you mean?"

The sensors on my ship indicate that the scourge has spread too rapidly. The scent of death fills the air.

"Very poetic. Are you saying we're all going to die anyway?" The thought alone shocked Knight. Connor looked like he'd just been punched in the balls. Emu swore in Spanish.

Killing the Angels should feel invigorating. You exacted your revenge, as did I.

"Are we going to die? Damn it."

The three Demons slowed as they neared one of their ships. Nualaan stopped to confront Knight and his human counterparts. A small device appeared in the Demon's hand.

Not all of you, no.

Chapter 55

"Andy, what the hell's going on?"

Connor's question hung unanswered as Knight vacillated over how to break the news. For once, Nualaan wasn't transmitting any helpful ideas his way. The vacuum of thought in his head freely absorbed the startling dread emanating from the razor-thin, shiny black device in Nualaan's gloved hand. As far as Knight knew, the Demons had gone silent.

But why?

"Mike, we've got a bit of a problem," Knight said carefully, still keeping his eyes on Nualaan. The Demon waved the small black tool over himself once, then twice. When finished, the smaller of the three Demons stepped forward. Nualaan ran the black device across the Demon's body once, twice, then three times.

"What kind of problem, Andy?"

The small Demon gracefully removed its spear from its sheath on its back. With one deft movement, the spear spun to point at its wielder. The weapon sparkled as the Demon drove the tip through its own chest. No audible scream could be heard, but Knight fell to one knee as a roaring anguish ripped through his own head, transmitted to him through Nualaan. The Demon jerkily twisted the shaft of the spear lodged in its torso. A brilliant flash exploded before their eyes.

When the light faded, only a spear remained on a scorched patch of earth.

"What the *hell*, Andy?" Connor yelled.

Knight regained his feet as Nualaan ran the ominous fate-decider over the taller Demon. This one stood about twelve feet tall, its armor similar in construction to Nualaan's, but a shade of reflective brown, instead of the metallic silver. Both Demons sported countless scrapes and tears where bullets had scarred their protective coverings. As Nualaan scanned his associate for a second time, an incredible wave of relief hit Knight, contrasting viciously with the fear broiling in his own gut.

Nualaan turned the device on Emu, who immediately dropped to his knees, crossed himself, and started mumbling and stammering prayers in his native tongue. When the Demon turned the scanner to Emu for a third time, every muscle and sinew in Knight's body wanted to lurch forward, to somehow interdict the inevitable.

Do not move.

Tears rolled down Emu's cheeks as Nualaan stepped past him, waving the device over Connor, who stood stiff as a board. The other Demon, the tall brown one, hovered close to Nualaan as he performed whatever test was taking place. After the third pass over Connor, Nualaan stepped in front of Knight. Trying to emulate his mentor in the face of death, Knight fought to hold the shakes in check. He didn't fully know if it was terror or anger that sought to fight against this injustice, but he remained stock still as the Demon scanned him only twice.

You are clean.

The sigh of relief, the release of unbelievable tension, felt like the sleuth gates opening in Hoover Dam. Knight put one hand on his face, and reached with the other to pat Connor on the back.

Do not touch him.

No!

Before Knight could even turn, Nualaan's arm jarred him in the chest, knocking him ten feet backwards. Gasping for breath, Knight pulled himself onto his knees. He lifted his head in time to see both Demons synchronously drive their spears through the hearts of his friends.

"Stop!"

The Demons ignored him. Connor's face twisted like he'd just smelled something foul. From his lips, only the slightest grunt escaped. Kneeling next to him, Emu screamed bloody murder, staring incredulously at the gnarled spear jutting from his chest. Wordlessly, the Demons twisted the spear shafts. Now Knight was on his feet, ignoring his lungs protesting for more air as he lumbered forward.

But he was too late.

The spears glowed an incredible blue before bursting into a flare bright enough to knock Knight back down. Recovering as quickly as possible, Knight crawled the remaining distance, but found only burned concrete to greet him.

"What the *fuck* was that?" he screamed.

They were infected.

Knight stayed on his hands and knees, staring at where his closest living friend had stood just moments ago.

"You didn't have to kill them."

They could have infected us. You would have done the same.

"Stop saying that. There had to be another way—"

This does not matter. Not now. Your planet is dying. We provided a far cleaner, painless death than that which would have found them soon.

Now Knight looked up at the Demon.

"Like the death I have to look forward to, you mean?"

You have a chance. You can join myself and Maarus. Our home world is also dead, but there are other places we can go.

"There's got to be a way to fix this—"

You can be the last of your species, but we must leave now. Already the lower atmosphere around your planet is becoming toxic.

"The last of my species?"

Karen, if you were still here, we could leave together. There might be a cure out there for you, a cure without Angels.

Your wife's death was not your fault.

I failed her when she needed me most.

Nualaan put a hand on Knight's shoulder as he crouched on the ground. The unusual display must've been picked up from watching Connor.

None of this matters in the grand scheme. Everyone makes mistakes, but your planet is doomed. We must go.

Knight stood.

"What about McGarvey? He had a hand in all of this. He gets to just live out the rest of his days in freedom?"

Death will find him soon enough without your help.

I'd prefer to put the bullet in his head myself.

With that, Nualaan and Maarus walked towards their spaceship. The sun now levitated low in the sky, its reflection displayed radiantly upon the side of the mirror-surfaced vehicle. The beauty of the sight distracted Knight until a break formed in the mirror. A black shadow traced down the side of the ship, reaching the bottom edge silently. Maarus disappeared into the shadow, effortlessly passing through. Nualaan walked to the dark shape, then turned to Knight. The gesture was very human.

Come.

Knight inched his way to the ship and peered into the infinite blackness. Never before had he seen the absolute absence of light. A strong hand on his back ushered him across the plane. A tingling sensation rippled across him from front to back, and then there was nothing. When Nualaan prodded him, Knight realized he still had his eyes closed. Upon opening them, he found himself inside a cockpit of sorts.

Two gigantic chairs loomed behind a blank console. Nualaan and Maarus seated themselves as a series of red lights danced across the sleek panel in the console.

Sit.

Where?

Look.

Confused, Knight glanced to one side and saw a ghostly green outline shimmering on the wall. He approached the peculiar shape and realized it was another chair, more simple in design than the ones the Demons used, but equally large. When he touched it, the green illumination disappeared. He pulled his hand back quickly.

As we grow closer together, I can highlight my instructions visually for you.

So you made it green?

Correct. Now sit.

Feeling like a six-year-old mounting his father's precious old recliner, Knight clambered up into the chair. At first, the surface was cold and rigid. After a few moments, the shape of the chair contoured to match Knight's posture, enveloping his back and legs. Despite the intense comfort of his chair, he recoiled at the movement.

Trust me. You are safe here.

Knight eased back into the chair and noticed a warm feeling centering around his lower back. His eyes grew heavy as the fatigue of the last few days overcame him. Thoughts of Karen, Brian, and Mike all floated around in his head, but he felt powerless to escape the pull of merciful sleep.

The sensor array indicates the swarm spores in the lower atmosphere will reach critical levels within the hour.

That got Knight's attention.

What does that mean?

That means the infectious particles will soon contaminate your entire race. Those who are not already condemned. There is only one course of action left to us.

"What can you do? I thought you said it was hopeless?"

Chapter 56

Nualaan stood and walked to the far side of the cockpit. In front of Knight's face, a simulated projection of the Earth appeared. Small red dots flashed at intervals, forming a wide net around the planet.

Maarus is remotely piloting all of our remaining ships around your planet.

The red dots.

Correct. Here, take this.

The projected view faded, and Knight could see Nualaan before him, holding something in his hand.

"What's this?" he asked, taking the object from the Demon.

A breathing mask. Hold it over your mouth.

The light object morphed gently over Knight's lower jaw and up over his nose. His first intake of breath failed, like he'd just had a plastic bag tied tightly over his face. Terror jumped all over him as he tore his fingers across the outer surface of the mask. Nualaan pulled his clawing hands away.

Just give it a moment. I should have warned you to take a deep breath first. I forget that this is all new to you. Our air requirement is not so different from your own, but first we must slowly acclimatize you to it. Hence, the breathing apparatus.

True enough, after ten seconds, cool air reached Knight's nose. His panic retreated until he tried to open his mouth, only to find it clamped shut by the mask.

I can't talk. I can't eat or drink. What am I supposed to do?

Calm down.

Nualaan placed a finger on the corner of Knight's jaw.

Open wide.

Now the mask bent, conforming to the new shape easily.

You can talk now, but it will be very muffled. I will show you later how you will ingest nutrients.

That sounds ominous.

You will find out soon enough.

Nualaan took his chair once more and reached up to the silver mask covering his face. A click sounded from where his glove touched the mask and a hiss of air escaped, but as the Demon's face was about to be revealed, Knight's entire view changed to an breathtaking shot from above the Earth. He hadn't even felt the spaceship take off. For all he'd known, they were still parked in Colorado.

That's amazing.

Enjoy the view while it lasts.

What do you mean?

A dull throbbing pulsed throughout the ship as Knight was forced to watch the Earth from outer orbit.

Uh, what are you doing?

We cannot let the Angels colonize your planet.

Panic rose again.

So what are you doing?

They are a plague in this universe.

Just tell me!

Each of our vessels is armed with a plasma cannon and explosive ordnances. We will destroy the planet's atmosphere, creating a totally uninhabitable environment.

You're going to kill everyone?

A deep sadness accompanied Nualaan's next words.

They are already dead, condemned by the Angels they so readily embraced.

Just like Knight and the rest of humanity, Nualaan and his people had fallen for the imposters.

So this just makes it faster? Cleaner?

There will be suffering, but far less.

Not that he had any say in the matter, but Knight said out loud, "Do it."

This was bigger than even the fate of humanity.

Dark orange beams tore from space all around the Earth, ripping gaping holes through the clouds. The beams danced and wove across the planet, etching a path of destruction. Knight's heart sank as he caught sight of two beams ripping across North America.

Are you sure that's going to work? It just looks like you're burning parts of it.

This is only stage one.

Staggering explosions engulfed the air above land mass and ocean alike. Purple clouds of burning fire expanded rapidly, spontaneously erupting into chain after chain of destruction. In seconds, the Earth was completely hidden underneath a blanket of fiery purple spiders, legs outstretched and intertwined in every direction. The awful beauty of his species' extinction both captivated and humbled Knight. He now was truly the last human left.

Sensing his desolation and relating to his abject loneliness, Nualaan offered his condolences.

It is for the greater good, brother. Now the species that follows the Angels will arrive to find their new home eradicated and useless. I only hope you never have to see those creatures in person.

The fact that the Angels themselves hadn't been the true enemy kept escaping Knight.

They'd best hope to never seen me in person either.

This elicited a laugh from Maarus, who had yet to communicate with Knight at all directly. Nualaan must've passed along his counterpart's feeling. The ethereal mirth felt odd to Knight, but he assumed he'd get used to it.

We will forge weapons for you. If an opportunity for further revenge presents itself, we shall pursue it.

The idea brought little solace to Knight as he watched the decimation of his planet recede in the distance. Still the image of the Earth blocked his entire view, not allowing him to look upon the Demons' faces quite yet.

Concerns over his companions' looks really didn't matter. His home was truly gone. Everything he'd ever known was gone. The emptiness was as black as the space he now traveled in.

He closed his weary eyes and let the chair morph around him as a mother embraces a child. Before drifting off completely, he wondered when the hammer would drop, when it would become fully evident that he was the last human alive.

Acknowledgments

I wrote this story over the course of a few years, but I would never have progressed beyond the planning phases without my good friend Franklin Fabrygel. He helped me flesh out the plot through numerous outline iterations and discovered an amazingly glaring hole when I was about a third of the way into writing Phalanx Alpha.

My lovely wife Sarah helped me with early story design decisions, and more importantly always supported all of my effort during some long days and late nights.

And I can't leave out the 4th Realm community. Kris Kramer, Marshall McKinney, and Patrick Underhill all had a hand in making this story a reality, each reading multiple variations and providing incredible feedback in order to create the final product.

The4threalm.com

If you would like to keep up with other books by this author, or other books from a number of talented storytellers, be sure to visit us at the4threalm.com! You can find more books, online reading, updates on our existing series, or even chat with the authors on our forums. The4threalm.com is a growing online community of writers, readers and fans, so be sure to stop by and let us know what you think, good or bad.

Seriously!

http://www.the4threalm.com

18563501R00243

Made in the USA
Charleston, SC
10 April 2013